DARREN SHAN

City of the Snakes

The City: Book Three

HARPER
Voyager

HarperVoyager
An imprint of HarperCollins*Publishers*
77–85 Fulham Palace Road,
Hammersmith, London W6 8JB

www.harpercollins.co.uk

This paperback edition 2010
1

First published in Great Britain by
Harper*Voyager* 2010

A catalogue record for this book is
available from the British Library

ISBN: 978 0 00 726135 2

Set in Meridien by Palimpsest Book Production Ltd,
Grangemouth, Stirlingshire

Printed and bound in Great Britain

Mixed Sources
Product group from well-managed
forests and other controlled sources
www.fsc.org Cert no. SW-COC-001806
© 1996 Forest Stewardship Council
FSC

FSC is a non-profit international organisation established
to promote the responsible management of the world's forests.
Products carrying the FSC label are independently certified
to assure consumers that they come from forests that are managed
to meet the social, economic and ecological needs
of present and future generations.

Find out more about HarperCollins and the environment at
www.harpercollins.co.uk/green

For:
Liam, Biddy & Bas – Snakes, Troops, Kluxers – all

OBE (Order of the Bloody Entrails) to:
Darren O'Shaughnessy and D B Shan – gone but not forgotten

Edited by:
Sarah Hodgson – running solo, like Capac, now

The City could not have been built without all of the architects
and tradespeople of the Christopher Little crew

part one

pretender to the throne

ONE – A TOAST

'The Cardinal is dead — long live The Cardinal!'

Cathal Sampedro and the three other men in my office applaud soundly as Gico Carl makes the toast. They're all grinning inanely — they love me to death. I smile obligingly and tip my crystal glass to Gico's. I'm not a champagne man by nature, but when the occasion calls for it . . .

'Ten years, Capac,' Gico beams, licking his lips nervously. I pretend not to notice the giveaway gesture. 'Seems like only yesterday.'

This is boring. I know they're here to kill me. I wish they'd stop wasting my time with small talk and just get on with it.

'Remember the night . . .' Cathal begins and I tune out. Cathal has the gift of making the most fascinating anecdote sound incredibly dull. His stories are best ignored if possible, and since I'm The Cardinal, lord of the city, I can ignore anyone I damn well please.

The Cardinal is dead — long live The Cardinal. It's been said to me many times over the last decade, occasionally by those who mean it, more often by fools like these who think they can replace me.

Ten years. A long time by most standards, but Gico - once loyal Gico Carl, the man I chose to succeed Frank Weld as head of the Troops – is right. It does seem like yesterday. I can recall every detail of Ferdinand Dorak's twisted expression as he stepped up to the edge of the roof of Party Central. Half excited, half fearful, thoroughly demented. 'Here's to a long life, Capac Raimi,' he cheered. Then, with one final 'Farewell!' he leapt and the reins of power passed to me. I've been fighting to cling on to them ever since.

I've had a lot of people killed since I took over, but nowhere near enough. Running a corrupt cesspit like this city is damn near impossible. No ordinary man could do it. You'd need several life-times to stamp your authority on these streets and make them your own. Fortunately I have those life-times, and more besides. I'll wear down the dissidents eventually, even if I have to die trying . . . repeatedly.

Cathal and Gico are rambling, quaffing champagne, working up the courage to kill me. They were fine servants of the original Cardinal. When I stepped in, they swore allegiance to me and for several years remained true to their oath. But their loyalties have swayed. Like so many, they've come to believe I'm not up to the task of leadership. They see the trouble I'm in, the strain the city's under, the threat of rival gangs, and they think the time has come to push me aside and install a new supremo.

Slipping away from the knot of assassins, I gravitate towards the balcony, brooding on how it's all gone wrong. For the first few years I ruled smoothly. I faced opposition, and assassination attempts were frequent, but that was to be expected. Things settled down as The Cardinal had predicted in the plans he'd left behind for me. It seemed that I was over the worst and I commenced planning for the next phase, expansion out of the city. That's when it all started to fall apart.

I study the dozens of puppets hanging from the walls. Dorak's macabre Ayuamarcans. He could create people. He had the power to reach beyond the grave, bring the dead back to life, and give them new personalities. A group of blind Incan priests – *villacs* – constructed puppets and aided Dorak in his resurrection quests. It sounds insane, but the Ayuamarcans were real. I know because I'm one of them.

I step out of the office. The balcony's a new addition. I've kept this place in much the same state as Dorak left it – sparsely decorated, a long desk, a plush leather chair for myself, simple plastic chairs for the guests – but I replaced the bullet-proof glass. When The Cardinal created me, he made me immortal. I can be killed but I always bounce back. As a man with no fear of death, I don't need to cut myself off from the world as my predecessor did. I like to step out here and gaze down upon my city. Normally it calms me, but not tonight.

Why am I struggling? Why the unrest on the streets? Why the renewed assassinations? Those days should be behind me. I haven't weakened. I've stayed true to my course, as my nature dictates. I've pushed ahead with The Cardinal's plans, improvising when I have to, using my initiative. I've been generous to my supporters, wrathful to those who oppose me, fair with all. I should be respected and obeyed as Ferdinand Dorak was. But I'm not.

The villacs shoulder much of the blame. The blind priests helped create me, with the intention of using me, but I'm The Cardinal's son, not theirs, and they resent that. They'd have me concentrate on making the city great, ignore the outside world completely. But I can't. I must have the world in all its glory. Nothing less will suffice.

The priests have become dangerous adversaries. Their power rivals my own, maybe even eclipses it. They're under-mining my authority, setting people and gangs against me. It was an uneasy relationship from the start, but recently it's deteriorated entirely. They used to send emissaries to consult with and advise me, but I haven't had word from them for eighteen months. There was no defining argument. They simply lost patience and have been doing all in their power to rock the boat ever since.

'What would you have done?' I murmur to the ghost of Ferdinand Dorak. 'Should I cut a deal? Make contact, grovel, surrender to their whims?'

Inside my head I hear him chuckle, and the clouds on the horizon seem to lift into an elongated sneer. I grimace. 'Dumb suggestion. You'd hunt them down and exterminate them like rats, and if you lost everything, so be it.' That's how he was. Failure didn't worry him, and the threat of it never held him back. It doesn't worry me either, but I'm faced with different dilemmas. The Cardinal had only one lifespan to consider, but I'll go on forever. I'll stand triumphant in the end, if only by outliving everybody else, and that makes me cautious. I can afford to concede ground to my enemies, knowing I've all the time in the world to regain it.

Were I human, I'd come down hard on the *villacs* and force a conclusive confrontation. All or nothing. But I'm super-human. I can wait. If I forced the issue, there'd be bloodshed. The city would burn. I'll avoid such dramatics if possible. Take my time. Endure the defections and betrayals. Reassert control gradually, imperiously, completely.

Gico Carl steps up beside me. Cathal lurks close behind, his features twisted with regret. This wasn't his idea. Gico talked him into it. Gico can be very persuasive. It's one of the reasons I elevated him so high, placing him in charge of the Troops. Too bad he lacks faith in me. He'll rue his betrayal soon enough, but that's little comfort. I'll have to ferret out a replacement for him. It's a headache I could have done without.

'Capac,' Gico sighs, draping an arm across my shoulders. 'You're a good lad, but it wasn't meant to be. "Too much, too soon", as they say.'

'You're a fool, Gico,' I smile as the other men step onto the balcony in a show of force. 'You think handing control over to the *villacs* is the answer?'

'They've nothing to do with it,' he grunts.

'You're acting alone?' I sneer. 'Then you're dumber than I thought. With the support of the priests you could have held on for six months, maybe a year. Alone, you wouldn't last a month.'

'We'll see,' Gico snarls, then nods sharply at Cathal. Ducking low, Cathal propels himself into the small of my back, knocking me over the ledge. Gico grabs my feet as I spin over the rails and shoves hard, to hasten my descent. The faces of both men are contorted with gleeful terror.

It's a fifteen-floor drop. Plenty of time to admire the scenery. I sail to earth relaxed, knowing it can't hold me. I smile against the rush of air. 'They'll have to do better than this,' I chuckle, then hit the ground and die in a shattering explosion of bones and shredded flesh.

On a train, approaching a grey, sprawling, menacing city. For a few minutes I don't know who or where I am. Then my memories return. I'm Capac Raimi, The Cardinal, recently deceased, freshly resurrected, on my way home. Coming back from the dead threw me for loops the first few times, but like most things in life, a man can get used to it.

A conductor passes up the aisle, asking for tickets. I fish mine out and hand it to him with a polite smile. I've never worked out how I re-form and wind up on this train, fully dressed, with a ticket from Sonas to the city in my pocket. It bothered me to begin with, but I've given up worrying about it. One of those mysteries of the universe I've learnt to accept without query.

It's been close to four years since my last execution. I'd aged slightly, gained a few pounds, developed a spray of grey hairs, picked up wrinkles around the eyes. But now I'm the way I was when I came to this city eleven years ago, bright, fresh, youthful. 'Hi, handsome,' I mutter to my reflection in the window as we enter a tunnel.

We pass Vidalus – a shanty town for immigrant Eastern Europeans – on the outskirts of the city. I check my watch — two p.m. It will be another forty minutes before we hit Central Station. Might as well lie back and make the most of the break. It'll be all systems go once I'm back in the thick of things.

Closing my eyes, I drown out the sounds, smells and sights of the city and think about immortality. Ferdinand Dorak had the power to bring dead people back to life, instilling them with talents and drives of his making. The *villacs* were the source of his power. Over the centuries, since coming to this city, they'd placed their fate in the hands of men they called *Watanas*, who could summon shades of the dead and create leaders to cement their control of the city. The Cardinal was the last of the *Watanas*, charged with the task of creating a leader who could meet the demands of the twenty-first century and all the millennia beyond. *Me.*

When The Cardinal created an Ayuamarcan, he was given a doll, a replica of the creation, with a heartbeat of its own. When the Ayuamarcan had served its purpose, The Cardinal wiped that person out of existence by piercing the doll's heart. A green fog then enveloped the city, eradicating memories of the Ayuamarcan from the minds of all.

I was created differently. To guard his empire indefinitely, he required an heir who could withstand the march of time. So he made me immortal. I'll live forever, aging slightly (he said I'd stop when I hit my early forties, though I revert every time I'm killed). I'm more resilient than most – minor wounds heal quickly – and though death knocks me back, it can't keep me down for more than a handful of days at a time.

It's a strange existence, but The Cardinal designed me to cope with the staggering implications. I don't like the hand which fate has dealt me, and I dread the loneliness the centuries will bring, as old acquaintances die and new generations come to regard me us an unapproachable god, but I'll get by. I'll have to. You can't mope around angst-ridden if you're doomed to last as long as the sands of time itself.

Jerry's waiting for me at the station, decked out in his uniform. I've told him he doesn't need to wear it, but Jerry Falstaff's a stubborn man, slow to change. 'Good to have you back, boss,' he says, helping me off the train, taking my bag (it changes with the reincarnations, keeping up with the latest fashions — a nice touch).

'How long have I been gone?' I ask, stretching, waiting for the crowd to disperse.

'You were killed at 23:14, Tuesday,' Jerry says matter-of-factly. 'It's now 15:03, Friday.'

'How's Gico bearing up?'

'Great.' Jerry grins. 'A natural leader.'

We follow the last few stragglers out of the station, to the waiting limo. Thomas holds the door open for me. Dry, faithful Thomas. He's been my driver almost as long as I can remember. Nothing shakes Thomas (though the bomb that took the two smallest fingers of his left hand seven years ago came close).

'Party Central, Mr Raimi?' he asks as I sit in.

'Party Central,' I concur, and discuss affairs of state with Jerry during the ride.

Jerry's one of the few who knows the secret of my immortality. The city's awash with rumours, but to most people that's all they are, fairytales circulated by a power-hungry despot to psyche out his opponents. Only those closest to me know about The Cardinal's legacy. I was on the point of letting

Gico Carl in on the big secret, but I sensed something weak in him. It didn't surprise me when he turned.

Jerry's a soldier, a long-serving Troop who came to my attention when he took a bullet intended for me eight years ago. Once he'd recuperated, I had Frank Weld – still head of the Troops in those days – assign him to the fifteenth floor of Party Central, where our relationship developed. He was shaken when I first displayed my Lazarus trick but now he takes my comebacks in his stride.

'What about Mr Sampedro?' Jerry asks as we draw close to Party Central, the fortress I inherited from the previous Cardinal. 'He's been led astray by Gico, but we could still use him.'

I consider Cathal Sampedro's fate, then shake my head. 'He's blown it.'

Jerry nods obediently and draws a pistol from his holster.

'It was Alice's birthday yesterday, wasn't it?' I ask.

Jerry looks surprised. 'I didn't think you'd remember.'

'Death's a small matter,' I quip. 'Birthdays are important. Do anything nice with her?'

He shrugs. 'We meant to go away for a couple of days, but your getting iced put paid to that. I took her out for a meal. She wasn't overly impressed, but she knows how it goes.'

We stop at the rear of Party Central and Thomas gets out to open my door. Frank Weld materializes out of the shadows, flanked by ten of the toughest-looking sons of bitches I've ever seen.

'Capac,' he greets me, grinning edgily. He's never come to terms with my indestructibility. My returning freaks the shit out of him, but he puts up with me because he senses – in a way Gico Carol and Cathal Sampedro can't – that I'm the future. Frank, like Ford Tasso before him, is a man propelled by instinct to identify and follow the strongest master.

Frank quit as head of the Troops three years ago. He

moved up in the organization, becoming overseer of my international interests. Although eternity is mine to play with, I'm limited physically to the boundaries of this city. If I spend more than three or four days away, my body unravels and I find myself back on the train. I can handle most of my global business from Party Central, and by arranging short trips abroad for face-to-face meetings, but it helps to have a strong lieutenant active in the field.

'Sorry to pull you away from your regular duties.'

Frank sniffs. 'Diplomacy's boring. I'm looking forward to running with the Troops again.'

'As long as you realize it's a temporary measure. As soon as I find a fit replacement, you're out of here.'

'If I didn't know better, I'd swear you wanted to get rid of me,' Frank laughs, then draws his gun, checks with his men – all armed with rifles – and leads us through the back yard, past a posse of Troops who look away and wait for this latest power game to reach its inevitable conclusion.

Gico's guards don't intervene when they spot us. The men we draft into the Troops are smart enough to know which way the wind blows. Besides, most were blooded by Frank, so even if they were prepared to take a shot at me, they wouldn't dare raise a hand against their old task-master.

In the past you had to check in your shoes at reception. The floors of Party Central are lined with some of the finest carpets you'll find this side of Arabia. Dorak was obsessive about them. I don't share his love, so we march to the room marked BASE in our shoes and boots, sparing not a thought for the priceless floor covering.

Mags is on duty. She's another of Dorak's finds. Best secretary bar none. I'd be lost without her. She looks up and smiles as we enter. I've never explained the truth about myself to Mags, but she's seen enough to guess. 'Glad to have you back, sir,' she greets me. 'I've lots of forms need signing when you're through with Mr Carl and his associates.'

'Why didn't you get Gico to sign them while he was acting CEO?'

'I had a feeling he wouldn't be acting for long,' she replies. Then she asks cheekily, 'Shall I check to see if he's receiving visitors?'

'I'm sure he'll make time for us.'

Breezing in without knocking, I find Gico, Cathal and two of their allies examining a map on the table which dominates the room. Four burly Troops are positioned by the windows. They raise their weapons when they see me, then lower them when Frank snaps his fingers.

'Good afternoon, gentlemen.' I smile lazily as their jaws drop. 'Hope I'm not interrupting anything important.'

'You . . . you . . .' Cathal gasps, taking a few involuntary steps away from me as if I'm some supernatural monster. Which I suppose I am.

'You four — beat it!' Frank barks at the Troops by the window. They stare at him uncertainly, then at the ten men behind him, then nod obediently and make themselves scarce.

'You just can't find the help these days,' I tut, locating my chair and slumping into it.

'We killed you,' Gico moans, face ashen. One of the men to his left is crying. The other's shaking his head numbly. Cathal has backed up to the window. If it was open he'd probably back all the way off the balcony and save us the price of a bullet.

'Some men are harder to keep down than others,' I murmur.

'We killed you,' Gico says again, stubborn to the last. 'You're dead. I pushed you over.' He looks to Frank and Jerry appealingly. 'We killed him!'

'Time to return the favour,' Frank grunts and gives the signal. His Troops circle the traitors.

'No!' Gico howls, trying to break through to me. 'You're dead! We killed you! We –'

A Troop clubs him over the back of the head and he falls limp to the floor. The others are swiftly subdued, even the normally fierce Cathal Sampedro. I tend to have that effect on people when I return from the dead.

'Take them to the yard,' Frank says, and his Troops bundle the prisoners out of the office, down the hall to the elevator. The executions will be short and unceremonial. No need for me to be present.

'Nice to be back?' Jerry asks.

'There's no place like home,' I agree, testing the chair, making sure Gico hasn't tampered with it.

'I'd love to stay and chat,' Frank says, 'but I've work to do. Three years is a long time. It'll take a while to get back into the swing of things.'

'You'll manage,' I reply confidently, then call him back as he heads for the door. 'One last thing. There's a photo I'd like you to look at.'

'This the guy you were asking about before?'

'Yes.'

The weekend before I was killed, I rang Frank, having guessed what Gico Carl and his companions were planning, to check that he was willing to return as head of the Troops. Whilst on the phone, I tested his memories of Paucar Wami — Dorak's most sinister and singular Ayuamarcan apart from me. I asked if he recollected a famous serial killer who'd terrorized this city and worked for The Cardinal. He didn't, but maybe the photo will jog something inside him.

'This was taken last Saturday,' I explain, digging through my drawers for the photo and tossing it across the desk. 'He stood close to a security camera out back and stared straight at it for a full minute.'

The photo's of a tall, lithe, extremely dark-skinned man.

Bald. Strange green eyes. Tattoos of coloured snakes adorn both his cheeks. He's dressed in dark trousers and a black leather jacket.

Frank breathes out heavily through his nostrils, then looks at me warily. 'That's a photo of Al.'

'Al Jeery?'

'Yeah.'

I shake my head. 'No. It isn't.'

I know Al Jeery as intimately as you can know someone you've never actually met. I became interested in him when he chose the name of Paucar Wami and adopted his guise. I've had him shadowed, researched and photographed in any number of compromising positions. This isn't him.

Frank studies the photo again. 'Sure looks like Al. Jerry?'

Jerry and Frank were both colleagues of Al Jeery's long ago.

'I've seen it already,' Jerry says. 'I thought it was him too, but Capac's right — it's someone else.'

Frank squints. 'Yeah, I see it now. His ears are smaller, his face is slightly sharper, his contact lenses are a darker shade of green.'

'I don't think they're contacts,' I say softly, retrieving the photo.

'Who is he?' Frank asks.

I'm reluctant to voice the crazy words, but I force them out. 'I think he's Paucar Wami.'

'That's the name Al uses,' Frank notes.

'I mean the original Paucar Wami. The Ayuamarcan who popped out of existence ten years ago when Dorak died.'

Frank and Jerry share an uneasy look. They never quite believed my tales of the Ayuamarcans. They've seen me return from the dead, so they know there's more to this world than meets the eye, but there are some things they find hard to get their heads around.

'Never mind,' I mutter. 'It's not your problem. Focus on

running the Troops. Leave me to worry about the ghosts of the past.'

Frank opens his mouth to say something, can't think of anything, salutes and exits. Jerry shuffles after the departing Frank Weld, leaving me alone in my eyrie to brood.

Paucar Wami isn't the only ghost who's come back to haunt me. There have been others. People who never truly existed, who died, who've lived these last ten years only in my memories. Until this one was captured on film, I thought I was imagining them. Now I'm not sure.

Sighing, I slide the photo back into its drawer and leave the puzzle for another day. There's much to be done. I've been gone less than three days, but a lot can happen even in that short a period. Time to catch up on the state of play, reassert my authority and let people know that The Cardinal's back from the dead . . . again.

TWO – THE RELIC

The city's most exclusive nursing home, Solvert's, is situated in a quiet corner of Conchita Gardens, a park built during Ferdinand Dorak's time. Dorak's wife, Conchita, pleaded with him to do something beautiful and unexpected for her birthday one year. He responded with the park. He could be a sentimental old goat where Conchita was concerned.

The Cardinal left behind a trust fund to pay towards the upkeep of the park, and I chip in with my own annual contribution, making up the shortfall, in tribute to the memory of Conchita Kubekik, who was a dear friend of mine.

Thomas drops me at the front of Solvert's. I'm recognized as soon as I enter and the staff scurry to look busy — nobody wants to get mixed up with a notorious gangster like me. Finally I flag a nurse and ask to see Ford Tasso. She gulps nervously and scampers ahead, leading the way. I could find it myself, but they don't like visitors walking around unattended. Ford isn't the only ex-gangster on their books. They worry about assassinations.

He's sitting outside in a wheelchair, under a leafy tree, enjoying the spring morning. He's an impressive sight, even from the back and seated, as broad and rock-like as ever.

I relied on Ford heavily when I took over. I'd still be depending on him if a stroke hadn't rendered him inactive.

I thank the nurse and cough to announce my presence. 'No need to throw a fit,' Ford wheezes. 'My ears are good as ever. I heard you coming.'

'Hello, old friend.' I bend to shake his left hand. His granite features haven't softened with time. If anything he looks rougher than ever, his face impassive and deathly grey on one side. The stroke hit him hardest down the right, paralysing his face and arm, almost destroying his leg. He can get around on his feet when he has to, but walking's slow and painful, his right leg drags leadenly with every laboured step.

'You must be in deep shit to come here,' he grunts.

I smile wryly. We both know I wouldn't waste time on a social visit. Sitting on the grass, I grimace. 'Deep as it gets.'

He pivots to face me and waits. It's been four years since the stroke. For six months he wasn't able to speak. Gradually he learnt to produce sounds, although at first his slur was so bad that even his full-time nurse couldn't understand what he was saying. With untold hours of practice and treatment, he's trained himself to speak again. He talks slower than he used to, and occasionally he'll stumble on a word, but he's more coherent than he has any right to be. The doctors didn't think he'd survive the first year. I guessed differently. Death will have to go a full twelve rounds with Ford Tasso before it forces him out of the ring.

'How's life?' I ask.

'Not bad. Still in sex therapy. I sustained an erection for three minutes a couple of days ago. My best yet.'

'Still refusing Viagra?' I grin.

'I don't mess with voodoo shit like that. Don't need it.'

'Why are you worried about your staying power anyway?' I ask. 'Not like you're going to get any action here.'

'I like to be prepared for anything,' he sniffs, then fixes me with his left eye (he lost sight in his right but refuses to wear a patch). 'Enough of the crap. What's wrong?'

'You heard about Gico?'

'Him and Cathal killed you and seized control. Didn't last long.'

'They never do, but that's not the point. Gico and Cathal were two of my best. I thought I could rely on them.'

'Maybe they got greedy,' Ford suggests, rubbing the flesh of his grey right wrist. His circulation is poor down the right. He has to work on his muscles continuously when he's by himself.

'No,' I mutter. 'Fear motivated them. They thought I wasn't in control. They saw me as a weak link. If my closest aides don't have faith in me . . .'

Ford nods slowly. 'I'd heard things weren't so hot. Tell me more.'

I fill him in on all that's transpired since my last visit two years ago. The city's heading for riots. Old gangs have splintered, new gangs have formed, fighting is rife. I've tried holding things together but they refuse to pay heed. I'm the most powerful force in the city but I'm not obeyed as Dorak was. People fear me but they don't respect me.

Ford listens silently. When I run out of words, he mulls the situation over, then asks, 'And the villacs?'

'Keeping low. I'm sure they're behind a lot of the unrest but they're doing it subtly, without showing their hand.'

Ford grunts. 'I told The Cardinal to take them out years ago, but he was always in awe of them.'

'It's not just the priests. Others oppose me, men who'd never have dared face up to Dorak. Eugene Davern's one.'

'The guy who runs the KKK?' Ford asks, surprised. The Kool Kats Klub has always been a hive of racists, but we never had to worry about them in Ford's time. Rich white kids talking big. Harmless.

'Eugene's moving up in the world. He's been uniting supremacist gangs under one flag for the last few years. They call themselves the Kluxers. I know,' I laugh as Tasso groans. 'Dumb name. But they're serious. They've abandoned the hoods and burning crosses of the Klan. Expanded steadily. Davern's never once asked for my blessing or sought my approval. He's an independent operator, and others are following his lead.'

'So eliminate him,' Ford barks. 'A dawn raid, corpses galore, Davern's head on a plate . . . that'll put paid to that.'

'We don't do it that way any more,' I sigh. 'The corporation's in the process of going straight. Taking Davern out would set us back ten or fifteen years.'

'Maybe things need setting back. Christ knows, you can afford to wait.'

'I guess. But . . .' I don't know how to explain it. Bloodshed doesn't deter me but I want to conquer by intrigue and cunning, not brute force. The game must remain interesting if it's to entertain me for eternity. My greatest fear is waking up one morning, the rest of time stretched out ahead of me, only to find myself with nothing to do.

Ford reads my thoughts and chuckles mirthlessly. 'You have to get real, Capac. Dispose of your enemies. Kill those who look at you crosswise. Be merciless. It's the old way but the only way.'

'Wise advice.'

'Which you'll ignore.' We smile at each other. He understands me better than anyone ever has, with the exception of my creator. 'So why come see an old fart like me if you're not gonna listen?'

I shrug. 'I thought you might have something more constructive to say. I was hoping the serenity of retirement would have opened your mind to fresh ways of thinking.'

'You can't teach an old dog new tricks,' he snorts, 'and

I'm as old as they come. Quit pissing around, Capac. Why are you really here?'

He's seen through me, as I knew he would. Time to come clean. 'I'm frightened, Ford.' A pause. 'I'm seeing ghosts.'

Ford doesn't remember the Ayuamarcans. Like everyone else in the city, he forgot about them in the wake of The Cardinal's downfall. But I've filled him in about them before, so he knows what I'm talking about.

'I've been catching glimpses of Ayuamarcans for weeks now,' I tell him. 'Y Tse was the first.' Y Tse Lapotaire, real name Inti Maimi, one of The Cardinal's rare failures. He was supposed to succeed Dorak but he didn't work out. A colourful figure when I originally knew him, he dressed in robes, daubed himself with paint, wore the most overstated jewellery he could find.

'He was in a crowd of people outside the Skylight. I'd gone over to greet some business associates but I had to wait to get in. Some rock star was staying and groupies had gathered out front. While I was relaxing in the car, I saw Y Tse. He was ten or twelve feet away, staring at me silently. At first I didn't recognize him – it's been a long time – but then he raised his arms above his head and bellowed, "The time is ripe, friend Capac!"'

'That means something?' Ford asks.

'He said the same thing to me the first time we met. The words struck me like a bullet. When he saw that I realized who it was, he smiled, waved, then disappeared into the crowd. I raced after him but the crush was too great. By the time it cleared, he'd vanished.'

Ford clears his throat. 'Might have been someone who looked like him.'

'No. A few days later I saw him again, lurking in front of Party Central. I sent Troops after him but they lost track of him after a couple of blocks. Said it was like he disappeared into thin air.'

'But they saw him?' Ford interrupts.

'They saw someone. They couldn't describe him accurately. Said they didn't get a good look at him. Then, a week later, I saw Leonora Shankar and Conchita.'

'Leonora's the woman you say founded Shankar's restaurant?'

'Yes.'

'And Conchita would be Conchita Kubekik, Dorak's alleged wife?'

I nod. As far as Ford and everyone else remembers, The Cardinal never married. They think Conchita Gardens was named after a local Indian girl.

'What were they doing?' Ford enquires.

'Swimming.' In response to his quizzical look, I elaborate. 'I go for a swim every Tuesday, Thursday and Saturday, schedule permitting. I use the Kargan pool — not conveniently situated, but it's longer than most. You can really stretch yourself there.'

'Fascinating,' Ford grunts impatiently. 'The women?'

'They'd been sitting by the side of the pool for ages. I didn't pay much attention. It was only when I paused at the end of a lap to catch my breath that I made them. I was dumbstruck. I stood in the water at the shallow end, mesmerized, for maybe five minutes, until they rose and slipped into the changing room. Then I charged after them and tore the place apart.'

'I bet that made you popular with the ladies,' Ford comments drily. 'But it was for nothing, right? You couldn't find them?'

'Not a trace,' I sigh. 'That's when I started to think I might be losing it. I had myself checked and drew a clear bill of health, but that was little consolation. I spotted them several times over the next few weeks, together, with Y Tse, singly. I ignored them. Didn't waste time giving chase. I figured, if they were products of my imagination, running after them was useless. If they were real, they'd make contact in their own time. Then this.' I pass the photograph of Paucar Wami to him.

'Al Jeery,' he says immediately. Ford knew Jeery too, before the guy lost his marbles and took to the streets as Paucar Wami. Thought highly of him. I wanted to drag Jeery in, find out what he knew about the Ayuamarcans. Ford convinced me to leave him alone — said the guy had been through enough.

'Look again,' I tell him, and he studies the photo some more.

'It's like Al,' he rumbles, 'but it's not. Some guy made up to resemble him?'

'Maybe. Or maybe this is the guy Jeery made himself up to look like — the real Paucar Wami.'

'I thought Wami was a myth,' Ford says uneasily. Like some other people, he has vague recollections of the serial killer. I don't know how fragments of Wami's existence survived The Cardinal's passing, but they did. He's not a substantial figure – he exists in the minds of those who knew him as a creature of shadows – but part of his evil legacy lives on.

'Wami was real, an Ayuamarcan. And on the basis of that photo, he's back.'

'You're sure it's not a ringer?'

'He's not someone you forget in a hurry. That's Paucar Wami. I'd stake my life on it. And if he's real, the others probably are too.'

Ford passes back the photo. 'I don't understand this – I never really did – but let's say it's on the level. Why does it bother you?'

'Wouldn't you be bothered if ghosts returned to haunt you?' I snap.

'Sure, but I'm human. I can be killed, so I'd have reason to worry. You don't.'

'I'm not so certain I believe that any more,' I mumble. 'The Cardinal made me immortal, but he reserved the power to destroy me. He could have wiped me out before he died, if he'd had a mind to. If someone else has the same kind of power – and if Wami and the others are real, only some-body as gifted as The Cardinal could have brought them back – maybe they can eradicate me too.'

Ford's good eye half closes. 'Didn't think of that.'

'I didn't either until this photo materialized. Now it's all I can think about.'

Ford chuckles bleakly. 'How does it feel to be faced with mortality again? Must be a shock after all these years.'

'Don't mock me,' I growl, but he only laughs at my tone.

'That explains why your knees are shaking. But why come to me about this? If the grim reaper's got you in his sights, what can I do to help?'

'The villacs must be behind this. I need to find them, confront them, stop them. But I can't chase the priests and run this city at the same time. I need someone to –'

'Whoa!' Ford stops me. 'If this is going where I think it is, forget it.'

'I need you,' I press. 'Frank's back in charge of the Troops. He'll do a good job, but he's not Cardinal material.'

'I'm not either,' Ford grunts.

'But you could fill in for me short-term,' I insist. 'You're still closely identified with Dorak. People would obey you. You could keep things ticking over while I sorted out my problems. Think about it – back in charge, everyone having to kiss your ass. You'd love it.'

He shakes his head, genuine regret in his live left eye. 'I'm past that. People wouldn't take orders from a cripple. I hate retirement. I talked about it a lot towards the end of my run, but now that I've tasted it, I think it sucks. I'd jump at the chance to return, but I'd be a liability. Look elsewhere.'

'There isn't anybody else,' I groan. 'I've been running the show single-handed, the way The Cardinal wanted. I don't have anyone groomed to step in. By the time I trained someone, it would be too late. I have to act now, before the villacs strike.'

Ford shakes his head again. 'I won't be held responsible for what'd go wrong. I'm useless to you.'

'What if I went down on my knees and pleaded?'

'You won't. It's not your style.'

'Bastard,' I mutter, then stand and walk away without a farewell, leaving Ford Tasso to the shade, his reminiscences and the wheelchair.

I didn't expect the old warhorse to accept my offer – at his stage of life, in his condition, he'd have to be insane to step back into the firing range – but it was worth a shot. With him at the helm, I could have pursued the villacs without worry. Now I'll have to struggle on alone as best I can.

What the hell are they up to and how are they managing it? I know from first-hand experience that the dead can return, but the same corpses rising twice from the grave is a bit much. Could the Paucar Wami in the photo have been a double, as Ford suggested? Leonora, Conchita, Y Tse too? I'm sure the villacs remember what the Ayuamarcans looked like. They might be plaguing me with lookalikes to distract me. Perhaps they want me to abandon my post, clearing the way for insurrection. They'll have a long wait if that's their game. Time, as the song goes, is on my side. I can wait those bastards out. They won't panic me into –

The car crashes a red light. Horns blare. We accelerate sharply. 'What's wrong?' I shout, looking out the rear window, checking for pursuit.

'Just taking you for a spin, like in the old days. Sit back and enjoy.'

My insides tighten — that's not Thomas. Throwing myself forward, I press my face close to the glass panel separating me from the driver. I only have a view of half his face, but it's enough to make a positive identification — Adrian Arne, an Ayuamarcan. He was my chauffeur when I first started working for The Cardinal. He's been RIP these last ten years. Now here he is, grinning broadly, not looking a day older.

'Adrian,' I moan, crashing to the floor as he takes a turn without braking.

'Miss me, Capac?' he asks mockingly. He's controlling the wheel with a couple of fingers, oblivious to the traffic.

'You're dead!' I gasp.

'So are you,' he retorts.

'What are you doing here? What do you want?'

He laughs ecstatically. 'I want to be James Dean.'

He takes his fingers off the wheel and presses down harder with his foot. The car roars ahead, veering sickeningly from left to right.

'We're going to crash,' I note dully.

'Do I look like I'm worried?' Adrian whoops.

'Where have you been? Do you recall the past? How have —'

'Too late!' he shouts, covering his eyes with his hands. 'We're doomed!'

There's a metallic, demonic shriek as we hit something hard and cartwheel through the air. We crash back to earth and the world explodes. Adrian goes up in a ball of fiery fury. A split second later, the fire engulfs me and I scream with pain and shock as I thrash, burn and die.

THREE – LADY OF
THE MAUSOLEUM

I slump in my chair on the fifteenth floor of Party Central and gaze at the face of the puppet I retrieved from the wall when I returned from my latest bout of death. It's Adrian's. The Cardinal used it to bring him to life. I raise its chest to my ear, listening for a heartbeat, but there isn't any. None of the dozens of puppets has a heartbeat. I've checked each and every one of them over and over again. It's all I've done these last few days.

My door opens and Jerry slides in. He stares at the puppets scattered on the floor and over my desk, then steps forward gingerly. 'Mr Raimi?' I don't respond. 'Sir?' No response. 'Capac!'

'What is it?' I sigh, lowering the doll but not letting go of it.

'Are you OK?'

I laugh shortly. 'Never better. What do you want?'

He clears a path through the dolls and crouches beside me. 'Snap out of this. You're acting like a loon and it's gonna be the end of us.'

His candour catches me off-guard. Jerry knows I value his advice but he's never spoken this bluntly to me before. It's a risk. I could have him executed for addressing me so plainly.

'What's up?' I ask, laying the doll on the table, directing

my thoughts away from Adrian, the car crash and the other Ayuamarcans for the first time since coming back to life on the train.

'We're on the brink of losing everything,' he hisses. 'Do you even know what's been happening?'

I shake my head.

'Eugene Davern invaded Hugo turf and annexed about seventy per cent of it.' The Hugos are one of the largest gangs in the city, loyal to me. They control most of the north-west, a largely undeveloped area, a valuable source of income in the years to come. Losing it to an independent operator like Davern is a serious blow and it jolts me out of my daze.

'Is he crazy?' I snap. 'He can't believe we'll let him take the north-west.'

Jerry shrugs. 'Apparently he does.'

'That's it,' I growl. 'He's been picking and poking at me too long. If this is designed to test how far I'm willing to let him go, he's misjudged terribly. Call the Troops and have them assemble in the –'

'Hello, Capac.' The voice comes from the balcony. Jerry and I spin towards it. Jerry's hand shoots to his holster and he draws his pistol.

'No,' I stop him, laying a hand on his.

'But –' he begins.

'It's OK.'

I step ahead of Jerry and face the girl on the balcony. In appearance she's thirteen or fourteen years old. Long, shiny blonde hair. An innocent, beautiful face, body covered from the neck down. But appearances can be deceptive. I know she's a woman, older than me, the victim of a cruel, unique disease.

'Hello, Conchita,' I croak. Conchita Kubekik – Ferdinand Dorak's ex-wife – was a special friend of mine. Seeing her again, after all these years . . . I almost feel human.

'Long time, big guy,' she grins. 'How's tricks?'

I stop at the door to the balcony. Conchita's leaning against the railings, playing with her hair, smirking. There's something not right. She has a glint in her eyes which I never noticed before. But there's no doubting it's her.

'Why are you here, Conchita?' I ask. 'How?'

'Two reasons. To pass on a message – Ferdy wants to see you – and to fly. How is easy — just spread my wings and dive.'

I frown, not certain what she's talking about. Then I remember Adrian ('I want to be James Dean') and my eyes shoot wide. 'No!' I scream and dash for her, meaning to clutch her to my chest and protect her — I promised The Cardinal I'd look after his wife if she survived. But I'm too late. She swings away from me with a laugh, hoists her legs over the railings and lets go. She yodels wildly and plummets fifteen floors, as I did myself not so long ago.

I don't chase to the railings. I just slump and shut my eyes to the nightmare.

'Capac?' Jerry says, bending to help me. 'Who was that? Are you –'

'Go and bring me her body,' I cut him short.

'But what about Davern and the –'

'Go. And bring me. Her body.' My tone leaves no room for argument. Jerry's seen me order people's deaths before. He knows, the mood I'm in, I could easily order his. Saluting with a snappy, 'Yes, sir!' he leaves me on the balcony and goes to sweep up the debris. After a few minutes alone, listening to the sounds of the city, I drag myself back inside to my chair and the silent, lifeless puppets.

There was no body. The ground was bare. I didn't believe Jerry. Insisted on checking for myself. Walked all around the building — nothing. Which means she disappeared midair, or someone cleaned up ultra-quick after her, or she really did learn to fly.

I retired to my office once I'd abandoned the search. Told Mags to let nobody disturb me, not even Jerry or Frank. Sat on the floor, surrounded by dolls, and gave myself over to madness. But it refused to take me, and after a slew of numb hours, I replayed my brief conversation with Conchita and recalled what she'd said before taking off. 'Ferdy wants to see you.'

'Ferdy' was Conchita's pet name for The Cardinal. I'm not sure what she meant – Dorak was human, so I can't imagine any way for him to return – but as I play her words over, I begin to think that I know what she wanted. Leaving my fortress of dolls and memories, I order a limo – Thomas is still off work, recovering from the crack over the head Adrian gave him before taking his place at Solvert's – and tell the driver to take me to the Fridge.

The Fridge is another of The Cardinal's grotesque play-things. A huge morgue, home to thousands who died in his employ or opposing him. The dead lie in refrigerated caskets, preserved against the ravages of time, awaiting Judgement Day and the call to arise. I've added my fair share of corpses to the pile but never visited personally until now.

The Fridge is camouflaged by the shell of an old building. Access is through computer coded doors. Inside, row upon row of metal caskets, stacked five high, twenty wide. The rows stretch ahead, seemingly without end, and rise all the way to the distant ceiling.

There's great excitement at my appearance. Staff crowd the landings overhead, eager to catch a glimpse. I guess I'm the next best thing to royalty in this city, and it's not often that my minions – apart from those who work in Party Central – get a chance to gawk at me.

I stand my ground where I entered, waiting for a guide

to come. It turns out to be the chief pathologist, Alex Sines. We've met before, at various functions, and a couple of times in Party Central. He's a pain in the ass but the best in his field.

'Capac,' he beams as if we're bosom buddies. 'You're the last person I expected to find. Come to check up on us, or is –'

'I want to see The Cardinal's coffin,' I interrupt.

That throws him. 'The . . .? Oh, you mean the other Cardinal. Mr Dorak.'

'Yes.'

He smiles falteringly. 'It's rather late for a visit. May I ask –'

'Just take me to him. Now. Before I replace you with someone who knows how to obey when he's given an order.'

Sines bristles but has sense enough not to bite back. He leads me through the maze of coffins. I follow silently, ignoring the onlookers, turning a deaf ear to their speculative whispers.

We end up at a crypt deep inside the Fridge. A small, octagonal, metal growth, the only free-standing structure within the building. Everyone else has to share. The Cardinal, in death as in life, resides alone. The entrance to the crypt is barred by a computerized door.

'I'm the only one who knows the combination,' Sines boasts, keying it in. 'The walls are lined with every kind of alarm imaginable. The Cardinal made sure his body wouldn't be vulnerable to grave-robbers.'

'What happens when you die?' I ask.

'I keep the code on file, in a secret location. My successor will be able to retrieve it.'

I step back as the door swings open with a series of heavy clicks. A light is shining inside. 'It comes on automatically when the door opens,' Sines explains in answer to my inquisitive look.

I edge forward. The Cardinal's coffin is set on an ornately carved slab of marble in the middle of the room. He used to say he didn't care what happened to his body when he died, but the specific instructions he left about what he wanted done with his remains proved that was a lie.

'Lock the door after me,' I tell Sines.

He blinks. 'The room isn't ventilated. A few hours inside and you'll run out of air.'

'That's OK. I'll signal when I want to leave.'

'There isn't a button you can press, and nobody would hear you if you hammered on the door or walls — they're too thickly insulated.'

I frown. 'Then give me an hour and come back. If I want to stay longer, I'll let you know when you open the door.'

'You're the boss,' Sines mutters, hits a couple of buttons and watches, troubled, as the door slides shut, entombing me with The Cardinal.

'And then there were two,' I mumble, turning to face the coffin.

No answer.

I circle the coffin. Long. Wide. Black. Ferdinand Dorak's name engraved on a silver plaque, along with birth and death dates, and a short epitaph – Nobody told me there'd be days like these. I laugh out loud when I read that. Nice to see the old bastard's sense of humour didn't desert him at the end. I skipped The Cardinal's funeral. Had other things to worry about, like running a city all set to blow in the wake of its former ruler's death.

'Where are you now?' I whisper, touching the coffin (it's warm, some kind of hard plastic, softer than I expected). 'Riding the devil's ass in hell? Tearing up the heavens? Simply rotting here?'

I don't know whether or not I believe in life after death. I'm proof that the dead can be brought back, but that doesn't mean they can move on. What happens to the billions of spirits not waylaid by the villacs? Do they find rest elsewhere, or did the Ayuamarcans, by their very existence, signify that this plane is all there is? The priests are powerful, but I can't picture them wrenching control of a soul from a god or devil. Perhaps they're only able to wield power over the dead because the dead have nowhere else to go.

Shaking my head, I check the lid of the coffin. It's held in place by screws which can be easily turned. Suppressing a shiver, I undo them all and gently slide the lid aside. I'm ready for anything – a living, grinning Ferdinand Dorak, a villac, an empty coffin – but all I'm faced with is a standard, grey-skinned corpse.

The Cardinal's hair is a mess, and his nails look jagged and long on his shrunken fingers, but otherwise he's much as I remember. His hands are crossed on his chest in the traditional manner of the dead. I check the smallest finger of his left hand. It used to bend away from the others each time he created a new Ayuamarcan. Now it's straight. Whoever's bringing the dead back to life, it isn't this decrepit stiff.

Curious, I press a couple of fingers to the flesh of the former Cardinal's left cheek. There's a thin snapping sound as the bone gives way. I pull back quickly before it crumbles. The Cardinal was in a pretty sorry state when they scraped him off the pavement at the foot of Party Central — a fifteen-floor drop takes it out of even the toughest son of a bitch. The undertakers did an incredible job piecing him back together for the televised funeral, but it's all spit and glue. One punch to the jaw and his head would explode.

I grin at the thought of desecrating the corpse – part of me hates The Cardinal for creating me and sentencing me to eternity – but I don't. He was only obeying his nature, as I've obeyed mine since taking over. The villacs are the real enemies, the sly bastards who manipulated us.

I lever the lid of the coffin back into place. I feel foolish for coming. Conchita's message must have had some other meaning. This has been a waste of time. Dead men can't see. As soon as Sines lets me out, I'll hot-tail it back to Party Central and refocus. There must be . . .

A groaning sound stops the thought dead. I spin towards the door but it's stationary. The sound isn't coming from outside but from in here.

Backing up against a wall, I stare at the coffin. I expect the lid to creak open, the way it would in a horror film, and the corpse of The Cardinal to stumble out. But that doesn't happen. Instead the entire coffin slides off the marble slab. At first I think it's magic, but then I spot a thin metal shelf supporting it and I realize this is technology at work, not the supernatural.

The coffin comes to a halt. Taking a couple of steps closer, I see that the marble slab is hollow. There are steps set within. As I stare into darkness, pondering this arcane twist, a head appears — someone's coming up. My throat tightens and I search for a weapon, but I gave up carrying guns and knives many years ago. No call for them when you're immortal.

Fighting the urge to lurch away from the slab and hammer on the door, I stand my ground, facing up to whatever horror awaits. As the figure mounts the steps, I realize first that it's a woman, tall, dark skin, long black hair. Next I notice that she's naked. As that sinks in, the even more incredible truth of her identity strikes me.

'Ama?' I wheeze. Her head lifts and her eyes settle on mine, but that's her only response. 'Ama,' I moan, taking a stag-gering step toward her. Ama Situwa was the love of my life, the woman The Cardinal created for me. She could have been Eve to my Adam, for a few decades at least, but I sacrificed her. Part of the price I paid when agreeing my demonic deal.

Ama puts a finger to her lips. Mouths the sound, 'Shhh.' I stop and stare. I want to cry but I've forgotten how. She lowers her hand, then stretches it out, offering it to me. I shake my head, afraid. She cups her fingers and beckons, smiling reassuringly. Trembling, scared of what will happen if I take her hand, terrified of what will happen if I don't, I slide my fingers into hers. She squeezes, then turns and starts back down the stairs. I hesitate at the top – it's dark down there, I can't see the bottom – but she squeezes my hand again and nods to say it's safe. I shouldn't go – this is insane, placing my life in the hands of a naked ghost – but I can't help myself. Reason has fled. The spirits of the past have claimed me as their own.

Holding onto Ama, I follow her down the stairs into the unknown, only dimly aware of the coffin sliding back into place overhead, plunging us into total, all-encompassing darkness.

part two

assassin

ONE – IN THE NAME OF THE FATHER

My father was a demon. He killed thousands of people, wicked and just, innocent and guilty — it made no difference to him. Paucar Wami was tall, black as the devil's heart, bald, with uncanny green eyes and colourful tattooed snakes running the gamut of both cheeks, meeting just beneath his lower lip. He butchered for pleasure and gain. He lived solely to destroy. Ten years ago he passed from the face of this earth and his unique strain of evil passed with him.

Between murders, Wami fathered a crop of children. I was the firstborn. I've spent the past decade trying to revive my father's twisted legacy. I've become his living ghost. I'm an assassin's shade, death to all who cross me.

My name is Al Jeery.

Call me Paucar Wami.

Friday, 23:00. I've been shadowing Basil Collinson since early evening. If the pimp sticks to his schedule, he should roll out of the Madam Luck casino shortly after midnight and head for a club. That's when he dies.

Basil's a poor gambler but he never drops more than a thousand in a single sitting. He's careful that way. Likes to maintain control of his life. Dresses in the same smart suit every day. Takes care of his wife and kids, hides the true nature of his business from them. Cuts a slice of his profits to all the right people. On drinking terms with influential police officers and lawyers. Even pays his taxes in full and on time.

Basil's only weakness is his violent appetite for the women who work for him. He has between fifteen and twenty ladies on the books at any given time, and though he sees that they're fairly paid, every now and then he takes one off for a weekend and goes to work on her. He drops the façade, hits the bottle and subjects his victim to a torrent of abuse and torment. Mostly they limp away nursing bruises and cuts, but occasionally he'll put one in hospital, and at least twice that I know of the damage has been fatal.

Pimps don't ruffle my feathers – live and let live – but murderers are fair game.

My motorbike's parked out back of the casino, ready if I need it, though I doubt I will. Collinson normally walks to a nearby club when he's done gambling. I'm waiting for him in an apartment on the fourth floor of the building opposite the casino. It belongs to a guy called George Adams. He works nights. Lives alone. He'll never know I've been here. I prefer to stake out prey from the comfort of an apartment or office. Beats loitering on the streets, disguised as a beggar, hidden behind layers of soggy newspapers and cardboard.

Midnight comes and goes. The air fills with the vicious beat of fuck-it-all music, guilty laughter, drunken cheers and jeers, the growl of taxis, occasional gunfire. The city's hotting up. There's been a lot of unrest recently. Gang clashes, street riots, attacks on police. Word is The Cardinal Mk II has gone AWOL. If it's true, it's bad news. I've no sympathy for Dorak's successor, but at least he held things together. If he's been killed or abducted, this city will erupt and the streets will run with blood.

Collinson exits through the arched, glittering doorway of Madam Luck. I check my watch. 01:23. Later than usual. Must have been on a winning streak. Letting myself out of the apartment, careful not to leave any trace, I slip down the stairs and tag Basil as he turns the corner at the end of the street. He's alone, which is a bonus. A companion would have complicated things. Now it's simply a case of picking the ideal moment to strike.

Keeping to the sides, stepping over broken glass and sleeping bums, I close on Collinson, unseen, unheard, a child of the shadows. Ahead, my prey hums and clicks his fingers in time to the tune. Chances are he wouldn't hear me even if he wasn't so self-absorbed. I've had nine years of practice. Only the very rare victim sees or hears me coming. To the rest I materialize out of the night like the monsters they were told not to fear when they were children.

Basil turns into Hodgson Street. Angling for the Nevermind club – '90s retro. He'll have to detour through Steine Avenue. The lights are inadequate there at the best of times. Useless these last four nights, since vandals smashed two of the lamps. That's where I'll take him.

I get close enough to Basil to identify the tune he's humming. Dylan's *Like a Rolling Stone*. A good song, and he carries it well, but I turn a deaf ear to it. Can't afford to think of him as human. He's a pimp, a killer, prey. I'm Paucar Wami, self-appointed executioner. I show no mercy. Fuck his taste in music.

Collinson hits the darkened Steine Avenue. Picking up speed, I stroke the varnished human finger hanging by a chain from my neck and slip up silently behind him, sliding a long curved knife from my belt. The blade's freshly honed. I take no chances. Murder's messy if you don't put your target down with a single swipe.

At the last moment Basil senses me. He begins to turn,

but too late. Bringing the knife up, hissing like the jungle cat I become at the moment of death, I slash it sharply across his throat, using the momentum of his swivelling head to drive the blade deep into his flesh, all the way across from right to left.

Basil's dead before he hits the floor, though it takes him a while to realize it. He jerks spasmodically, blood arcing high into the air from his severed throat. I stand clear of the spray, letting the wall take the burst, watching emotionlessly as his legs and arms go still. When he's at rest and the flow of blood has subsided to a steady trickle, I step forward and crouch, working quickly. I'm wearing disposable plastic gloves. Dipping my index finger into the pool of blood spreading around his head, I rip the front of his shirt open, then scrawl on his chest (pausing to re-bloody my finger several times), 'This is what happens to pimps who maltreat their women. P.W.'

Done, I close Basil Collinson's eyes and say a silent prayer over him. 'This son of a bitch is yours, Lord. Do with him as you will. Just don't send him back.' The prayer's instinctive. I mutter similar words over many of those I kill. A force of habit I've never bothered to break, though I should — wasted seconds.

Standing, I check I haven't been seen, then slip away, offering myself to the shadows of the streets and alleys. As usual they accept me, and soon I'm invisible to all but the city itself.

I wake early, before seven. I'd have appreciated another couple of hours, but once I'm awake there's no slipping back to sleep. Better to get up and on with the day than lie here thinking about Collinson and the other lives I've taken. I can reconcile myself to the life I lead when I'm active

(when I'm Paucar Wami)

but if I sit back and brood, doubts flood in, and doubts

will be the end of me if I give them their head. I have to keep busy. My sanity depends on it.

Temperatures have been hotter than usual for this time of year, but it's cold this morning and I start with a series of push-ups to warm up. I break three hundred before the first beads of sweat flow. I've spent most of the last ten years exercising. Approximately six hours of sleep each day, a couple of hours wasted on eating, washing, cleaning and shopping, the rest working-out or pounding the streets. No leisure time. I don't read, watch TV or listen to the radio. Sometimes I dip into newspapers, do research in libraries, and scan computer files to check on certain facts, but otherwise I'm continually on the move, acting and reacting, thinking only of the challenges to hand.

I finish with the push-ups and segue into sit-ups, focusing on my abdominal muscles. I'm in great shape for a man pushing fifty. I have to be. The streets devour the weak. I must be stronger than those I hunt and kill.

My eyes flick to the photograph hanging on the wall at the foot of my bed. This is a small apartment, a bedroom, living room, kitchenette and bathroom. The wallpaper was old when I was young. The smell from the alley is suffocating in hot weather. But it's home. I deserve and long for no better.

In the photo, an off-duty police officer has an arm draped paternally around the shoulders of a young, amateur actress. They're beaming at the camera. I've loved both of them, in different ways, and hated them more than I've loved. The woman died by my hand before I became Paucar Wami. The man is missing, presumed dead, but I believe he's still alive. My sole purpose in life is to find him, put a gun to his temple and blow his brains out. On that day the killing can stop, and so can I. Until then I act out the part of my father and roam these streets without rest, hunting, killing, searching.

I start on neck-rolls. Whisper softly to myself as I rotate my head, a word or short sentence each time my chin touches my chest. 'Paucar. Wami. I am. Paucar Wami. The night. Is mine. No rest until. He dies.'

He — Bill Casey, the cop who destroyed me, who robbed me of everything I ever had and was, reducing me to this pale shadow of my inhuman father in the process. I have Bill's small left finger – the digit which hangs from my neck – and one day, if he's out there, I'll have the rest of him too.

I think about Bill and Paucar Wami every day, every hour. Even when trailing prey, they're foremost in my thoughts. Everything I am, I owe to them. Everything I do is in response to the hell of their creation.

Wami was my father, a legendary serial killer, beloved of The Cardinal. A beast who tormented and murdered to pass the time. Somewhere along the line his path crossed with Bill Casey's. I haven't worked out what Wami did to Bill – I suppose he butchered someone close to him – but it drove Bill mad. He swore revenge and spent decades plotting a bizarre retribution. Befriending me as a child, he guided me through much of my life, keeping me close by his side, only to strip me of everything I valued when the time was right, slaughtering those close to me, pinning the blame on Wami in the crazy belief that I'd take up arms against my father and kill him.

I confronted Bill once I'd unmasked him. When I asked why he didn't kill Wami himself, he cited poetic justice. That didn't make sense then, and it hasn't grown any clearer with the passage of time. Unless Bill's alive, and I can find him and squeeze the truth out of him, I doubt it ever will.

My head comes to a rest. I take several deep breaths, then head for the kitchenette to prepare breakfast. A simple meal – dry cereal, toast, slices of cold meat. Food doesn't interest me. I eat to keep my body – my engine – ticking over. It's fuel. Without it, I'd stop. And stopping's something I can't allow myself to do, not until Casey's severed head rests on a spear before me.

And if he really died in the blast he engineered – the blast which left my body scarred and burnt – and didn't plant a corpse in his place? Then I'll carry on until I grow old and withered, and perish on the streets of blood which I have chosen to make my own. Either way, there can be no rest. Not for the wicked.

I was an alcoholic once. In the nightmare months after Bill's awful revelation, I almost gave myself over to the bottle. That would have been the easy way out. I often wish I'd taken it. But I hung tough, and gradually, when only the abyss loomed large in my life, the *plan* presented itself.

My father wasn't human. The original Cardinal, Ferdinand Dorak, said he'd created Paucar Wami out of thin air, assisted by blind, Incan priests who've controlled this city for centuries. He said he'd created others too — Ayuamarcans. Whenever he destroyed one of his creations, a green fog crept over the city and gnawed away at people's minds, eliminating all memories of the unreal person.

I don't know if The Cardinal was telling the truth or if he was a hundred per cent bugshit, but there was *something* supernatural about Wami and the others. I'm the only one who remembers the Ayuamarcans. When The Cardinal died, those that were left faded out of existence and memory, except for Wami, whose legend lived on vaguely.

The *plan* was to recreate the serial killer, and thus lure Bill out of hiding. Since Bill had devoted so much of his life to destroying the hated Paucar Wami, I figured he wouldn't be able to stop. He'd pursue his crazed quest, even if he was no longer sure who he was chasing. The trouble was, with Wami gone – banished to the realms of nothingness when The Cardinal died – there was no one for him to chase, no reason for him to come out of hiding.

So I gave him one.

Following the food with half a pint of milk, I edge into the tiny bathroom and relieve myself. While washing my hands, I study my reflection in the mirror. I'm dark-skinned like my father, very similar in appearance. The main differences — Wami was bald, with green eyes, and sported tattoos of twisting, multi-coloured snakes, one down either cheek, their heads locking in the middle beneath his lower lip.

I started with the hair. Scissors and a razor rid me of that. Green contact lenses for the eyes. Then the tattoos (which, as a bonus, hid the worst of my scar tissue). It took a while to find a tattooist capable of replicating my father's serpentine design, and several lengthy, painful sessions to ink in every last coil, scale and link, but eventually it was done and I took on the full look of Paucar Wami, down to the leather jacket and motorbike which were favourites of his.

All that remained was to kill.

I used to remove the contact lenses each night, before retiring, but now I leave them in, not caring about the damage that must be doing to my eyes. They help keep me in character. Such small touches have become second nature. They have to, if the disguise is to work, if I'm to truly become the killer I seek to mimic and tempt my tormentor out of hiding.

I realized it wasn't enough to look like Paucar Wami. To be him, I had to act as he had. I had to murder. At first, when the madness was fresh upon me, I thought to kill indiscriminately. The world had treated me cruelly and I meant to react in kind. I imagined myself butchering bloodily, freely. I got as far as shadowing a randomly picked woman to her home, slipping in at night while she was asleep and pressing my knife to the soft flesh of her throat.

I went no further. After an eternity of indecision, I withdrew, having shed no blood, to marvel at how close to true evil I had sailed. If I'd killed her, I genuinely would have become my father, and in time I'm certain I would have abandoned thoughts of revenge and lost myself entirely to viciousness.

Instead I ran home, moaning and weeping, and prayed for death. I almost took my life in the dark hours that followed, but the blade that had wavered at the woman's throat crept away of its own accord every time I raised it to mine.

Over the next few days, between fits of rage and remorse, I found myself readjusting my *plan*. I couldn't bring myself to kill the innocent, but I knew from experience that I was capable of dispatching the guilty. I'd killed during my years working for The Cardinal, as one of his Troops, and when I'd been betrayed by a woman in league with Bill and the *villacs*. This city's full of criminals, deserving of death. If I left the innocent alone and set my sights on the scum . . .

Coming out of the bathroom, I wipe my hands dry, get down on the floor and launch into a punishing set of squats, hard and fast, thinking, 'Machine. Machine. Machine.' Al Jeery grimaces as I break the hundred mark. Paucar Wami licks his lips and asks for more. His wish is granted. Two hundred. Three hundred. Four . . .

The New Munster hotel. 14:00. Three ground-level rooms packed with booksellers and buyers. Long tables overflowing with first prints and rare editions. Very little in the way of popular or pulp material — this is a fair for serious collectors. Most of the clientele are middle-aged and formally attired. Very little cash exchanges hands. It's all credit cards these days.

I mingle unobtrusively with the rich as they fawn over the tomes, discussing print runs, volume conditions and prices. They also talk a lot about other fairs. Apparently Paris is the hot city at the moment, wonderful finds lying in wait on dusty shelves for those prepared to look. They take no notice of me, assuming – if they assume at all – that I'm with security.

I've removed my contact lenses, covered my tattoos with flesh paint, and I wear a wig of tight black curls. A shabby but acceptable suit. Neat shoes. Sometimes it's better to go abroad as Al Jeery. These people would flee in terror at the sight of my nocturnal face.

I've been to dozens of fairs over the years, and I visit all the bookstores in the city on a regular basis. Books were Bill's great love. He had a massive collection of first editions, a collection many of the people here today would happily steal, mug or even kill for. When he disappeared ten years ago, he took the books with him. That's how I knew he
(*probably*)
wasn't dead. He often said he didn't care what happened to his books once he died, so since he'd taken the time to spirit them away before blowing up his house, I assumed it was because he hadn't yet finished with life.

I don't really expect Bill to show his face at a fair like this, but I come anyway, to mingle, observe, hope. These people get around – some have flown in from distant cities and countries, just to circulate for a few hours in search of a missing volume – and they tend to know, or know of, everybody within their exclusive circle. Maybe one of them has run into Bill, or knows somebody who has, and I'll overhear them talking about him. A thin straw to clutch at, but when you're as desperate as I am, you'll clutch at anything.

I spend four hours in the dry, studious, murmur-filled rooms, circling silently, eavesdropping, studying faces. I ask no questions of the buyers – I tried that in the early days, but it only aroused people's suspicions – though sometimes I'll stop by a quiet table stacked with the sort of books Bill favoured (Steinbeck, Hemingway, Dickens) and linger a few minutes, prompting a bored proprietor to start a conversation.

On such occasions I'll casually steer talk around to an old friend of mine – 'Bill Casey. A police office. Had a full set of Hemingway firsts.' – and gauge their reaction. Some recall him, but all believe that he died in the blast. Nobody's heard word of him in the decade since.

As the fair draws to a quiet close, I make my exit. I'm not disappointed but I feel downhearted. It's at times like this that I realize just how blindly I'm casting about for my old friend. He has all the world to hide in, and I've no clue where he might be. The odds against me finding him are immense. If I was in control of my senses, I'd cut my losses and call it quits. But I'm not. Haven't been for ten years. So I'll continue, like the senseless, dogged, single-minded beast that I am.

The city's an ancient, sprawling, troubled beast. Founded by Indians, it's been built up over the centuries by the Incan priests who fled from the conquistadors and made their home here. They rule from the shadows, which maybe explains why the city is dark and menacing at heart. Chaos flourishes here, nurtured by the *villacs*, who ladle power out among the various gangs, pitting black against white, Italian against Spaniard, the Irish against everybody. Street laws hold the gangs in check, but those laws change abruptly in accordance with the dictum of the priests.

The last weekend's been especially rough. Major clashes in the north-west between the Kluxers and Troops. The Kluxers are an offshoot of the Ku Klux Klan, led by Eugene Davern, the guy who owns the Kool Kats Klub. Five years back, I'd have said Davern was crazy if he thought he could take on the Troops. But power's been slipping through the new Cardinal's fingers. Individuals have defied him and he hasn't cracked down hard. The belief on the street is that Capac Raimi's weak, out of touch with the pulse of the city. Revolt's been on the cards for ages.

Davern and his Kluxers are the start. I hate those KKK sons of bitches – I've strung up more than a few of them these past nine years – but they're a powerful force and Davern's a shrewd leader. I doubt they can defeat the Troops alone, but if other gangs riot and Raimi's forces are split, they might just pull it off.

Not that The Cardinal will notice. Word has strengthened over the weekend. It now seems certain Raimi's no longer running the show. Some say he's been killed, others that he quit, more that he disappeared mysteriously. Whatever the truth, he's not *in situ* at Party Central any longer. I don't know who *is* in charge, but I don't envy him. The city's facing its worst bout of mayhem since the race riots of some decades back. I pity the fool charged with the hopeless task of averting it.

It's almost dawn, Monday, and I've been on the go since Saturday evening, bar a few hours of sleep yesterday. Although most of the trouble's been confined to the north-west, there's been a knock-on effect all over, especially here. Eugene Davern may have rid the Kluxers of many of their icons – they've abandoned the white hoods and burning crosses – but leopards don't change their spots. If they overcome the Troops and annex the north-west, the next area they're likely to target is the black-dominated east.

People in this part of the city are edgy, and that edginess manifested itself over the weekend in violence. Gangs are fighting to expand their boundaries and recruit new members, preparing for the war they think is coming. Street kids are mugging freely, making the most of things while the going's good, before the lynchings start. A police precinct was besieged when one of its officers remarked in a radio interview that the Kluxers taking over would be the best thing that ever happened.

The city hasn't erupted – the Troops are still the force all others are measured by, and they've been working hard to hold things in place – but it isn't far off. If Davern can drive the Troops out of the north-west, expect ballistics.

I've spent the weekend doing what I can to calm things locally. I'm known and feared all over the east. I'm the Black Angel . . . Mr Moonshine . . . the Weasel. I kill mercilessly (very few know that I only punish the guilty — I take credit for the deaths of innocents whenever possible). I'm a creature of the night, a son of the shadows. Unstoppable. Utterly vicious.

I've taken advantage of my reputation and patrolled the streets relentlessly, breaking up fights and gatherings by intervening directly or simply showing my tattooed face and coughing ominously. I shouldn't interfere. My father cared nothing for the welfare of others. To truly be him, I should focus only on killing. Paucar Wami relished bloodshed. Setting myself up as a vigilante is counter-productive. I should leave the east to the gangs, keep my head low.

But this is where I grew up. These are my people. Even though I have few friends, and mix with the locals as little as possible, I feel attached. There isn't much of the old Al Jeery alive within me, but just enough lingers somewhere beneath my skin to make me do what I can to help between executions.

Monday, 22:00. I snatched several hours of sleep earlier and feel much fresher. I disguised myself as Al Jeery when I woke and went to do some shopping. I wear the make-up whenever I want to pass among ordinary people. Remove the contacts, don a wig, plaster the sides of my face with flesh-coloured paint to hide the snakes, dump the leather jacket. I'm unrecognizable this way.

After a quick dinner I dispensed with the wig and make-up, slipped the contacts back in and took to the streets again, exiting my apartment by the fire escape and dark rear alley, as I always do when in Paucar Wami mode, careful not to reveal myself to any of my neighbours. I checked on a few of the worst trouble spots – things have calmed down, though I doubt the peace will hold – saw I wasn't needed and returned to the business of meting out terror.

I'm on the prowl for a homosexual, homicidal rapist. He's struck four times in three months. Brutally rapes his young male victims, then stabs them through the heart with an ice pick. A savage piece of work. More than worthy of the slow death he's going to endure when I get hold of him.

Even as I think that, the small trace of a human within me whispers that there can be no justification for murder. Even though the people I kill are the lowest of the low, they have the right to be tried by law. I'm labouring under no delusions — what I do is wrong, unjust, immoral. If there's an afterlife and a judgemental god, I'm for the big drop. There can be no room for vigilantes in a civilized society, even one as beset by brutes as this. I'm no better than the scum I kill. If anything I'm worse, because I know what I do is wrong.

I turn down Cyclone Avenue, hugging the shadows, watching, waiting, at one with the night. Most of the buildings in the east date back to the 1950s. Old, tired, ugly, many in a state of slow collapse. The whole sector needs to be bulldozed and put out of its misery. That said, in the dark, with the crumbling brickwork, barred or splintered windows, and garbage-spattered streets obscured by the shady streaks of the night, it can almost pass for pleasant. Darkness becomes this city.

The rapist has struck in a different spot each time, no discernible pattern, but always in the east, between ten and midnight. I've been hunting for him since his second victim was discovered, slotting the search in around my other duties, scouring likely alleys, those which are ill-lit and rarely used. Luck will need to be on my side if I'm to find him, but in my experience luck comes to those who work for it. I don't always get my man – the Mounties can lay sole claim to that distinction – but few evade me once I focus on them.

The streets are as good as deserted. Mondays are traditionally quiet, and after the weekend we've endured, tonight's even quieter than usual. I'm beginning to think I should head for home when I enter a cul-de-sac and spot two figures ahead, one on the ground, struggling and moaning softly, the other on top, thrusting with his hips and panting.

I slide against a damp, moss-encrusted wall and creep towards them. While I don't jump to conclusions – although this looks like rape, I've come across couples engaged in equally violent but consensual intercourse before – I do draw my knife and prepare for the worst.

Closer. The figure on the ground is male, black, fourteen or fifteen. Gagged and bleeding from a cut to his head. Trousers yanked down around his ankles. The man on his back swats him, hissing, stabbing at him with his penis. I don't think he's penetrated, and I also no longer think this is consensual. I've seen masochists put themselves through worse than this, but I've never seen naked terror in their eyes, the way I see it in the boy's.

'That's enough,' I say softly, stepping away from the wall, keeping my knife low by my side where the rapist can't see it.

The man stops, startled, then pushes himself away from the boy and spins to confront me. He's wearing a dark wool cap, pulled over his ears and forehead. A long, bulky jacket, open down the front. His trousers are crotchless. His exposed penis points at me like a dagger, uncommonly stiff.

'Bastard!' the rapist snarls. He reaches behind the boy and grabs a short but finely pointed ice pick — my man!

'I've been looking for you,' I grin bleakly, sheathing my knife and drawing the .45 I keep for encounters such as these. Only a fool goes up against an ice pick with a knife.

'Bastard!' the rapist snaps again – a man of limited vocabulary – and starts towards me, pick held high.

I raise my gun to shoot but stop as I catch a clearer glimpse of his penis. I realize why it looked so strange. It isn't real — it's a strap-on dildo. As the folds of the rapist's coat shift, it clicks — I'm dealing with a woman!

Momentarily startled, I forget to fire, and she's upon me. She swings for my left arm with the pick. Luckily for me, she misjudges and it scrapes off my leather jacket harmlessly, to whistle across the expanse of my chest. She curses and reverses her movement, fluid, swift. But not swift enough. I step out of the way of the pick. She stumbles from the force of the missed blow. I take three more steps back, raise my gun again and fire before she recovers. Not a finely judged shot, but at this range it's almost impossible to miss.

An unexpected zinging sound is followed immediately by a deeper, thudding noise — a bullet burying itself in flesh. The rapist collapses with a muffled shriek, dropping her pick, falling backwards, hands flying to her stomach, coming away sticky with blood.

I close on her, ready to shoot again if I have to. The kid is on his feet, pulling up his trousers. He hasn't taken the gag out. 'Go,' I grunt. 'Don't look back.' He says nothing, only nods gratefully and flees.

The woman – no, the *rapist* is mewing softly. I must think of her purely as the murdering defiler that she is. I was raised to be polite to women. Got to forget that. Focus on the task. Finish her off or wait for her to die.

As I study her, I see that the dildo no longer juts out straight from her groin. It's bent to one side. The bullet must have struck the fake penis, then ricocheted upwards – the source of the zing. I can't prevent a wicked grin. She who lives by the dildo, dies by the dildo.

Noises behind me. My smile vanishes. I pivot, gun raised. When I see three half-naked old women entering the cul-de-sac, staring hungrily at the woman on the ground, I relax and step aside.

The women dart past me and fix on the stricken rapist. She ignores them when they fasten their claw-like fingers on her – she has other things to worry about – and only screams when they bite into her flesh. Her shrieks are short-lived. One of the Harpies is on her mouth in seconds, covering her lips with her own, kissing her silent, smothering her cries. In no time at all the rapist succumbs to the inevitable and yields beneath the onslaught. Her limbs go still. Her eyelids stop fluttering and the emptiness of death takes the place of living thought.

The Harpy draws back, bits of the rapist's lips and tongue dangling from her teeth. She gurgles triumphantly, then joins the other two in their feast, tearing warm flesh from the corpse with her hands and teeth, swallowing it raw.

I avert my gaze and nod politely at the primly dressed, middle-aged woman who has followed the Harpies into the cul-de-sac. 'Mrs Abbots,' I greet her.

'Mr Wami,' she responds with a wan smile. She observes the Harpies at feed, then turns to me with a worried frown. 'She was alive when they started?'

'Yes.'

'Was she a bad person?' Her face contorts in anticipation of the answer. She does her best to keep the Harpies away from the innocent, but sometimes they feed on the corpses of the good as well as the bad.

'She was a child-raping murderess,' I sniff, and the worry deserts her.

'I'll let them feed in peace then.'

Jennifer Abbots walks to the mouth of the cul-de-sac and waits for her charges to finish eating. After a last glance at the rapist and the Harpies – one of the cannibalistic ladies has dug through to the intestines and is reeling them out like a sailor drawing in his nets – I join her.

I first ran into the Harpies four, maybe five years ago. I'd just killed a guy who'd been selling spiked heroin when a quartet of crazed, near-naked women descended on him, ripped off his clothes and carved him up with their claws and teeth. I was repulsed and drew my gun to fire on them. I'd seen a lot of dark deeds during my time, but nothing as foul as this looked.

Jennifer stopped me. She threw herself at my arm and knocked my gun away, yelling, 'No!' As I scrabbled for the gun, she fell to her knees, clasped her hands together and wept. 'Please, I beg you, no. They don't mean any harm. They can't help themselves. They only feed on the dead.'

That struck a chord. It was ridiculous, but put across with such earnestness – as if feeding on a person was fine as long as they were dead – that I stopped and studied the woman, crying and dirty from the dust of the street, pleading with me to spare the feasting cannibals. I saw the rosary beads hanging from her neck, the grey in her hair, the anguish in her face. And I lowered my gun and let her talk.

The four women stripping the flesh from the bones of the dead dealer had been inmates in an asylum for the deranged. Privately run, very down-market, the sort of institute you read about in tabloid exposés, staffed by unqualified nurses, patients fed on watered-down porridge and stale bread, bedclothes washed once a month, orderlies having their wicked way with the unfortunate women. As if the situation wasn't grim enough, the staff had a run-in with the manager and walked out *en masse*. Whether because he expected them to return, or just didn't have the funds to hire replacements, he took over the running of the asylum himself. The relatives of the inmates didn't find that out until later. Few visited regularly, being either unwilling to face their incarcerated kin or unable, as in the case of Jennifer, who had to work three jobs to pay for the upkeep of her house and cancer-stricken husband.

For a couple of weeks the manager struggled by, buying food and drinks from nearby supermarkets, using laundromats to wash the sheets a few at a time. Perhaps he could have carried on indefinitely, but the strain must have got to him, because he died of a heart attack while preparing dinner one night. He was only discovered three weeks later, when a local councillor running for re-election wandered in with the intention of obtaining positive press shots of himself with some of the less privileged members of the community.

Nobody knows how long the crazed inmates tolerated the hunger pangs. Some held out to the end — there were nine to begin with, and three died of starvation. The other half-dozen, having raided and emptied the cupboards, fridges and freezers, turned in the end to the only remaining food source — the manager and their dead companions.

'How's life?' I ask Jennifer as we stand guard and wait for the Harpies to finish eating.

'So-so,' she answers. It's been several months since we last ran into one another and she looks healthier than she did. 'Rose died just before New Year, poor dear.' Rose was the mother of one of the Harpies. She'd been helping Jennifer care for the three remaining members of the cannibalistic clan.

'You're looking after this lot by yourself?'

She shakes her head. 'A very kind friend of mine, Mr Clarke, has taken responsibility. He's let them move in with him and he sees to their day-to-day needs. I've been able to relax for the first time in years, though I chip in with my share of the duties, which include chaperoning them when they go on the prowl.'

The councillor hushed up the scandal, terrified of being associated with a media nightmare. Bribing the photographer to keep his mouth shut, he contacted the relatives of the surviving inmates, told them what had happened and gave them the option of quietly coming to collect the survivors. Four responded, two didn't. Jennifer and Rose, unwilling to leave any of the ladies to the discretion of the councillor – he promised to place them in a first-rate home, but they didn't trust him – each took one of the 'spare crazies' home along with their own relative.

With the survivors cleared, the councillor torched the nursing home, destroyed the evidence, put the mess behind him and focused on his campaign (in the end he lost by a thousand votes and hasn't been heard of since).

Jennifer and Rose weren't sure what to do with their charges. If they'd admitted them to another nursing facility, they would have had to explain where the women had been previously. The ladies were quieter than they'd been in the past, so Jennifer and Rose decided to tend to them by themselves until they could work something out.

The four weren't difficult to care for. Apart from the occasional hysterical fit, they were model patients. Jennifer and Rose were both working women, but they arranged their shifts so that one was free while the other was busy. It wasn't easy, but they managed, and everything ran smoothly until Rose fell asleep one afternoon while minding the four, and woke to find they'd vanished.

One frantic phone call later, Jennifer met Rose on the street and they went searching for the missing lunatics. They knew the women couldn't get far – with no money, and dressed in simple gowns, they weren't going to make much of a break for freedom – but the worry was that they'd attract attention, leading to all sorts of uncomfortable questions.

They searched the streets on foot, working in methodical

circles. Nearly six hours later they found the quartet, crouched behind a garbage bin, sucking on the bones of a derelict who must have frozen or starved to death days before.

Jennifer and Rose were shocked, but since there was nothing they could do without calling the authorities and confessing, they opted to make the best of a bad lot, dumped the body in the bin and shepherded their stuffed, sated charges home.

Over the coming months, they realized the ladies' taste for human flesh wasn't going to go away. They'd get restless, stop eating, complain and act up. They grew violent if denied their cannibalistic pleasures. The only way to keep them quiet was to take them out, locate a fresh corpse and let them at it.

So that's what Jennifer and Rose did.

The first of the Harpies finishes her meal, staggers away from the others, sits at Jennifer's feet and burps. It's Rettie, Jennifer's sister. One of the Harpies died a couple of years ago. Jennifer never told me what of. I've a sneaking suspicion it might have been indigestion.

I don't wholeheartedly approve of the Harpies, but they do no harm, feeding only on the dead or those – like the rapist tonight – who are as close to it as makes no difference. It's a dog-eat-dog world. Who am I to pass judgement on a few mad old women who've taken that credo literally?

I tried curing the ladies of their craving once. I used to be able to help people with mental difficulties. As a younger man, I could absorb their fear and hurt, and ease their pain. But I couldn't work my charms on the Harpies. Didn't even get to first base. I think I lost that gift around the same time I abandoned my humanity. Monsters can't cure, only kill.

As the others reach their fill and desert the body of the rapist, Jennifer starts towards it with the intention of carting it away for disposal. I stop her with a gentle hand. 'That's OK. I'll get rid of the remains.'

'Are you sure?' Jennifer asks.

'Yeah. Spare your back. You're getting too old for this. You should hire someone younger to help.'

Jennifer laughs. 'It's not exactly a post you can advertise for.'

I grin. 'Guess not.'

'Besides, I can't complain. Mr Clarke, God bless him, has relieved me of most of the stress. I have things easy compared with how they used to be. This would be a harsh, lonely life if we had no friends.'

'Yes,' I sigh, and stand aside as she leads Rettie and the other two Harpies away, to wherever they now call home. I muse on the dark wonders and variety of the world for a couple of minutes, then roll on a pair of gloves, bag scraps of the rapist's clothes, flesh and bones – not forgetting the dildo – and grab hold of the bloody remains of the dead woman. She doesn't weigh much now that she's been stripped to the bone. I hoist her onto my shoulders and go looking for a decent-sized dumpster or furnace.

Just another average night in the city.

TWO – OLD FRIENDS

I sleep in late. Putting an end to the rapist pleased me, and I sleep the sleep of the

(*almost*)

just. I half-wake a couple of times, but doze off again without opening my eyes, smiling in the gloominess of my stuffy room, enjoying the warmth and comfort of my bed.

It's after midday when I rise and launch into the first set of the day's exercises. Squats. I'm up to two hundred and thirty-six when someone knocks on the door.

I come to a cautious halt. I'm not expecting visitors, and unexpected guests are rare around here. Religious missionaries don't venture this far east – they gave up on us long ago – and nobody's dumb enough to come collecting for charity. My neighbours aren't in the habit of dropping in – they care as little about my affairs as I do about theirs – and the rent isn't due for another two months.

Rising, I pad to the door and pause with my hand on the knob. I don't have a chain or latch, so I address my visitor through the thin wood of the closed door. 'Who is it?'

'Jerry Falstaff.'

Unlocking the door, I open it and gesture him in. It's been

three years – more – since he last looked me up. My curiosity's instantly aroused.

Jerry walks straight to the only chair in the tiny living room and takes it. 'The décor hasn't improved,' he notes, casting an unimpressed eye around.

'I was never big on interior design.' I close the door and take up a position opposite him, standing to attention the way I used to when I was one of Jerry's colleagues in the Troops. Jerry's come a long way since then, further than either of us ever imagined. The new Cardinal took a shine to him. Jerry mixes with the high and mighty these days, though he doesn't bear the look of an important man. He's the same Jerry Falstaff I remember, slightly overweight, clothes a bit loose, a small grin never far from his lips. A bit greyer at the temples perhaps.

'Looking good, Al.'

'I keep in shape.'

'And then some.' Jerry coughs meaningfully and I take the hint.

'Can I get you something to drink?'

'Thought you'd never ask. Got any beer?'

I fetch a couple of cans from the fridge, one for each of us. Ten years ago I was dry, avoiding all forms of alcohol in the sure knowledge that one slip would be my downfall. These days I can indulge in a social drink (though I rarely do) and leave it at that. I have greater demons to wrestle with.

'Busy?' Jerry asks, sinking a third of the can and burping.

'Yes.'

'Things have been tense lately. I hear you're keeping a lid on the situation in these parts.'

'I've done what I can.'

'Didn't think community watch was your kind of business.'

'Riots are good for nobody. How are things going with the Kluxers?'

Jerry grimaces. 'We've forced them back a bit. They've established a toe-hold, but we showed we weren't ready to let them roll in and take over. It's an uneasy truce but it should hold for a few weeks.'

'And then?'

'Who knows?' He smirks humourlessly. 'Actually that's what I'm here about.' He pauses, giving me a chance to ask questions, but I say nothing. I can't imagine what he's after. 'We've been good to you, haven't we?'

'*We?*'

'Me and Frank. Ford, before he retired. As a rule we're opposed to vigilantes. We had every right to crack down on you, especially since you targeted so many of our valued associates.'

I nod slowly. 'I can't argue with that.'

'But we've kept out of your way and granted you the freedom of the city.'

'That's true.'

Jerry sips from the can and speaks over the rim. 'You know about Capac going AWOL?'

'I've heard rumours.'

'He went to the Fridge Saturday before last. Asked to be admitted to Dorak's crypt. When the doctor who let him in returned, he wasn't there. Vanished into thin air, or so it seemed. We found a passageway beneath Dorak's coffin, a set of stairs leading down into a maze of tunnels. He must have gone down — or was taken. We tried to track him but it's immense, full of traps and dead ends. He hasn't been seen since.'

'A tragedy,' I mutter drily. Inside I'm thinking that underground tunnels plus an Ayuamarcan plus mysterious disappearance equals *villacs*.

'It will be if we don't get him back,' Jerry says seriously. 'He has his critics, but Capac's The Cardinal, the only one

who can hold this shit-can of a city together. He . . .' Jerry
shakes his head. 'But that's not for me to say. You'll be told
more later. I want you to come with me, Al.'

'Where?'

'Party Central.'

'Why?'

'Ford's back. He's taken control.'

'Ford Tasso?' I ask stupidly. 'I thought he'd been crippled
by a stroke.'

'He's semi-paralysed but he can get around. It isn't easy,
and it'll get harder by the day, but right now he's the one man
everyone's willing to rally behind. Ford's name still carries
weight. The shock of seeing him stagger out of retirement gave
all of our enemies pause for thought. It even drove the Kluxers
back — as soon as Davern realized he'd be pitting himself
against Ford Tasso, he turned tail. That won't last – he's too
tempting a target, old and fragile – but it's bought us time.'

Tasso bossing the gang around at Party Central again was
something I never thought to see. I assumed he'd simply
pass away quietly and that would be the end of the Ford
Tasso legend. Seems he didn't bother to read the script.

'I'm glad he's back,' I say honestly. 'It's nice to hear the old
bastard's still up for a fight. But what's it got to do with me?'

'He wants to see you,' Jerry says.

'Why?'

'I think he wants your help. He seems to believe you might
know where Capac is, or how to find him.'

'I don't.'

Jerry shrugs. 'That's what I figured, but –'

'No buts,' I interrupt. 'I know nothing about your Cardinal's
disappearance. I've no wish to get involved. Tell Tasso that.'

'Al,' Jerry chuckles, 'it hasn't been so long that you've
forgotten how things work. I was told to bring you in, not
deliver a message.'

My eyes narrow. 'What if I don't want to come?'

Jerry sighs. 'I'm not fool enough to try and force you. But I went out of my way for you once. Put my life on the line.' That was ten years ago, when everything around me was going to hell. Jerry helped me put part of the Bill Casey puzzle together. Unlike many of the players in that game, he wasn't manipulated by Bill or the *villacs*. He only got involved because he wanted to help.

'OK,' I mutter. 'Do I have time to get dressed?'

'Sure,' Jerry beams, returning to his beer. 'You might want to stick on your wig and cover those snakes too. I don't bear you any ill feelings for the contacts of ours you've taken out, but there are some at Party Central not as forgiving. If they see Paucar Wami walk in, they might start shooting.'

Grunting sourly, I go get ready for my meeting with the fill-in Cardinal.

Jerry still drives the same old van that he drove ten years ago, though the engine's been replaced and new leather seats have been fitted. Traffic's bad, so it takes us forty minutes to reach Party Central. The fortress is much the same as ever. Twenty floors of reinforced concrete, steel and glass. Raimi made a few structural alterations – such as the balcony on the fifteenth floor – but by and large it hasn't changed. Two costumed doormen still operate the front doors, but the ten Troops who used to flank them aren't to be seen. I'd heard the new Cardinal wasn't as security-conscious as his predecessor.

Inside it's buzzing. The huge tiled lobby's full of people talking, arguing, booking appointments, waiting to be met. In Dorak's day everyone had to take off their shoes and leave them at reception, but Raimi scrapped that asinine rule and the desk where people checked in their footwear has been replaced by a row of computers, where execs can surf the web, work on their files, or kill time playing games.

Although the Troops on the doors have been removed, there are more guarding the lobby than ever before, blocking entrances to the elevators and stairs, patrolling relentlessly, weapons openly displayed. By the slight air of confusion, I can tell these aren't regulars. Tasso must have drafted them in.

'Expecting trouble?' I ask Jerry as we weave through the crowd.

'And getting it,' he replies. 'Frank wanted to put guards back outside the doors but Ford said it would be admitting to the world that Capac was gone.'

'I thought Frank didn't work here any more.'

'Capac asked him to step into Gico Carl's shoes. Frank agreed, on a temporary basis. Now he wishes he'd kept the hell out, but he's stuck with it.'

'How's he getting on with Tasso?' There was never any love lost between them.

'Surprisingly well,' Jerry says. 'There's no time for friction. You'd swear they were long-lost brothers if you didn't know better.'

The private elevator to the fifteenth floor is protected by a dozen armed Troops. They part as Jerry approaches, but their gazes linger suspiciously on me and I hear the creaking of fingers as I pass, tightening on triggers. If I was a man who worried about dying, I'd be very nervous right now.

I recognize the elevator operator — Mike Kones, a friend of Jerry's. The three of us shared many shifts in the old days. Working an elevator's not my idea of a satisfying job, but Mike was never the most mobile of men and this is a pre-stigious position. He looks content. We nod to each other but don't say anything.

Frank's waiting for us at the top. It's been six years since our paths crossed. He's put on a lot of weight – too many corporate lunches – and his hairline's receding, but he looks happier and calmer than when he was head of the Troops.

'Al,' he greets me with a genuine smile and a firm hand-shake. 'Great to see you. How've you been?'

'Not bad. You?'

He pats his bulging stomach and grins. 'Getting by.' He faces Jerry and his smile thins. 'Trouble.'

'Pena?' Jerry guesses and Frank nods. 'Ron Pena,' Jerry explains for my benefit. 'Manufactures designer drugs. Fancies himself as a successor if Capac doesn't return.'

'He's making his move,' Frank says darkly. 'Ridiculing Ford, saying he's too old, demanding he step aside. Most of the people who matter are in there — Pena summoned them. If they side with Pena, Ford's through.'

Jerry's face darkens. 'If Pena takes over, we're fucked. He'd try and do deals with Davern and his like. Screw every-thing up.'

'I told Ford that,' Frank grumbles. 'I said we should deny his request for an audience. He wouldn't listen. Told me to admit him. I don't think he realizes the threat Pena poses. He doesn't understand that things have changed. The gangs aren't automatically obedient any longer.'

Jerry chews his lip and glances at me. 'Think we should wait out here until it's over?' he asks Frank.

'No. Ford said you were to enter as soon as you arrived. If we don't obey his orders, we can't expect anyone else to.'

BASE – The Cardinal's office – is jammed with Raimi's disgruntled generals. Men in suits mingle with hoods in jeans and slashed shirts, but nobody looks out of place. The Cardinal's empire embraces both the legitimate and illegal, and these people are accustomed to the curious mix.

All eyes are focused on the pair at the centre of the room. Ford Tasso sits in The Cardinal's vacated chair, stony face impassive, right arm slung lifelessly across his waist. Ron Pena circles him like a lawyer, gesturing expansively, a picture of youthful arrogance and strength, berating the old man.

'We know how important you were to Dorak and Raimi,' Pena barks, 'but you're a cripple now. We can't live in the past. You're not fit to walk, never mind run a corporation like this. Stand down, for fuck's sake, and let those of us who know what we're doing take command. You're a joke. The only reason you haven't been attacked is that all our rivals are falling about laughing.'

Tasso sighs an old man's sigh and shakes his head meekly. The right side of his face is a stiff mask – paralysed from the stroke – and the eye there rests dead in its socket. 'You're right,' he mutters, his voice a slurred imitation of what it used to be. 'I thought I was helping, but I see now it was an old fart's folly. I wasn't a man to lead in my prime, so I'm hardly fit for it in my twilight years.'

Sympathetic murmurs and chuckles fill the room. Pena beams condescendingly at the crippled elder gangster and lays a comforting hand on his shoulder. Frank curses beneath his breath and looks away, disgusted. Jerry and I share a wry glance — we know Tasso better than Frank does. We don't buy the act.

'Help me up, Ron,' Tasso croaks, struggling to rise. 'Get me back to Solvert's. A few of us play poker every Tuesday. I might make the first hand if I hurry.'

'That's the spirit,' Pena laughs, taking hold of Tasso's dead right arm and hoisting the old man to his feet. 'Stick with your card games. Leave the running of the city to those best suited to –'

Tasso's left hand strikes for Pena's throat. His huge fingers dig into flesh and he squeezes. Pena gasps, eyes widening, and drops to his knees. Tasso holds him up, supporting the weight of the younger man's body with his one good hand, fingers whitening from the pressure as he crushes. Pena makes savage choking noises and slaps at the hand around his throat. Tasso ignores the feeble gestures. Around the room, jaws drop. Nobody steps in to save Ron Pena.

Half a minute later, the job's finished. Tasso lets go of his dead challenger, who flops to the floor. He turns slowly and painfully, his right leg nearly useless, and glares with his working eye at those who moments before were ready to pension him off.

'If anybody else has anything to say about my leadership qualities,' he snaps, and this time his voice is as firm as ever, 'say it now, to my face.' Silence reigns. He kicks the corpse at his feet, then hits a button on the desk. 'Mags. Send in a disposal unit. Shit needs scraping off the floor.'

'Yes, Mr Tasso,' comes the voice of his secretary. Seconds later, four Troops march into the room, pick up Ron Pena's remains and cart him away.

'*Well?*' Tasso shouts. 'Am I in charge of this fucking ant-hill or not?' There's an immediate flurry of answers, everybody hurrying to swear allegiance. 'In that case, stop wasting time, get out on the street and spread the word that it's business as usual at Party Central.' The gathered heads of the corporation start to file out. 'Gentlemen,' he calls them back. 'If I even *think* that any of you are plotting against me, I'll have your heads for bowling balls, your wives for whores and your children for house-slaves.' A few of the men begin to chuckle. Then they realize he's not joking and their laughter dies away in gurgles. Tasso turns his back on them and limps to the balcony for a breath of fresh air.

'A force of fucking nature,' Frank whispers admiringly.

'I told you he'd crack the whip,' Jerry smirks.

Tasso makes his slow way back from the balcony. The strain in the huge man's face is evident, but so is the relish. He's loving this.

'Algiers,' he nods.

'Ford.'

'Been a while.'

'You're looking good.'

He snorts. 'I look like a fucking wreck. You two!' he barks at Frank and Jerry. 'What are you doing here?'

'Awaiting orders,' Frank says.

'Don't you have any initiative? I've just throttled the chairman of one of the most profitable pharmaceutical firms in the city. The race to replace him has already begun. I want one of our men in there. See to it.'

'Yes, sir!' Frank salutes smartly.

'Right away, Mr Tasso!' Jerry mimics Frank's salute.

'Pair of fucking clowns,' Tasso grumbles as they exit, but the left side of his mouth lifts into an amused half-smile. 'Take a load off, Algiers.' I grab a plastic chair and sit opposite him as he eases himself into the soft leather chair. 'How's life been treating you?'

'Better than you,' I comment.

He chuckles. 'I'm a mess, sure as fuck, but I'll take punks like Ron Pena any day, crippled or otherwise.'

'Pena was a nobody. Will you be able to take Eugene Davern when he comes?'

Tasso grimaces. 'Let's not dwell on that. Get you something to drink?'

'I'd rather skip the preliminaries and find out why you called me in.'

'As you wish.' Tasso rubs the wrist of his right arm, then moves up to the elbow. 'You heard about Capac and the Fridge?'

'Jerry filled me in.'

'Ever meet him?'

'Raimi?' I shake my head. 'Saw him a couple of times.'

'A strange kid,' Tasso reflects. 'Cold and alien inside. Dorak was a mean son of a bitch, but he was human. I don't know what the fuck Raimi is.'

Tasso tosses a doll at me. It's a dead ringer for Capac Raimi. It reminds me that this room used to be full of dolls — absent now.

'I locked them in a cupboard,' Tasso explains as I stare at the bare walls. 'Never could stand those fucking mannequins. Had to put up with them when I was playing second fiddle to The Cardinal.'

'But when the cat's away . . .'

'Exactly.'

I turn the doll around, examining it idly. 'Think he's dead?' I ask.

'He can't be killed.'

I smile, keeping my eyes on the doll so that Tasso won't see the grin. 'You never struck me as the gullible type.'

'I'm not. But I'm telling you, Capac Raimi can't be killed. He's immortal.'

'I've heard the rumours. I don't believe them.'

'I've seen it first-hand. He's been shot, knifed, blown to pieces, pushed off that balcony. The fucker keeps coming back. I don't know how, but he does. His remains dissolve away and a few days later he forms a new body and returns. If you think I'm going senile, check with Jerry and Frank. They've seen it too.'

I shift uncomfortably in my chair. 'If that's true, why are you worried?'

'He's never been gone this long. Normally he returns within three days. At a stretch, four. Never longer. This time he's disappeared. I don't know where he is. And I don't think he's going to make it back on his own.'

'But if he can't be killed . . .'

'I don't know how to explain it!' Tasso roars. 'If I could, I wouldn't need to turn to you.'

'Speaking of which . . . What do *I* have to do with your missing Cardinal?'

Tasso's left hand creeps to his right shoulder and he kneads the flesh firmly. If he was sitting at an angle to me, the right side of his face would show all the vitality of a corpse.

'Capac came to see me the week before he vanished,' Tasso says. 'He was agitated. The city's going to hell and he wanted to halt its slide. He believed the *villacs* – they're blind priests –'

'I know who they are,' I chip in softly.

'– were responsible for the unrest. This wasn't the first time they'd clashed. Capac had his own way of doing things. The *villacs* didn't approve. He felt they were undermining his authority. He asked me to step in for him, freeing him to deal with them. I refused. The following weekend he wound up at the Fridge and nothing's been seen of him since.'

I dwell on that a while. 'Why return to the hot seat now, when you wouldn't before?'

'Guilt,' he answers directly. 'I thought Capac could handle things. I didn't take his offer seriously. If I had, maybe he wouldn't be on the missing list and this city wouldn't be on the brink of war.'

'It's a bit late in the day to put things right.'

Tasso shrugs (only his left shoulder rises). 'If I'm late, I'm late. Point is, I'm here and I need your help.'

'I still don't understand what you think I can do. I've no idea where Raimi is.'

'You can find out,' Tasso says evenly. 'I think the *villacs* have him and I think you're the one person who can deal with those blind sons of jackals and persuade them to set him free.'

'Why would you think that?' I frown.

'Stuff Capac told me over the years. I know about the Ayuamarcans, your father and how, aside from Capac, you're the only survivor of Dorak's phantasmagoric army.'

'You remember Paucar Wami?' I hiss.

'Not clearly, but Capac told me all about him.'

I'm trembling. That won't do. I need to be composed. I count silently until I'm in control. When I reach twenty-two and my hands are still, I speak. 'Even if there's a link between Raimi and me, what makes you think I could find him?'

'I've been here since Friday,' Tasso says. 'But it was only last night, when *this* was dropped on my desk, that I thought about you.'

Tasso tosses an envelope to me. Warily, I slide the flap open. A large poker card slips out — the jack of spades. An ordinary card in most respects, except two tiny photos have been glued over the faces of the jacks, one of Capac Raimi, the other of me, in Al Jeery guise. Across the middle of the card runs a printed message, written in red ink on a white strip of paper. 'The bloodlines WILL merge.'

I read the message twice, glance again at the photos, then place the card back in its envelope and return it to Ford.

'You're right,' I say quietly. 'The *villacs* have him.'

'Any idea what it means?' he asks. 'About bloodlines merging?'

'The priests have a vision. They want to make this city the centre of the world. They believe in a sun god, and they think he'll bless them if the conditions are right and ensure their longevity until the end of time. That can only happen if three bloodlines come together in a chakana of blood — Blood of Flesh, Blood of Dreams, and Flesh of Dreams.'

'I haven't the slightest fucking clue what you're babbling about,' Tasso says.

'Raimi told you how the Ayuamarcans were created, how Dorak and the priests wove them out of thin air, moulding their features after people he saw in dreams?'

'Yeah,' Tasso says cautiously.

'Capac's supposed to be a creature of the dream world — hence, Blood of Dreams. The *villacs* are human — Blood of Flesh. As the spawn of an Ayuamarcan and a human, I'm meant to be the blood of Flesh *and* Dreams — Flesh of Dreams. The way they told it, if I hooked up with them and Raimi, and we worked as a chakana – a three-tier team – this city would be ours and we'd rule forever.'

Tasso looks perplexed. 'I'm still not sure I follow. But you've confirmed what I thought — you and Capac are mixed up with the *villacs* and thus with one another. That's why you've got to look for him. If I send others, the priests will kill or repel them. Those bastards only spare those they have a use for. If they've a use for *you*, you might be able to go places the rest of us can't.'

'Maybe,' I concede guardedly. 'But I'm not interested in Raimi or the priests. The less I have to do with them, the better.'

'You're turning me down?' Tasso asks blankly.

'Nothing could make me throw in my lot with those blind bastards,' I answer directly. 'Money won't sway me and threats won't scare me. I won't get involved and that's all I have to say about it.'

I rise, aware that I'm taking an enormous chance, prepared to fight if I have to, sure I won't get very far. But Tasso makes no move to stop me. He lets me get to the door, then says, just loudly enough for me to hear, '*Bill Casey.*'

I come to a halt, eyes closing as I groan. Deep down I knew he had something up his sleeve. I just didn't think it would be this compelling.

Turning to face him, I wait for him to continue.

'You fascinated Capac,' Tasso says. 'When you adopted Wami's look and name, he had you investigated. He found out everything he could about you, much of it from Dorak's files — the old Cardinal had a shit-load of material on you.

'Bill Casey admitted in a letter to the cops that he fucked up your life. He told them he masterminded the murders of your girlfriends and ex-wife. But he never provided a reason. Capac guessed it was linked to your father. He figured Paucar Wami hurt Bill Casey, and this was Casey's warped way of hitting back at his tormentor — through his son.'

'Smart thinking,' I comment icily.

'Capac's as cunning as they come,' Tasso huffs. 'What he didn't understand was why you assumed your father's position. Casey tormented you, but he died in the explosion that almost killed you. That should have been the end of it. Unless, of course, he wasn't really dead.'

Tasso slides the photo-decorated jack of spades out of the envelope and studies it while elaborating. 'Capac figured Casey must have rigged the explosion and walked away, that your Wami disguise was a ruse to tempt him out of hiding, so that you could settle the score.'

'A certified genius,' I snarl.

'There's more,' Tasso says, laying the card down. 'As The Cardinal, Capac had informants everywhere, ears and eyes in places the rest of us don't even know about. He set his people looking for Casey.' A carefully calculated pause. 'They found him.'

My strength deserts me. I stumble against the door and pant for breath, eyes shut, fighting off the madness bubbling to the surface. 'Bill's alive?' I wheeze.

'And living in this city.'

My eyes open. Everything goes cold. *Where?*

Tasso stares at me evenly. 'I'll only tell you that once Capac's been safely returned.'

'No!' I bellow. 'Tell me now!'

I start towards the old man in the chair, insane with vengeful desire, not about to be denied. I'll tear Tasso limb from limb if that's what it takes. If he thinks he can dangle Bill in front of me like a carrot, then snatch him away, he's seriously fucking mistaken.

'Don't do it, Algiers,' Tasso says softly, and the unexpected gentleness in his voice unnerves me. 'If you attack, I'll fight to the death. I'll kill you or you'll kill me. The latter's the more likely outcome, but it won't get you Casey's address. It'll only earn you an early execution at the hands of my Troops.'

There's no arguing with that. I wish I could throttle it out of him, but I know him too well. Violence isn't the answer, not this time.

'A deal,' I growl. 'The address first. If it's on the level, I'll see to my business with Bill, then search for –'

'Negative,' Tasso barks. 'Capac first, then Casey. That's the offer. Take it or leave it.'

Inside my head I count to ten. Thinking of Bill and his sad expression when he explained how he set about wrecking my life. *Twenty*. Remembering the explosion, the aftermath, slowly coming to the realization that he might still be alive. *Fifty*. Dwelling on ten years of murder and craziness. *Eighty*. Looking ahead, exploring alternatives, seeing only one way forward.

On *ninety-six* I let out a long breath. 'If you're bluffing . . .'

'I'm not.'

'OK.' I pull up the chair I was using earlier and position it in front of the makeshift Cardinal. I sense eager demons gathering around me, in anticipation of the chaos and bloodshed that's sure to follow. 'Tell me where you want me to start.'

THREE – DÉJÀ VU

It's been a long time since I played detective. Ten years ago a woman was murdered in the Skylight hotel, and The Cardinal (nudged by the *villacs*) assigned me the task of finding her killer. That was my one and only case. It was enough. I learnt and suffered more during the course of that investigation than any shamus should. A true baptism of fire. I swore I'd never endure such torment again.

But here I am, at the heart of another mystery, facing the same dangers as before. At least this time I'm aware of the risks and don't have as much to lose – my previous trial robbed me of my friends, my lovers, my entire way of life. But I'm sure, if the *villacs* are behind this, they can find some fresh way to stick a knife into my back and twist it.

I spend most of Tuesday in Party Central, interviewing those closest to the missing Capac Raimi, getting a feel for the man. Tasso tells me Raimi had been seeing faces from the past — Ayuamarcans. He believed the ghosts of the dead had been revived again. Tasso shows me a photo of Paucar Wami – the real deal, not me in disguise – but I dismiss it.

'That could have been taken any time,' I snort.

'But Capac saw him a few weeks ago. These pictures are from a security camera, and cameras don't lie.'

'Sure they do,' I retort. 'The *villacs* probably hired a ringer to startle Capac, then slipped old footage of Wami into the camera to make it seem real.'

'I don't know,' Tasso mutters. 'Capac seemed convinced.'

'More fool him,' I grunt and move on.

Shortly before Raimi struck out for the Fridge, a woman appeared in his office and 'freaked the living shit out of him', in the words of Jerry Falstaff. Raimi knew the woman. They exchanged words but as he moved towards her, she jumped from the balcony. Jerry was assigned the task of cleaning up the mess. When he took a team downstairs, he found no trace of her broken body.

'Could it have been a projection?' I ask.

'No chance,' Jerry says.

'So what happened? She disappeared midair? Sprouted wings and flew?'

Jerry smiles sourly. 'It's more likely a net was extended out of a window to catch her. But I never did have a fancy imagination. Maybe it *was* wings.'

Jerry's level-headedness is refreshing. It's comforting to find that not everyone in Party Central has succumbed to the forces of witchcraft and voodoo, that some can reason logically. That said, when I quiz him about Raimi's immortality, he reads from the same book as Ford Tasso and Frank.

'The guy returns from the dead — fact. Every time he's killed, he comes back a few days later on a train from a place called Sonas. He re-materializes on the train, though we've had people on it, watching for him, and they've never seen him regenerate. He somehow does it when nobody's looking.'

'You know how crazy that sounds?'

'Of course. Early on, I searched for logical answers – clones, lookalikes, twins – but the truth's the truth. Capac Raimi comes back from the dead. You learn to accept it when you've been around him a while.'

Arguing's pointless – Tasso, Frank and Jerry can't be shaken from their absurd belief – so I don't bother. Instead I gather what relevant facts I can – who his friends were (he didn't have any), where he liked to hang out (apart from trips to a gym with a pool, he worked non-stop), and if he had any untoward habits (clean as a whistle) – then return home with midnight fast approaching. I spend a few hours writing up notes and playing with theories, then hit the sack, where I toss and turn, obsessing about snakes, dead people, blind priests, sun gods and a nine-fingered ex-cop — alive and in the city.

I rise before dawn, tired and irritable, and squat in the shadows of my living room, thinking about Bill, wondering what he looks like now, what he's doing, where he's spent the past ten years. Tasso's news both thrills and depresses me. Thrills, because the years of murder and madness haven't been a waste — my quest is justifiable and revenge can be mine. Depresses, because Tasso could be lying – or Raimi could have lied to him – and I have a sick fear that even if it's true, Bill will drop dead of old age or flee before I can descend on him in all my fury.

As desperate as I am to get my hands on Bill, I put thoughts of him on hold. I've a deal with Tasso to honour. Raimi must be found before I can focus on my dearest friend and most hated enemy. Where to start in my search for the missing Cardinal?

As the sun rises I focus all my mental faculties on the Raimi problem, and the answer soon presents itself. Start where Raimi was last seen — the Fridge. After a quick breakfast and a hundred push-ups, I cycle to the morgue. I'm in Al Jeery guise, so I use the bicycle I've had for fifteen years. I save the motorbike for when I'm Paucar Wami, storing it in a nearby garage.

I'm no stranger to the Fridge, its false exterior (it looks like a deserted factory) and gleaming, coffin-lined halls. I've dropped off many bodies here, friends and foes of The Cardinal and his crew. I even have my own access code, though it has to be renewed every three months and only admits me to a small, self-contained section at the rear of the morgue.

Once I've parked and entered, I tell one of the assistants that I'd like to see Dr Sines. He's head honcho, though he was just one of many pathologists on the books when I first made his acquaintance ten years ago. He's one of the select few who knows that Paucar Wami and Al Jeery are the same man.

'Mr Jeery,' he greets me with a curt nod, coming from an operating room, his hands encased in blood-smeared plastic gloves.

'Dr Sines.' We've known each other for a decade, but have never dropped the formalities. Sines is an associate, not a friend. I prefer it that way. I'm safer without friends.

'Dropping off or picking up?' he quips. A standard joke.

'I've been hired to find Capac Raimi. I want to see where he disappeared.'

Sines stares at me. 'I didn't think you were into detective work these days.'

'I'm making an exception this once. I have clearance. You can check with Jerry or Frank if you don't believe me.'

'If it's all the same, I will. Nothing personal.'

One phone call later, Sines leads me through a maze of casket-lined corridors to Ferdinand Dorak's crypt. 'We've had a hell of a time since Raimi vanished,' the doctor mutters, peeling off his gloves as we walk and discarding them. 'Hordes of Troops swarming around, interviewing everyone, upsetting everything. I've been quizzed on five separate occasions. I suppose you'll make it an even half-dozen?'

'I don't think I'll bother. I know how clueless you are.'

'Very droll. You should have been a comedian.'

We arrive at the crypt. Octagonal, heavily reinforced, a computerized lock on the door. Sines keys in a code and after a number of clicks it swings open.

'Want me to come in with you?' Sines asks.

'Yes. I want to see the stairs under the coffin.'

We enter. A cold, dry room, The Cardinal's coffin resplendent in the centre, on a huge slab of marble. I examine the inscription – 'Nobody told me there'd be days like these' – then the coffin and marble.

'There's a lever at the bottom of the stairs,' Sines says. 'Until the Troops came ferreting around, that was the only way to open it. They busted a few locks, so now the coffin slides aside if you push.' He lays a hand on the head of the coffin and demonstrates. It slides two-thirds of the way off the marble slab before coming to a halt, revealing a dark chasm and a set of stairs.

'This wasn't here originally?' I ask, staring down into the darkness.

'No. They burrowed up from beneath.'

'How come nobody noticed?'

'The room's soundproof,' Sines explains. 'Besides, nobody passes by much – The Cardinal made sure he was put in a secluded part of the building. What gets me is how they knew where to dig. Only three people have access to the architectural plans. Each has been cleared by the Troops. Whoever did this didn't find out about it through official channels.'

Several flashlights are set on the floor in a corner of the room. I fetch one and click it on. 'I'm going to the bottom of the stairs,' I tell Sines. 'I won't be long.'

'What will I do if you don't come back?' he asks nervously.

'Make up a good story for the Troops and pray they believe

you.' I climb up onto the slab, swing my legs over, find the top step of the stairs and start down.

There are forty-one steps to the bottom, where a short tunnel ends in a door. The lock's on the other side but the Troops must have kicked it open on one of their visits because the door swings inwards when I push. I step through and shine my light around. I'm at a junction, five crudely cut passages branching out to who-knows-where. Three of the passages are marked with crosses, where the Troops explored. Tasso told me they found nothing but more junctions and tunnels before giving up.

'You're here, aren't you?' I whisper, turning off the torch and letting the darkness engulf me. 'They're keeping you where no one can find you. You're the ace up top, but they rule beneath. These tunnels are theirs. I wonder what they're doing to you?'

I cough self-consciously. One of the side-effects of spending so much time on my own – I've started talking to myself. I haven't got to the stage where I'm answering yet, but it can't be far off.

I linger a minute, feeling the darkness as if it has a tangible, physical presence. I'm sure I'll be down these tunnels again before this investigation's over, but for the time being I have no use for them. I'm not going to find Raimi by walking directionlessly into the darkness. I'll have to work to root him out. The *villacs* won't make it easy for me.

I climb back up the stairs, wondering where to turn next. I proved no slouch in the detective stakes last time, but I'm no super sleuth either. The priests will have to strew the path with clues if I'm to progress, otherwise I'll run around in circles. But I'm sure they'll help me along, as they did before. The game means nothing to them, only the result. So it's surely just a matter of time before . . .

On cue, as my head comes level with the sixth step from

the top, I spot a photo standing at an angle. Smiling at the timing, I grab the photo and continue to the top.

'What's that?' Sines asks, spotting it immediately.

'Someone's been careless with his holiday snaps,' I murmur, studying the photo in the harsh light of the crypt. It's a young, attractive woman. She looks familiar but I can't place her. Party Central looms in the background. She's holding a newspaper. I'm sure, once I get it under a magnifying glass, I'll be able to check the date — the obvious intention of the people who placed the photo there.

'Where was it?' Sines asks, taking the photo from me.

'On the stairs. When was the last time anyone was down there?'

'Yesterday. No . . .' He pauses. 'Late Monday. Four Troops. Lamps, ropes and other equipment had been left at the bottom. They went to retrieve them.'

'They wouldn't have missed this. It's been placed here since then, or one of them left it.'

Sines shakes his head. 'I was here when they came up. It wasn't them.'

'You're certain?'

'Positive.' He hands back the photo.

'Then I won't bother questioning them.' I start to tuck the photo away. Stop at a memory flash and hold it up to the light. 'I know her,' I mutter. 'I met her years ago. She worked at . . .'

The name clicks, but I say it only to myself, seeing no need to inform the good Dr Sines. *Ama Situwa*, daughter of Cafran Reed, who ran what was once maybe the city's kookiest restaurant. I haven't been there in ten years. I don't even know if Cafran's exists any more. But it won't take me long to find out.

To my surprise, not only is Cafran's still going strong, but its original owner has held on and is happy to talk with me.

Cafran Reed looks older than his years — grey, stooped, feeble. He spends most of his time in the restaurant – which hasn't changed much, as gaudily coloured as ever – but a manager runs it for him now. Cafran merely mixes with the staff and customers, testing the food, fussing over the music (mostly pop songs from the 1960s and '70s), waiting for death to claim him.

'Ama Situwa?' he responds blankly when I ask.

'You haven't a daughter?'

'Alas, no.' He smiles sadly. 'I wished for one but it wasn't meant to be.'

I show him the photo I picked up in the Fridge. 'Recognize this woman?'

He has to put on his glasses before he can comment. Studies the photo at length. No hint of recognition in his tired old eyes. 'Sorry,' he says.

Cafran invites me to stay for lunch but I reject the offer. Too busy. I'll eat on the move, a sandwich or bagel to keep me going.

Outside, I use my cell phone to dial the number Tasso gave me yesterday. He answers on the second ring. 'Algiers?'

'I want you to check something for me. The list of Ayuamarcans I saw was an old copy my father had stolen from the files of Party Central. Do you have a more up-to-date –'

'I know all the names,' he interrupts. 'I used to scan it regularly, hoping a name might jog my memory. Shoot.'

'Ama Situwa.'

He grunts. 'One of the last to be added. I asked Capac about her but he never said whether he knew her.'

'Thanks.' I head for home, where I check the newspaper in the photo under a magnifying glass. It indicates that Ama Situwa – an Ayuamarcan, dead ten years – was standing in front of Party Central less than a week ago. I lay the photo aside and don't worry about it. I know what can be done with digital enhancement. The date on the paper means nothing. I won't believe the shades of the dead have returned until I see one in the flesh. And even then I'll reserve the right to be sceptical.

I patrol the streets as my father, flashing photos of Capac Raimi and Ama Situwa, asking people if they've seen or know anything of them. My contacts are legion. As Paucar Wami, I'm known to thousands of gang members, store owners, bums, clubbers, pimps, prostitutes and various other creatures of the night. Most fear me and answer openly when I question them, wanting to be shot of me as quickly as possible.

They all know Raimi – or of him – but haven't seen him since he vanished, nor have they any idea where he might be. No one recognizes the woman. I ask if the blind priests in the white robes have been active of late – I only put this question to the more clued-in of my contacts – but nobody's spotted them on the prowl.

The street folk are worried. Although the city has stabilized since Tasso took control of Party Central – that became common knowledge during the last twenty-four hours – the veterans know the lull is temporary. The keg's still primed to explode, and those who live or work on the streets will bear the brunt of the blast. I urge them to listen for rumours of Capac Raimi and watch for the woman in the photo, but most are too concerned with their own welfare to focus on anything else. I won't be able to rely on them.

Thursday passes. Friday. Lots of travel, as Al Jeery and Paucar Wami, covering both the day and night worlds. I've never confined myself to the east, but that's where I'm most powerful and I feel uneasy spreading myself further, covering so much ground. Wami's known and feared in all sectors, but not as respected as in the east. Challenges to my authority are more likely elsewhere. I have to tread carefully. Be polite. Rely on bribes as well as threats. Ask permission of the more influential gangs to canvas their territories. It'd be different if I was tracking prey. I could move in, make my hit, slip out. But this investigation could run for weeks or longer. Some degree of diplomacy is called for.

Between flashing snaps of Capac and Ama, I study the faces of old men on the streets and through windows, my gaze lingering coldly on those bearing even a passing resemblance to Bill Casey. I don't have the time to fixate on Bill – I have to concentrate on the quest to find Raimi – but I can't stop looking for him. I also ask a few discreet questions. If he's hiding in the city, someone other than Raimi and Tasso must know where he is. If I find the ex-cop by myself, all bets are off. Tasso – anyone – can have me once I'm through with Bill. I'll be done with this world. It can do to me what it likes after that.

But nobody's seen him. Those who knew him believe he's dead. I plant seeds of doubt – say I've heard rumours that he survived – and leave them to sprout.

In the meantime I continue hunting for Tasso's lost leader, pounding the streets, offering bribes, listening to the dark whispers of the city in the hope that they'll tell me where Raimi is.

Saturday. I leave my apartment early, carrying my bike with me, in Al Jeery mode. I trot down the stairs, whistling, and nod to a disinterested neighbour on the ground floor. They never see me as Paucar Wami — I always exit and enter by the back alley and fire escape then. Nobody here knows about my double life. Or if they do – if someone spotted me slipping out of my window one dark but cloudless night, and made the connection – they keep it to themselves, knowing that to cross swords with Paucar Wami is to guarantee the kiss of death.

Mounting my bike, I set out to visit Fabio, an ancient pimp who knows more about the seedy secrets of the city than anybody. The old pimp's on his last legs. If he's to be believed, he celebrated his one hundred and thirteenth birthday this year. Even if he's exaggerating – and Fabio never was one to stick too closely to the facts – he can't be far short of that remarkable age. He's been going as long as anyone remembers. He was a big shot in the days before The Cardinal. When Dorak put him out of business, he turned to pimping and has maintained a stable of women ever since – although in reality these last few years the more loyal of his ladies have been maintaining him, as his strength and eyes have steadily failed. His ears are as good as ever though.

Fabio's quarters look no more rundown than they did thirty years ago, and his favourite rocking chair still stands on the rickety porch out front, though he rarely uses it now, as even getting from his bedroom to the chair is a struggle. Two teenagers – a boy and girl – are on the porch, talking in low voices. I cough loudly as I approach, so as not to alarm them. The boy looks up quickly, identifies me and smiles. 'Hi, Al.'

'Drake. Who's your girl?'

'Name's Lindie,' she answers, 'and I ain't this fool's *girl*.'

'Are too,' Drake grunts.

'Shut up!' she snaps.

I smother a laugh and ask if Fabio's in. 'Nah, he's out rollerskating,' Drake chortles, then looks guilty. 'Don't mean no disrespect. Sure he's here. Mom's taking care of him.'

Flo's been good to Fabio. Although she still ostensibly works for him, it's been a long time since she turned a trick. Her and a couple of others tend to the ailing pimp, feed him, wash up after him, keep the house in order. They're genuinely fond of the old goat – Fabio always treated his women decently – but the fact that he's rumoured to have a fortune stashed away somewhere probably doesn't hurt.

Flo's in the kitchen, doing the laundry. She beams and gives me a big hug when she sees me. 'Good to see you, Al. Fabio was asking about you only yesterday. He'll be delighted you've come.'

'How is he?'

'No better, no worse.' She shrugs. 'A *bit* worse. His voice went last week – couldn't say a word for a few days – but it came back again. His doctor don't know how he's alive – says he should be long dead and buried – but Fabio just laughs and says he'll go when he feels like, not a minute before. Tea or coffee?'

'Can Fabio drink beer?'

'He ain't supposed to, but he does anyway.'

'Then I'll share a beer with him.'

Flo fetches a couple of bottles. She's a sweet woman. And Drake's a good kid. I helped him out some years ago. His brutish father had left him traumatized. My healing powers were functioning then. I got inside Drake's head and relieved him of his nightmares. He's never looked back. Last year his father was released from prison and came poking into Flo and Drake's affairs. I warned him off. Didn't hurt him – for all his faults, he's Drake's father, and the boy didn't want to see him harmed – just told him in no uncertain terms what would happen if he didn't catch the first train out.

Fabio's lying flat on his back, eyes closed, breathing shallowly. He looks every one of his hundred-plus years, skin tight around his jaws, skeleton-thin, hands twitching feebly on the bedcovers.

'I don't want to wake him if he's sleeping,' I whisper to Flo.

'Too late,' Fabio snaps. He cocks his head – neck muscles

quivering wildly – and grins horribly. 'I was having a lovely dream – in a sheikh's brothel and still able to get my pecker up – but you've blown that. Sit down and spin me a few lies while I wait to drop off again.'

I take the chair beside the bed and gently squeeze the old man's hand. I help Flo prop him up – he complains bitterly until we get him settled *just right* on the pillows – then she opens his beer, sticks a straw in it and leaves. 'If he starts choking,' she advises me on her way, 'give his balls a quick tug.'

'See what I have to put up with?' he moans. 'Mind, that's the closest I get to screwing any more, so I can't grouch.'

Fabio's almost completely blind and his eyes stare ahead at nothing while we talk, discussing pills, doctors, old friends, the neighbourhood. He's as up to date with local events as always. The fragile pimp might be confined to bed and on the verge of death, but his ear's as close to the ground as ever.

'Heard you been hired by Ford Tasso to hunt for The Cardinal,' he says after a while. I shouldn't be surprised but I am.

'Where the hell did you hear that?'

'I got my sources,' he chuckles. 'That's a bad business, Algeria. Those guys play for high stakes. You don't want to get stuck in the middle.'

'I know,' I answer softly, 'but I haven't a choice.'

Fabio's head tilts sideways. 'Now, I *know* you can't be bribed or blackmailed. And I'm pretty sure threats don't work. So how can it be that the fearsome *Paucar Wami* don't have a choice?'

'Tasso has information which I must have. He'll only exchange it if I find Raimi for him.'

Fabio thinks a moment, then says, 'This to do with Bill Casey?'

'Are you sure you're dying?' I ask suspiciously. 'You're too sharp for an ancient son of a bitch with one foot in the grave.'

He laughs delightedly. 'Body mightn't be worth shit, but I still got a brain. Only thing you've cared about this last decade is finding that dead man's living bones. Ain't nothing else I can think of that'd get you skittering about on Ford Tasso's business.'

I nod wearily. 'Tasso says he's alive and in the city. Won't tell me any more unless I return Raimi to him.'

'Could be lying,' Fabio notes.

'I doubt it. He knows what I'd do if he played me for a sap.'

'Ford Tasso ain't the sort who worries about retribution.'

'He does where Paucar Wami's involved,' I contradict him, gently stroking my left cheek, careful not to disturb the paint. 'Everyone fears Wami.'

An uneasy silence descends. Fabio's never understood my need to become the legendary killer, and he feels uncomfortable whenever the topic's raised.

'Anyway,' he breaks the silence, clapping my forearm with a frail hand. 'You didn't come to pass the time of day. You want to know if I've heard anything about Raimi?'

'Yeah. Though I'd have come regardless. I was overdue a visit.'

'Can't argue with that,' he smirks, takes a sip of beer through his straw, and leans back further into his pillows. 'Don't have much to tell. I know he went missing in the Fridge, through an underground passage, and I don't think any of the gangs are behind it — nobody round here knows shit about who took him or why. Other than that, I can't help.'

'Any theories on who'd have it in for Raimi?' I ask.

'Hell, Algeria, everyone has it in for The Cardinal. They

need him – he holds this shit together – but that don't stop them hating him.' He pauses. 'Mind, there's a hell of a difference between those who'd wish him gone and those with the balls to take him on. Eugene Davern might be powerful and dumb enough to try. Those blind priest friends of yours could have done it too.'

I grunt neutrally and let the reference to the *villacs* pass. 'You think Davern could be involved?' I ask instead.

'Maybe. Doubt he is, not by the way he backed down in the north-west when Tasso took over, but if Raimi don't return and warfare erupts, Davern's the most likely to ride it out. That gives him good reason to want Raimi out of the way — and extra good reason for you to be careful if you go sniffing around after him.'

I spend a further half hour with Fabio, talking over old times. He's deteriorated a lot since my last visit. His voice cracks every so often, and there are times when his thoughts wander. Resilient as he is, I doubt he'll see out the summer. Death's been a long time coming for Fabio, but now that it has him in its jaws, it's swiftly grinding him down.

Talking tires the ancient pimp. When he starts to doze, I trail off into silence, then rise silently and leave. I slip Flo some cash, tell her to call me if she needs anything, let myself out – Drake and his girl have moved on – and stroll away, idly planning for the funeral which is surely close upon us.

I hadn't seriously considered the possibility that anyone other than the *villacs* had abducted The Cardinal. I still believe the priests were behind it – the card Tasso received supports that theory – but perhaps they operated through a third party. If they did, Davern seems as logical a choice as any, and as worrying – if the Klan-spawned Kluxers come to prominence, they're bound to target the black gangs in the east.

Having slipped back into Paucar Wami's flesh, I spend the

rest of Saturday learning more about Eugene Davern. I know him by reputation only, and though I've taken out a few of his men in the past, those I killed were peripheral to his operation, and he had sense enough not to make an issue of their deaths. He's an easy man to investigate. My contacts practically line up to spill the beans on the ex-Klansman. Within hours I know the whereabouts of several of his hide-aways, the names and addresses of three of his mistresses and the nights he visits them, how many men he has with him at any one time in any one place. He guards himself cleverly, but if I need to get to him, I can.

If Davern authorized the kidnapping of Capac Raimi, there are very few men he dare trust with such a charge. According to the grapevine, there are only four he trusts implicitly. His younger brother, Ellis. His best friend since childhood, Dan Kerrin, who isn't a Kluxer. And two of his closest lieutenants, Hyde Wornton and Matthew 'Millie' Burns. If I don't come up with anything else, I'll start shadowing the quartet in case one of them is sitting on Raimi.

I'm exploring a warehouse of Davern's on the docks when my phone vibrates shortly after midnight. I check the digits but don't recognize them. That troubles me – strangers shouldn't have access to my number – but I answer anyway.

'Yeah?' I grunt, not giving my name away.

'Is this Paucar Wami?' a man asks nervously.

'Who wants to know?'

'Terry Archer. I'm night manager of the Skylight.'

I know him. Haven't seen him in a long time. No idea why he should be ringing me or how he got my number. 'What do you want?'

'Ford Tasso told me to call and gave me your details. We . . .' Archer stops to lick his lips.

'Go on,' I prompt him.

'There's been a murder. One of our customers has been

killed. A woman. Her back was sliced up into a sun-like symbol.' I go cold, my mind snapping back ten years. 'She was killed in room –'

'– 812,' I finish, staring ahead blankly into the darkness of the warehouse.

'Yes,' Archer says, surprised. 'How did you know?'

'I'll be with you as soon as I can. Don't let anybody near the body.'

'I've already sealed off the room. Nobody gets in without my –'

I cut him off. Within a minute I'm out of the warehouse and on my motorbike, tearing across the city, propelled by the spirits of the bloody past.

The Skylight underwent a renovation last year. It was shut for almost six months while old rooms were demolished and rebuilt, walls repainted and papered, fresh carpets laid, new furniture moved in. The Skylight's reputation as the city's key draw for the rich and famous had dwindled since Ferdinand Dorak's death, but now it's streets ahead of its rivals again, more luxurious than ever, up to date with all the latest technology and boasting five extra floors.

One thing hasn't changed — no CCTV. Anonymity is guaranteed in the Skylight. The doors are guarded by Troops, but that's it as far as security goes.

Terry Archer's waiting for me in reception, puffing on a Marlboro. Life goes on as normal around him — word of the murder hasn't leaked yet. I draw startled stares and a few gasps when I enter – people don't expect Paucar Wami to walk boldly into the Skylight – but nobody interferes.

Archer's flanked by two Troops, who grip their weapons tightly and eyeball me mercilessly. I'm sure they're two of his best, versed in the ways of fighting and killing. I'm just as sure I could take them without moving into middle gear.

'Mr Wami,' Archer greets me, ditching the cigarette and extending a hand.

I ignore it – Paucar Wami doesn't shake hands – and snap, '812. Now. And lose the bodyguards.'

Archer gulps loudly, then nods at the Troops. 'I'll take him up myself.'

'Are you sure, sir?' one of them asks. 'Maybe we should come along to –'

'Ten of you couldn't save him if I had murder on my mind,' I cut in, then start for the elevators ahead of Archer, who wastes a moment chastening his Troop, before hurrying after me, catching up as the doors slide shut.

We say nothing until we're on the eighth floor. I march towards the room, remembering the way from before. 812 was where my girlfriend, Nicola Hornyak, was left to die. It's also where my ex-wife, Ellen, was murdered.

'When was she found?' I ask.

'Less than an hour ago,' Archer says, trotting to keep up. He's put on weight since I last saw him. 'I rang Mr Tasso immediately – that room has a history and I guessed he'd want to know about it – and he put me on to you.'

'Was the room signed out to anybody?'

'Yes, but . . .' He grimaces.

'Tell me,' I grunt without slowing.

'It was booked under the name of Al Jeery,' he says quickly, 'but I'm sure he has nothing to do with this. I know Al and he's not the sort who –'

'Enough!' I come to a stop. So they – whoever *they* are – used my name, just in case memory failed me. The extra touch was unnecessary. An insult.

I study Terry Archer. He knows me as Al Jeery but doesn't recognize me in my Paucar Wami guise. I want to keep it that way. 'I'll check on Jeery,' I growl. 'If he's innocent, he has nothing to fear. If he isn't, I'll deal with him.' Archer nods, terror in his eyes. 'And don't tip him off in advance.'

'I won't!' Archer gasps. 'I swear!'

We reach 812 and Archer passes a golden card through the computerized slot. A light blinks twice. He produces another card – also gold, but with red stripes in the upper left corner – and swipes that as well. 'I double coded it, to be extra safe,' he says smugly. With a beep the door opens and we enter, lights coming on automatically. A flat screen TV on the wall broadcasts a message. 'Welcome to the Skylight, Mr Jeery. We hope you enjoy your stay.'

On the bed, a naked woman lies face down, hands tied together over her head, a gag in her mouth. Her back has been cut to shreds and a rough circle can be glimpsed through the dried blood, several straight lines running from its rim, representing the rays of the sun.

'This happened before,' Archer says, closing the door. 'Nine or ten years ago, two women were killed in exactly the same –'

'I know,' I stop him, moving closer to the bed, studying the floor for clues. 'I want the room dusted. The woman too. A full examination. Call Alex Sines at the Fridge. Tell him to come in person. I want him to report directly to me.'

'What about Mr Tasso?' Archer enquires.

'If Tasso wanted to be personally involved,' I bark, 'he wouldn't have sent you to me.'

Archer cringes at my tone and says no more.

I carefully tilt the dead woman's head to one side and study her face, emotionlessly taking in the familiar contours and eyes, noting how relaxed she looks in death. I bet Sines finds strong drugs in her system when he slices her open. Nobody dies serenely when in pain. She must have been doped out of her senses.

'Know her?' I ask Archer, gently lowering the head. Al

Jeery wants to close her eyelids. Paucar Wami sneers at the sentimental touch.

'No,' he says shakily.

'I do.' Standing, I unroll the plastic gloves and pocket them. '*Ama Situwa*,' I sigh, not loud enough for Archer to hear, then make a quick exit, to retire for the night and consider what the hell this means.

FOUR – PAPERWORK

Ama Situwa. Ayuamarcan. Lost to the world ten years ago. Returns

(*how?*)

and gets killed in the Skylight

(*why?*)

in room 812. Not much of a biography. No hints of who she was or how she lived. Was there a specific reason she was chosen to die instead of anyone else that I know? And is the corpse *really* Ama Situwa? I still don't buy into this resurrection business, though it's getting harder to discredit. She could be someone who merely looked like the woman I remember. An elaborate red herring.

Sines will be able to help on that front. He'll take fingerprints, dental impressions and DNA samples. Check them against the records. I'm sure there are no files on Ama Situwa – the *villacs* did a thorough job of removing all traces of the Ayuamarcans – but if this is another woman, we might strike lucky.

I doze off while sitting next to my tiny living room window, contemplating the various twists and possibilities. I dream of room 812 in the Skylight and the three women who've been murdered there, Nicola Hornyak, Ellen Fraser and

(*until proven otherwise*)

Ama Situwa. In my dreams I'm present at the executions, which blend together into one nightmarish scene of perpetual murder. I stand by the foot of the bed as Nicola's tied down. I hear Ellen scream. She calls my name and I reach to help, but I'm powerless. A large woman – Valerie Thomas, one of the *villacs'* tools – pushes me away and laughs. A blind priest wraps his arms around me and holds me as Priscilla Perdue carves a symbol into Ama Situwa's back, her knife impossibly large, the blood impossibly red. As it pools on the floor, faces form – Capac Raimi's, Leonora Shankar's, mine. No, not mine . . . my father's. The real Paucar Wami smiles at me and murmurs, 'Reasons for a refund, hmm, Al m'boy.'

As I'm trying to think of a reply, Wami's face explodes in a geyser of blood which splatters the walls and ceiling. The blood covers me. It's hot. I scream. And suddenly *I'm* lying on the bed and a *villac* is carving the flesh of my back to pieces. Incredible pain. He's chanting. I'm screaming. Nicola, Ellen and Ama Situwa stand in a semi-circle in front of me, naked, making love, laughing at my misfortune. The carving lasts an eternity.

'Flesh of Dreams,' the priest sings, and the women echo him. I cover my ears with my hands (not thinking to attack my tormentors with them), but the sounds penetrate the bloodstained flesh and bones. High-pitched, shrill, driving me to the verge of madness. I open my mouth to shriek. Blood gushes. And still the ringing of the women's voices . . . ringing . . .

My eyes snap open but the noise follows me out of my dream. Heart racing, I look for blind priests, then realize it's only my phone. Letting out a shaky breath, I wipe the last images of the nightmare from my thoughts and dig my cell out of a pocket. 'Hello?' I answer, checking my watch. 04:19.

'Jeery? It's Dr Sines.'

I sit up. 'What's wrong?'

'Your corpse — the woman in the Skylight.'

'What about her?'

'She vanished.'

For a moment I think I'm still dreaming, but that impression is short lived. 'Where are you?' I ask.

'The Fridge.'

'I'll be right over.'

As I slip on my shoes, I think I hear someone whisper, 'Flesh of Dreams.' But it's only a residue of the nightmare.

'How the fuck could she disappear?' I roar, punching the door of Sines' office and kicking a spare chair out of my way. I've been here ten minutes and my rage has increased with every passing second. The doctor sits at his desk, impassive, waiting for my fury to pass. If he's afraid of me, he masks it well.

'Tell me again what happened,' I snarl, leaning on the desk, putting my face close to his, watching for the slightest trace of a lie.

'I've told you three times already,' he says, meeting my gaze without blinking.

'So tell me a fourth!'

'You think it will help?'

'Start talking or *I'll* help *you* through the fucking window.'

Sines sneers. 'Quit chewing the scenery. It doesn't become you.'

'You think this is a joke?' I yell. 'You think this is a fucking –'

'Sit down. Stop shouting. Take deep breaths. Hold your hands out until they stop shaking. Then I'll tell you again — for the last time,' he adds pointedly.

I want to rip out his eyes, but that wouldn't do any good, so I pick up the chair, sit and breathe. Eventually my teeth stop chattering and the veil of rage lifts. 'I'm sorry I shouted.'

Sines nods. 'Better.' He launches into his story, keeping it brief. 'I oversaw the initial examination of the corpse in the Skylight, as you requested. Made sure the area was dusted for prints and that nothing was disturbed.'

'Did you dust the body?'

'Yes, but only to check for obvious, clumsy traces of her killer. There weren't any. I was saving the indepth study for when I got back to the Fridge. Once I'd done all I could in the Skylight, I had her transferred to a gurney, then downstairs to the hearse.'

'Why a hearse?' I interrupt. 'Why not an ambulance?'

He withers me with a smile. 'Ambulances are for hospitals, where they treat the living. This is a morgue. We don't have much use for resuscitative –'

'OK,' I snap. 'I only asked.'

'As I was saying,' he continues, running an arrogant hand through his hair, 'we transferred the body to the hearse. I was with it the entire time. We collapsed the legs of the gurney, slid it inside, strapped it down, locked the doors. The driver and I sat in and set off. We made good time. Opened the doors when we got here, slid the gurney out, and the body wasn't there.' He coughs. 'I can't explain how, but it vanished in transit.'

'Just like that?' I snort.

He glares at me. 'I know how it sounds, but there's no way it could have fallen out or been abducted. We were with it the whole way. You can check the hearse, but I assure you there are no false panels or gaping holes in the floor.'

'Bodies don't vanish into thin air,' I remark icily.

'I agree,' he sighs, 'but as Sherlock Holmes was fond of saying, when all other probabilities have been eliminated, what remains, however improbable, is the real shit.'

'I don't think he put it quite that way,' I smile.

'You could be right.' Sines stands and heads for the door.

'Let's go give the hearse the once-over. You won't believe me until you've seen it for yourself. Who knows, you might find something I overlooked. To be honest,' he mutters with uncharacteristic humility, 'I rather hope you do.'

The hearse is inviolate. No secret panels in the sides, a solid floor, reliable lock. I suggest someone might have forced the lock while the hearse was stopped at traffic lights. 'Impossible,' Sines says. 'Traffic's non-existent at four in the morning and we were in a hurry to get back, so we broke a few rules of the road and didn't stop for any lights.'

'Somebody on the roof? They could have worked on the lock while you were driving, slid out the body and . . .' I stop, realizing how weak that sounds.

Sines shrugs. 'I thought of that too. It makes more sense than the suggestion that the body simply vanished, but it fails to account for the alarm.' Sines closes the doors at the back of the hearse, locks them, then takes out a different key and tries to insert it into the lock. A siren blares, which the doctor quickly silences by hitting a button on the hearse's key fob.

'We've had bodies stolen before,' he explains. 'The alarms have been standard issue for twenty years. They're updated annually to keep ahead of those with a talent for break-ins. To cling to the roof of a moving car, and not be seen, and unlock the doors without triggering the alarm . . .' He shakes his head.

I stare at the lock, then circle the hearse again, racking my brain for an explanation. Sines watches expressionlessly. When I return, he says, 'Know what I'd recommend as a doctor?'

'What?'

'Go home. Sleep it off. The mystery will still be here in the morning. It won't be any clearer, but you'll be in better shape to deal with it.'

And since there's nothing else I can do except stand here and go mad, I follow the good doctor's advice.

Surprisingly, I sleep soundly, no nightmares, waking in the early afternoon on an excessively hot Sunday. Over a bowl of cereal, I reflect on my visits to the Skylight and Fridge, and where I go from here. The more I think about it, the more I'm drawn to the theory that Ama Situwa (or whoever was killed in the hotel) wasn't a random plant. The previous women killed in 812 were both closely linked to me – my girlfriend and ex-wife – so I'm sure there's a reason why this latest sacrificial lamb was chosen, other than the fact that we met briefly ten years ago.

To get to the heart of that reason, I'll have to find out more about Ama Situwa. If the woman in 812 was a ringer, I'll deal with that later. For the time being I'll take the line that it was really Situwa.

It isn't difficult deciding where to start. As an Ayuamarcan, her name will have been wiped from all city records and nobody will remember her. The only place I might find a history of her is in Party Central, in the personal files of the original keeper of the Ayuamarca secrets.

Ford Tasso isn't surprised when I turn up demanding an audience, but he makes me wait almost an hour while he deals with more immediate problems. Somebody's been hitting key members in the organization, business executives, generals in the Troops. The assassin strikes without warning and without fail. At first Tasso thought it was one of Davern's men, but the Kluxers have also come under attack. Five of Davern's closest aides have been killed, including his best friend, Dan Kerrin. It seems there's a third player in town, stirring things up, but nobody has a clue who it is.

Eventually I'm admitted. Tasso's lying on a newly installed couch, an ice pack over his eyes, massaging the dead flesh of his right arm and shoulder. He looks fit for the grave. 'I used to complain about the nursing home,' he groans as I take a seat. 'Didn't know how lucky I was. I'd give anything to go back.'

'What's stopping you? You've given it your best shot, but you're old and lame. Nobody would blame you if you called it a day.'

'*I'd* blame me,' he growls, removing the ice pack. 'And less of the "old and lame" shit.' His good eye is red and bleary. I doubt he's slept more than a handful of hours since we last met. I don't know what he's running on. I guess he's like the dinosaurs — too stupid to know when he should lie down and die. 'I had Sines on the phone earlier, telling me what happened. Reckon he's fucking with us?'

'Not Sines,' I answer confidently.

'Any idea who took the body and how?'

'It could have been the *villacs*. They have the power to screw with people's minds. They might have hijacked the body at the Skylight, then brainwashed Sines and the driver to believe it vanished mysteriously *en route*.'

'Don't see why they'd go to so much trouble,' Tasso growls, 'but that's better than anything I can think of. So, what next?'

'What shape are the files in on the floors above?' I ask.

'Better than they used to be. Dorak must have had some sort of system but he never revealed it to anybody. It was a nightmare when he died — shit everywhere. Raimi's had people sifting through the mess, filing relevant articles together. They're nowhere near finished, but if they can't find what you're looking for, they can maybe point you in the right direction. What are you after?'

'The woman in the Skylight was Ama Situwa.'

Tasso's eye narrows. 'The one on the Ayuamarca list?'

'Yeah.'

'I thought they were all dead.'

'So did I. We were wrong, or it was someone made up to look like her. Either way, it's time I learnt some more about Miss Situwa. You said Raimi believed he was seeing Ayuamarcans before he disappeared. If I can find out where they – or the impostors – are coming from, it might lead me to your missing Cardinal.'

Tasso nods thoughtfully. 'The files are yours. Most of the Ayuamarca material has been lumped together. I can get a secretary to lead you to it.' He raises a warning finger. 'There's a lot of sensitive shit up there, Algiers. Don't go looking where you ain't meant to.'

'Ford,' I grin, 'don't you trust me?'

'Get the fuck out,' he snarls in reply.

The Ayuamarca file is massive, more than a dozen oversized folders bulging with fact-sheets, detective's reports, newspaper clippings, photographs, DVDs and The Cardinal's own hand-written notes. All of the files have one thing in common — the people they relate to have no background histories, as befits creatures who were allegedly brought back from the dead.

I never realized how many people Dorak supposedly created, or how many positions of authority they filled. Three mayors, two police chiefs, several senior judges, the presidents of some of the most influential banks and companies, many gang leaders. Whenever The Cardinal couldn't crack a rival legitimately, he invented an Ayuamarcan and sent him to his rival's camp as an insider, with orders to cause maximum disruption.

I could spend weeks examining these dusty ledgers and files, learning about the city and the men and women who shaped it over the course of the last half century. But I've a mystery to unravel. Some day, maybe, I'll come back and browse. Right now there's Ama Situwa to account for.

Her file isn't bulky – she only entered the fray a year before Dorak died – but it's thorough. Height, weight, measurements, hair clippings, receipts, hundreds of photos — including several of her making love with Capac Raimi on the stairs of Party Central.

That reminds me of something I'd forgotten. Ama Situwa was on the roof when The Cardinal made his fatal plunge. I was listening in on his final conversation with his successor, and from what I picked up, Situwa was Raimi's true love. He condemned her to oblivion with the other Ayuamarcans by demanding Dorak leap to his death, but it wasn't an easy decision. I can't believe I hadn't remembered that before. Maybe I'm starting to catch the forgetfulness bug at last. I might end up like everybody else if I'm not careful, no memories of Paucar Wami, Leonora Shankar or the others.

I scour Situwa's file for clues to where she or her looka-like might have chosen to hang out. The Ayuamarcan lived with her supposed father, Cafran Reed, but I've already had words with him. There were a few restaurants and bars she favoured, so I jot down the names — I'll visit them and flash Situwa's photos around, in case she's been back recently. I also take the names and addresses of her hairdresser, the beauty parlours she graced, shops she frequented, and the gym where she kept in shape.

Not many friends. Plenty of business acquaintances – Reed was grooming her to run his restaurant – but bosom buddies were scarce. A waitress at Cafran's, Shelly Odone, was closest to her, but they were hardly blood sisters. They went for occasional meals together, hit the clubs every so often. Still, the real Situwa might have looked her up, so I copy down Odone's address – noting in brackets that it's probably changed after so many years – and pencil in the names of a few of her casual friends, on the off-chance that one knows anything about her.

And that's it. I go through the file two more times but there's nothing else to be gleaned. No sisters or daughters (if the woman I saw in the Skylight was a ringer, it's possible she was a relative). No mention of the *villacs*. No links to criminal organizations.

I lay the file aside and massage my eyelids. My eyesight's as good as ever, but lately I've found my eyes pain me if I focus on small print too long. I'm getting old. I'll have them seen to if the condition worsens. It shouldn't pose much of a problem. Just change my green contacts for prescription lenses.

My contacts . . . Paucar Wami . . .

I lower my hand and glance around furtively. I'm alone in an office on the seventeenth floor, where the secretary left me once she'd carted in the files. Tasso warned me to stick to the facts pertinent to the case, but the opportunity to learn more about my father is too good to pass up. In particular, it would be interesting to find out the names of his other children. Apparently he sired many sons and daughters, in this city and further abroad. He never told me their names, or how many there were, but I'm sure his *master* would have known.

I check the names on all the files but Wami's isn't among them. I go through them again, looking inside each folder in case his is nestling inside another — no joy. Pressing a button, I summon the secretary, a plump and genial woman called Betsy. 'Are these all of the Ayuamarca files?' I ask.

'I think so.'

'Could you check again? Or, better still, take me to where the files are kept, so I can look for myself?'

She hesitates. 'I think I should check with Mr Tasso first.'

I shrug. 'If you want to bother him, go ahead. I can wait.'

She frowns. 'I know he's busy . . . He *did* say you could have unlimited access to the files . . . OK,' she decides. 'But I won't leave you alone.'

'Perish the thought,' I smile and follow Betsy out of the office.

We pass several other secretaries as we make our way to where the files are stored. They're busy working on the pillars of paper that stretch to the ceiling in some places, dismantling the towers, making notes of what's in each, carefully re-stacking or re-filing them.

'Is this a twenty-four-hour operation?' I ask.

'Pretty much,' Betsy answers. 'There are only twelve of us — Mr Raimi says that twelve's the most Jesus trusted, and what's good enough for Christ is good enough for him.' She giggles at the soft blasphemy. 'We work in groups of six, twelve hour shifts, though we take long breaks.'

'Do you work seven days a week?'

'Alternate weekends off, and very long holidays.' We come to a rectangular gap, four feet across by eleven or twelve deep, between two six-foot high pillars of paper. Betsy stops. 'We keep the files here.'

I walk into the gap, eyes peeled for an overlooked file, but there isn't any. 'Is this the only place they're stored?'

'There could be others elsewhere, but these are all we've found so far.'

'Who stacked them?'

'We all chipped in, but I did more than most. Mr Raimi was very concerned about these files and he spent a lot of time up here, overseeing their transfer. As a senior secretary, I worked closely with him.'

'Did he ask you to keep any files separate from the others?'

'No.'

'He didn't take any himself, to stack elsewhere?'

'No.' She blushes — lying.

'Come on,' I smile. 'You can tell me. I have the authority.'

'Mr Raimi might not like it if I —'

'Betsy,' I interrupt. 'The Cardinal's missing. I'm trying to find him. If you don't tell me, you'll be hindering, not helping.'

She sighs and nods. 'There was one file he pulled.'

'Paucar Wami's?' I guess.

'No – his own.'

That's disappointing, but it makes sense. A man in his position would want to keep his secrets hidden where only he'd have access to them.

'But now that you mention it,' Betsy adds, 'he also asked me to look for a file on Paucar Wami.' She leans in close and whispers, 'He was a notorious serial killer. The things he's supposed to have done . . .' She shivers.

I hide a grin – if I wiped my cheeks clean, Betsy would be in for one hell of a shock – and ask if she found the Wami file. 'No. We've searched high and low but we haven't unearthed it yet. Mr Raimi thinks it was stolen, though he never said who he suspected.'

I have a strong hunch — the *villacs*. They mustn't have wanted him learning about Wami and his heirs. So much for brushing up on 'dear ole pappy's' past and tracking down my brothers and sisters. Oh well, it's a distraction I can do without. Better to stay focused on the case.

'What are these other files?' I ask, gesturing to the towers of paper surrounding the barren rectangle.

'The files on the left are unrelated,' Betsy says. 'Those on the right and at the rear contain details of people mentioned in the Ayuamarca files — family, friends or business associates of the Ayuamarcans.'

That's interesting. I might learn more about Ama Situwa's friends through these. Digging out my notebook, I reacquaint myself with the names I jotted down, then scan the indexed spines. 'I could be at this a while,' I tell Betsy. 'You can slip away if you want.'

'No thank you,' she smiles. 'It's not that I *don't* trust you, but I *can't*.'

I read up from the bottom of the second pillar on the right. The names are ordered alphabetically. I'm looking for a Sarah Ceccione, a sales rep friend of Situwa's. I jump to the end of the B's and begin on the C's. 'It looks like the one I want is near the top,' I mutter. 'Could you get a ladder or . . .'

I stumble to a halt, eyes settling on a name far more familiar than Sarah Ceccione's. Heart beating fast, I grab the file by the edges and tug.

'Hey!' Betsy pushes me away with unexpected strength. 'You'll bring the whole lot tumbling down.'

'I don't care,' I grunt, trying to get at the file.

Betsy blocks me, a no-nonsense expression on her face. '*I* care,' she huffs. 'I'll have to tidy up after. Tell me which one you want and I'll remove the others, nice and neat, and get it out for you without creating a mess.'

My fingers twitch – I want it in my hands *now* – but it's best to keep Betsy on side. 'That one,' I croak, pointing with a trembling finger. 'The file marked *Bill Casey*.'

FIVE – DETOUR

The train clears the suburbs and enters the great beyond. I stare out of the window at an expanse of bare fields, then pull away from the glass and spend the rest of the journey gazing down at my lap. I guess I've grown agoraphobic from so many years spent hemmed in by the walls of the city. The last time I was this far out was five years ago, when I followed a couple of joy riders until they ran out of gas. They'd mown down a four year old. I disabled the pair, drove to a nearby village, came back equipped with a hammer and nails, and crucified them. A quaint day in the country, Paucar Wami style.

I'm on my way to meet Leo Casey, Bill's younger brother. I never knew Bill had a brother — he always gave the impression that he was an only child. He had a sister too – Jane – but she's deceased, along with his mother and father.

Last night I locked myself into the office on the seventeenth floor of Party Central with the Bill Casey file. Wouldn't allow myself to open it until my hands had stopped trembling. When I did, I found it wasn't the goldmine I'd anticipated. It didn't list Bill's current whereabouts, or comment on whether or not he'd survived the explosion ten years earlier. The disappointment could have been crushing, but as Paucar Wami I'm immune to most emotions. It took a few minutes to snap into character, but once I had – by stroking the tattooed snakes on my cheeks over and over – I was able to settle down and assess the file for what it was, as opposed to what I'd wished it might be.

The file hadn't been updated in decades. It focused on Bill's relationship with Paucar Wami and filled in some of the gaps I've long been puzzling over, concerning how Bill got mixed up with my father. If the details are correct, a teenaged Bill Casey crossed paths with Wami by chance as the serial killer was abducting a girl. Bill tried to kill him but failed. Instead of retaliating, Wami took an interest in the teenager and devised an ingenious method of torture. He sent Bill photos of people he intended to kill, and told him he could save them by performing some cynical, harmful task, such as breaking a blind violinist's fingers, spiking baby food with glass, or bullying a mentally handicapped guy.

The viciousness of the tasks increased in degrading stages. Bill performed some dreadful deeds – Wami even made him rape a girl – in his desperate desire to spare lives. He sought the help of the police, but the cop he went to – none other than Stuart Jordan, our current police commissioner – was one of The Cardinal's pawns. When word reached the Great One, he made sure Bill's pleas went unheeded. Wami was a vital cog in Dorak's machine and he would have sacrificed a thousand like Bill Casey to protect his number one assassin.

The file didn't tell how it ended. A page had been ripped out, and at the top of the next lay a single, perplexing, seemingly unconnected line. 'Margaret Crowe is back safe with her family.' After that it skipped a few years, recommencing with the news that Bill had joined the police. The rest of the file followed his early career. I think it continued in another file, but I found no trace of that one.

I ran 'Margaret Crowe' through the computer, along with

the dates, and came up with a high-profile media story of a nine-year-old who'd been kidnapped, tied up and held in darkness for a couple of days, then released without harm. I don't know how that ties in with Bill and the ordeal he underwent at the hands of Paucar Wami, but I'm on my way to find a man who might.

Leo Casey's led a troubled life, judging by the short entry at Party Central. In counselling of one kind or another since he was a teenager. He's been arrested for shop-lifting, fighting, on drunk and disorderly charges several times, and served two years for selling narcotics whilst on parole. He hasn't had any run-ins with the law since then, but that has a lot to do with the fact that he's spent most of that time in a rehabilitation clinic, St Augustine's, in a town called Curlap, two hundred and forty miles north of the city.

There wasn't a direct train to Curlap until Wednesday – I didn't like the idea of driving – but the 11:14 on Monday goes to Shefferton, which is only twenty-two miles from the town. I booked my ticket over the internet, went home to grab some sleep and pack a bag, and here I am, on my way north on a rare rural excursion.

The train pulls into Shefferton on time. I disembark and take in the locale — a tiny town, sleepy, deserted-looking. I feel dizzy – I need the grime of a big city! – but I quell my sense of unease by concentrating on my mission.

I hire a taxi from Shefferton to Curlap. The driver's inquisitive – asks about my job and where I live – but I say little, grunt in answer to his questions, and sit on my fingers so they don't creep to my scalp to scratch beneath my wig. It always itches in the heat, and today is set-your-hair-on-fire hot.

The driver doesn't know St Augustine's, but stops in Curlap and gets directions. I ask him to wait, even though I don't know how long I'll be. 'Take all the time you like,' he smiles.

'I'm the most patient man in the world when the meter's running.'

St Augustine's has the appearance of a children's school. White walls, a blue, tiled roof, fairytale windows, picket fences, carefully maintained trees set far enough back from the building not to cause damage should they fall. There's even a play area, partly visible from the front path, with swings and slides.

A bell tinkles softly as I enter. A woman in a baggy T-shirt and shorts stands up behind the reception desk and smiles welcomingly. 'Help you, sir?'

I walk over, noting the brightly painted walls and child-like drawings pinned to them. 'Hi. I'm Neil Blair. I was hoping to have a few words with a patient of yours.'

'We call them "guests" here,' the woman corrects me.

'I'd like to see a "guest" then.' I grin as warmly as possible.

'Are you a relative?' she asks, then sticks out a hand before I can answer. 'My name's Nora.'

'Pleased to meet you, Nora,' I respond, shaking her hand. 'No, the man I'd like to see is the brother of a close friend of mine. I've lost contact with this friend and I'm hoping Leo can help me track –'

'Leo Casey?' she interrupts brightly.

'Yes.' I get ready for the curtain to come crashing down but Nora isn't the least suspicious.

'Gosh, it's been a long time since Leo had any visitors. He'll be delighted. Have you known each other long?'

'Actually, we've never met.' It always pays to stick close to the truth when spinning a lie. 'I don't even know if his brother told him about me. But I was in the neighbourhood – I'm a basketball scout – and I recalled Bill telling me this was where Leo lives, so I thought –'

'A scout!' Nora gasps. 'I'm a *huge* fan. Ever discover anyone famous?'

'No,' I chuckle ruefully. 'I feed the smaller teams and universities.'

'I know a guy you *have* to check out,' she says, scrabbling for a pen and paper. 'He's a bit on the mature side – twenty-three – but he's brilliant. Would have turned pro years ago except for an injury.'

'I'll have a look at him,' I lie, taking the scrap of paper from her and squinting at the name as if genuinely interested. 'Now, how about Leo? Is it possible to see him, or do I have to book an appointment or check with his doctor?'

'Goodness no,' she laughs. 'Most of our guests stay with us voluntarily. They can have all the visitors they like. Besides, Leo's an orderly.'

'I thought he was here for treatment.'

'He was – is – but he likes to keep busy, and he's utterly trustworthy. He started helping out a few months after arriving. He fitted in so well, it wasn't long before we put him on the payroll.'

Nora has a free tongue, so I work on her some more. 'What exactly was Leo treated for?'

'Now *that* I can't reveal,' she says regretfully.

'Sorry. I shouldn't have asked.'

'That's OK.' She purses her lips. 'I can say that we specialize in depression. We tend not to take on those who are seriously disturbed, just those who feel confused, a little lost or sad. We make them feel part of a family.'

'Does Leo ever talk about his real family?'

'Yes,' she answers hesitantly. 'But I probably shouldn't speak too much about that.'

'I understand.' A young woman with a troubled look passes through reception and waves curtly at Nora. I note gold rings and a necklace with small diamonds embedded in it. 'Does it cost much to stay here?'

'Oh yes,' Nora chuckles. 'We make special arrangements

for certain individuals, but by and large you don't come to St Augustine's unless you're rolling in it!'

'Bill pays for Leo, doesn't he?' I chance the query, expecting her to say she can't discuss such matters.

'No,' she surprises me. 'I'm not sure who sponsored him when he arrived, but he pays his own way now, out of the money he earns. He's one of the special cases — having been with us so long, and having served so capably, we cut him a serious discount.'

'Has Bill ever come to visit Leo?' I ask, trying to sound casual.

'No.' She frowns. 'Actually, I believe Leo told me his brother was dead. Didn't he die in an accident some years ago?'

'That was an uncle,' I lie smoothly. 'Same name. A freak explosion.'

'Yes, I remember the explosion. Could have sworn it was . . .' She shakes her head. 'Never could trust this brain of mine. Do you want me to page Leo?'

'If you wouldn't mind.'

Nora presses a button, then stands again, peeling the folds of her T-shirt from her armpits. She's sweating, even though the reception's air-conditioned. I'm sweating too, but at the prospect of learning about Bill Casey.

'All our staff wear electronic wristbands,' she says, wriggling her left wrist. 'They vibrate when activated. Much more convenient than a tannoy system.'

When Leo finally shows – ten minutes after his first summons, and having been paged twice more by the good-natured Nora – he takes me by surprise. He's not much older than me but he looks like a man of eighty. An exhausted, trembling wreck, bald on top and white at the sides, grey, wrinkled skin, stooped and slow.

'Sorry it took so long,' he apologises. 'I was with Jacqueline. She was talking about her son. I couldn't leave in the middle.'

'Of course not.' Nora points me out. 'Leo, this is Neil Blair, a friend of your brother's.'

'Bill?' Leo asks, regarding me uncertainly.

'I knew Bill years ago,' I say, offering my hand – which he takes – and lowering my voice so that Nora can't hear. 'I've been out of the country a long time. I only learned of his death a few months ago. I was hoping I could talk about him with you, if that's OK?'

'Sure,' Leo says. 'I like to talk. Do you want to come through and sit out back? It's a lovely day — be a shame to waste it indoors.'

'I was thinking the exact same thing myself.' I turn to Nora. 'Thanks for the assistance.'

'Don't mention it. Look in and say goodbye before you go.'

I follow Leo to the garden. He circles around the play area to a bench in the shade of a tree. 'Who are the swings and slides for?' I ask as we sit.

'The guests,' he says. 'Mrs Kaye – she runs St Augustine's – is a great believer in the power of play. She thinks it's necessary to revert to the joys of childhood if the tribulations of adulthood prove too much to take.' He smiles ruefully. 'I spent a lot of time on those swings when I first came. Didn't go on the slides too much. Never did like slides.'

There's a pause. Leo checks me over, no wariness in his eyes, merely curiosity. 'I don't recall Bill mentioning your name.'

'Were you close to your brother?' I counter.

'Yes. We didn't see as much of each other as we'd have liked — Bill's job kept him city-bound, while I've always preferred open spaces. Actually,' he coughs, 'I've a phobia about that city. Not cities in general, just that one. But we kept in touch. Bill was great for writing. Sent me a couple of letters and, later, dozens of emails every week. I miss him terribly.'

Leo's grief would be hard to fake. I suspect he knows nothing of his brother's possible survival, but I press ahead regardless. I have no room for sympathy where Bill Casey's concerned.

'I want to come clean with you, Leo,' I say softly, not entirely sure how best to proceed, playing it by ear. 'The reason you don't recognize my name is that it's an alias. I didn't want anyone knowing my real reason for being here.'

'Oh?' His forehead crinkles. 'I'm intrigued.'

'My real name's Al Jeery.' I watch closely for how he takes that.

Leo scratches the dry, wrinkled skin of his chin. 'That name I *do* recall. You were one of Bill's best friends. He wrote about you a lot. The way he went on, you could have been his son.' He chuckles. 'Bill was like that. If he developed a warm spot for someone, he loved them completely.'

'Yeah.' I force a sick laugh, recalling the deathly pale faces of Nicola Hornyak and Ellen, how Bill calmly and coldly destroyed my life.

'I don't get it,' Leo says. 'Why the subterfuge?'

'Did Bill ever tell you what I did for a living?' I ask.

'I don't think so. But my memory's not the strongest.'

'I'm a private detective.'

'Really? How exciting. Is it glamorous, like in the films and on TV?'

'No. Long, tedious hours and you never get seduced by beautiful *femme fatales*.' Not true. I was taken for a ride by a chic she-bitch on my only previous case. But I'd rather not dwell on that.

'Are you on a job now?' Leo asks.

'Kind of,' I answer slowly. 'It's personal, and I'm sure there's nothing to it, but . . .' I clear my throat and nudge closer. 'I've heard rumours that Bill's alive.'

Leo blinks. 'Alive? No. Bill died in an explosion. The police said terrible things, that he killed people, that it was suicide. I never believed them – he couldn't have murdered, not after what happened to Jane – but I know he's dead. They found his body. Bits of it. He was blown to pieces and burned. He . . .'

Tears form in Leo Casey's tired old eyes and drip down his coarse cheeks. If he's putting on an act, he's a master performer, even better than his brother, who played the part of my friend to perfection while all the time planning to strip me of everything that made me human in order to sic me on my father. 'He can't be alive,' Leo croaks. 'He'd have come to see me. He'd have written.'

'Easy,' I soothe him, taking his hands and massaging them. His fingers are like a witch's, long, thin, bony. 'It's just a rumour, but I had to check it out.'

'Who's saying such things?' Leo snarls, anger getting the better of his sorrow. 'Who's making up lies about my brother?'

'A dirtbag. You don't know him. He's scum, but as I said, I had to check, to be certain. Now I can go back and deal with him.'

'I don't understand,' Leo moans, his anger fading as swiftly as it rose. 'Why would anyone make up something like that?'

'Bill had enemies. They're trying to pin the blame for more deaths on him. I'm determined to expose their lies, stop them insulting Bill's memory.'

'Bastards!' Leo spits, then looks contrite for having sworn. I don't like playing this broken man – I'd feel more comfortable if he wasn't so trusting – but I've come too far to back off. I'm sure he doesn't know where Bill is, but he mentioned their sister and I want to find out what he meant by 'he couldn't have murdered, not after what happened to Jane'.

'Bill didn't talk much about his past,' I say as Leo dabs at his eyes with a large handkerchief. 'Barely mentioned you and Jane — she was your sister, wasn't she?'

'Yes.' Leo sighs miserably. 'I'm not surprised he didn't talk about it. None of us liked remembering those horrible days. Our mother – God rest her soul – made us swear never to talk of it in her presence.'

'Could you tell me what happened?' I ask gently, buzzing with curiosity.

Leo's face darkens. 'I don't want to.'

I bite down on a furious grimace. 'I understand.'

'My doctors encouraged me to talk about it when I first arrived,' he says, 'but when they saw how much it pained me, they taught me how to deal with it without confronting it head-on. That's where a lot of my troubles lay, either running from those memories or dwelling on them too much. They still haunt me, but nowhere near as much as they used to.'

I nod, then clear my throat, hating myself for opening old wounds, but needing to know. 'I was with Bill at the end.'

Leo stares at me oddly. Then his eyes light up. 'Of course! God, how could I be so dense? *Al Jeery*. You were with Bill when . . .' His eyes go dull again.

'He was in so much pain,' I murmur. 'Death was a relief.'

'Do you . . .' Leo gulps. 'Do you have any idea why he did it? The police said he killed people and blew himself up, but I don't . . . I never believed . . .'

I could destroy him with the truth. Part of me wants to – to hurt Bill as he hurt me – but I came here to learn, not to harm. 'The police got it wrong,' I mutter, the lie bitter on my lips. 'Bill had been tracking a killer. He found and executed him. One of the killer's partners framed and butchered Bill in retaliation. I tried telling the cops but they wouldn't listen.'

'I knew it!' Leo gasps, crying again, but with relief this time. 'I knew there was more to it than they said. Bill wasn't evil. He didn't take his own life.'

'Of course not,' I agree with a wan smile, then frown. 'The

last person he mentioned was Jane. He said he was sorry for what happened, that he was looking forward to seeing her in the next world. I tried asking him about her but it was too late. He . . .' I leave the rest unsaid and keep a sly eye on Leo, hoping he'll take the bait.

Leo wrestles with it in silence, then his features relax. 'It was the summer of the riots,' he says in a soft voice, referring to a time when the city endured several months of race-related violence. More than a hundred people died, and much of the city – especially in the east – was burnt to the ground. 'It was hot then, like now. Jane was nine. She loved the sun. Couldn't wait for the holidays, so she could go swimming every day. Then she went missing. She was kidnapped.'

I start to smile, feeling the pieces of the puzzle fall into place, but quickly hide it before Leo sees. 'Go on,' I say encouragingly.

'Another girl went missing at the same time — Margaret Crowe. She turned up a few days later, shaken and afraid, but alive. Jane didn't.'

Leo stops, his eyes twin pools of pain. I wait for him to continue. When he doesn't, my prodding is somewhat sharper than intended. '*And?*'

'Nothing,' he whispers. 'She stayed lost. The police searched for a long time. We searched too – my step-father hired private detectives – but she was never seen or heard from again. For a long time we believed – hoped – she was alive, but a year after she was taken, we received something in the post . . .'

His expression is so dreadful, I'm not sure I want him to carry on. I almost ask him to stop but he blurts out the rest before I can. 'It was her hair. Tied with her favourite ribbon. There was a note. "Hair today, gone tomorrow. Ho ho ho".'

My eyes close comprehendingly. There's no mistaking my father's sick sense of humour. I see now how Bill ended up so twisted with hate. At the peak of his taunting of Bill, Wami must have kidnapped the girls. He probably told Bill to kill Margaret Crowe or he'd kill Jane. Bill wasn't able to do it, so Wami released the Crowe girl and killed young Jane Casey.

The mystery has eaten away at me for ten years. I still don't understand why Bill sought such a warped form of revenge – setting me after Wami in the hope that I'd kill him – but I now know what lay behind it. In a strange way, knowledge of the tragedy is a relief. At the back of my mind I nursed the suspicion that Bill had been lying when he said he ruined my life to get even with Wami. I thought he might have been truly evil, and had simply toyed with me for kicks. At least now I know his claims of revenge were genuine, that I suffered for a heartfelt reason, not because some inhuman psycho was in search of a thrill.

'The family fell apart,' Leo says hollowly. 'The hair confirmed that she was dead. Paul, my step-father, collapsed with a stroke a few days later. He lived another three years, paralysed and speechless. He had to be spoon-fed. My mother blamed herself for the death and took to self-torment, physically punishing herself with flames and knives. We had to commit her. Some months later, shortly before Paul died, she took her own life. In many ways it was a blessing.'

'And Bill?' I ask quietly. 'How did *he* take it?'

'I don't know,' Leo says. 'Bill cut himself off emotionally from the rest of us, long before we got proof that she'd been killed. He wouldn't join in the search. He never gave any sign that he thought she was alive. He detached himself and went into private mourning.'

Because he knew about Paucar Wami. He knew there was no hope. I can see it from Bill's viewpoint – Jane's life was his to spare, but his humanity stayed his hand. He hadn't been able to kill Margaret Crowe, so his sister died in her place. What a terrible burden. No wonder he threw himself into revenge so thoroughly — it must have been the only way he could continue, the one way he could stave off madness and function as an ordinary human being. Without revenge to occupy him, he'd have crumbled completely.

(Part of me tries to comment on the similarity between Bill's situation and my own, but I silence that voice instantly.)

'Did Bill ever mention someone called Paucar Wami?' I ask, knowing it's a pointless question. Leo wouldn't be sitting here quietly if he knew the name of his sister's killer.

'Yes,' Leo says, startling me. 'How strange that you should know about that. He often moaned the name in his sleep, and once I found him scratching it on a wall in our garage. He was using his fingernails. His fingers were torn and bloody, but he went on, even after I tried pulling him away.'

'This was when you were still a kid?'

'Yes.'

For a moment I'm confused — why hasn't Leo forgotten about the Ayuamarcan? Then it hits me. Only the memories of the people in the city were wiped clean by the *villacs'* mystical green fog. Those living outside weren't affected.

'Did you ever ask Bill about Wami?' I enquire.

'Once. He said Paucar Wami was the devil, and if he ever heard the name on my lips again, he'd slice out my tongue.' He looks up, his eyes bloodshot and wet with tears. 'Do *you* know who Paucar Wami was?'

'A killer. I think he murdered your sister.'

Leo nods weakly. 'I guessed as much. He's the man Bill killed, isn't he?'

'Yes,' I lie, maybe the kindest word I'll ever speak.

'I'm glad,' Leo says firmly. 'A murderer like that deserved to die.'

I rub the muscles at the back of my neck and let out a

tired but satisfied groan. 'I hope I haven't stirred up too many unpleasant memories.'

'No,' Leo smiles. 'I'm glad you came. I feel better knowing the truth. It's like you've given Bill back to me after those other people tried to take him away with lies.'

I study Leo's eyes and see a peace in them which wasn't there when I arrived. His life will never be perfect – it can't be, not with all that he's suffered – but it won't be quite as grim as it was. Part of me envies him that peace, but for the most part I'm pleased for him.

'I'll go now,' I say, standing and stretching. Then I remember the story I fed him and quickly tie up the loose ends. 'Those bastards won't get any further with their stories about Bill. I'll put a stop to them.'

'Don't worry about it,' Leo says. 'Let them lie all they want. I don't care now that I know the truth.' He leans against the tree and sighs. 'Would you mind if I didn't see you off? I'd rather sit here and rest awhile, think about Bill.'

'That's fine. It was nice meeting you, Leo.'

'You too, Al,' he murmurs, closing his eyes and snuggling up to the tree.

I watch the wretched old man for a few seconds, thinking about Bill, Paucar Wami and the dark secrets of the past. Then, skirting the central building – I don't feel up to another conversation with Nora – I locate my driver and tell him to get me back to the station as quickly as he can. I'm anxious to return to my ugly, cramped but familiar and comforting hovel in the city.

SIX – KKK

It's a relief to be back. When I got off the train last night, I walked home, even though it took ages. It was like a stroll through paradise, soaking up the noise and stench of the city, relishing the feel of the pavement beneath my feet, the crush of the crowds outside cinemas and in public squares, the intensity of the lights, the overpowering, converging buildings which block out most of the sky and make me feel as if I'm inside a dome. It's not healthy, this fear I've developed of the world beyond. Addictions are dangerous, and addiction to a city – especially one with as polluted a soul as this – is downright perverse. But I can't help myself. I've devoted my last ten years to darkness and insanity, and in the eyes of the world I'm a monster. I need somewhere to hide from those condemning eyes — a lair.

It was late when I got home, and I was tired, so I stayed in and wrote a report of my meeting with Leo. I read through it several times once it was finished, in case it would spark any new ideas. Then I burnt it. This apartment has been burgled twice and might be again — it's not the safest of neighbourhoods. I wouldn't want such a sensitive document falling into someone else's hands.

I'd like to pursue the Bill angle – I toy with the idea of

abducting Leo and putting out word that I have him and won't release him unless Bill shows his face – but I can't risk pissing off Ford Tasso. If he learns I've been hunting for Bill instead of for his Cardinal, he could bring the full wrath of Party Central down upon me.

So, putting the mystery of Bill and Paucar Wami to one side, I return to the Capac Raimi puzzle. I spend Tuesday locating Ama Situwa's friends. Most are easy to track down. I contact them by phone and ask about her, pretending to be an insurance agent, trying to find her in order to pay out on a premium. Only one of them – Shelly Odone – can recall Cafran Reed's temporary daughter.

'Ama and I were great friends. We enjoyed some wild nights on the town.' She giggles at the memories. Shelly lives abroad, with the man she married eight years ago. She left the city shortly before Ferdinand Dorak died. She wasn't here when the brainwashing fog was working its wonders. That's why she remembers Ama.

'Did you ever hear from her after you moved?' I ask.

'No. I rang the restaurant a few times, but she must have had a major row with her father because he wouldn't even admit to having a daughter. Will you let me know if you find her? I'd love to hear what she's been up to.'

No luck with Situwa's favoured restaurants, bars, clubs, beauty salons, shops or gym. I do the rounds of all of them, Wednesday and Thursday, in Al Jeery guise, again pretending to be an insurance agent.

I break from my investigations on Thursday evening, to attend a book auction. Many rare first editions in the biggest sale to hit the city in six or seven years. I weave in and out of the crowd of excited punters in my security guard clothes, scanning the faces of elderly men, searching for Bill. I leave an hour before the conclusion, bemused by the frenzied bidding and increasingly crazy prices fetched by the novels.

Later, as Paucar Wami, I visit a couple of the bars and clubs which I hit earlier, and convince the managers to pass me copies of their surveillance discs, which I'll sift through, watching closely in case Ama made an appearance and was caught on camera. A shot in the dark, but I have to try. I'll sift through the society columns in papers and magazines too, studying photos. I can do that in Party Central — they have copies of all the city's periodicals on file. It won't be fun, and I doubt it'll lead anywhere, but it's all part of a detective's sorry lot.

Friday morning, I purchase a pair of TV sets and DVD players, using the credit card Mags sent me the day after I accepted the case. I have them delivered and I ask the team – a middle-aged man and his teenage son – to hook up the equipment. They say that they know nothing about that, they're just the monkeys who lug this stuff around. One generous tip later, they become instant experts, and I'm soon in business.

I crack open a beer, then settle back and play two discs simultaneously, eyes flicking lizard-like from one TV to the other, drinking in faces, comparing them to Ama Situwa's, dismissing most automatically. A few cause me to hit the pause button, but on closer study they aren't my woman and it's back to the action, watching, waiting, blinking as seldom as possible.

One of the discs runs out before the other. I let the second get to the end before ejecting both and inserting a fresh pair. A short break to rest my eyes, then it's back to the discs, the silence of the apartment disturbed only by my breathing and the soft whirring of the DVD players.

I'm on my fourth set of discs when my cell rings. I'm glad of the distraction. I'm accustomed to long, lonely vigils, stalking prey, but a live stakeout can be exciting, despite the hours of inactivity. This is just a drag.

I check the incoming number but don't recognize it. This influx of unfamiliar callers is annoying. 'Hello?' I answer neutrally, ready to be Al Jeery or Paucar Wami, depending on who the caller's looking for.

'Al? It's Flo. I got your number from Fabio's book. Hope you don't mind me calling.'

'Of course not. Is he dead?'

'No,' she sighs, 'but he's not far off. I thought you might like to be with him at the end. You don't have to come, but –'

'I'll be there,' I interrupt softly. 'He's at home?'

'Yes. He made us promise we wouldn't move him to a hospital. He wanted to die in his own bed.'

'I'm on my way.'

Switching off the TVs, I eject the discs and hide them behind the loose panels at the back of my wardrobe – not a great hiding place, but they should be safe from amateur burglars – then slap on my Al Jeery facepaint and wig, remove the green contacts, take off the severed, varnished finger hanging from my neck, and hurry downstairs with my bike.

The house is crowded with Fabio's friends and relatives, all come to cheer the old pimp off, as he would have wished. Beer and whisky flow like water. Spirits are already high. Pulsing music blares from Fabio's CD player – he developed a taste for R'n'B late in life – and the space closest the speakers is full of younger mourners, bopping their heads. The older members occupy rooms nearer the back, where they complain to each other about the noise.

Flo and Drake are playing host, along with a handful of others who helped look after Fabio in his twilight years. They pass around food, clear away empties, keep the peace between the young and old, and guard the entrance to Fabio's bedroom, making sure he isn't overcrowded.

'Can I sit with him awhile?' I ask Flo during a quiet moment.

'Sure,' she smiles wearily. 'We're giving everyone a few minutes with him, to say goodbye and wish him well, but you can stay as long as you want. You're one of his favourites.'

'It's good to have friends in high places,' I grin, then head through. I find him unconscious, as he's been for most of the last twenty-four hours. Zeba — one of Fabio's ladies — tells me they don't expect him to open his eyes again.

'We asked if he wanted us to call you over, the last few times he was awake,' Zeba says softly, wiping sweat from his forehead. 'He said not to bother. Said you knew each other too long for sentimental shit like that. Said there wasn't nothing you could say now that you hadn't said before.'

'Cantankerous to the end,' I snort, laying the back of my hand on his cheeks, one after the other, feeling the coldness of death in them. 'Any idea how long he has left?'

'A few hours. His body's all busted. I reckon he's only hanging on for one last blast of music. Soon as them young-sters stop playing the songs, he'll up and quit.'

'Maybe we should let them play on indefinitely,' I suggest.

'Nah,' she smiles. 'He's done here. Let the old tomcat go. It'd be cruel to keep him hanging on. He's got better places to be.'

I sit with Fabio until the end, while others file in and out, shepherded by the eagle-eyed Zeba. Sometimes I hold his hands, sometimes I wipe his brow, but mostly I sit back and watch people make their farewells. I don't say anything. He was right — there's nothing new either of us could say. Fabio's my oldest friend, even there for me before Bill Casey, the only one I never alienated since becoming Paucar Wami. I worried sometimes that the *villacs* might use him to hurt me, but thankfully they let him be.

Another old friend, Ali, enters and we exchange a few

hushed words. He runs a bagel shop beneath the apartment where I used to live. I still drop in occasionally, in Al Jeery guise, though it's been a few months.

'How are you, my friend?' Ali asks.

'Good. And you?'

'I cannot complain.'

'I didn't know you knew Fabio.'

'I don't,' he says. 'I just saw the crowd and joined the party.' He laughs, then smiles sheepishly when Zeba glares at him. 'Fabio was a good customer of mine. And I of his. We exchanged . . . services.'

'You swapped bagels for ladies?' I smirk.

'Yes,' he blushes. 'I always believed I was getting the better of the bargain, but Fabio said many men had finer women to offer than he, but nobody in this city could slap together as delicious a bagel as me.'

'He had a point.'

'I will miss him.'

'Me too.'

'And the women.'

I choke on a laugh. 'I think you'll find a few of those else-where.'

'Yes,' Ali sighs. 'But it will not be the same. I will always think of Fabio when I am enjoying the embrace of a fine woman.' He giggles impishly and winks at me. 'Well, maybe not *always* . . .'

Finally, Fabio passes. There's no climactic finale or dramatic last gasp. His breathing has been getting softer, to the point where his chest no longer seems to rise or fall. Flo replaced Zeba an hour ago and has been checking his pulse every five minutes, holding a mirror over his lips and nose. This time she shakes her head, tears forming. 'He's gone,' she says flatly.

And that's the end of that.

*   *   *

I want to slip off home but Flo asks me to stay. It would be impolite to say no, so I remain as she and Zeba see to his body, stripping and washing him one last time, before dressing him in his best clothes — Fabio always placed great importance on appearance. A mortician will fix him up tomorrow, but the ladies are determined to keep him in good shape in the meantime. We should be able to get him cremated soon, maybe at the weekend or early next week. There's a long waiting list at the crematorium, but one of Fabio's many grandsons is on the staff.

I leave the women to their ministrations – rather, they shoo me out of the room – and mingle uneasily with the other guests. I know most of them (as Paucar Wami it's my business to know people), but very few know me. They're aware that I'm a close friend of Fabio's, and a few of the older guests recognize me from when I was a kid, but nobody knows who I am at night.

After half an hour of strained small-talk, one of Fabio's great-grandsons takes me aside. Fabio never married, but he sired many bastards, who in turn bred like rabbits. I don't know how many grandchildren and great-grandchildren he had – I don't think the old buzzard knew himself – but it's in excess of a hundred.

I know Kurt Jones, AKA Bones Jones, the one who sidetracks me. A small fish in one of the smaller gangs. Fabio liked him. Most of the pimp's descendants had gone legit. That pleased him, but left him with little in common with them. Bones was one of the few he could click with.

'How you doing, Bones?'

'Not bad, man. Business is good. Could be better, but hey! You ain't in the market for digital cameras, are you? I got a load going dirt-cheap.'

'I can maybe take one if the price is right.'

'Nah, man, I'm into bulk trading.'

'Sorry.'

'That's OK.' He glances around, drags me away from the others and lowers his voice. 'I don't know why he told me to tell you this, but I was shooting the shit with the F last week, and there was this one thing he said I had to take it to you. I came over your place Monday but you was out and I been busy since.'

'What's it regarding?'

Bones' voice drops even further. 'Ever hear of a dude called Paucar Wami?'

I stiffen. 'What about him?'

'Shit I heard. Rumours. You probably don't know this, but someone's been offing people close to Ford Tasso and Eugene Davern.'

'So?'

'Word is Paucar Wami's taking them down.'

'You think Wami's killing Tasso and Davern's confidants?'

'Not me, man, I don't think shit. It's what I heard. I told the F – he always liked hearing about Wami – and he said I had to tell you.'

'Thanks, Bones. I owe you.'

It's not unusual for me to be blamed for killings I've nothing to do with, and normally I allow such rumours to circulate unchecked (good for business), but this is a complication I can do without. When Tasso gets word of it, he'll want to know if it's true. I'm sure I can convince him of my innocence, but once seeds of doubt have been sown, relationships are never quite the same. I'll have to move to quell the rumours, and fast.

I make my apologies to Flo, tell her to call me if she needs help with the funeral arrangements, then slip away from the party – which is hitting full swing – and return home. I shed my wig and face-paint, become Paucar Wami, and take to the streets to sort this shit out.

*   *   *

It's worse than I thought. The rumours have been spreading for a couple of weeks. I'd have twigged to them sooner if I hadn't been so wrapped up in my investigations. According to the gossip mongers, I'm not only responsible for wiping out some of Tasso and Davern's key men, but I've been putting together a gang of my own, backed by a mystery benefactor, with the intention of turning the Troops and Kluxers against each other, letting them slug it out, then moving in to finish them off and seize control.

It only takes a few hours to track the stories back to some of their sources, and I spend the pre-dawn hours Saturday grilling several people who've been busy feeding the rumour mill. They confess freely, with only a minimum of prompting (being jolted awake in the middle of the night by a legendary killer tends to loosen the stiffest of tongues). They were bribed to spread the lies, but they don't know who paid them or why. They received orders and payment in plain envelopes. I check the notes, all of which run much the same way. 'This is the news. Let it be heard. More money to follow.' Underneath, the rumours — Paucar Wami has been killing Ford Tasso and Eugene Davern's men . . . he's formed a gang of his own . . . he kidnapped The Cardinal . . . etc.

I'm baffled to begin with – I don't know what anyone stands to gain by this – but then a glimmer of an idea strikes me. By framing me for his disappearance, maybe Raimi's kidnappers hope to turn Ford Tasso against me. If that's the case, it raises a conundrum. I've been working on the assumption that the *villacs* took Raimi, to tempt me back into their warped games. But if they did, they'd surely want to keep me active. They'd hardly instigate rumours which might lead to Tasso terminating my contract.

Is somebody else involved? Was Raimi kidnapped by a third party? Maybe the priests are looking for Raimi too, got me involved because they thought I might be able to help

find him, and the real kidnappers are now trying to undermine me.

It's almost 08:00 when I go to bed, brooding about the
rumours, the *villacs* and possible others. After ten or fifteen
minutes I fall into a troubled sleep . . .

. . . which I snap out of abruptly at 09:16 when my front
door's kicked in and three men with guns burst into my
apartment.

I'm rolling out of bed in an instant, snatching my .45 from
beneath the pillow where I always keep it, taking a bead on
the men who've fanned out. My finger tightens and I prepare
to blow away the man on my right. But they aren't firing.
They have the drop on me but they're holding off. And they
look terrified.

As I pause, bewildered, a fourth man enters. Clad in a
white fur coat, the hem swirling around his ankles, he strolls
past the three with guns. His blond hair and blue eyes belong
on a model. He oozes self-confidence and wealth. He smiles
at me as if we're old friends, casts an eye around and sighs.
'How you people live in such squalor is beyond me. Have
niggers no sense of self-worth?'

I almost let him have a full clip in the stomach. But if I
open fire on him, his men will retaliate. I wouldn't survive
the shootout.

The man in the fur coat pulls over a chair and sits. His
manicured fingers pick at the folds of the coat as he grins.
'Hyde Wornton,' he introduces himself. 'I'd say I was pleased
to meet you, but that'd be a lie. The only niggers I like are
those with a rope around their necks and nothing but air
beneath their feet.'

Hyde Wornton. Eugene Davern's lieutenant, one of the
men I considered following in the hope of tracing Capac
Raimi. This is bad. Wornton has a foul reputation. One of
the more zealous Kluxers, he keeps the spirit of the Klan

alive and well, even while Davern struggles to suppress it. A dangerous man at the best of times.

'What do you want?' I snarl.

'That's "Sir" or "Massah" to you, nigger,' he says pleasantly.

'Call me that again and you die,' I tell him.

'I don't think so,' he laughs. 'You're smarter than that. You won't throw your life away just because someone calls you a nigger or a coon.'

'You're a dead man,' I whisper. 'Not today, but soon. That's a promise.'

'Never met a darkie who could keep a promise,' he giggles, then gets serious. 'You know who I work for. Eugene – Mr Davern to you – requests the pleasure of your company. Pronto.'

'Eugene Davern can go fuck his whore of a mother,' I retort, enjoying the dark cloud which disturbs Wornton's expression.

'Careful,' he hisses. 'Make a crack like that again and I'm apt to start something ugly, regardless of the consequences.'

'Just tell me what you want and quit with the dramatics,' I drawl.

'Your ass in my car, now.'

'If I refuse?'

Wornton shrugs. 'It's obvious I don't want to start a shooting match. If you don't come, we walk. But it's taken a lot of time and money to track you down, to link the feared Paucar Wami to the meek Al Jeery. Now that we have, you're up shit creek. If you don't jump when we say, we tell everyone what we know and that's bye-bye alter ego, farewell hideyhole. You'll be exposed, with nowhere to run, and your enemies will descend on you like a swarm of locusts and free your clean white bones of their degenerate black skin.'

'I'd heard you were a bible-thumper,' I sneer but inside

I'm cursing. They have me by the balls. I'd never have survived this long without being able to retreat from the madness of the streets when needs dictated. Even Paucar Wami has to have a place where he can rest up.

'We don't *have* to make this general knowledge,' Wornton says. 'Only a few of us know about you and we've sworn to Eugene that we won't reveal the truth.' His nose crinkles. 'Personally, I'd rat you out as soon as look at you, but Eugene's the boss and we know the value of loyalty, unlike some races I could mention.'

I ignore the slur and consider his proposal. 'What does Davern want?'

'Damned if I know. Maybe he's looking for a new shoeshine boy.'

'Why should I trust you?'

'Hell, nigger, you can't!' Wornton whoops. 'I could give you my word, but my word's only sacred if given to one of my own. I'd think nothing of lying to a nigger. Still, if it'd make you feel safer . . .'

'Fuck you,' I snap, then put my gun away. 'Give me a few minutes to change. I'll meet you out front presently.'

Wornton nods to his guards. They edge out backwards, not lowering their weapons, and Wornton follows.

'Hyde,' I stop him. 'I know you white boys have a thing for black men, so if you want to stay and jerk your chain while I'm changing, I won't object.'

His apoplexy almost makes me glad that my cover's been blown.

Wornton doesn't remove his coat in the car, even though the heat has me sweating through my T-shirt. He sits up front with the driver, while the two other goons sit either side of me in the back. Nobody speaks. We end up at the Kool Kats Klub, Eugene Davern's restaurant, which opened in the 1980s as the Ku Klux Klub. It's remained true to its origins, though the burning crosses in the windows and the occasional hooded customer or waiter are relics of the past.

I'm marched into the restaurant by a side door, past several startled members of staff, to a room at the rear of the building where Eugene Davern awaits. To my surprise, I'm not relieved of my weapons, merely waved in by a sardonic Hyde Wornton, who mutters, 'Best of luck, *nigger*,' before closing the door after me.

Davern's hovering in front of a glass display case, full of articles about the restaurant. He's in his early forties, tall – at least six-five – and in good shape. His dark hair's swept back with gel and he sports a stylish moustache and goatee. Dressed immaculately in a cream suit. His hands are in his trouser pockets. He doesn't take them out or step forward to greet me.

'You're wondering why you haven't been disarmed,' he says, grey eyes cold and penetrating.

'Yes,' I answer sombrely, wary of this intelligent, quietly threatening man.

'I've let you keep your weapons because I do not fear you. This is my domain, and here I fear no man. Besides, you aren't a fool. My men know where you live. You've spent ten years living a double life. I have the power to let you continue or expose you. That power must be respected. Killing me would be self-destructive.'

'How did you find out about me?' I ask.

'Irrelevant,' he sniffs. 'Let's talk instead about why you're here. I wish to strike a bargain.'

I blink, confused. 'What sort of bargain?'

Davern steps away from the display case. Gets up close and studies my face, the coiled serpents, my unnatural green eyes. He keeps his hands in his pockets. He doesn't look as hateful as Hyde Wornton, but I get the impression that he's even more arrogant, that he thinks as little of me as he would an ant.

'You've killed men who were important to me,' he murmurs. 'Men I've worked with for many years. Friends like Dan Kerrin. We grew up together. Closer than brothers. And you butchered him in his bath, leaving his bloody, naked body for his wife to find.'

He voices the accusations passionlessly. I find that more worrying than if he was screaming abusively.

'I didn't kill Dan Kerrin,' I say evenly. 'Or the others.'

'You deny it?' His left eyebrow lifts marginally. 'I thought Paucar Wami was a man who boasted of his kills. You even take credit for other hits, don't you?'

'If people are willing to accredit them to me, I let them — it's good for business. But I don't lie. I didn't kill your men.'

Davern smoothes his goatee with the ball of his left thumb. 'Are you hungry? Would you care to break bread with me?'

I'm startled by the change of tone but don't let it show. 'I'll gladly eat with you,' I tell him, 'but only if you swallow before I do.'

Davern laughs and leads me into the dining room, past the day's first customers – their outraged mutters when they spot me are music to my ears – to one of the private areas where a table is laid for two, overflowing with croissants, cereal, fruit, silver bowls of butter and preservatives, five pitchers of milk and fruit juice, various loaves of freshly baked bread.

'Rather different to what I assume you're accustomed to,' Davern says, taking a seat and breaking a fresh loaf of seeded bread in two. He passes half to me, slices his open and smears it with thick, soft butter. I wait for him to bite into it before scraping a thin layer of butter over mine.

'What do you want?' I ask, washing the bread down with

a glass of purple juice — again, only after Davern has tested it first.

The owner of the Kool Kats Klub and head of the Kluxers doesn't answer immediately, but chews on a currant cake. Then he says, 'You're lying about Dan but that doesn't matter. There will come a day when I'll seek retribution, but for the time being I wish to talk peace.'

He pauses. I think about denying the charges again, but I'm not that bothered whether he blames me for his friend's death or not. I'm more interested in this deal of his.

'I know about the Snakes,' he says softly.

'Snakes?' I repeat.

'*The Snakes*,' he hisses. 'I congratulate you on the way you've recruited and guided them, keeping them a secret for so long. Such initiative is rare. I'm sure you're not working alone – armies require funding, and you're not rich – but in the absence of any other visible leader, I'm prepared to deal with you directly.'

I've found through experience that it's wiser to say nothing where you're ignorant of what's being discussed. Let the other person ramble and maybe you'll learn something. But I'm so dumbstruck by what he's saying that before I know it I'm mumbling, 'I haven't a clue what you're talking about.'

Davern smiles thinly. 'Don't insult me. I don't know how many you've gathered to your cause, or how you plan to deploy them, but I know they exist and that they keep to the tunnels, out of sight and hearing. And I'm sure you plan to unleash them soon, otherwise why kidnap Capac Raimi and target Ford Tasso and me?'

'Honestly, I don't know what –'

'Don't lie to me!' he shouts, cheeks reddening. 'I won't sit here and be lied to by . . .' He stops abruptly.

' . . . a nigger?' I finish for him icily.

'Now that you mention it, yes,' he says, regaining his

composure. 'It would be pointless to hide my prejudices. That said, I've come to realize there can be no clean division of the races. Black and white have come together, and while I don't approve of the mingling, only a fool or a romantic such as Hyde rages in the face of it. This city will never again be ruled by one race. It's time we reconciled ourselves to that and got on with forging new, mutually beneficial relationships with one another.'

'A touching speech,' I snicker.

'An honest statement of truth,' he counters. 'I won't pretend to like your dark-skinned brethren, but I acknowledge the fact that I have to share the reins of power with them. And I'm prepared to. I'm willing to strike up a partnership with you and your followers. There's more than enough action in this city for both of us. Once Tasso and his Troops are out of the way, we can discuss an equitable arrangement. The north and west for me, east and south for you? The docks split fifty-fifty?'

I shake my head. 'You're talking of things I know nothing about. I haven't recruited a gang. I'm just a vigilante. This talk of partnership means nothing to me. I'm not into power games.'

Davern's expression hardens. 'Don't fuck with me,' he growls. 'I'm not a man you fuck with. In ten short years I've gone from being a chorus boy in the Klan to head of my own army, second in strength only to the decaying forces of Dorak's Troops. This restaurant was my sole source of income twenty years ago. Now I run much of the city. You think I came this far by letting punks shit on me? I've made a valid proposition. If you don't greet it with the grace it merits, I'll have you taken out back and executed like the upstart that you are.'

I nod slowly. 'Now you're talking my language.' I draw my .45 and lay it on the table. His eyes narrow but he shows no other discernible concern. 'You want to start a shooting match, go ahead. But this talk of gangs and taking over the city falls on deaf ears. I'm not into that shit.'

Davern cocks his head. 'If I didn't know better, I'd swear you were on the level. You must teach me how to lie so smoothly. Very well, you refuse to discuss an entente. I respect that. There are other players and you don't want to pick sides too soon. In your position, I'd do the same. But take heed.' He wipes crumbs from his lips with a silk napkin and stands. 'I have options too. There are others I can ally myself with. I'd rather link with your Snakes, but if I have to strike a deal with the white-eyed devils, I will.'

His mention of the blind priests intrigues me, but I say nothing, not wishing to start Davern off on another rant.

'You can go when you finish eating,' he says as he leaves the table. 'I won't ask any of my men to drive you back, but there are a number of cab ranks close by. I'm sure you'll find a hard-up driver who won't object to giving you a ride.'

'Davern,' I stop him as he reaches the door. 'What about Al Jeery?'

He pauses. 'It would drive you underground if I went public. I'm tempted to, if only to force you to admit your ties to the Snakes.' He waves a dismissive hand. 'But I like having you where I can find you, so we'll keep your identity a secret for now. But if you don't play ball, that can change swifter than a hummingbird's fart.'

He exits.

I linger a while, enjoying the meal, taking advantage of my unlikely host's hospitality, wondering what Eugene Davern was talking about, why he thinks I'm a competitor and possible ally of his . . . and who the hell the *Snakes* are.

SEVEN – REQUIEM FOR A PIMP

Sunday, traditional day of rest — but not for me. I spend it as I spent yesterday afternoon, pounding the streets, pumping informants, determined to find out more about the Snakes.

Nobody knows anything. I'm greeted with blank stares and shakes of the head wherever I go. There are several snake-themed gangs – the Fangs, the Serpent's Kiss, the Coils – but no simple Snakes.

The only known subterranean gang is the Rats. A small gang, nine or ten members, with a demented apocalypse fixation. They've been down the tunnels for fourteen years in anticipation of a nuclear attack. They live on the waste of the city – roast rat's a speciality of theirs, hence the name – only rarely straying above street level when driven by floods or to forage for clothes and medicine.

I know the Rats – they've aided me on a couple of occasions when I've chased quarry down the tunnels – and they can't be the Snakes Davern was talking about. The Rats have as little interest in the world above as the rest of us have in theirs. But thinking about them gives me an idea. They know the tunnels better than anyone. They might be able to put me on the track of the missing Cardinal or help me search for him.

I go looking for the Rats late Sunday but don't find them. They're nomads, with temporary bases all over the city's underworld, so it can take a while to track them down. I leave messages at the four campsites I visit, asking them to contact me, then return to the streets to quiz the late-night revellers for word of the Snakes.

Back home I shower thoroughly – the stink of the tunnels is vile – then crawl into bed and stare at the ceiling until I fall asleep.

Monday. Fabio's funeral. His grandson pulled strings to bump the dead pimp up the waiting list. They considered having the ceremony yesterday, but delayed it twenty-four hours, so that they could contact all of his relatives and friends, giving everyone the chance to attend.

Fabio was Catholic – something I only found out since he died – and there's a mass said for him in his local church, St Jude's. It's an immense gathering. Thousands of mourners pack the church and streets outside. I've never seen such a crowd for a funeral. (There were hundreds of thousands for Ferdinand Dorak, but I missed that, being laid up in hospital at the time.)

The priest says a Latin mass, the way Fabio requested. I tune out after the first few mystifying minutes. Flo asked me to say some words but I declined. Speaking in public was never my thing.

I sit near the front – Flo nagged me forward – surrounded by three of Fabio's children and their progeny. The kids behave themselves, sitting silently like little angels. I'm impressed, until one of Fabio's sons explains as we're standing outside the church afterwards, waiting for the coffin. Fabio set aside a considerable stash over the decades, with orders to share it among the young — but only the ones who behaved at his funeral. I laugh out loud when I hear that, and don't feel guilty. Most people are laughing and joking, as Fabio would have wanted.

It takes half an hour to get the coffin to the hearse – everyone wants to touch it for good luck, or to express their farewells – and another half hour for the hearse to clear the block. Only a fraction of the crowd has been invited to the crematorium. The chosen few gather on the steps of the church. There are seventy or eighty of us, Fabio's children (no room for grandchildren, bar one or two favourites) and nearest friends.

When the crowd clears enough for us to push through to our vehicles, we make our way to the crematorium. I've brought my motorbike, even though I virtually never use it when in Al Jeery mode. It's a long ride and I'd miss the start of the service if I cycled.

I park out back, flash my invitation to the guard on the door, and join the rest of the mourners in a large chamber, the walls of which are draped with billowing curtains. Flo and Zeba stand inside the door to the chamber, greeting and directing the mourners. I get shunted to the third row from the front on the left, next to the wall. I don't have a great view of the coffin, which suits me fine. I hate funerals.

When everyone's settled, the priest from St Jude's steps up and delivers a final, heartfelt tribute to Fabio. He avoids hypocrisy – says he knows how Fabio made a living, and as a man of God he can't approve – but admits respect for the pimp. 'He was a man of honour who kept his word and did no harm unto others — unless they did it to him first!'

At the end of his speech, he clears his throat and blushes. 'I, uh, normally I'd hang around until the end, but Flo and Zeba have a special send-off in mind and I can't really . . .' His blush deepens. 'I'll wait outside,' he mutters and scurries away to whispers of confused amusement.

Zeba faces us. She's weeping but grinning at the same time.

'We all know Fabio was a womanizing bastard,' she grunts, and is greeted by a round of cheers and claps. 'His final wish was to go with a flourish, and though he never said what he intended, Flo and I have come up with something we think he'd like.'

As Zeba sits, a door at the side of the chamber opens, the lights dim and 'Hey Big Spender' starts to play over the tannoy. As we crack up, six chorus girls enter, faces covered with masks — life-size photos of Fabio. They kick their stockinged legs high, split skirts parting to reveal flashes of thigh, glittering tops tight around their breasts.

The girls gyrate in front of the coffin, race down and back up the aisle, then gather in a line and strip. Many of the men are hooting encouragingly, some of the women too. Practically everyone's smiling and laughing, though a lot of the smiles are flecked with tears. The first girl whips off her top to a raucous cheer. Then the second, the third, all the way down the line, until the six are naked from the waist up, dancing lewdly, masks of Fabio still in place, wiggling their breasts and hips.

In all the unexpected excitement, I almost miss Fabio's exit. As the strippers jiggle down the aisle, his coffin glides backwards on a conveyer belt, through a pair of laced curtains, never to be seen again. I salute him as he goes, wishing him luck wherever he winds up.

'If that doesn't satisfy the horny old goat, nothing will,' one of his daughters in the seat ahead of me mutters to her husband.

'What'd really make his day,' he murmurs, 'would be if they slipped back there and jumped his dead bones.'

As I'm laughing at their comments, the music dies, the lights come back up, the strippers gather their clothes, bow one final time to the mourners and start to leave. Those closest to the aisle are already on their feet, in a hurry to get back to Fabio's house for the wake. Since I'm by the wall, I stay seated and wait for the way to clear. As my eyes wander, I notice one of the strippers standing nearby. It's hard to tell with the Fabio mask, but I get the impression she's staring at *me*.

I stare back at the stripper, smiling awkwardly, trying not to ogle her breasts. Then she removes her mask and I forget her breasts entirely. It's Ama Situwa!

As my jaw drops, she sends the Fabio mask flicking towards me. Instinctively I duck to avoid it. When I look again, she's gone. Not waiting to question my sanity, I bound from my seat, leap over the people in the rows ahead – ignoring their indignant roars – duck through the door and race down a corridor.

It branches at the end. The right fork leads to a room where I can hear loud conversation and laughter – the strippers. I doubt that Ama Situwa will return to her colleagues – I can always trace them through Flo and Zeba later if I have to – so I turn left and pick up speed.

The corridor leads to the rear of the crematorium, no further forks or doors. I burst out into sunlight, drop to my knees in case anyone's waiting with a gun and raze the area with my gaze, desperately wishing I'd packed my .45. I spot Situwa at the far corner of the building to my left, tugging on a T-shirt. She's on a moped. I start towards her, realize I've no hope of catching her on foot – the engine's already running – so turn and dart for my motorbike in the parking lot.

By the time I clear the lot, I'm sure Situwa will have vanished, but to my delight I catch sight of her overtaking a car which has stopped for an amber light. Cutting lanes – almost getting wiped out by a van – I come down with a jarring thud on her side of the road, take a few seconds to straighten, and set off after her, ripping through the gears, eyes locked on the figure in front.

Within a minute I've already closed the gap by half and know she's mine for the taking. Secure in this knowledge and thinking clearly – aided by the fresh air – I ease up on the throttle. I close the gap another seventy or eighty feet over the next few minutes but maintain that distance, giving her the run of the city, to see where she'll lead me.

As we bypass traffic, I ponder the situation and come to the obvious conclusion that this is a set-up. The woman wants me to follow her. She's leading me somewhere specific and I bet friends of hers will be waiting when we arrive. The intelligent thing would be to cut her off, knock her from her moped, interrogate her on territory of my own choosing. But I let her keep her lead, eager to know who she's running to.

She heads for the city centre. I start to think she's leading me to Party Central but then she takes a turn for the docks. That would be a good spot for an ambush – plenty of deserted warehouses – but then she turns again, away from the river. I stop speculating and simply follow.

Several minutes later she pulls up at the base of the Manco Capac statue and leaps from her moped. I draw up beside the abandoned bike, stand my own beside it and pad after her, closing the distance to forty feet by the time she reaches the door at the foot of the statue and races inside.

The Manco Capac statue is the city's largest monument, standing an incredible nine hundred feet high, an immense tribute to the founding father of the Incas. Construction commenced a decade ago but the doors were only opened to the public the year before last. I've never been inside but I've heard a lot about it — it's home to a supposedly world class Inca museum, and the views of the city are allegedly second to none.

I pause at the entrance. There's a sign proclaiming the statue closed for the day, but the door's unlocked and there are no guards. This feels bad but I'm not about to turn tail now. I might be weaponless, but my hands are the hands of a killer, so I'm never truly unarmed. Wiping my palms on my trousers, I take a calming breath, then start up the stairs after Ama Situwa.

After a long climb, I stop at a steel door. I flex my fingers, take hold of the handle, pull the door open and throw myself through, rolling across the floor, anticipating action.

Nobody here.

I stand warily and study my surroundings. I'm in the lowest section of the museum, where a gift shop and an Inca-themed restaurant predominate. No sign of Ama Situwa. I step up to the window of the gift shop and check the display. Useless bric-a-brac, but on the left I spot a thick-headed walking stick, and just behind that a belt of ornamental knives. I kick in the glass – no alarm sounds – and grab the walking stick and knives. The stick's hefty and will serve as a club. The knives are flimsy but better than nothing. I strap on the belt, slide out a knife and hold it by my side, and advance.

The statue is hollow and tiered with crystal floors of different colours. On each floor a dazzling array of cabinets and display stands boast all manner of Incan ornaments and tools, garments and jewellery, maps and information sheets. I ignore all of it and search for Ama Situwa, who's lost me amidst the aisles of memorabilia and artefacts.

I move up floors cautiously. I sense she's waiting for me at the top but I don't rush. The museum's deserted, lit by dim security lamps. My footsteps echo loudly. I don't try to muffle them. Whoever's waiting with Ama Situwa knows I'm coming, so the element of surprise isn't in play.

Finally I leave the last of the display cabinets behind and come to a door marked 'SOLARIUM. Authorized Personnel Only'. I know all about the statue's solarium. A lover of everything Incan told me about it many years ago, when work on the statue was in its infancy. A circular room full of mirrors designed to harness the full blast of the sun and amplify it. Access is restricted and allegedly no bribe will get you past the security guards if you haven't been given the go-ahead by the relevant authorities.

There are no guards on the door today, but I pause before entering. The glare of the mirrors is meant to be blinding and visitors have to wear coloured goggles. The glass of the roof is tinted, cutting down the glare, but it can be retracted at the push of a button. If I go up, unprotected, and somebody pushes that button . . .

I have to risk it. Situwa could be hiding on any of the floors beneath – I gave them only a cursory once-over – but I know in my heart that she's waiting for me in the solarium, along with whoever sent her to me as bait. I could try to wait them out, but this is their game, not mine. I must respect the rules.

Pushing through the revolving door, I find myself on a set of narrow, steep stairs. I swap my walking stick from my left hand to my right as I climb, and the knife vice versa, just to give myself something to think about while ascending.

At the top of the stairs I hit the domed solarium. The walls are embedded with mirrors. The glass roof is tinted a dark grey-blue colour. The floor of the room is mostly covered by a huge, circular stone. A strangely carved block juts from the centre of the stone, maybe five feet high. Standing in front of the block, a long knife held between his hands, is a robed, blind *villac*. At the base of the stone, legs dangling over the side, rests Ama Situwa.

'Welcome, Flesh of Dreams,' she greets me, smiling blankly. I get the feeling she isn't in control of herself. She's being manipulated.

'Who are you?' I ask, striding forward. Before I reach her, she swings her legs up, rolls away from me and comes to her feet. I stop at the edge, remembering a similar stone from many years earlier. The *villacs* called it the *inti watana*. When I tried to mount it, I received a crippling electric shock.

'You have a keen memory, Flesh of Dreams,' the woman with Ama Situwa's features says. 'This platform, like the other, will repulse those who set foot on it uninvited. You may test it if you wish, but I would not advise it.' She doesn't sound like a woman. Her voice is deep and masculine.

'Who are you?' I ask again.

In answer she removes her T-shirt, slides out of her skirt and slips off her shoes and stockings.

'Who are you?' I ask for the third time.

'Ama Situwa,' she answers.

'Ama Situwa's dead.'

'Yes.' She smiles a corpse's grin. 'And today she dies again.'

The naked woman walks to the priest at the centre of the platform. He steps to one side and she jumps and hauls herself onto the stone block. Drapes herself across it, facing me, body arced, pubis high. The *villac* walks around the block, muttering words in a language I don't understand.

The priest comes to a halt at the front of the block and sets the blade of his knife to the flesh of the woman's throat. She doesn't look alarmed, merely stares calmly at the ceiling, breathing steadily.

'Stop,' I say softly. 'You don't have to do this. Let's talk.'

The *villac* ignores me, presses down, then drags the blade from right to left, severing the woman's vocal cords. Ama Situwa's body jerks but she doesn't beat him off. She holds her head as still as she can while he makes a second cut, then a third, slicing deeper each time, right the way through the neck, until her head flops over the edge of the block, connected to her body by only a thin flap of flesh.

I watch the sacrifice neutrally. I've killed too many people to feel sickened or appalled. If the priest meant to shock me, he failed.

Ama Situwa's blood runs down the sides of the block, soaking into the stone of the platform. The *villac* steps away, knife hanging by his side. Dropping the knife, he raises his arms above his head and chants. I consider launching one of my own knives at him – I could hit him from here, though I don't think the cheap blade would do much damage – but choose to wait. I want to see what he does next.

While I'm studying the priest, I spot movement at the centre of the platform. My gaze flicks to the block, back to the priest, then returns to the block, my eyes widening. I thought the movement was Ama Situwa's body shifting, or another priest entering the solarium, but it's nothing so simple. A tiny cloud of green fog has formed around the dead woman's body and rises to the ceiling, dispersing as it does. As I watch, mystified, I realize that the body on the platform is growing translucent, fading away. She's disappearing, flesh and bones transforming into tendrils of a vapid green fog which drifts upwards and separates, becoming invisible dust motes, until both woman and fog are no more.

'What is this shit?' I gasp.

The *villac* smiles. The sacrifice didn't impress me but this did. The priest can't hide a gloating snicker.

'It's an illusion,' I moan. 'This room's full of mirrors. You simply . . .' I trail off, knowing it has to be trickery, yet sensing in my heart that it isn't. The priests wouldn't waste their time on cheap conjuring feats.

As my brain reels, the *villac* turns, walks to the far end of the platform and jumps down. I click back into action and race around the huge stone, determined to catch the priest and force answers out of him. The priest faces me with his white, expressionless eyes. I drop my makeshift club and prepare to go to work with the knives. Before I can, a mirror drops from the ceiling and slots into place in a groove in the floor, blocking my path.

I curse at my reflection and smash my right elbow into the mirror, meaning to force my way through. But the glass is shatterproof. I grit my teeth against the impact of the blow and clutch my arm to my chest, squeezing the flesh above the elbow to combat the pain. I flex my arm a few times, then retrace my steps, coming at the priest from the opposite direction. It's a waste of time – another mirror will drop, I'm sure – but I have to try.

I notice several mirrors around the edges of the room lifting to reveal hidden compartments. In each rests a mummified corpse, strapped to a chair. I ignore them and focus on the *villac*. His arms are outstretched and he's muttering. I glimpse another mirror descending. I throw myself forward, hoping to beat it to the punch, but it slots into place and I bounce backwards.

Hissing with fury, I rest on the floor a moment, considering my next move. As I lie there like a wounded dog, another mirror drops into place behind me, trapping me. I don't react immediately, but get my breath back, then stand and appraise the situation. I'm surrounded on three sides by mirrors, on the other by the charged *inti watana*. There doesn't seem to be a way out, though I'm sure one will present itself. The *villacs* didn't lure me here simply to strand me.

As if somebody's reading my thoughts, the mirror in the wall slides up, revealing one of the hidden compartments. I start towards it, then stop, confused. There's no corpse in this one, just another mirror which casts my bald, tattooed reflection back at me. That doesn't make sense. There must be a way out. Perhaps a panel in the floor or . . .

I stoop to check the floor, then freeze. My reflection hasn't moved. It stands the same as before, grinning. But I haven't grinned since I saw Ama Situwa in the crematorium.

Straightening, I study the figure, noting the bald head, green eyes and tattooed snakes on its cheeks. A highly accurate representation of me in my Paucar Wami guise. The thing is, I'm currently masquerading as Al Jeery, snakes painted over, wig in place, contact lenses removed. This isn't a reflection. It's a life-size replica. But why put it here? What do they hope to –

The right arm of the *replica* shoots up. Its fingers grip my throat and tighten. Its face comes alive. Its green eyes fix on mine and its lips lift in a mocking sneer.

I punch at the hand and kick at the legs of my assailant, but he takes no notice. Instead, leaning forward, he smirks in a way I remember only too well and says in a voice I've heard many times in my nightmares, 'Long time no see, Al m'boy.'

A blast of inhuman fear numbs me and I stop struggling. This isn't a replica — it's the real Paucar Wami!

As my senses dissolve, Wami's fingers flex and the supply of blood is cut off. I slip to the floor. Dark waves wash over me, obscuring all. The last thing I see is the evil grin of my long-dead father. Then nothing, except for shadowy, slithering, nightmarish snakes.

part three

unholy reunions

ONE – THE SNAKES

I've been lying awake, eyes open, for several minutes before I realize it. The darkness is so absolute that I mistook it for the darkness of my dreams. Groaning, I sit up and massage the swollen flesh around my throat. I've throttled men unconscious before, but this is my first time on the receiving end.

Swallowing stings, but I force myself to dry-swallow mechanically, and after a while the pain recedes and I'm able to breathe naturally, with only a minimum of discomfort. What I wouldn't give for a glass of water.

Getting to my feet, I turn in a slow circle, arms outstretched, probing with my fingers — nothing. Bending, I pat the floor, getting a feel for where I am. Hard earth, damp, musky. I fan out with my hands but the area's clear. I check for my belt of knives but they've been taken from me. The walking stick too.

Sitting again, I allow my thoughts to wander back to my encounter with the past in the Manco Capac statue, and try convincing myself that what I saw wasn't – couldn't be – real. Paucar Wami's lost to the mists of time and reality. It must have been a lookalike. There's no other logical answer.

But what about the Ama Situwa double? And the others Capac Raimi said he saw in the weeks leading up to his disappearance? Finding one person who looks similar to another is difficult. Finding a host of them, for a group of people . . . I don't even begin calculating the odds. Something's going on, something I can't account for, and the best way to deal with it is to let it slide. First things first. I have to find my way out of here, wherever *here* is.

Rising, I sniff the air for any scent of a draught. 'Hello?' I croak, grimacing at the flare-up in my throat. 'Hello!' I shout, voice almost breaking — it feels as if I'm vomiting glass. Ignoring the pain, I listen for echoes. They come, faintly, from my left. Facing that way, I shout again, a wordless grunt this time, and the echoes are clearer. I hear nothing when I roar in the other directions, so I head left, hands stretched out in front. I count my steps silently, in case I need to retrace them. Five . . . eight . . . fourteen . . .

On my thirty-fourth step my hand strikes a brick wall, wet with condensation. I examine it with my fingers, then test the ground for puddles. I find several and – having dipped a finger in and tested the water, which tastes bitter but other-wise OK – I lean down and sip from one of the larger pools, quenching my thirst.

Refreshed, I stand, wipe my lips, choose a direction at random, lay my palm against the wall and walk, brushing the brick lightly with my fingertips, feeling for gaps or cracks. I think of nothing but the wall, pushing all other thoughts from my mind, as hard as that is.

I've no idea how long I was out or what the time is — my watch has been taken from my wrist and my cell's gone too. Instead of worrying about it, or where I've been taken, I count my paces, making my world exist of nothing but the wall, the darkness and footsteps.

Forty-seven steps into my count, I run into another wall and come to the end of my path. I make a ninety degree turn and continue walking and counting.

One hundred and seventeen steps later, my hand slides into space. I turn and take two steps forward. I stick my right hand out — wall. Stretching forth my left, I shuffle that way . . . a bit more . . . wall. I'm in a passage.

Standing in the middle, I can touch both walls. Keeping to the centre, I start walking, feeling for openings on either side. After six hundred and fifty-nine steps the walls give way to emptiness. Exploring, I discover a four-way junction. I focus on each tunnel in turn, listening closely, peering through the darkness for the slightest flicker of light. There isn't any. No sounds either apart from the dripping of water. Then, as I'm examining the passages a second time, an extremely faint noise – perhaps a human cry, maybe only a rat squeaking – carries to my ears from one of the tunnels.

My choice made for me, I start ahead cautiously. This passage is the same width as the last. I'm progressing as before, hands outstretched, when the ground ends and I drop. Stifling a yell, I grab for the bricks of the walls. Then my feet hit and I relax. It was a short fall. Drawing in my hands, I stoop and feel the ground — concrete. I run my fingers forward into air, then down to more concrete. I'm on a step, the first, I suspect, of a set of stairs. Standing, I slide onto the next step, feel for the edge with my toes, find it and carry on down, deeper under the earth, in search of the origin of that elusive sound.

Fifty steps . . . a hundred . . . one-fifty . . . I'm only four shy of the two hundred mark when they finally run out and I hit level ground. I'm in a tunnel with an arched roof. I can tell because it's lit by the most welcome torch I've ever seen, burning faintly ahead of me. The desire to rush to the light is strong, but I fight it and study the terrain. The tunnel runs in both directions, seemingly without end, but this is the only torch. Turning right, I walk to the torch. It's set in stone, the head a replaceable wick, which runs down into an encased container. No way to remove it. I'll have to continue without it and hope there are other torches ahead to light my way.

Concentrating solely on finding a way out, ignoring thoughts of my father, Ama Situwa and the *villacs*, I proceed, hand no longer on the wall, navigating by the glow of the torch, which gets fainter the further I progress. I'm almost surrounded by total gloom again when I hear sounds from somewhere ahead. This time the noise is definitely human — men arguing loudly. Hurrying, I come to the mouth of another tunnel. There are no torches in this one, but fresh air wafts through it, and the sounds of the men are stronger than ever.

The tunnel's long – I quit counting steps now that I'm no longer scouting blind – and the voices dwindle as I close in on them. By the time I reach the end, the argument has come to a halt, but there are grunting, scuffling sounds. I pause, listening intently. I thought there were only two men, but by the varying noises, I revise that figure upwards. Then, since there's nothing else to do, I step forward to face whatever awaits.

I find myself in a large, man-made cavern, ninety feet wide, maybe a hundred and fifty long, with a high ceiling. The walls are bare, save for candles. The floor's covered by a thick, green, padded mat.

There are fifteen men and three women inside the chamber. All are young – the youngest looks thirteen or fourteen, the oldest no more than twenty-five – and most are black. Their heads are shaved and down the cheeks of each runs a tattooed snake similar to mine, but monochromatic, plain blue, red, green, etc. All eighteen are clad in jeans and dark T-shirts. They're barefoot.

I believe I've found the Snakes.

The young men and women are sparring in pairs or threes.

They punch, kick and twist with remarkable agility. Their
fists and feet are unprotected and leave cuts and bruises
where they connect too sharply, but nobody takes any notice
of the wounds, getting up when knocked down, fighting on,
pausing only to wipe blood away when it gets bothersome.
They say nothing as they spar, although every so often one
of the older members chastises a younger participant for
making a mistake. The girls and boys contest equally, taking
and meting out their fair share of the punishment, no
allowances made.

I watch in silence, unseen, for several minutes. Finally I'm
spotted by a young woman who steps aside to remove her
ripped T-shirt. She pulls it off over her head, baring her
breasts – none of the men bats an eyelid – then turns back
towards her partner to continue — and sights me. She stops,
hands dropping by her sides, and stares at me expressionlessly. Her partner turns to see what she's looking at and
soon everyone is facing me, silent, impossible to read.

Stepping forward, I come to a halt five feet short of the
nearest member of the group, a tall, lithe, dark-skinned man
in his early twenties. I croak, 'Where am I?'

The man says nothing, just raises a hand and strokes the
red snakes on his face, eyeing me suspiciously.

'Do you have a name?' I'm finding it hard to speak.

In response the man walks around me, sizing me up, noting
the marks on my throat. He's rippling with muscles but there's
an air of uncertainty about him – he's trying too hard to act
cool – and I sense from the way he moves that he's untested
in real combat.

The man stops behind me. I feel his breath on the back of
my neck but I don't turn to face him. The woman with the
bare breasts steps forward, her left hand going to my groin,
hard brown eyes staring directly into mine, watching closely
to see if her nudity or the contact unsettles me. They don't

and I stare back calmly, unaroused, waiting for her to quit
with the games.

'How did you get here?' she asks, removing her hand.

'I walked.'

'Who are you?'

'I asked for your name first.'

The girl raises her right hand and makes a signal with her
thumb and middle finger. In reply, eight of the group fan
out behind her, four to her left, four to her right. They
surround me, dangerous intent in their expressions.

'Your name,' the woman says.

I consider lying, but see no reason not to tell them. 'Al
Jeery.'

The woman relaxes, as do those around her. 'You're
expected,' she says and turns her back on me, looking for
her sparring partner. They resume their contest. Within
moments the other sixteen have also returned to their original positions and training continues as before.

I stare at the men and women, mildly astonished. 'Who's
expecting me?' I ask. No answer. I grab one of the younger
men and whirl him around. 'Who the hell –'

He flicks his left hand towards my face, fingers stiff. I have
to move swiftly to avoid being blinded. Slapping his hand
away, I snap out of range. As I steel myself for a counter-
attack, he recommences sparring. I feel like drawing him out
and laying him flat, but that would be pointless. There are
no answers here. Best move on and seek them further ahead.

Circling the trainees, I come to a door in the opposite wall
of the chamber. The handle turns smoothly. Sparing the
sparrers one last, bewildered glance, I step through into a
brightly lit corridor, let the door swing shut and press on.

There are several doors in the walls of the corridor. I open
each as I come to it. Store rooms, more corridors, all dark

and empty. No signs of life. At the end I come to a set of swing doors. Pushing through, I enter a kitchen where a handful of men and one woman – dressed, shaven and tattooed the same as those in the sparring hall – work in silence over old-style stoves, baking bread. One of the men spots me and scowls. 'You can't come in here!'

I ignore him and wander forward, noting microwave ovens in the background, a curious mix of new and old utensils, three huge freezers running along one wall, two refriger-ators along another. The man with the scowl moves to block me. 'You can't come in here,' he repeats, softly this time, anticipating a fight.

I take stock of the chef and realize he's as dangerous as those in the cavern, if not more so. I have to be careful. 'My name's Al Jeery,' I mutter.

The chef relaxes. 'We've been expecting you.'

'You know who I am?'

'You're Al Jeery,' he laughs.

'Is that all you know — my name?'

He nods. 'We were told you'd be joining us.'

'Who told you?'

He pulls a face, as if he thinks I know the answer and am testing him. 'Probably the same person who brought you here.'

'And that's . . .?'

'You know,' he chuckles and returns to his dough, which he kneads clumsily. I think he's more of a warrior than a chef.

I watch the men and woman work for a while, then ask the chef for his name.

'Ray,' he says.

'Ray what?'

'We only use first names here.'

I change tack. 'How many are you cooking for?'

'The eighteen of phalanx 5C.'

That could be the group I encountered earlier. 'How many phalanxes are there?'

'I don't know.'

'Which do you belong to?'

'4A.'

'How many in your group?'

'Eighteen, the same as the others.'

'How many of you are there in total?'

He smiles. 'You already asked me a question like that. I still don't know.'

'Who does?'

He shrugs. 'The Cobras.'

'Cobras?'

'The captains of the triumvirates. There are three phalanxes per triumvirate.'

He's mixing Greek and Roman terminology, but I let that pass, doing the maths. Eighteen multiplied by three is fifty-four. If there are at least five triumvirates, that makes two hundred and seventy — not counting *Cobras*.

'Where did you come from?' I ask Ray. 'How did you get here?'

He shakes his head. 'We don't ask questions like that.'

'Who controls the Cobras?'

A flicker of irritation crosses his face. 'I don't have time for this.'

'Who should I report to?'

'I don't know.'

'Who were you told to send me to?'

'Nobody. We were just told you were coming and not to interfere with you.'

'Where can I find the Cobras?'

'They have their own quarters. I don't know where. They come to us, not the other way round.'

'Is there some kind of central meeting place?'

Ray walks me to the swing doors and points out a door on the left. 'Take the corridor through there. When you get to the third door on the right, turn off. That leads to the main hall, though I doubt you'll find anyone there now.'

'What time is it?' I ask.

'Ten to four. Everyone will be in training or on assignment until six.'

The last time I checked my watch was in the Manco Capac statue and it was a few minutes shy of midday. Less time has passed than I thought. I thank Ray for his assistance. He grunts and returns to the kitchen. I start for the door, then stop, follow Ray and ask for a glass of water. I slide a knife from a counter without anyone seeing, then go looking for the main hall.

Ray's directions were true. Within minutes I'm standing inside the entrance to an enormous cavern which I recognize. I was here ten years ago, summoned by the *villacs*. It's much the same as I remember, walls adorned with symbols, many blood-red depictions of the sun, a huge, gold, sun medallion hanging from the ceiling over a round stone platform, like the one in the Manco Capac solarium, only larger, maybe a hundred and twenty feet in diameter. Three thrones sit at the centre of the platform. Around the circumference, mummies are lashed to chairs, though there are gaps. The priests must have moved some of their dead ancestors up to the compartments in the solarium.

I approach the platform warily, scanning the shadows of the candle-lit cavern for *villacs* and Snakes. I appear to be alone. Skirting the platform, keeping my knife low, I edge further into the cavern, feeling isolated and exposed.

'You found your way here quicker than I expected,' someone says from the darkness above. I raise my knife and

peer uselessly into the layers of blackness which mask the
ceiling. 'Put away the knife,' the speaker says and a rope drops.
'You won't need it.'

A man shimmies down the rope and lands cat-like. He
turns and smiles. He's older than the others I've encountered, in his thirties. He's bald, and sports light blue snakes
on his cheeks, but he wears a leather jacket over his T-shirt.

'Are you a Cobra?' I ask, not lowering the knife.

He raises a thin eyebrow. 'You learn quickly. Yes. I
command the second triumvirate. You know about those?'

'I've gathered the basics. How many triumvirates are
there?'

'Seven. We're in the midst of forming an eighth.'

That bumps the numbers up to almost four hundred. No
wonder Davern's worried about the Snakes.

'Who commands and finances you?'

The Cobra smiles. 'Ask no questions, told no lies. Come,
Mr Jeery, the master awaits.' He offers the rope to me.

'I'm not climbing up there until I know what's going on,'
I tell him.

He shrugs. 'Then you'll stay here and rot.'

'Who are you taking me to?'

'You'll see when you get there.'

'Is it . . .?' I can't bring myself to say the name.

The Cobra's smile fades and he jerks the rope. Since I've
no real choice, I take it and start up, followed by the Cobra,
to a balcony. Once there, I turn, stop the Cobra from
mounting, and press my blade to his throat.

'I want answers and I want them now,' I snarl, but he
laughs at the threat.

'Kill me if you must, Mr Jeery, but you won't scare answers
out of me. Nobody fears death down here. We're taught to
accept it.'

I'm tempted to slice his throat for the hell of it, but that wouldn't bring me the truth. Standing back, I let him climb and fall into place behind him as he marches to the end of the platform, into another tunnel.

'How many tunnels are there?' I ask after we've wound our way through several more passages.

'That's a question I couldn't answer even if I had a mind to,' the Cobra says. 'I've been down here six years and I'm still discovering new routes.'

'Six years is a long time to spend underground,' I note.

'Yes,' he agrees, just a touch of bitterness to his tone.

'Did the *villacs* build these tunnels?'

He considers the question, then nods.

'Do they still control them?'

Clicking his tongue, he shakes a finger at me. We advance down one dark tunnel after another, twisting and turning. Finally we come to a door and the Cobra stops. 'We've arrived. I'll leave you. Proceed as you wish.'

'Wait,' I stop him. 'What's your name?'

'Cobras don't have names. Not as far as you're concerned anyway.'

He leaves.

I stand in the gloom a few moments, then push open the door. I enter a short corridor, both sides lined with human skulls, a few with scraps of flesh still clinging to the bone. The tops have been sliced off all of them and candles set within. I'm not given to superstitious fears, but my spine tingles as I walk the short stretch to the door at the opposite end of the corridor.

Driving the fear from my mind, I focus on the door and open it. Stepping inside, I study my surroundings. I'm in a fair-sized room, a single bed in one corner, knives, chains and other weapons in another. The third corner's bare. In the fourth rests a desk decorated with human bones — dozens of them are pinned to the legs and around the rim. At the desk sits a man with his back to me. He's breathing lightly, busy with something. Stepping closer, I peer over his shoulder and see that he's prising the eyes from the sockets of a dead child's head.

'Have you ever killed a child?' he asks conversationally.

'No,' I sigh.

'They afford great sport.'

There's no answer to a statement like that. Looking away, I wait for him to speak again, which he does presently. 'You know who I am?'

'I know who you claim to be.'

I sense his smile. 'Surely you do not doubt your own eyes and ears?'

'I know how easy it is to mimic a man. I've been doing it for ten years.'

'The appearance, yes, but not the voice,' he retorts. 'I have eavesdropped on you many times. You never mastered my dulcet tones.' He swings round and faces me. This close, there's no mistaking him. The face, the eyes, the snakes can all be copied, but that expression of sheer, gleeful, inhuman evil is unique. I've never come close to matching it and I don't believe anybody else could either.

'Salutations, Al m'boy,' Paucar Wami says, then spreads his arms and grins his most charmingly twisted smile. 'Don't you have a hug for your dear ole pappy?'

TWO – PAPPY

'You're dead.' The words sound ridiculous said to him in the flesh. I'm sitting on the edge of the bed, across from my father, a man ten years deceased. He hasn't moved from his seat at the desk.

'No,' he says thoughtfully, fingers toying with the child's head as he speaks. 'I have been, and shall die again soon I'm sure, but for the time being I live.' He chuckles. 'You could say this is one of my better days.'

'Where have you been?' I ask.

'Most of the time . . . deceased. The rest down here, training my boys and girls to be good little killers.'

'You recruited the Snakes?'

'A few, but most were brought to me by the priests. I am the figurehead leader, the assassin who returns from beyond the grave. The priests slaughter me in front of the Snakes every so often, then resurrect me. It impresses my followers no end. I also make impassioned speeches and participate in training. And occasionally I accompany a phalanx on a raid to the upper world, where I glory in death's wondrous embrace once again.'

'You killed Tasso and Davern's men?'

'Some of them. The Snakes took care of the rest.'

So Davern was right. Paucar Wami *did* kill his men. It was just a different Paucar Wami to the one he assumed.

'I don't understand this. You were an Ayuamarcan. You should have died with The Cardinal. Hell, you did! How have you come back?'

'I have not *come*,' he answers, eyes dark. 'I have been *brought*.' He tosses the child's head away, stands and stretches. He's exactly as I remember. Hasn't aged a day. He should be an old man, but time doesn't weigh heavy on him. He looks younger than I do.

'Much up here –' he taps the side of his head '– is darkness. My memories are elusive. I know you are my son, my firstborn, but I cannot recall your mother or watching you grow. I have flashes of us ten years ago, working as a team, but I do not remember how our paths crossed or the common goal we pursued.'

'You don't remember Bill Casey?' I ask quietly.

He frowns. 'In dreams, sometimes, I think that name, but I do not know why. Who is he?'

'A police officer.'

'An adversary of mine? A man I killed or who tried to kill me?'

I shake my head wordlessly. I want to think he's playing with me, but I see in his eyes that he's not. He really doesn't know.

'We'll return to Bill,' I mutter, praying for calm. This is a surreal encounter and it would be easy to run mad in the face of it. I have to remain lucid and take it on its own terms. 'Tell me about yourself . . . the last ten years . . . what happened.'

'That is a long story.'

'We have time.'

'Yes. More than you could imagine. At least *I* have.' He strokes his snakes the way I've so often stroked mine since having the tattoos. 'Ten years ago I died. My last minutes are clear in my mind. You were with me at Party Central. I wanted to stop The Cardinal killing himself, because I knew that my life was bound with his. He created me. When he died, I would perish with him.

'I tried to stop him jumping but I was powerless. He leapt. A green mist enveloped me. I had a sense of the world fading, then nothing. I was dead.'

His eyes cloud over with anger and confusion.

'Did you kidnap Raimi?' I ask, getting ahead of myself but keen to know.

The killer shakes his head. 'The priests were clear on that point — I was never to harm the new Cardinal. The punishment if I disobeyed was death.'

'I thought you could bounce back from death.'

'As I said, I can be brought back, but only by the *villacs*. If they choose not to resurrect me, I face real, final death. While I do not fear my end – I have always regarded death as a lover, not an enemy – I am in no rush to embrace it.'

'Tell me more about the resurrection process. How do they bring you back? Is it painful? How much do you remember of the past?'

His eyes are cold. 'It is seven or eight years since I was first revived. I have no memories of the months before that — death is nothingness. I woke in darkness. At the time I remembered no previous life. I screamed like a newborn, instinctively aware that I should not be. A light entered my world. I saw men in white robes, with white eyes. They probed my face with their fingers. I was tied down but I struggled with my bonds and broke free. I killed three of them. As I pursued the fourth, green mist obscured my vision and I returned to nothingness.

'Some months later they brought me back again. This time I had memories. I was also more expertly chained. Through an interpreter, a priest said they would release me, but if I disobeyed their orders, they would undo my form as they had before.

'I gave my word that I would behave. The priest and some of his companions took me on a tour of these tunnels. He said they were recruiting an army, warriors who would model themselves after my legendary example. The *villacs* wanted me to work with them and act as a totemic leader. He promised untold riches and opportunities if I cooperated.

'Being a level-headed man, I heard him out. When he was done, I strangled him and a few of the others, took one hostage and went in search of a route to the surface. Within minutes the green haze enveloped me again. I could only scream as my body unravelled and emptiness reclaimed me.'

Wami goes quiet. His left hand is clenched tight. The knuckles are almost white with tension. 'Existence is a prison as conceived by the priests,' he snarls. 'I live by their terms, obedient to their whims. Can you imagine how demeaning that is?'

'My heart bleeds for you,' I sneer, thinking of all the innocents he killed, finding it impossible to pity him.

He glares at me, lips lifting over his teeth. 'I suppose you think this is a fitting end for your dear ole pappy.'

'Actually, yes.'

He grins menacingly. 'But you rejoice too soon — it is not the end, only a beginning. The third time I returned, I knew I could not fight the priests. I did as they bid and spoke to their recruits, promising them the city. I let them kill me in front of the young men and women, to kindle a superstitious awe within them.

'I was not kept alive all the time. Months would pass when they had no need of me. During such times I was left to rot in limbo. I feared such periods, afraid they would not bring me back, but there was no point arguing, so I accepted my lot and waited for better times. Those times are almost here.'

He crosses the room and crouches beside me. Squeezes my knee, green eyes fierce in the dim light. 'They have promised me freedom. A few more months and I can roam the world as I used to. I must return to mortality – there will be no further resurrections – but I will be free to live and kill in the time I have left.'

'You trust the *villacs*?'

'Of course not,' he snaps, 'but in this instance they will honour their word. They have sworn on their blood and that is sacred to them. If all goes well and you do as they say, I will be –'

'Wait a minute,' I stop him. 'What do *I* have to do with this? I've no interest in seeing you back on the streets. Fuck family ties. I'd rather see you dead than free to take more lives.'

'Al, m'boy,' he moans theatrically, 'why do you say such horrible things to me? Don't you know I love you? You're breaking my heart.'

'Bullshit,' I sniff. 'Now tell me what I'm supposed to do and how I can help earn your freedom.'

Wami's eyes narrow. 'I do not recollect you being this disrespectful.'

'Ten years ago I needed you but I never felt anything for you other than revulsion. You knew that then – it amused you – and I'm sure you know it now. So quit with the indignant act and give it to me straight.'

'Very well,' Wami sniffs. 'The *villacs* want you to . . .'

The door to the room opens and a blind priest enters, clasping a curved dagger to his chest. Hatred springs to the surface within me and I dive for him, meaning to take the knife and slit his gut. My father holds me back with a powerful hand and shakes his head.

'Sit, Al m'boy, or I shall take my belt to you.'

'You might have to bow and scrape to these bastards,' I spit in reply, 'but I don't. Let me go or I'll –'

'I throttled you once today,' he says sternly. 'I will do so again if I must.'

The calm menace in his voice brings me to a halt. I've not feared anyone these last ten years. But faced with the man I've spent so long mimicking, I'm reminded how much wilder and sharper he is. I did a great impression of him, but this is the real thing. He's fiercer than I could ever hope to be. Crossing him would be foolish. Dropping back onto the bed, I glare at my father as he faces the priest, but make no move to interfere.

'Welcome, O wise and blind-as-fuck Great One,' Wami greets his visitor. His mocking words are tinged with tension. Death must be truly terrible if the threat of it can cause Paucar Wami to tremble. The *villac* says nothing, but holds out the knife. The killer takes it obediently. 'Who would you have me kill, O fashion-retarded lord?' The priest smiles thinly at Wami's jest, then points to the killer's chest. Wami's lips tighten. 'No.'

The *villac* barks something in his foreign tongue and points at Wami's chest again. The assassin grimaces and looks at me. 'See the shit I have to put up with?' he sighs, then presses the tip of the dagger to a point below his heart and drives it home to the hilt, its curved blade slicing upwards as it enters. He gasps with pain, drops to the floor, convulses . . . and dies.

As my father's chest subsides and the light fades from his eyes, the *villac* steps forward and toes the corpse's head to one side, so his eyes are facing away. 'That man can be an awful irritation,' he says in perfect English, 'but he knows how to kill himself with style.'

The priest's simple words astonish me more than my father's suicide. 'You can talk!' I gasp stupidly.

'We could always talk,' he replies. 'We just never bothered to learn your language – your words are bitter to our tongues. But times change and we have re-thought many of our ways since the passing of the last *Watana*. Most still cling to the language of our fathers, but some have learnt to speak as you do.'

As I stare at the *villac*, lost for words, my father's corpse shimmies and turns to green fog, as Ama Situwa's did in the Manco Capac statue. Within moments it's a cloud of glittering particles, which slowly disperses in the air.

'Paucar Wami returns to nothingness,' the priest laughs cruelly. 'He dreads the emptiness of the beyond, but this time his stay will be short. We will bring him back soon.'

'How?' I ask.

The *villac* taps his nose. 'That would be telling. Come.' He pushes the door open. 'There are people you must meet.'

I start to follow him, then stare at the spot where Wami disappeared and stop. 'Why did you make him kill himself?'

'You miss him?' the priest enquires slyly.

'I just want to know.'

The *villac* shrugs. 'Partly to prove that we have the power of life over death. You know that by now, but knowing and believing are different things. We need to be certain you have no doubts. But also it was practical. Wami thinks we can only speak Incan. If he knew better, he might torture one of us for information.'

'You're afraid he can hurt you?'

'No, but he can inconvenience us.' The *villac* taps a foot, sightless eyes as steady as ever. 'Come. Time is passing. Your children await.'

I don't know what he means, but there's nothing to be gained by defying him. Suppressing my questions, I follow the blind priest into the corridor of skulls, closing the door on one section of the bewildering puzzle and subjecting myself to the myriad mysteries of another.

THREE – A DESTINY

The *villac* leads me through a series of long, twisting tunnels, back towards the giant cavern with the monstrous *inti watana* stone. Many of the tunnels are lit – for the benefit of the Snakes, I presume – and I seize the opportunity to study the *villac's* featureless face, extremely pale skin, light brown hair and delicate hands.

'What's your name?' I ask.

'I have none,' he answers. 'I am a servant of Inti, and he requires no names. He recognizes his sons by the burning fires of their souls.'

'Inti? Oh yeah, the god of the sun.'

He stops and his empty eyes narrow slightly. 'You do not believe?'

'No. In this day and age I'm surprised to find anyone who does.'

The priest smiles. 'If our powers are not god-given, how else do you explain us bringing the dead back to life?'

He starts walking again. I follow silently, unable to think of a reply.

As we draw closer to the cavern, I hear many people muttering, whispering and shuffling. I slow down. 'Come,' the priest encourages me. 'There is nothing to be afraid of. We will not harm you.'

'That's not what worries me.' I nod in the direction of the voices – I keep forgetting he can't see – and say, 'That sounds like the Snakes.'

'Of course.'

'I thought we might be going to meet Capac Raimi,' I test him.

To my surprise he answers directly. 'Not yet. You aren't ready to take your place by his side. When you are, we will introduce you.'

'You have him?'

'Yes. Now come. Your children are restless. We must not keep them waiting.'

Letting the Raimi confirmation slide, I follow the priest to an opening in the side of the huge cavern, where I stand, hidden in shadows, observing the scene below. The cavern's crowded, yet nowhere near full, with the hundreds of young men and women of the Snakes. All seven triumvirates must be here. The men outnumber the women by roughly fifteen to one and there are even more blacks to whites. All are bald and tattooed, clad in T-shirts and jeans, except for the Cobras who also sport leather jackets.

The Snakes are lined up in ranks behind the giant *inti watana* stone, on which stands a lone *villac*, head bowed, three buckets at his feet. The troops are standing to attention, but slackly. Many talk softly and shuffle on the spot. The Cobras patrol the ranks, admonishing those who get out of order but allowing the softer murmurs and shuffling to continue.

I step back from the ledge, troubled. 'What are they waiting for?'

'Their leader,' the priest replies. 'They worship him, but he appears rarely, preferring to work through us. They've been told he is to address them today.'

'They're waiting for Wami?'

'Yes.'

'You can resurrect him this swiftly?'

'No. Mama Ocllo works fast, but not that fast.'

'Who the hell's Mama . . .?' I stop, eyes widening. 'You want *me* to face them.'

The priest smiles. 'You're sharp, Flesh of Dreams. Yes, we wish you to play your father here, as you have above.'

'No,' I snap. 'I won't.'

I don't know why I react so violently. I'm always inclined to say no to any proposal of the *villacs*, but it's not just that. I sense a trap.

'They will be disappointed if their leader does not show,' the priest demurs.

'Like I give a fuck.'

'You should. The Snakes are only important to us because of *you*. If you show no interest in them, we will dispense with their service. That would necessitate elimination. We'd introduce some fatal, fast-working poison to their food.'

'You'd slaughter your own soldiers?' I snort.

'But they're not ours. They're Paucar Wami's.'

'You'd do it too,' I growl disgustedly. 'Murder them at their dinner table and leave them to rot.'

'We do what we must,' the *villac* says pompously.

I shrug. 'So kill them. What do I have to lose?'

'Some friends,' the priest purrs, 'and many brothers and sisters.'

'Brothers and sisters my ass. Just because most are the same colour as me, it doesn't . . .' I grimace. 'You're not talking figuratively, are you?'

'Forty are of your blood. We reaped the harvest of Paucar Wami's bastards, drawing all that we could. They don't know he sired them. We recruited them the same as the others and treat them no differently.'

I stumble back to the opening and gaze upon the massed ranks. With their shaven heads, tattoos and uniforms, they could all be his children, even the paler members — Wami chose white women as well as black.

'What makes you think I care about half-siblings I've never met?' I ask gruffly.

'Ties of blood are usually impossible to ignore.'

'You won't kill them,' I challenge him. 'If I don't play along with your plans, you'll have to turn to another of Wami's children. You won't kill those you need.'

'But we don't need them,' he retorts. 'We have already chosen our alternatives in case you fail us. Those few will be spared. All others are expendable.'

I breathe in deeply, silently cursing the *villacs* and their knack for getting under my skin. First they use Raimi and Bill to draw me in. Now they introduce me to forty of my closest relatives and tell me they'll be executed like vermin if I don't toe the line. I hate these white-eyed dogs, but I can't help but admire their cunning.

'What do you want?' I sigh, as if they've called my bluff. In fact they haven't. As loath as I am to let these kids die, I will sacrifice them if the priests demand too much of me. But I don't want *them* to know that. Not yet.

'We want you to take your place on the *inti watana* when it is raised above the folds of the earth, and help us rule this city. But that's a position you must come to voluntarily. For now we wish you merely to parade before the Snakes as their master.'

'I just have to pretend to be Wami, then I can go?'

'Yes.'

'If I do this, will you tell me where Capac Raimi is?'

'No.'

I don't like it – I feel the walls of a trap closing in – but I decide to play along, to learn more about the Snakes and where they fit in with the priests' plans.

Without making a performance of it, I slip off my wig and wipe the paint from my face with a handkerchief. Normally I use moisturizing lotions to remove it, but here I settle for spit. As I'm rubbing hard with the handkerchief, a second *villac* appears and hands me a T-shirt, leather jacket and jeans. I strip and put them on, then the first priest reaches into a pocket and produces a pair of green contacts.

'You think of everything, don't you?' I snipe.

'We try,' he replies.

I sourly slip them in and the transformation is complete. Show time!

A third *villac* is waiting for me in the cavern, with a microphone. 'I won't need that,' I wave him away.

'It is not so much to clarify as to disguise,' the English-speaking priest from the tunnels says. 'Your father always addresses them this way. It muffles his words, as it will yours. Without that distortion, sharp ears might note the differences in your voices. This way we hope to –'

'– cover your asses,' I finish for him.

He smiles stiffly. The priest with the mike attaches it to the neck of my T-shirt, the control box to my waistband, then reaches for my left ear.

'What's he up to?' I scowl, slapping his hands away.

'A receiver, for instructions. We will tell you what to say.'

I let him fit the piece in my ear. As soon as it's in place, a voice comes over it. 'Testing, one-two, testing.'

'Who's that?' I ask.

'One of our brothers,' the first *villac* replies. 'Is it working?'

'Yes.'

'Then proceed. Words will be fed to you as and when you need them.'

'What do I do?' I ask nervously — I was never comfortable speaking in public.

'Walk to the *inti watana*. Examine your troops. Be Paucar Wami.'

The priests withdraw. I'm alone, hidden by shadows. There's an exit close by. I could make a break for freedom. But where would I run to? The answers are here.

Steeling myself, I head for the huge circular stone. I'm spotted immediately. There are excited gasps, then the sound of heels snapping together. I tread softly, glancing only briefly left and right as I converge on the young soldiers and pass through their ranks. Each of the Snakes lifts his or her head a couple of inches when I pass, saluting me. The Cobras, standing out from their charges, drop to one knee and rest their palms flat on the floor, heads bowed. I search for the Cobra of the second triumvirate, the one who guided me to my father's room, but they all look the same when viewed crown-on.

As I near the platform, the *villac* on it lifts his head and walks to the edge to greet me. 'Spread your arms wide,' a voice whispers in my ear, and this time it's the voice of the priest who led me to the cavern. 'Let him press his finger-tips to yours and kiss the place on your chin where the heads of your tattoos meet.'

Spreading my arms as ordered, I stop at the platform and lean forward as the blind priest touches his fingers to mine. Muttering something unintelligible, he puts his lips to the spot below my lower lip and kisses the heads of my tattooed snakes. There's a soft hissing sound and when he draws away his tongue flicks out at me – it's *forked*.

I almost draw back from his serpentine tongue, but Paucar Wami never flinches, so I hold myself steady. Then the priest opens his mouth to chant some more and his tongue is normal again. Maybe it always was and I just imagined the fork.

The *villac* drones on for several minutes. I stand without moving, arms outstretched, awaiting further instructions.

Finally he stops and walks to the three buckets, which he transfers to the edge of the platform.

'Face the Snakes,' comes the voice. 'Say what I tell you.'

I turn and repeat the words of the *villac* as they're fed to me. If I was doing this as Al Jeery, I'm sure I'd stumble and stutter. But as Paucar Wami I'm fearless and eloquent, a natural orator.

'Our time is almost at hand. For long years we have existed anonymously. That is soon to change. Those who matter in the city have heard of us and grow anxious. Soon all will tremble at the sound of our name.'

My voice echoes around the cavern and is absorbed by eager ears. Many of the young men and women are grinning. A few even nudge their companions and wink.

'But we must be patient a while longer,' I caution them. 'Our enemies turn on one another like dogs, but we must wait until they are fully engaged before we act, lest they sense our threat and unite against us.'

'Face the *villac* on the *inti watana*,' the voice whispers. I do as instructed, then continue.

'In preparation for your rise, you will now be blooded. You have come through much, but there is much still to endure. Let this be a reminder of what you have sacrificed, and a promise of what you will enjoy.'

The buckets are filled with blood. It could be the blood of animals, but I'm sure it isn't. 'Vegetarians should leave the building,' I mutter, unprompted, and there are ghoulish giggles.

'This is the blood of the conquered,' the voice says, and I repeat the words obediently. 'The blood of the weak and impure. To cleanse this city, you must first taste of its foulness. Hold the blood down when you drink. Those who cannot stomach it have no place here and will be cast out.'

Three *villacs* march from the side of the cavern, chanting

as they walk. They accept the buckets from their colleague on the platform, then weave through the ranks, offering the blood to each Snake in turn, not moving on until the soldier has drunk and kept down the thick red liquid. I speak as they administer the blood.

'Take a mouthful, no more, no less. Those who cannot drink of this city are not wanted, but nor are those who would drink too much. Only those who can drink in moderation are desired.'

I wait for more instructions, but there are none, so I stand and watch as the Snakes complete the bloody ritual, lips red, faces impassive. Nobody rejects or vomits up the blood. Maybe they've tried it before. I'm prepared to accept an offering if it's made, but the buckets aren't presented to me.

When the last of the Snakes has drunk, the buckets are returned to the platform and the *villac* stacks them behind the thrones. I'm told to mingle with the troops, making comments or asking questions. 'But none about *us*,' I'm warned.

I prowl the ranks arrogantly, as my father would, studying the soldiers, trying to spot relatives. They stand three abreast, six deep, a gap between each phalanx, a larger space between each triumvirate. At the rear stand eleven separated members, rawer than the rest. New recruits, the beginnings of the eighth triumvirate.

I recall how the sergeants in the Troops treated me when I first joined. I stop at the back of one of the phalanxes and tap a burly teenager on the shoulder. He turns his head inquisitively and I punch his jaw hard, knocking him to the floor. 'Did I tell you to look around?' I roar.

'No, sir,' he responds, face flushed, almost grinning through the pain — it's an honour to be singled out by their leader, even for punishment.

'Get to your feet.' He stands. Medium height, heavy build, a wide, open face. Slightly foggy eyes. 'What's your name, boy?'

'Leonard, sir, first phalanx, sixth triumvirate.'

'Been with us long, Leonard?'

'Three years, two months, six days, sir.'

'An impressive memory.'

'I keep track on a calendar.'

I lean in close. 'Tonight, take that calendar, tear it up and burn it.'

He hesitates. 'But . . . sir . . . it belongs to –'

I club the back of his head. 'I didn't ask for a debate. I gave an order.'

'Yes, sir!' he shouts.

I swivel away from him and address the others. 'That goes for the rest of you. Focus on the present. Embrace it. Breathe it. Become it. Cut yourself off from the world of time. If you do not, you belong to that world, and that means you don't belong to *me*.'

By the shine of their faces, I see that I've made an impression, and I feel the ridiculous stirrings of pride in my chest. I quickly quash it. These are pawns of the *villacs*, thus my potential enemies. I should cut the Patton shit. Get the inspection over with quickly and . . .

I'm hurrying past the eleven newcomers at the rear when one catches my eye. I move up close, making sure I'm not mistaken, and he takes a worried step back. '*Drake?* What the fuck are you doing here?' Flo's boy gawps, astonished to be addressed by the legendary Paucar Wami. 'Answer me!'

'I . . . I'm a Snake . . . sir.'

'How long have you been here?'

'A couple of weeks. I sneak back home every few days, but –'

'Does your mother know about this?'

'Of course not.' His spirit rises and he faces up to me squarely.

I start to ask what he thinks Flo would say if she knew,

then remember who I'm meant to be. I step back from Drake. 'Tell me why you're here, boy. What brought you to this notorious den of thieves . . . this disreputable pit of snakes?' There are amused laughs. But Drake is deathly serious.

'I want to protect my mother, sir.'

'How?'

'By learning to fight. The city's about to blow, but we've got nobody to fight for us, to stand up to the Troops or the fucking Kluxers.'

'Fucking Kluxers,' is echoed by several Snakes. I silence the murmurs with a wave of a hand.

'Go on,' I tell Drake. 'Say it so that everyone can hear.' Making it sound as if it's for the crowd's benefit, not mine.

'The Snakes will protect their people in the east,' Drake says seriously. 'We'll push back the Troops and Kluxers, and anybody else who threatens those we love. We'll control the gangs. We'll see peace and order restored. We'll kick the ass of anyone who fucks with us!'

He shouts the last line and is greeted with cheers. I wait for them to die down before whispering harshly, so it's only just audible, 'And then?'

Drake pauses. 'Sir?'

'What will you do when the streets are yours? Will you return to your mother or retreat back here to the depths?'

'That's enough,' the *villac* hisses in my ear.

I ignore him. 'Tell me what happens next.'

'I don't know, sir. No one said.'

'Who will tell this boy?' I roar. 'Who knows? Who has thought this through?'

'Jeery!' the *villac* screeches. 'If you don't quit right now, I'll –'

A young woman raises a trembling hand. 'Yes?' I ask her, tuning out the priest.

'We control, sir,' she says confidently.

'You win the streets, then keep them?'

'Yes.'

'How do you think your relatives and friends will react to that?'

She frowns.

'The public might back us against the Troops and Kluxers, but what happens when they want to return to normal, only to find –'

The English-speaking *villac* rushes into the cave. 'Sapa Inca!' he shouts. 'You must come with me. There is trouble. We need you elsewhere.'

'I am addressing my troops,' I growl. 'I don't like being interrupted when –'

'The Kluxers have attacked one of our posts. You must come.'

The Snakes mutter angrily at mention of the Kluxers, and I know the *villac* has me. If I don't accompany him, it will seem like I care more about talking big in front of my supporters than protecting them from their enemies.

'OK,' I mutter irritably, then raise my voice one last time. 'But think on what I have said. Obedience is essential if you are to serve me, but a keen mind is just as important. My followers must be able to reason as well as obey.'

Turning my back on them, I trail after the priest, who hurries to an exit in the side of the cavern, where the darkness of the tunnels awaits. I don't look back at the Snakes — Paucar Wami never looks back.

Once out of sight and earshot of the young soldiers, the *villac* relaxes.

'What does "Sapa Inca" mean?' I ask.

'That is how we refer to Paucar Wami. It is the name we used long ago for our war leaders.' His lips crease in a sneer. 'Speaking as you did was foolish. I warned you not to cross us.'

'You told me to behave as Paucar Wami would,' I counter.

'The performance was admirable,' the priest agrees, then adds cuttingly, 'to a point. But prompting them to question their long-term goals was inflammatory. As soldiers it is their place to jump when we tell them, not ponder.'

'That's where you and I differ. I think they've a right to know what they're getting into, what may come of it.'

'When the Snakes are yours,' the priest sniffs, 'you may treat them as you wish. But until that time, I would ask that you respect —'

'What do you mean, when the Snakes are *mine?*' I cut in.

'The Snakes have been recruited to serve Paucar Wami,' the priest says. 'He acts as a figurehead, a symbol they can unite behind. But surely you do not think we would place such power in the hands of a psychopathic killer.'

'Listen,' I begin sharply, 'if you think *I'm* going to lead your army, you —'

The *villac* raises a small pipe to his lips, blows hard and sends a cloud of pink dust flying into my face. As I cough and splutter, motes fill my lungs and my head goes light. My legs give way and the walls dissolve. 'Bastard!' I shout, but the word is a whisper. I try to hit the priest but my fist blurs and my fingers turn to steam. I have a sense of unbecoming, of floating . . . then no sense of anything at all.

When I come to, someone's holding my hand, leading me through a narrow tunnel. The drug's still in my blood and my head throbs. Stopping, I wrench my hand from my guide's and fall to my knees. I beat the floor with my fists, gritting my teeth, and that helps clear my head. The *villacs* drugged me before, and that time it was a long-lasting trip. But this drug isn't as strong, and though the world around me shimmers at the edges, I'm able to recognize reality and cling to it.

'Are you alright?' my guide asks, bending to help. A woman's voice. I slap her hands away and force my eyes to focus.

'Who are you?' I gasp.

'A friend. I'm taking you to the surface. We're going home.'

I'm too weak to fight. Allowing the woman to grasp my elbows, I let her haul me to my feet, then lean on her for support. As we start forward, I examine her face and recognize it. 'Ama Situwa,' I murmur, wondering if I'm really able to tell the difference between fantasy and reality after all.

'Yes,' she replies.

'Are you real or a vision?'

She doesn't answer immediately. We come to a set of stairs. She pauses at the first step, looks sideways at me and says softly, 'I'm not sure.'

We smile shakily at each other. I squeeze her hand for comfort and she squeezes mine. Then we climb.

FOUR – CONVERSATIONS WITH THE DEAD

Wednesday, just after midnight, my apartment. Ama's in the kitchen, making sandwiches. I told her I could do it, but my legs are still weak and she insisted I sit and rest.

It was Monday when I encountered my father in the Manco Capac statue. When I came to, found the chef and asked the time, he told me it was afternoon. Which it was — but Tuesday, not Monday. I was out of commission an entire day.

Ama and I didn't talk much during our climb. We emerged behind a rubbish tip, where my motorbike and Ama's scooter were waiting. I asked Ama how they got there but she didn't know. She wasn't even sure how she knew the way up — she claimed to be navigating by instinct.

She slides in from the kitchen, tray of sandwiches in one hand, a bag of cookies in the other. 'These are stale,' she says, 'but they'll be OK if you dunk them.'

'There's a twenty-four-hour store on the next block. I could –'

'Don't bother. These will be fine.'

I sip the coffee she brewed earlier and chew on the sandwiches. Ama nibbles at a cookie but doesn't touch her drink. Her eyes are serious and dark.

'Do you remember the statue?' I ask delicately.

She nods. 'The priests made me lure you there, then offer myself as a sacrifice. I had no control over what I was doing. Sometimes when they bring me back, I'm a zombie and they can . . .' She trails off into silence and frowns. 'Do you know what I'm talking about?'

'Yes. I met my . . . Paucar Wami down there.' No point telling her he's my father if she doesn't know. 'He explained how the *villacs* bring him back from the dead and force him to do their bidding.'

'It sounds crazy said like that,' she smiles. 'I was hysterical the first few times. Now I pretend I'm like anybody else, and when they tell me I have to die, I act like it's no big deal, just falling asleep.'

'How many times . . .?' I wince. I've a splitting headache.

'You need rest,' Ama says. 'We can talk about this in the morning.'

'I'd rather –'

'Morning,' she says firmly.

'Yes, nurse,' I grin, then get to my feet and hobble to bed, aided by Ama. I sit on the edge, breathing deeply, eyes shut against the pain.

'Who are the pair in the photo?' Ama asks, referring to the shot of Bill and a young Priscilla Perdue which hangs over my bed.

'Old friends,' I sigh without opening my eyes.

A pause as she takes in the rest of the room. 'There's a finger on your dressing table.'

'I know.'

Ama slips off my shoes and helps me out of my T-shirt. Her breath catches when she sights the scars on my chest and back – most from the explosion a decade ago – but she doesn't ask about them. Her hands are on the buttons of my jeans when I stop her. 'I'm not wearing shorts.'

'I doubt you've anything I haven't seen before,' she says, but turns her back while I wriggle out of the jeans and slide beneath the covers.

'I don't have a sleeping bag,' I tell her as she faces me again. 'You'll have to make do with the couch. Of course, if you'd rather, I could –'

'No. You need a good night's sleep.' She starts to leave. Stops and looks at me. 'Was I naked in the statue?'

'I think so,' I mutter.

She smiles. 'Bashful, Mr Jeery?'

'You were naked.'

'So I definitely don't have anything *you* haven't seen before.' Her smile fades. 'You've no idea how lonely it is. They keep me locked in a room when I'm alive. I dread the isolation. I don't want to sleep alone tonight.' I raise an eyebrow. 'I'm not talking about *that*! I just want someone to cuddle up to. It's been a long time since I had anybody to cling to in the dark.'

'I understand,' I answer softly. 'It's been a long time for me too.' I throw back the covers.

She undresses quickly, turns off the light and gets into bed beside me. We lie facing each other but not touching for a few seconds. Then she drapes an arm around me. I lay one over her. And we fall asleep, foreheads pressed together, clinging, dreaming . . . one.

Ama's gone when I awake, though the shape of her body is clear in the lines of the sheets. Lurching out of bed, ignoring the pain in my head, I rush through the rest of the apartment. Not here. I stand in the living room, panting, trying to figure out if she disappeared in a cloud of green fog, was abducted, or . . .

The front door opens and Ama walks in, dressed in the same shirt and beige trousers as last night, carrying a brown paper bag from the twenty-four-hour shop on the next block. She stares at me, standing naked in the middle of the room, then laughs. 'You shouldn't have been so shy when undressing — you've nothing to be modest about.'

My hands dart to cover my nakedness, then I hop back into the bedroom and pull on a pair of jeans, before trailing her into the kitchen.

'I got milk, fresh cookies, bread, sliced meat, and these.' She tosses a packet of aspirin to me.

'Thanks,' I mutter, popping a couple and letting them dissolve.

'Head any better?'

'Still hurts. Throat too, though not as much as it did.'

'The bruises are beauts. You're lucky he didn't kill you.'

'It wasn't luck. He knew what he was doing.' I cough. 'We didn't have a chance to swap histories. I'm not sure how much you know about me or –'

'You're Al Jeery. Paucar Wami is your father. You pretend to be him.'

'The *villacs* told you?'

'No. It's something I know. There are lots of things I know but can't explain. I think the priests programme me before they revive me.' She finishes unpacking and turns. 'Sorry if I startled you by not being here. I was going to wake you but you looked dead to the world.'

'Leave a note next time.'

'Yes, boss.' She walks to the bathroom and flicks on the light. 'I was going to take a shower earlier but there wasn't any hot water.'

I check the time. 'The hot-water tank is shared by all the tenants,' I explain. 'Most people use it before work, so it's normally empty by half eight. It should be OK now but you won't get long out of it, five or six minutes.'

'That'll do. Want to use it too?'

I sniff my armpits. 'Yeah.'

'Want to share?'

'Don't tempt me,' I grimace.

I step into the shower as soon as she's out, turn the heat up high and scrub myself clean of the stench of the tunnels. The water runs cold after a minute. I shiver but don't get out. After a long soak, I turn it off, towel myself dry and fetch a fresh pair of jeans and a T-shirt. Once clad, I catch up with Ama, who's back in the kitchen, preparing breakfast.

'Can I ask you something?' I enquire, standing in the doorway.

'Shoot.'

'How did you know you could trust me?'

Ama butters a slice of bread. 'You only kill guilty people. You're not evil like your father. That's one of the things I *know*. I also know you won't take a lover, afraid that the *villacs* would use that person to hurt you, so I knew you wouldn't make a pass at me in bed.'

'And you didn't feel like making a pass at me?' I scowl.

She laughs. 'Don't take it personally. I don't have a choice. I was created to love someone else.'

'Capac Raimi?' I guess.

'Yes.' She grabs another slice of bread. 'We've a lot to talk about. It's going to take a while. Let's have some breakfast first.'

We eat on the couch. A simple meal — cereal, sandwiches, milk. Ama discusses her relationship with The Cardinal as we eat.

'My memories of Capac are vague. A conversation we had on the docks, raiding Party Central, meeting in a restaurant where I worked.'

'Cafran's,' I interject.

She frowns. 'I don't remember.'

'You don't recall the owner, Cafran Reed?'

She thinks a moment. 'No.'

I file the information away. I can tell her about him later. Right now I want to find out about her life underground with the Incas.

'I know Capac's an Ayuamarcan and what that means. I also know he was different, that he didn't die when the rest of us did.'

'Do you recall him sacrificing you for his career?' I ask.

'Yes.' Her face goes bleak. 'When I came back originally – two or three years ago – I hated him. Now I know better. He was only doing what he was made to. He had no choice. The Cardinal created him to be cold and focused.'

'You still love him?' I keep my voice neutral.

'I can't *not* love him. I see that love for what it is – manufactured, unreal – but I can't deny it.'

'Do you know where he is?'

'Party Central, I imagine. But,' she adds softly, 'I have a recurring dream of meeting him in a cold, dead place and leading him down stairs into darkness.'

'The Fridge?' She stares at me blankly and I let it drop. 'Tell me about coming back to life. Any idea how they do it?'

'No. When I first returned, I was terrified. I recalled my previous life and that I'd died, but I had no recollection of the years between. That hasn't changed. Death is nothingness, no sense of time or space.'

'Where do you come back?'

'A small room, dark and red. There are many women, one in particular . . .' Her face creases as she tries squeezing out more memories. 'Sorry. That's as much as I remember. I'm always woozy when I return. Someone leads me to my room – close to the cave of the *inti watana* – and I rest there.'

The room and the women interest me. All the *villacs* I've met are men. But they must have partners to procreate.

I never thought about it before, but now that I do, it makes sense that they'd mate with Incan women. They wouldn't want to taint their precious bloodlines by breeding with ordinary females.

'Do the women come to the cave of the *inti watana*?' I ask.

'I've never seen them there. Why?'

It's time to tell her about her missing lover. I talk swiftly, describing his disappearance and my search for him. She's troubled by the news, but not overly.

'The *villacs* have him,' I finish. 'If I could kidnap a few of their women, I might be able to force them to release him.'

'Why go to so much trouble?' she says. 'He's immortal. They can't kill him, not really.'

'But they can hold him captive. Force-feed him. Keep him as a prisoner until the end of time.'

She frowns. 'He could kill himself. Cut his wrists or bash his head off a wall.'

'Not if he was bound and drugged.'

Ama hisses. 'Those sons of bitches. I bet they used me to lure him down. I've often wondered why they went to the trouble of reviving me. Now I know — to get their hands on Capac.'

'If that was their only use for you, they wouldn't keep you on now that they have him.'

'Unless they want to use me against somebody else,' she murmurs, and her eyes meet mine.

'Don't worry,' I grin. 'I'm not going to ruin myself on your account.'

'Charming.' She finishes her milk and studies me over the rim of her cup. 'You still haven't said where you fit into this. Why do you care about Capac?'

'Influence. If I save The Cardinal, I'll have a friend in the highest of places.'

She smiles smugly. 'You're lying. But that's OK. We all have secrets.'

She's sharp. I'll have to be careful around her.

'What do we do now?' Ama asks. 'Seems to me your investigation's come to a close. You know that Capac's underground but I don't think anyone except the *villacs* can pinpoint his exact location.'

I nod. 'I can try grabbing one of their women and using her in a deal, or maybe capture a priest who speaks English and torture him. But the *villacs* own the tunnels. I doubt I can take the fight to them down there and triumph.'

I fall silent, mulling it over, but no ideas present themselves. 'I guess there's only one thing for it,' I sigh. 'I'll go to Ford Tasso, tell him what I know and let him take it from there.'

'You think he will?' Ama asks sceptically.

'No,' I grunt. 'I'd never be so lucky.'

Ama comes with me to Party Central but stays with the bikes in an alley at the rear of the building. I enter as Al Jeery and head for the fifteenth floor. The corridors are teeming with Troops and anxious execs. I push past them unnoticed, elbowing several out of my way at the door to Tasso's office – they're packed tight around it, clamouring for an audience with the fill-in Cardinal.

'Hi Mags,' I greet the tired-looking secretary. 'Any chance of fitting me in?'

'You kidding?' she snaps. 'I spent all of yesterday trying to reach you. You're the one person Ford *does* want to see.' Hitting the intercom, she says, 'Al's here.'

Tasso roars at the other end, 'About fucking time! Send him in!'

On my way, I swivel to avoid three terrified men – they race out of Tasso's inner sanctum as if the devil himself was after them – then close the door on the chaos. Tasso's sitting in front of the desk, neck stiff, good eye glaring. His left hand is busy massaging his right arm. 'Tell me what you know about these fucking Snakes,' he growls by way of a greeting.

'When did you learn about them?' I ask, drawing up a chair.

'Night before last. A bunch took out a squadron of Troops on patrol in the east. Left a warning with the bodies. "Stay out of the east — the Snakes." Within hours the streets were wild with rumours, about how there are hundreds of the fuckers, all trained killing machines, led by the legendary vigilante, Paucar fucking Wami. Who are they, Algiers? And why the fuck are you heading up a fucking army?'

'If you really thought I was their leader, we wouldn't be talking — you'd be washing my blood from your hands.'

'Too fucking true,' he snorts, then grins horribly. 'What's going on and where have you been?'

I give him an abbreviated account of my run-in with the real Paucar Wami, the *villacs* and Snakes. I say nothing about Wami being able to die and come back to life, nor of Ama's similar abilities. He can make that leap himself, or else assume they've been in hiding for ten years. He quizzes me closely about the Snakes. How many? Are they armed? What are their intentions? I answer honestly, telling all I know, finishing with the observation that they could do a lot of damage.

'Tell me about it,' he groans. 'I was just figuring out how to deal with Davern, then this shit hits. Where the fuck did they come from? You can't assemble a force that size without attracting attention.'

'The *villacs* are masters when it comes to secrecy. They've been building the Snakes for years, recruiting slowly, targeting young men and women who want to be part of something big, who know how to keep their mouths shut, who are able to slip away without creating a fuss.'

'I could send Troops down the tunnels to flush them out,' he muses.

'I wouldn't advise it.'

'You don't think we could take them?'

'Not down there. At best you'd suffer a hammering. At worst you'd piss them off so much, they'd do something nasty to your Cardinal.'

'You're sure they have Capac?'

'Yes.'

He scowls. 'What are they after?'

'They want to protect their homes and families.'

'Not the Snakes,' he growls. 'The fucking priests. Why have they raised an army? What are their plans?'

'To set them against you and weaken your stranglehold on the city.'

'But why? No matter how strong these Snakes are, they're not gonna drive us out. Hurting us only makes it easier for Davern and his Kluxers to strike. Chaos serves nobody, so why generate it?'

'Are you asking me or thinking aloud?'

He chuckles tonelessly. 'A bit of both. Any ideas?'

'No. And I'm not bothered. I was hired to find a man. I found him. Will you keep your side of the bargain?'

'Where is he?' Tasso enquires coolly.

'In the tunnels. I won't get closer to him than that. Nobody will.'

'That's not enough. The deal was for you to bring Capac back, not point me in his general direction. Deliver him and I'll give you Bill Casey. You get nothing for coming close.'

'That's not fair,' I mutter.

'Fuck fair. You were hired to do a job, Algiers — do it. And Al?' he says as I rise angrily. 'Do it quick. If this shit continues, I mightn't be around to honour our deal much longer.'

*   *   *

I take Ama to a restaurant, Sultry Sally's, situated by the river. We study the menu leisurely – this is Ama's first date in ten years and she's savouring the moment – before ordering. When the waiter departs, Ama asks me to tell her what Ford Tasso said.

'Who's Bill Casey?' she asks when I get to the part about Tasso not giving up Bill's location unless I hand him Raimi.

'An enemy. The reason I got drawn into this mess.' I start to tell her about the past, finding my girlfriend murdered in Party Central, The Cardinal hiring me to investigate her death, the way my life fell apart, discovering the identity of the man responsible, becoming Paucar Wami in the hope that Bill was still alive and could be lured out of hiding. The tale sees us through starters and the main course, and I only wrap it up as dessert arrives.

'Jesus,' Ama whispers when I finish. 'What do you think Wami did to drive him to such lengths?'

'I'm pretty sure he killed Bill's sister. He had some sick game going with Bill. He forced him to commit crimes, and spared victims in return. I think it was meant to culminate in murder. He kidnapped a girl and told Bill to kill her. When Bill didn't, Wami slaughtered his sister.'

Ama's face whitens and she puts down her spoon. 'That's awful.'

'Yeah. It doesn't excuse what he did to me, but I feel sorry for him, or at least for the boy he was.'

'Do you think . . .?' Ama stops. 'No. It's not my place to ask.'

'Go on. I can take it.'

'Is revenge the answer? Perhaps you should drop it and flee. Build a new life for yourself and try to forget about him.'

'If I was sane, that's what I'd do. But I'm not.'

'You seem fairly sane to me.'

'Only on the outside. Inside I'm afire with madness. That's why I can cut a deal with the *villacs* or a monster like my father. A sane man would have limits, lines he wouldn't cross. I have none.'

Ama picks up her spoon and tucks into a bowl of ice-cream. 'If he's really alive, and you find him, what will you do after you kill him?' I stare at my slice of cheese cake and don't answer. 'Al? Did you hear what I –'

'To all intents and purposes, I died ten years ago,' I murmur. 'I've subexisted since then as my father's ghost. Once I finish with Bill, I'll be done with this world. I don't deserve a place in it.'

'You'll kill yourself?' she asks hollowly.

I force a bleak smile. 'Eat your ice-cream.'

We're silent for the rest of the meal, and during the lull I fall to thinking about what to do with Ama. I need to focus on the search for Capac Raimi. I must be alone to think, plan, act. But I can't just dump her. There must be some diplomatic way . . .

I hit on the solution as I'm paying the bill. Outside, as we mount our bikes, I tell her to follow me. Cutting through the traffic, we make good time to Cafran's. Ama frowns at the sign and stands by her scooter. 'Recognize it?' I ask.

'It seems familiar but I don't know why.'

'Let's go in. There's someone I want you to meet.'

Cafran Reed is sitting at a table near the kitchen, engaged in conversation with a waitress. He doesn't look so old when he's laughing, though his fragile frame shakes with each chuckle. I cough to introduce myself and he looks up. 'Al Jeery. Nice to see you again. I hope you'll dine with us this time.'

'Afraid not. I've just eaten. Mr Reed, I'd like to introduce you to a friend of mine, Ama Situwa.'

Ama steps forward, smiling. Her smile falters when she

faces Reed. His smile slips too. 'Have we met before?' he croaks.

'No,' Ama says stumblingly. 'At least . . . I don't think so.'

The pair stare at each other, unaware of the link they once shared, but somehow sensing a previous connection. I break the silence. 'Ama's a waitress. Are there any openings here?'

The old man blinks. 'We're not short of staff, but . . . yes. There's a place for her if she wants it.' The waitress sharing his table looks at him oddly.

'Excuse me a moment, Mr Reed,' Ama says and draws me aside. 'What the hell are you –'

'Cafran Reed didn't sire you,' I interrupt quietly, 'but ten years ago you and he believed he was your father.'

The colour drains from Ama's face. 'God,' she moans. 'That's why I recognize him! He . . .' Her throat seizes.

'I want you to stay with him, Ama. You wouldn't be in the way in my place, but you'd be a distraction.'

'But he doesn't remember me, and I remember nothing about him.'

'Use this time to catch up. I wouldn't mention the fact that you were once his daughter – you'd confuse him – but you can get to know him again and forge a new relationship. He's a lonely old man, missing someone he doesn't know existed. He needs you. And you need him — you told me you were lonely.'

'But the priests . . . Capac . . .'

'I'll tell you if I find him,' I promise. 'I'll keep you informed, and call on you for help if I need it — and I think, before the end, I will. But for now you'll be better off here.'

Ama nods slowly. 'Very well. I'll stay. For a while.'

I bid Cafran farewell, give Ama my number and depart, pausing at the door to look back at the old man and his long lost 'daughter'. They're staring at each other, silent, slightly fearful, but touched with hope. I think they're going to get on fine.

Pushing through the door, I wipe a dopey smile from my face, cast thoughts of Ama Situwa and Cafran Reed from my mind, and hurry to my bike. I slip off my wig and wipe my face clean of paint as I walk, insert my contacts, hang Bill's severed finger around my neck, and become Paucar Wami by the time I hit the saddle and kick the engine into life.

FIVE – RIOTS

I spend hours in my apartment writing up a report of all that's happened, detailing my sighting of Ama at the crematorium, following her to the Manco Capac statue, my father, the voyage underground. It helps to have it on paper. Sometimes I see things written down that I overlook when they're only inside my head.

But not this time. Though I pore over the notes until four in the morning, analysing and adding to them, I see nothing that might lead me to Capac Raimi, or any clues as to how I should proceed. I know the *villacs* have him. I know he's in the tunnels. But how to determine his precise location? I could blunder down with a flashlight and keep searching, but that could take years — or forever, if the priests are moving him around. There must be a less hit-or-miss method.

I'm drawn again to the idea of using the Rats. The subterranean gang might know where to look. I'll track them down and ask for their assistance. That can be my first step. Take things from there.

I read through the notes one last time before I destroy them (wary of thieves getting their hands on such sensitive information). This time I pause at the phrase, 'Sapa Inca'. Why are the priests so sure I'll lead the Snakes? They know

I'm not interested in power. They offered me a controlling stake in this city before and I turned them down flat. What makes them think I'll comply this time?

Late Thursday, after much searching, I find the Rats in the bowels of a derelict football stadium in the northwest of the city, abandoned twenty years ago in favour of a new structure. All twelve of the Rats – a couple of new recruits have joined since I last saw them – are present, cooking strips of dog over a large fire.

Their leader, Chunky, spots me first and shouts, 'Po!' That's their nickname for me, a shortened version of Paucar. I force a grin as he embraces me, trying not to gag on the stench of the sewer dweller. Chunky drags me over to the fire and offers me a slice of half-raw dog. I take a few bites – not that disgusting – and wash it down with their home-made beer. The beer's worse than the dog – Chunky once started to tell me how they brewed it, and I had to stop him before I threw up – but I drain half a cup of it and belch approvingly.

'Got yer messages,' Chunky says, running a hand through his greasy hair, then down the front of his ragged cardigan. The Rats make their outfits from clothes they find in the tunnels and rubbish dumps. 'What can we do for ya?'

'I'm looking for someone. Thought you might be able to help.' I quickly tell him about The Cardinal, that he's being held by the *villacs*, and offer to reward the Rats generously if they help me find him.

Chunky hears me out, then shakes his head. 'Sorry, Po. Ain't on. We don't fuck with the priests, 'specially now they got an army behind them.'

'You know about the Snakes?'

'Sure. Knew about them long before anyone else. There's advantages to living beneath the streets, and not just beating the bombs when they fall. We've seen the Snakes grow and we've steered clear — snakes eat rats! Besides, they won't stay down here forever. They'll move up top eventually.'

'What about Raimi? Any idea where they might be keeping him?'

'Nope. We could maybe find him by shadowing the priests, but they ain't the sort we want to get on the wrong side of.'

'Name your price,' I tell him.

'Sorry, Po, ain't nothing could persuade us to make enemies of them blind bastards. We'll have to share these tunnels with the priests long after you and the rest of the crowd above have been blown to bits in the big blast.'

'OK,' I smile. 'But if you see or hear anything while you're foraging, will you let me know?'

'Might, if I don't think it'll rile the priests. Want to hang a while? We captured a couple of koala bears from the zoo and we're barbecuing 'em later. They smell like piss but they're pretty good with gravy.'

'I'll give it a miss,' I mutter, feeling my stomach tighten.

'Your loss,' Chunky chuckles.

I bid Chunky and co. farewell and head back to the normal world. I spend the rest of the night checking with my contacts, asking if anyone's heard about Raimi, but all the talk's of the Snakes and how everything's going to change now that a new force is in play. In the end I head home and sleep soundly, without a hint of a nightmare, until I'm woken shortly after six by the sound of gunfire, and arise to discover the city in a state of civil war.

The trouble started with the assassination of four gang leaders last night, all from small gangs in the east. Brutally slaughtered at home, by parties unknown, for no clear reason. Their followers took to the streets, enraged, looking for someone to blame. Encountering each other, they clashed and violence flared. Other gangs joined in and a bloody battle developed, engulfing several blocks. The fighting could have been contained by the police, but around the same time two police stations were attacked and set alight, again by persons unknown. Forces rushing to deal with the street fights had to be diverted. Then, as if things weren't chaotic enough, another two gang leaders were executed, along with a number of priests, medics and community workers. By dawn the streets were clogged with furious gangsters and citizens baying for blood. In the absence of a definable foe, they took their grievances out on each other, and the fighting quickly developed into a savage, unchecked free-for-all.

As I patrol the streets, observing the warfare, I find it hard to believe that things got this bad this quickly. Windows of shops and cars have been smashed to pieces and many have been set on fire. Looters are making off with anything that isn't tied down. The smoke of a thousand fires blocks out the sky, giving the appearance of dusk. People I know – good people – are in the thick of the action, beating, maiming, even killing. A madness has washed over them and I can't explain it. Everyone knew the city was heading for riots, but I don't think anybody anticipated a blow-up of these proportions. It doesn't make sense.

There's little I can do to counter the chaos. My presence normally makes people pause, but nobody's taking the slightest notice of me today. I'm just another face in the crowd. I break up a couple of especially vicious fights, where children are at risk, but quickly realize I'm wasting my time – the combatants scatter, run a few blocks, re-group and find someone new to attack.

I decide to take a break and check on those I care about. I slip back to my apartment, become Al Jeery, then head to Flo's, where I learn that Drake was an early victim of the violence and has been rushed to hospital. The hospital's only three blocks from where they live. Hurrying over, I dodge the people fighting out front – nurses locked in combat with a street gang – and push my way along corridors cluttered with bleeding patients bleating for assistance.

The nurses on reception look scared and harried. They're guarded by a ring of security officers who hold back the crowd, but the ring looks as if it could break any moment. A few of the braver nurses and doctors wade through the walking wounded, picking out the more serious cases for treatment.

Slipping past the guards – not difficult in the uproar – I gently nudge aside a woman with a large gash in her head and ask the receptionist which room Drake Martins is in. 'Are you shitting me?' she barks. 'We got World War III erupting and you want to go visiting!'

'He's a friend. I'd like to see how he is.'

'I don't care what you'd *like*. Get out of my face before I –'

Behind us, a man screams insanely, draws a rifle and fires. A guard goes down clutching his leg. The crowd splinters, shrieking and wailing. The man with the gun – a large white male, eyes wild – moves in to finish off the guard. I've had enough of this shit. Drawing my .45, I wait for a clear line of fire, then pop him in the upper right arm. He curses, drops the rifle, stoops to reclaim it. I step forward and kick his head, knocking him out. I make sure the guard's OK, then return to the desk, where the receptionist regards me with new respect.

'Drake Martins.'

'Give me a minute,' she mumbles, consulting her computer. 'He was admitted before the rush. Ward 3, room 5B. Take the stairs — the elevator's out of order.'

'Much appreciated.' I glance around at the crowd in the lobby. I've caught their attention, so I might as well make use of it. Scanning those nearest me, I pick six who look like they can handle themselves. 'You, you, you, you, you

and you!' I shout. 'Come here.' They obey instantly. I fan
them out in a half-circle, fitting them in between the guards,
who watch mutely. 'Work with the guards. Help keep order.
Understand?' They nod uncertainly, then face the crowd and
assume solid stances. I don't know how long they'll last, but
they'll keep the peace for a while.

Hurrying up the stairs, I jog to Ward 3 and find Drake.
Flo's by his bed. There are blankets on the floor, on which
excess patients lie, some groaning, some unconscious, some
staring blankly at the ceiling.

'Doing anything later, gorgeous?' I grunt, touching Flo's
shoulder.

'Al,' she smiles through tears. 'I tried calling but I lost your
number.'

'I'll give it to you again before I leave. How is he?'

'He'll be OK,' she sighs, wiping sweat from his face. 'We
were attacked. They wanted Drake. They thought he was in
a gang, but that's crazy, I'd know if he was.' I let that slide.
'He helped me out a window and down the fire escape. They
knocked him off when he was trying to follow. Ran when
they saw him hit the ground – thought he was dead. I did
too, but he got lucky. The doctor only gave him a quick
examination, but she said it wasn't as serious as it seemed.
She was meant to check on him again but we ain't seen her.
I guess she's busy elsewhere.'

'It's turning into a real busy day.' I roll up Drake's left
eyelid. He groans and blinks, half-waking. 'Take a break,' I
tell Flo.

'That's OK, I don't –'

'Take a break,' I say firmly. She frowns, then leaves. I pop
in my contact lenses and remove my wig, then slap Drake's
cheeks just hard enough to wake him. When he's conscious,
I lean close so that nobody else in the packed room can hear.
'Are the Snakes behind this?'

Drake blinks and focuses. When he sees my green eyes and shaven scalp, he freezes, not even noticing the fact that my tattoos are covered up. 'Sapa Inca!' he gasps.

'Are you fit to continue, soldier?'

'I think so, sir,' he says, trying to rise.

I push him down. 'No, you're not. But you will recover soon. Report to the priests when you are able.'

'Excuse me, sir,' Drake says, a quiver in his voice, 'but why are you here?'

'I heard you had been singled out for attack. I thought those who assaulted you might know of our plans.'

'No,' he snorts. 'They were just neighbourhood kids, itching for a fight. They know I'm in a gang but they don't know which.'

'They don't know that the Snakes initiated the riots?'

'No, sir.'

That confirms my suspicions. 'Do you know why we instigated this uproar, why we destroy that which we are supposed to protect?'

'I'm not sure,' Drake replies cautiously. 'We were told it's necessary, that we have to demolish before we can build. I know the Snakes will step in soon, make our presence known and calm things down. I guess, in the long run, it'll be for the best, but I wish . . .' He trails off into silence and bites his lip, afraid he's spoken out of place.

'That's OK, soldier. I share your sentiments. I will be discussing this with our white-eyes *friends* later. Maybe we can put an early end to the fighting.'

'I hope so,' he says. Then, as I stand to leave, he calls me back. 'Sir, will you warn my mother not to drink the water?'

'What?'

'The tap water. I meant to warn her but I didn't get a chance. I don't want anything bad to happen to her.'

'Of course,' I mumble, then let myself out, the pieces of

the puzzle clicking together as I remove the contacts and put on the wig again. The *villacs* didn't just order the executions – they polluted the water supply. I wasn't imagining the madness. These people really are insane, at least temporarily. I've no idea what the priests added to the supply, or how far it might drive those who ingest it, but I don't think it will cause a serious imbalance. Just enough to turn this part of the city on its head for a few days, so they can send in the Snakes and become heroes of the hour.

I warn Flo about the water, give her my number, then rush from the hospital and head for the nearest radio station, to spread the word and do what I can to thwart whatever grand, twisted scheme the *villacs* have cooking.

The station manager dismisses me as a psycho until I put a knife to his throat. I still don't think he believes my story, but with his life on the line, he agrees to broadcast my warning, urging people to stick to bottled water. Within minutes of the story airing, it's picked up by a TV show and word spreads swiftly. Whether or not people pay heed is another matter, but at least they've been warned.

I release the manager and depart the building, looking for a quiet spot where I can make a call. Finding a deserted café, I dial Ford Tasso's direct number. It rings sixteen times before he answers with a curt, 'Yes!'

'It's Al.'

'I know who it is. What do you want?'

'You've heard about what's happening?'

'Is that a trick fucking question?'

'You've got to do something to stop it.'

'Such as?'

'Send in the Troops. They'll be more effective than the cops.'

'Have you been drinking that contaminated water?' Tasso

laughs. 'The sight of the Troops would send everyone wild. It'd be like throwing water on an oil fire.'

'At least people would have a real target to rally against. Right now they're attacking each other. Hundreds of innocents are dying. If you send the Troops in, everyone will unite –'

'– and wipe my men out!' Tasso barks.

'You can withdraw them before they're massacred. All I'm asking for is a respite. These people have been drugged but I don't think the effects will last. Distract them. Stop the killing. By dawn tomorrow it'll have blown over.'

'No.'

'But –'

'I'm not prepared to risk the lives of my Troops. Besides, moving my forces there would leave me open to an attack by the Kluxers.'

'If you don't quell the riots, the Snakes will take control of the east. You'll face a war on two fronts.'

'The Snakes won't work with the Kluxers. They hate each other. It'll be war, a war neither can win by themselves. Sooner or later Davern or his counterpart will come to me for help.'

'Playing both ends against the middle, Ford? A dangerous game.'

'Leave me to worry about the games, Algiers. You focus on finding Capac.' He cuts the connection, leaving me to curse his name to the smoke-obscured heavens and kick the nearest wall with frustration.

I spend the afternoon and evening as Paucar Wami, doing what little I can to restore the peace. I shouldn't get involved, but I can't stand by and let looting, raping and killing go ahead unheeded. These are my people. If I can protect some few of them, I must.

After hours of action, I knock the heads of a pair of muggers together and break their fingers. Leaving them in the gutter, I head for home. I need food and rest — I've a long, taxing, bloody night ahead of me.

I smell the visitor when I open the door, the musky stench of the underground impossible to disguise. I pause in the doorway and consider retreat, but this is my home and I'm not about to give it up lightly. Entering, I shut the door and switch on the light in the living room. The real Paucar Wami smiles at me from where he stands by the window. 'A fine night, hmm, Al m'boy?'

I go to the kitchen, fix a sandwich, fetch two cans of beer from the fridge and toss one to my father. He catches, opens and raises it to his lips in one smooth movement. I flop on the couch and munch my sandwich. 'How long have you been back among the living?'

'Since this morning.' He belches and eyes me, amused. 'You don't seem fazed by my ability to return from the dead.'

'When you've seen one zombie, you've seen them all.'

'You have changed. The Al I remember had no time for the occult. He would have been busy seeking logical solutions to explain my existence.'

I shrug. 'I've learnt to take the world for what it is. If corpses return to life, so be it.'

Wami observes me intensely. His eyes linger on the finger hanging from my neck but he doesn't ask about it. 'If I did not know better, I could almost think I was gazing into a mirror,' he remarks approvingly. 'You look older than me – you need to hide those wrinkles – your face isn't quite as angular as mine, and some scars show through your tattoos, but otherwise you're a near perfect likeness.'

'Mother always said I favoured your side of the family.'

He laughs. 'And you've developed a sense of humour! You have done the old man proud.'

I'm not sure whether he's being sarcastic or paying me a genuine compliment. I don't much care. 'Why are you here? Did your masters send you?'

'No man can call himself my master,' Wami growls. 'The priests command me but it is a temporary arrangement. Their hour of control will pass, as Ferdinand Dorak's did. I am my own man.'

'You're deluding yourself,' I sneer. 'You're their puppet and always have been. Now be a good boy and spit out whatever message they gave you for me.'

His face darkens and his lips curl. I stare at him impassively. 'They said they started this riot and they can finish it,' he mutters bitterly, dropping his gaze. 'If you pledge allegiance, they will send in the Snakes and restore order.'

'Do you know they plan to oust you in favour of me? The Snakes are designed to be led by me, not you.'

'I would not have it any other way,' he says. 'I savour my own company. I could not tolerate leadership. You can have your pitiful Snakes.'

'But I don't want them. Tell the *villacs* to go fuck themselves.'

Wami throws back his head and laughs. His white teeth flash in the light of the bulb. 'You should choose your words carefully when dealing with your enemies, Al m'boy. There is a time for honesty and a time for diplomacy.'

'Then put it diplomatically to them. I don't give a rat's ass.'

My father's eyes narrow. 'That is foolish. I hate the priests but I respect them. You think the world cannot hurt you, that because you do not fear death, no one can tell you what to do. That is not so. As free as you have become, you are not invulnerable. By no means give yourself over to the Incan devils, but work with them. We all must make concessions at various times.'

I shake my head. 'I won't dance to their tune. They want me to lead the Snakes – I won't. They want me to work with Capac Raimi – I won't. They want me to make this city theirs – I won't.'

'Very well.' Wami stands. 'I have passed on their message and you have given your reply. I think they expected no different.' He strides to the window – when it comes to entering and leaving a room, I guess it's a case of like father, like son – then stops. 'Out of curiosity, where have you been?'

'On the streets, doing what I can to help.'

He frowns. 'Why?'

'I grew up here. I know these people. I care.'

'Caring is dangerous. The *villacs* might use it against you.'

'They can't. There's a limit to my sympathies. I'll help where I can, but if the priests threaten my neighbours and make it a condition that I do as they say or they'll go to war on those I know . . .' I shrug.

'Calculated care,' Wami muses. 'A curious concept. Do you intend returning to the streets tonight?'

'After I've rested and eaten.'

'Would you care for a partner?'

'You want to help me restore peace and order?' I ask suspiciously.

'Fuck that,' he laughs. 'These people's plight is of no interest to me. But it has been a long time since I had the run of the city. The *villacs* did not tell me to hurry back, only to return once I had finished with you.'

He playfully kneels and puts his hand on his heart. 'Let me run beside you, Al m'boy. I swear I will follow your lead and only kill those you deem fit. I will be your right-hand man. Together we can do more than you could by yourself.'

'That's true,' I murmur. 'But could I trust you?'

'I give my word that I will be obedient, and my word is as strong now as it was ten years ago.'

'But two Paucar Wami's would be confusing.'

'Slap on your paint and wig and be Al Jeery.'

'I won't – can't – kill as myself. You'd have to don the disguise.'

'Very well. Your will is mine, O great and noble Caesar.'

'And cut the wise-cracks,' I snap, returning to the kitchen.

'That may prove more troublesome,' he chuckles. 'But for you, Al m'boy, I will try. Now, where do you keep the weapons?'

We prowl the night like a pair of panthers, gliding silently above and around the chaos on the streets, observing, monitoring, interceding when I judge fit. I'd forgotten how swift and ethereal my father can be. His feet barely seem to touch the roof-tops and pavements. Sometimes, as we're moving, I close my eyes and it's impossible to know he's there.

His fingers twitch occasionally as we study the fighting, and I know he'd love to be in the thick of it, cutting loose, making up for the years he's missed. My father was created for one purpose only, to kill. Holding himself in check at a time like this, when the opportunities for murder are countless, must be torture. But he remains true to his word, acting only when I say, restraining himself when we strike.

We pull rioters off three cops who've been detached from their unit, and guide them to safety. We spy a leering man leading two children down an alley. His intentions are sickly clear. We stop him before he assaults them and crucify him to a door, using nails from a nearby crate.

The night air's hot and smoky. Sweat has drenched the back of my T-shirt but not my father's. He's as cool as ever, breathing in the thick, toxic air as if it was blowing fresh off a mountain.

We've been on patrol for almost two hours and still haven't killed. I sense Wami's growing impatience. I'd like to feed him a victim, to ensure he doesn't snap and go off on a slaughter spree, but I'm not going to single out anyone for execution unless they truly deserve it.

Finally, half an hour later, we spot a gang of five youths torturing an old man. An old lady, presumably his wife, lies on the street beside him, raped and butchered, her naked body a bloody, shredded mess.

'Now?' Wami asks politely, testing one of the knives he took from my kitchen.

'Now,' I agree darkly.

'Let me go first,' he says, moving to the edge of the roof, pocketing the pair of sunglasses I gave him to camouflage his green eyes. 'You pick off any runners.'

There's a pipe down the wall which I expect him to use, but he merely steps off the edge and drops three storeys, landing like a cat, ready for combat. I'm tempted to leap like him – anything he can do . . . – but I don't want to end up in hospital with a broken leg, so I take the pipe.

By the time I hit the ground, two of the gang are down, clutching their throats, dying. Wami moves upon the third, blocks a knife as it's thrust at his face, ducks, grabs the young man's penis and testicles – he's naked from the waist down, his lower body red from his rape of the old woman – and rips them off.

As Wami drops the sexual organs and moves on to his fourth victim, the fifth man makes a break for freedom. He rushes past the spot where I'm standing in the shadows. I stretch out a hand, a sharp blade held rigid between my fingers, and press it to the side of his neck. His momentum forces the blade in deep and he hits the ground heavily, blood spraying from the opened artery, limbs thrashing.

Leaving the dying boy, I check to make sure my father doesn't need any further assistance – he's put the fourth teen down, and has returned to the third, to feed him his severed manhood – then go to see if the old man's alive. He is, but one of his eyes has been gouged out and there are ugly wounds to his chest and stomach.

'Easy,' I whisper as he tries to struggle to his feet.

'Elsa?' he wheezes, gazing at me imploringly.

'Dead.' I hold him down, trying to judge the severity of his wounds.

He goes limp in my arms. 'They wanted money,' he sobs. 'I gave it. But it . . . wasn't enough. They dragged us out and . . .'

'Save your breath. You're going to live, but only if you –'

'No,' he gasps. 'Don't want to. Not without . . . Elsa.'

I hesitate, but only briefly. 'Are you sure?' I ask. He locks gazes with me, sees the intent in my eyes, and smiles peacefully. I make it quick and painless, then lay him beside his wife and cover her body with scraps of clothes I find lying nearby.

'A touching scene,' Wami murmurs. He's standing directly behind me.

'I thought you'd spend more time on your playthings,' I retort, wiping my hands clean on my trousers.

'I am rusty. I hit them too hard. But not to worry — the night is young and there are more to be killed. I will find my touch before we are through.' He steps over the dead pair and studies my face. 'You killed impassively, Al m'boy. Very commendable.'

'I did what I had to,' I answer simply.

He clears his throat. 'It may be an imprudent question, but can I ask how many you have despatched since taking to the streets all those years ago?'

'I gave up counting.'

'A hundred? Two hundred? More?'

'I don't keep track. I kill when I have to but I take no pleasure from it.'

Wami can't hide a look of disappointment. 'Not as advanced

as I thought,' he mutters. 'You live with death but do not love it. To truly be me, you should savour each murder. To kill mechanically is not enough. You must kill lovingly.'

'If I did, I'd become you for real. Then I'd care about nothing but the killing, and the reason for putting myself through this would be lost.'

'What *is* that reason?' Wami asks.

I tug gently on the finger hanging from my neck. 'You haven't remembered any more about Bill Casey?'

'The policeman,' my father sighs. 'I thought about him in the quiet moments since the priests resurrected me, but my memories are no clearer now than before.'

'When you recall who he is, you'll know why I had to become you.' With that, I spin away and take to the rooftops again, leaving him to make of the puzzle what he will.

We monitor, intervene, break-up and kill until the sun rises and Saturday dawns. We keep conversation to a minimum, conferring only when it's time to take life. I sense Wami wracking his thoughts for memories of Bill, but he asks no more about him. I'm not sure how many we execute between us – I allow the memory of one kill to blend with the next – but somewhere between fifteen and twenty. All guilty. All deserving of their fate.

As the sun rises and the east quietens for the first time since the outbreak of violence, my father returns my sunglasses and wig, and says he'd better head back underground. 'The *villacs* will not approve of my being out all night, but they will accept it. If I remain absent much longer, however, they might recall me by that most irritating of devices — extinction.'

'They can kill you even when they aren't near you?' I ask. 'Yes.'

'Ever worked out how they do it?'

'I would not be scraping my knee to them if I had,' he

growls. 'You will know if I unearth the source of their power, because the streets will be lined with white-robed corpses.'

'What do you think their next move will be now that I've rejected them again?'

My father shrugs. 'They have set one sector of the city on fire in a bid to bend you to their will. Perhaps they will burn the rest.'

'It won't make a difference.'

'That is their affair, not mine.' He offers his hand. I consider refusing it, but he kept his word during the night and his assistance proved invaluable. 'Our paths will cross again soon, Al m'boy,' he predicts as we shake hands.

'I don't doubt it.'

'I hope we can run together again. This night has been a pleasure.'

'We'll see,' I mumble, releasing his hand and lowering my gaze. 'You helped me, and I'm grateful, but you have to understand, I'm not like you. I only do this because . . .'

Looking up, I stop. I'm alone. Wami has slipped away, unseen and unheard. Sighing, I sheathe my weapons, wipe my hands clean of the worst of the blood, and head for home, to shower and sleep, until it's time to rise again and kill.

SIX – CRY OF THE HARPY

I'm woken by my phone. Groaning, I answer to find Ama Situwa on the other end. 'I tried calling you last night but your cell was switched off. I was worried sick. I would have come looking for you, but there are police blocks everywhere.'

'I'm fine,' I sigh, rubbing my eyes and yawning.

'Where were you?'

'On the streets. Damage limitation.'

'I think the Snakes started the riots.'

'I know they did.'

'I'm scared, Al. If they can provoke something like this . . .'

I walk through to the kitchen and run the tap. I'm reaching for a glass when I recall the pollution and kill the flow. 'Any news about the water?' I ask.

'I heard a reporter say it should be safe to drink by early afternoon, though the mayor's advised people not to take any chances.' A pause. 'Are things as bad as the media make out?'

'Yes.' Then, changing the subject, 'How's life with Cafran?'

'Wonderful. We're getting on famously. I've rediscovered my waitressing skills too. I did a full shift last night, though I kept ducking out to call you.'

'Don't bother about me. I can take care of myself.'

'I can't help it. Maybe I should come over and . . .'

I talk Ama out of that idea and promise to keep in touch. When she finally lets me go, I return to bed and slip back asleep immediately.

The riots continue through the weekend. Gangs claim streets by breaking up the roads and erecting crude barricades to keep out traffic. Booby traps and ambushes are set for police or soldiers unfortunate enough to be ordered in. Buildings are annexed, looted or gutted with fire. Fights flare hourly. The polluted water's no longer working its antagonizing charms, but by this stage most people don't need a chemical irritant to make their blood boil. Their homes have been destroyed, their friends and relatives injured or killed. They're fired-up for revenge. Some have the good sense to drop everything and get out, but most remain, hackles up, teeth bared, hell bent on giving as good as they get.

I'm kept busy assisting those who need it, guiding refugees who want to leave to safety, cracking down on looters, killing those intent on evil.

I've tuned my TV sets to local news stations and leave them switched on when I'm home, keeping abreast of developments. As I eat a late Sunday dinner, Stuart Jordan, our crooked-as-they-come police commissioner, pops up, wearing the grim but stoic expression he's been perfecting since the riots erupted. He promises a swift end to the violence and says he's in the process of drafting in more soldiers. If the rioters don't play ball, he vows to level them, along with as much of the east as he needs to. A reporter asks if he's worried about injuring the innocent. He growls, 'In war, there are no innocents!' With luck the quote will return to haunt him in the next election.

As the report continues, I note the worst-hit areas, where

I'd be best employed. To my amusement, there's a short piece about 'the dreaded Paucar Wami', warning people to be on the lookout. There are CCTV shots of me in action last night, killing two men who lobbed home-made bombs through the windows of a church full of people being treated for injuries. No mention of the church – the men are portrayed as upright citizens – just a number of pictures of me callously finishing them off.

I can't complain. With surveillance cameras in place all over the city, I should have been highlighted long before now, and would have been if not for the fact that I have allies in high places — Ford Tasso and the *villacs*. I'm surprised this piece made it through. The editor must be new to the game. I'm sure someone will explain the rules to him before he has time to run a repeat.

Stepping clear of the furniture, I warm up. My body's taken a lot of punishment these last sixty-odd hours and I'm feeling the strain — I'd give my back teeth for a full massage. Then I return to the fiery cauldron of the streets, hugging the walls and roofs, slipping by and through the baying crowds, looking for trouble and moving to quell it, resting only when I have to, thinking and operating as a machine.

Most of the rioters have retired by three in the morning. Ambulances and fire brigades move in to mop up and are allowed to operate unopposed. Stuart Jordan had the uncommonly good sense not to send his armed squads in. There must be new advisers on his staff. I continue my rounds for a couple of hours, enjoying the relative serenity, before circling back to my apartment. My legs drag as I climb the fire escape. Bed will be a blessing after this.

A note has been pushed through my letter box. No name or address. Frowning, I slit it open and look for a name at the bottom — Eugene Davern. My eyes slide back to the top and I read quickly. He wishes me well and offers his sympathies for any friends or relatives I may have lost in the fighting. He says these riots are good for nobody, and if there's any way he can help, I'm to let him know and he'll do what he can. 'The prejudices of the past need no longer apply,' he writes with fake sincerity. 'It's time for our people to come together and forge a new, lasting, peaceful union. I extend the hand of friendship — accept it, and let's put an end to this madness.'

I crumple the letter into a ball and toss it in the bin. Davern must have guessed that the Snakes started the riots, and figures they'll come out of this as the dominant force in the east. The letter's an invitation to join forces with him against the Troops.

I consider letting Ford Tasso know about Davern's overtures. He's sitting back smugly because he doesn't think there's any chance of the Kluxers and Snakes forming an alliance. He might be more willing to help if he knew Davern wanted to strike a deal with his traditional enemies. Alternatively, it might send him off in a panic after the Kluxers, leading to riots elsewhere. That would divert Stuart Jordan's forces, making it easier for the Snakes to take control.

All this intrigue is giving me a headache. I'm not cut out for it. All I want is to smoke out Bill Casey and get even with him. Why the hell can't the clowns of this demented political circus look elsewhere for a ringmaster?

Night again. I shave my skull and face before heading out. I haven't had a chance the last few days, so bristles fall thickly into the basin. I slip into a fresh pair of jeans and a clean T-shirt. The local laundromat was firebombed in the riots, so I do my laundry in the small sink in the kitchen. I wring out the socks and T-shirts and hang them on a rack inside the living room to dry.

After a simple meal I grab a few knives, reload my .45 and let myself out. I'm not expecting much trouble – word has leaked that Stuart Jordan's planning a Tuesday raid, so most of the rioters are holding themselves in check for the big showdown – but the first few hours turn out to be some of my most testing. Lone agents – burglars, muggers, rapists – have taken advantage of the lull and scuttle around like malevolent spiders, hitting the weak while the strong aren't looking. I have my hands full keeping track of them.

I take a break about one in the morning, grab some sandwiches and a Coke from a busted vending machine, and sit on the shell of a burnt-out car. The street lights are out – much of the east is in darkness – and I have as clear a view of the night sky as I'll ever get in this city. I'm admiring the stars when a woman shrieks. As I come alert, there's another cry, softer this time, and I relax, recognizing the call of a feasting Harpy. Finishing off the last sandwich, I go looking for the cannibalistic ladies.

I find the three old women in a side door of a shopping precinct, feasting on the remains of a cop who must have been dumped there during the weekend. Jennifer Abbots stands nearby, keeping watch, patiently waiting for them to finish. 'Good evening, Mrs Abbots,' I call as I approach, not wishing to startle her.

'Mr Wami,' she smiles. 'I'm glad you haven't been harmed.'

'You know what they say – only the good die young.' We stand in silence for a while, watching the Harpies eat. 'You should choose more carefully next time,' I advise her. 'Letting them feed on a cop is a bad idea. His colleagues will take it poorly if they find him half-eaten.'

'I know,' she sighs, 'but there's no stopping them when they get the scent. Luckily I found a lot of bottles filled with gasoline nearby – some anarchist's stash, I suppose – and I've borrowed a few to soak him with before I set him alight. That should destroy the evidence.'

I nod approvingly. 'Managing OK otherwise?'

'Yes. The girls were keen to get out all weekend, but I held them in until the trouble died down. One of Rettie's teeth played up last week. I had to take her to a dentist for the first time in years. He was shocked by the bloodstains and scraps of flesh. He'd have called in the police, but Mr Clarke bribed him.' She frowns. 'I can't say I approve of bribery, but in this case I had to make an exception.'

I hide a smile. It's OK in Jennifer's mind for her sister and Harpy friends to strip the dead of their flesh, but bribery's a serious offence.

'Did she have to get the tooth removed?' I ask.

'No, just filled.' As we're talking, Rettie finishes her meal and comes over to squat beside her sister. 'Rettie,' Jennifer coos, 'show Mr Wami your tooth.'

The Harpy tilts her head and opens her mouth wide. To be polite, I peer into her red maw and pass favourable comment on the gold filling.

'Mr Clarke made him use gold,' Jennifer chuckles. 'He says it's more ladylike.'

'I must meet this Mr Clarke of yours sometime,' I smile. 'He sounds like a character.'

Rettie closes her mouth, pulls a book out of the folds of her clothes and plays with it, opening the covers and peering at the words as if she can read. Jennifer yanks the book from her and wipes blood stains from the pages. 'Bad girl, Rettie!' she snaps. 'This is Mr Clarke's. You know you're not supposed to take it.'

'Perhaps she'll make a scholar yet,' I laugh, then spot the spine and pause. 'Can I have a look at that?' Jennifer passes the book to me and continues to scold her sister. I study the title – *Heart of Darkness* – and run a finger over the creased cover. It's old and worn. I turn to the title page but it's been ripped out. 'This looks valuable,' I mutter.

'It probably is,' Jennifer says. 'It's a first edition, I think.'

My fingers freeze and the night seems to darken around me. 'What makes you think that?'

'Most of Mr Clarke's books are first editions. He's a collector. He'll be furious at Rettie for taking it. Maybe I can slip it back before he realizes.'

My head spins. I gaze at the Harpy by my feet and a switch clicks. 'Is "Rettie" short for "Margaret"?' I ask, my voice a broken whisper.

'Yes,' Jennifer says, rubbing her sister's head, gently tugging her hair to chide her for taking their friend's book.

'Your name before you married — was it Jennifer Crowe?'

Jennifer stares at me, mildly surprised. 'How did you know?'

I start to tremble. Rettie is Margaret Crowe, the girl Paucar Wami kidnapped all those years ago, the girl a tormented teenager was meant to kill in exchange for his doomed sister's life.

'What's Mr Clarke's first name?' I wheeze.

'William,' she says, and I laugh sickly.

'Your friend . . . Mr Clarke . . . William,' I croak. 'Does he ever make a mistake and refer to himself as *Bill*?'

SEVEN – KILLER'S SECRETS

Jennifer doesn't object when I ask if I can accompany the Harpies home to meet *Mr Clarke*. I tell her I think I know him, and want to say hello. She has no reason to suspect my real motives. She packs the bloody ladies into her small car while I fetch my motorbike, then leads the way across the city, out to the suburbs, driving slowly in order not to lose me.

I keep my thoughts blank while trailing her. I warn myself not to get excited. It's possible that the bibliophile William Clarke isn't the bibliophile Bill Casey. But I know in my heart that I've found him. After all these years, a mad cannibal has shown me the way. If I wasn't so terrified by the prospect of the encounter, I'd howl with glee at the absurdity of it.

After a long, fretful drive – I keep thinking the car will crash or explode, taking the secret of Bill's whereabouts with it – we pull up at a sorry-looking excuse for a house, set in the middle of nowhere, surrounded by industrial wasteland. I gaze wonderingly at the boarded-up windows, the corrugated iron roof, the warped door which doesn't quite meet with the frame most of the way round. Why has Bill chosen to hole-up in a dump like this?

'It's not so bad inside,' Jennifer says. She lets the Harpies out and they amble around to the back. 'It's cold in the winter but dry. And nobody comes here. That's the most important thing.'

'Is Mr Clarke there now?' I ask, fingers tickling the handle of the knife jammed inside my belt.

'He should be. He doesn't go out much. He's a lonely old man. I believe you're the first visitor he's had in all the years he's lived here.'

'And I'll be the last,' I mutter, too low for Jennifer to hear. 'Could you do me a favour and take the girls back to your place tonight? I'd like to have *William* to myself. We've a lot of catching up to do.'

'I suppose,' she says hesitantly. 'I don't like changing their routine but I guess it can't hurt this once.'

'I appreciate it.' I don't know what she'll do when she returns and finds her friend's brains splattered across the floor, but I can't say I care. As much as I like Jennifer, the extermination of Bill Casey takes precedence over everything.

I wait until she's rounded up the Harpies and driven away before pushing the creaky door open and entering. I'm clutching the copy of *Heart of Darkness* in one hand and a knife in the other. The house is dimly lit and smells of blood and sweat. I explore the downstairs area quietly, drifting from room to room. No doors in any of the frames. Three beds are set close to each other in the largest room. Another is packed with spare sheets, pillows, towels and other such items. All the rooms feature laden bookshelves.

'Jennifer?' comes a tremulous voice from the top of the stairs.

My fingers tighten on the knife at the sound of the voice, which I recognize instantly. Moving to the side of the stairs, I wait for him to descend. My heart's beating more quickly then usual. I concentrate on slowing it down. I want to be

as cool as Bill was when he faced me ten years ago and
admitted responsibility for the destruction of my life.

'Jennifer?' he asks again. A long pause. Then footsteps,
slow, coming down the creaking stairs. 'I have nothing of
value. Nor am I armed. You may take what you wish, as
worthless as it is, or if you're hungry and looking for a place
to stay, perhaps I can . . .' He trails off as he reaches the foot
of the stairs and peers at me through the gloom. 'Who's
there?' he whispers.

I step forward, revealing myself, and he draws back, eyes
widening, hands shooting to his wrinkled mouth. He's much
thinner than when we last met, and stooped with age. His
hair's grey and unkempt. He looks ill.

'Hello Bill,' I hiss, closing the gap between us, until he's
backed up against a wall. I lay a hand on either side of his
arms, imprisoning him. 'Remember me?'

'Snakes!' he croaks, eyes watering as he gazes with horror
at my tattoos. 'Please . . . don't . . . not the snakes . . .
please . . .'

'Forget the snakes,' I snarl. 'Forget the bald head. Forget
the –' I remove my green contact lenses. '– eyes. Look at *me*.
Do you remember *me*?'

The old man gradually stops shaking. His tears dry. 'Of
course,' he sighs. 'I've been waiting ten years for you to find
me. How have you been, Al?'

I step away, disgusted by his amiable tone. 'Don't *Al* me,
you fucker! Do you remember what you did, how you
screwed me over?'

His smile fades. 'For a moment, I didn't. Sorry. I forgot
I'm your enemy, that you've come to kill me. The mind deterior-
ates when you're my age. Oh well, I've no one but myself
to blame. You may execute me now if it suits you.' Closing
his eyes, he spreads his arms, Christ-like, offering himself.

I almost kill him – my knife quivers in my hand, thirsting

for blood – but it's too soon. I need to hear what he has to say in his defence. I have to make him talk — make him scream.

'You don't seem surprised to see me,' I grunt, lowering my knife.

'I've been expecting you every day for a decade,' he replies. 'I knew you'd find me. No matter how old and feeble I got, I never feared death, because I knew it wouldn't take me until I'd sorted things out with you. I could have lived a hundred years if you hadn't come.'

'Open your eyes,' I growl. 'I want you to look at me when you die.'

'As you wish.' His lids open and his eyes settle on the finger hanging from my neck. His left hand twitches. Next he studies my tattoos and scalp, and frowns. 'I'd heard about the get-up. Can't say I approve. It doesn't suit you, Al. Why do you go about like this, calling yourself that terrible name?'

'You know who Paucar Wami was?'

He shrugs. 'He was a killer. I never worked out whether he was real or a bogeyman, or why you chose to model yourself after him.'

My breath catches. He doesn't remember! I always dreaded this, that he'd forget his reason for ruining my life. I prepared myself against the eventuality, but it still comes as a shock. For a moment I want to grab him by the neck and choke the truth out of him, but that would be a waste of time. People who don't remember the Ayuamarcans can't have their memories jogged. But there are other ways to get to the facts. I have to be sly.

'What's upstairs?' I ask.

'My living quarters. The ladies reside down here. I don't allow anybody up, not even Jennifer when I'm sick and can't get out of bed.' He grins coyly. 'But I'll let *you* up, Al.'

'Lead the way,' I nod, and follow him up the stairs,

matching him step for step, knife by my side, ready to cut him down if he makes a false move. I stop when I get to the top and stare at the walls, all of which have been crudely painted with snakes. There are serpents of every kind, colour and length. Some are incredibly detailed, beautifully portrayed. Others are childish squiggles.

'My scaly companions,' Bill chuckles, moving to the closest wall to stroke the coils of a long boa constrictor.

'Did you paint them?' I ask.

'Yes. It's how I pass the time. I'd go crazy without a hobby. I've white-washed these walls three or four times and started again from scratch. I suppose it's an unhealthy obsession – it feeds my snake-haunted nightmares – but it keeps me busy. Keeps me sane.' He laughs when he catches my expression. 'I know what you're thinking — a guy who paints snakes all day long has to be crazy. And that's true. But there are different shades of craziness. I've had the kind where all I do is storm around, screaming and harming myself. This kind is infinitely preferable.'

He walks to a doorway at the end of the corridor. I follow edgily, nervous of the snakes. I pause suspiciously at the entrance. Just because Bill's crazy (there's no doubt about that, he's not putting on an act), it doesn't mean he's stupid. He may have set a trap. But I don't spot anything to be afraid of. This is a simple bedroom with a thick mattress laid on the floor, a chair in one corner, shelves to the ceiling loaded with books.

'Welcome to my palace,' Bill says, squatting on the edge of the bed and gesturing towards the chair. I remain standing.

'Is this place wired?' I ask.

'Of course. We're off the beaten track but we've been running on electricity for a long time. You don't think . . .' He groans. 'Oh. You mean wired for explosives.' He shakes his head. 'I have my old tools in the cellar, bombs and bugs, but I no longer play with them. I lack the enthusiasm. I don't read much either, except to the ladies, but I never could bring myself to get rid of the books.'

'Speaking of which . . .' I toss the Conrad novel to him. He catches it, studies the cover and smiles ruefully.

'I bet you got this off Rettie. She enjoys my recitations the most. I never read this to them – their lives are dark enough – but I keep it downstairs with the bulk of my collection. She must have swiped it when I wasn't looking.'

'You should have blown up the books with the rest of the house,' I tell him. 'They're how I knew you were alive. I'd have surrendered my grip on life a long time ago if I hadn't noticed they were missing. And now they've led me to you.'

'A costly vice,' he agrees, laying the book down. Then he says quietly, 'Are you going to kill me now, Al?'

'In time. I want to talk first. There are things you must tell me. About the past, your life, the snakes.'

'Don't ask about *them*,' he snaps. 'I won't talk about *them*.'

'Oh, I think you might,' I chuckle and drag the tip of my knife along the crumbling wall.

Bill laughs. 'I'm too old and crazy to be threatened. What could you do to hurt me?' He unbuttons his shirt, revealing a chest riven with scars and burn marks. 'I've punished myself beyond the point where I even feel. You can put me to the test but it won't work. Nothing can loosen my tongue if I choose to hold it.'

I look from his tortured chest to the drawings on the walls, then stare into his eyes. I grin viciously and hiss, 'I can feed you to the snakes.'

His face whitens and he buttons up the shirt, fingers trembling. I've found his weak spot. He's mine.

'Where do you want to start?' he mutters.

Drawing out the chair, I sit, cross my legs, lock gazes with him, and say softly, 'Tell me about Jane.'

He wasn't expecting that. His face tics and the trembling of his feet on the floor is like a drum snare. '*Jane?* What's she got to do with anything? I thought you'd want to know about the blind priests and why I betrayed you.'

'I already know. In fact I'm willing to bet I know more about it than you.' I lean forward challengingly. '*Do* you remember why you did it?'

'The snakes,' he whispers, eyes far away. 'You were a servant of the snakes. I tried to destroy them. By harming you, I hoped . . .' His senses seem to swim back into place. 'No, not exactly. There was someone I meant to hurt by exploiting you, but I've forgotten who he was. That's the madness, I guess.'

'So tell me about Jane.'

The veil of fear sweeps across his face again. 'Why?' he groans. 'She has nothing to do with this. That was long in the past, long before I set after you.'

'Tell me what you remember about Jane and her death,' I persist. 'I know what happened but I want your version of it.'

'You *know?*' He stares at me, and the terror in his eyes surpasses any I've seen before, even in the faces of those I've killed. His fear's so great, I almost take pity and spare him the painful trip down memory lane. But I need to hear him say that his sister was killed and that's why he set out to destroy me. I might even squeeze out his reasons for coming after me and not my father, though that would be a bonus, not a necessity. I'll settle for the confirmation.

'You were a teenager,' I start him off. 'You'd finished school. You were living with your mother, stepfather, brother and sister. It was summer. You were leading an ordinary life. Then . . .'

'The snakes entered my life,' Bill croaks. His hands have crept together and his fingers squeeze and tear at each other while he speaks. 'They made me do awful things. I saved lives. I mugged, stole, bullied – worse – but I saved others from the snakes by serving them. Can a villain be a hero? Is a man wicked if he performs a lesser act of evil to prevent a greater one?'

'I'm not interested in a moral debate,' I growl. 'I don't know if you were good or bad, hero or demon, and I don't care. Tell me about Jane and Margaret Crowe.'

'Rettie . . .' He smiles sadly. 'I visited her often in the nursing home before I went into hiding. It was so sad, what happened to her and the others. I kept an eye on Jennifer and Rose when they took the survivors into their care. It was clear that they'd need help, so I befriended Jennifer, using a pseudonym. I knew it was risky, that you might trace me through her even though she didn't know my real name, but I had to do what I could to protect poor Rettie.'

'Wami kidnapped Rettie and Jane, didn't he?'

Bill frowns. 'It was the snakes. They hid behind a man's features but I don't know whose. You think it was Paucar Wami?'

'It doesn't matter. Someone kidnapped them. Told you to kill Rettie or he'd kill Jane. You couldn't, so he murdered her. Right?' My fingers grip the handle of the knife. I'm readying myself to bring the decade of self-torment to an end. I might kill myself as soon as he's dead, or spin off into madness even deeper than his. I don't know. It's impossible to look that far ahead. But first the execution. That much I'm sure about.

Bill's shaking his head, crying, confused. 'Jane,' he sobs. 'I loved Jane. I did it . . . for her . . . to save . . . I'd have done anything to bring her back . . .' He falls off the bed and crawls to where I sit impassively. Grabs my legs and howls. 'Hear my confession! Please . . . I can't stand it any longer . . . will you . . .?'

'Yes,' I answer bleakly, and lay the edge of my blade to the dry flesh of his mottled throat. 'I'll grant absolution as well.'

Bill's features relax and he sobs gratefully. I let him cry, waiting patiently. I've all the time in the world now that the moment has come. I'm in no rush. Let him make his confession and go to meet his maker clutching the illusion of spiritual cleanliness.

'The snakes kidnapped Rettie and Jane. They told me to kill Rettie to spare Jane. I tried all I could think of to defy them. I even tried to kidnap you.'

'*Me?*' I interrupt, surprised. 'What the hell had I to do with it?'

'You were important to the snakes, even as a baby. I tried to steal you, to trade you for the girls, but it didn't work out. I was left with no choice. I had to do as the snakes bid. I couldn't let Jane die.'

Bill stops shaking and his eyes close. His chin drops a few inches. I have to lower the knife before he inadvertently slits his throat on it.

'It happened here,' he says softly. 'The snakes brought her to this house. That's why I came back. There was no roof or upper floor then. I had the floor restored and a roof put on when I returned. But back then it was a shell.

'The snakes tied her to a chair in the living room,' he continues. 'They shaved her bald – like you – and blind-folded and gagged her. They made me strip naked, made me torment her with weapons and . . . myself. You understand?'

'He made you rape her?' I frown.

Bill flinches, but nods. 'It was a living nightmare, all the worse because a sick part of me enjoyed it. That's why the snakes chose me — they sensed evil inside me and they wanted to coax it out. When it was finished and they could wring no more entertainment from me, they made me kill her.' Bill weeps pitifully.

'This doesn't make sense,' I mutter, then prod his chest with the tip of the knife. 'Hey, old man, look at me.' He doesn't respond. 'Look up now!' I jab him and his head lifts wearily. 'What you've told me doesn't tally. They wanted you to kill her but you didn't. You couldn't. That's why your sister was slaughtered. You didn't kill Rettie. She's here, alive, with the Harpies.'

'Yes,' Bill says. 'Naughty Rettie. She took my book. I must scold her, but not severely. She doesn't mean to be bold. It's just her nature.'

'Then what's this crap about killing her? If you're playing for sympathy . . .'

He scowls. 'This is my last confession. You think I'd waste it on games?'

'Then what —'

'It was simple,' he interrupts. 'Rettie's life for Jane's. As confused and desperate as I was, I did as they ordered. Jane was my sister. I couldn't let her die, even if I had to torture, rape and murder to save her. I knew there could be no forgiveness. I meant to kill myself afterwards, the only fit punishment I could think of. But I had to do it. Jane . . .'

He breaks down in a fit of tears. I let him cry, trying to work out the angles but failing. As his fit passes, without needing to be prompted, he wipes the tears away and says hollowly, 'The snakes swapped them.'

My eyes narrow. 'What?'

'The girls were similar in looks and build. With her hair shaved, her eyes blindfolded, her mouth gagged, dressed in Rettie's clothes, I mistook Jane for the other girl.'

My hand drops and I pull back from Bill, eyes filling with horror.

'The snakes gave me a girl to torment. To save Jane, I killed the one they put before me, thinking it was Rettie. But it wasn't. The snakes switched them.' He looks up at me and grins the grin of a man who's been to hell and is trapped there still. 'I tortured, raped and butchered Jane, mistaking her for Rettie Crowe. When it was over, the snakes revealed the truth, then stood by and cackled while I wept over the bloody remains of my poor, damned sister.'

With that the old man finishes, closes his eyes and calmly waits for me to put him out of his misery.

part four

sons of the sun

ONE – AFTERMATH

I push my bike to its utmost limits and chew up the streets at ninety miles an hour, a hundred, faster. I defy red lights and one-way systems, take bends without braking, challenging the city to blast my wheels from under me and send me crunching to my death.

The police are soon after me, sirens wailing. They set up road-blocks which I dodge automatically, brain ticking over mechanically, analysing the routes ahead, anticipating the blocks, detouring before I come upon them. Part of me wants to ride into an ambush and go down in a hail of gunfire like a Wild West outlaw, but another part resists and pleads with me to cling to life. While the two halves wrestle with one another, I fly one step ahead of death, ready to stop, turn and greet it with open arms if my darker desires win out.

Thoughts of Bill whistle between the spokes of my wheels. They're faster than my bike – faster than anything – but they don't overtake me, content to tag along, tickling the back of my neck, whispering, 'No escape, not even in death.'

I turn into a long open stretch and spot a burning barricade. This is an entry point to the east, blocked off by the locals. Nobody's manning it this early in the morning. As soon as I see the flames, my decision is made. With a suicidal grin, I aim for the centre of the mound of old tyres, tables, wardrobes and chairs, and hit the gas.

I'm doing eighty-seven when I hit. I close my eyes as I plough through the molten mess of rubber, wire and wood. Splinters strike my hands and cheeks. Something hot singes my left ear. The air is thick and unbreatheable.

I burst free of the barricade, still alive. Irate, I brush glowing embers from my face and scalp, then probe the damage with my fingertips. Lots of cuts and nicks. A small chunk gone from the lobe of my left ear. Otherwise unharmed. Cursing the inadequacies of the fools who built the barricade, I push on, picking up speed again, cutting corners tighter than ever. I've lost the cops — they won't venture this far east. Now it's just me and death in a straight-up contest.

I snake and snarl through the streets, so fast that the houses, shops and signs blur. If I'm to die, this is as good a place as any. I'm glad it's early and that the riots have confined most people to their homes. There's almost nobody on the streets, so when I crash, I'll hopefully not harm anyone else.

Finally, as I'm beginning to think that my bike's conspiring against me, I hit a dead dog as I scream around a corner. My wheels choke, the bike coughs and suddenly I'm flying. My bike spins lengthways through the air, back wheel over front, shattering the iron grille and window of a shop, continuing into the store, cutting a destructive swathe through the display. I pitch along next to it, but smash into what's left of the grille and bounce back to the pavement. Air whumps out of me, my head whips backwards and I snap into blackness. *Yes!*

No.

My bike's finished, but I'm not. I return to consciousness within minutes and struggle into a sitting position, groaning with agony, hating this world for clinging onto me. As an alarm blares uselessly – no police will answer – I assess the damage. Grazed elbows and knees – the material of my jacket and trousers cut to shreds around the bloody protuberances – and a deep gash across my forehead, from which blood runs thickly. My back feels as if a sumo wrestler used me as a trampoline, but incredibly I can't feel any broken bones.

I stand, and though I'm light-headed and wobbly on my feet, I don't fall. I let the gash in my head bleed, hoping I'll lose too much blood and collapse, but when I lift a hand and test it, I feel it scabbing over and I know I'm going to live.

What the hell does a guy have to do to die around here?

With a wry chuckle, I accept the world's refusal to acknowledge my deathwish. As much as I long to embrace the eternal darkness, it's clear that some higher force in this universe thinks I should hang on for a while yet, and who am I to argue with a power like that?

I stumble through the wreckage of the shop and check my bike. It's a write-off. The frame's buckled, the handlebars lie somewhere under a mound of leather jackets and gloves, the tank's busted, wires hang exposed, engine parts bleed pitifully. I find a pen and paper on a counter and scribble a note, promising to pay for the damages. I pin it to the wall with a knife, then hobble out and start the long, painful walk home.

A shower. Caked blood rinses away, turning the water at my feet a dark reddish brown. Hot becomes cold. I stay where I am, head propped against the wall, letting the chill of the spray numb the worst of the pain.

Eventually I turn off the water and crawl, dripping wet, to bed. I can't lie on my back – too painful – so I turn facedown and shut my eyes. Sleep isn't on the agenda, but it's easier to lie peacefully than to sit or stand.

I remain prostrate for most of the day. It's cloudy outside, and it rains lightly in the early afternoon, the first shower since April. The planned Tuesday raid by Stuart Jordan's forces fails to materialize – maybe the rain put him off – and it turns into a damp squib of a day. People mop up the worst of the carnage, shop in stores on the outskirts which have escaped the riots, and grumble about the rain.

My cell rings. It's the third time someone's called. I ignored it before, but now I reach over and answer. 'Hello?' I croak.

'I phoned earlier but I guess you were out.' Ama.

'I was here. Didn't feel like talking.'

'Are you OK?'

'Not really. I'm tired. Of everything. Would you do me a favour?'

'What?'

'Hire someone to kill me.'

There's a long pause. 'Is this a joke?'

'No.'

Another pause, then, 'I'm coming to see you.'

'No, don't . . .' I stop. She's already hung up. Groaning softly, I drop the phone and wonder whether or not to let Ama in when she arrives.

Some time later I've just about decided not to admit Ama, when she knocks and calls my name. My legs swing over the edge of the bed and next thing I know, I'm creeping to the door to open it.

'Jesus!' she gasps at the sight of me.

'No,' I chuckle hoarsely. 'Just me.'

'What happened?' she asks, pushing in and turning on the light, standing on her toes to examine the cut on my forehead.

'Came off my bike.'

'You crashed? When? Are you hurt? Have you seen a doctor?'

'I'm fine,' I scowl. 'There's nothing broken. I'm bruised

and winded, but with a bit more rest I'll be good as ever, worse luck.'

I retreat to my bedroom, where I sit tenderly on the bed and prod glumly at my wounds. Ama follows slowly, frowning. 'What do you mean, "worse luck"?'

'I'm sick of living. I wanted to crash. I wish my neck was broken. My spine. My skull. I want to be dead, Ama. I can't take this life any longer.'

'Al,' she says quietly, crouching. 'What's wrong?'

'For ten years I've hated and hunted — for nothing. He was pitiful, not evil. I thought I'd imagined the worst, but the truth was worse than anything I dreamt. I understand him now, and that's the most godawful feeling in the world.'

Ama takes my hands. 'You're not making sense, Al.'

'That's the trouble,' I moan. 'It *does* make sense. For ten years it didn't. I was able to hide in madness, thinking it my friend. Now I see clearly, but I don't want to. Better to perish and not see at all.'

'*Al!*' She squeezes my fingers. 'Tell me what happened. Explain. I want to help but I can't if you won't tell me what's wrong.'

I look into her eyes, calm and pure, and realize that I want to tell her. I thought it was a story I'd take to my grave

(*sooner rather than later*)

but now I find myself desperate to share. 'You remember my ex-wife, Ellen?'

'Vaguely. We were friends. She was killed in the Skylight. You came to see me about her. It's how we first met.'

'She was murdered by a woman who was working for Bill Casey. Bill was my best friend, the closest thing I had to a loving father.' I take a breath, put my thoughts in order, then start over. 'I guess it began, for me, with a fishing trip . . .'

*   *   *

I tell Ama the whole story, leaving nothing out — Bill, Paucar Wami, everything. I even tell her of the offer the priests made, for me to share this city with Capac Raimi, and how I turned them down. It takes hours, and I'm still going long after midnight, but I bring her bang up to date, finishing with Bill's revelation and crashing my bike. She's silent for a long time, holding my hands, staring dead ahead, thoughtful. I wait for her to make a comment.

Finally, without glancing at me, she asks, 'How did you feel when you killed him?'

I crack a ghastly smile. 'I didn't.'

Her head shoots round. 'You didn't kill him?'

'I couldn't. Not after what he told me. I tried. I've spent ten years hating him, killing in an attempt to lure him out of hiding, with the sole purpose of executing him. But when I looked into his eyes and saw the insanity, the terror, the *pain* . . . He begged me to kill him – followed me out of the shack, weeping, pleading – but my hands wouldn't lift against him.'

Ama starts to cry, but she's smiling through the tears. 'You took pity on him!' she exclaims, hugging me tight.

'No,' I wince, pushing her away. 'He's suffering more than any man I've seen. Execution would have been a mercy. It's crueller to let him go on, tormented by dreams of snakes, wondering why he destroyed me, hating himself. I let him live because it's worse than killing him, not because I pity the bastard.'

She shakes her head. 'Tell yourself that if you want – you might even believe it – but I see the truth in your eyes. You understand why he did it, that he was tied to his course, just as you've been to yours for ten years, and you forgave him.'

'No!' I shout. 'He killed Nicola Hornyak. One of his servants butchered Ellen. He brought me to my knees, took away everything I valued. I hate him. I let him live to punish him.

I . . .' My throat tightens. My shoulders shake and my eyes fill with tears. 'What have I done? What have I become? Ten years hunting a broken old man who raped and murdered his own sister while trying to save her. Ten years of killing, madness, hate . . .'

'But it's over,' she murmurs. 'You can rest, get out, start clean. It's taken ten years, but you're free, Al. You're *free!*'

I stare at her, then bawl like a child, a scream that's been building inside me for a decade, a howl of rage, despair and loss. Clutching Ama to me like a life buoy, I bury my head in her lap and roar into the folds of her dress. Within seconds it's dark with tears and crumpled from where my teeth close and open, but Ama doesn't push me away. Instead she hugs me and whispers, telling me it's OK to yell and cry. And I do, losing myself in grief, cutting out the world and its hurt, giving myself over to the waves and rhythm of release, until, in the early hours of the morning, my head still in her lap, her arms wrapped tight around me, I can cry no more, and fall into a dark, dreamless, demonless sleep.

When I wake, the nightmare's over. For ten years I've lived it, each day a new instalment of terror, fear, hatred. That dreadful driving force is gone. There's pain, regret, longing – I wish I could have those wasted years back – but no thirst for vengeance. As I lie face-down in the grey gloom of the morning, I mutter into the pillow, 'I am Paucar Wami,' but the words are meaningless. That part of me died during the night and evaporated in the light of the dawn. I need never again stalk the streets or kill as my father. I don't know if I can be the person I was before the madness, but I'm no longer a monster.

I stretch and groan, muscles aching, joints stiff, head on fire. I sit up and the sheets fall away. Ama enters. 'I thought you were going to sleep all day,' she says, setting down a cup of tea and coming over to examine my scar. She's taken off her dress and only wears a long shirt over her underwear. 'How do you feel?'

'Shaken. Sore. Small and weak. But alive.' I grin at her and she must see the realization of freedom in my eyes, because she returns the smile and kisses my forehead, just beneath my scar and above my eyebrows.

'Glad you didn't die in the crash?' she asks softly.

'Yes.' I take her hands and kiss them. 'Thank you.'

'For what — being here?'

'And listening. And understanding. And helping *me* to understand.'

'Don't get sappy on me, Al,' she chuckles.

'Without you, I might never have known that I was free.'

'You would,' she replies. 'It just might have taken you a bit longer to figure it out. So, what do you want to do on your first day of freedom?'

'So many things,' I sigh. 'Put right the wrongs of the last decade. Bring back to life the people I killed. Say sorry to those I terrorized. Get rid of these horrible fucking snakes.' I stroke my tattoos, then my scalp. 'Grow my hair back.'

Ama laughs. 'You can't do all that in a day.' Her smile fades. 'Some of it you'll never be able to do.'

I nod soberly, thinking of the dead.

'But let's not waste time worrying about that,' she snorts. 'What's it to be – a walk in the park? A swim? Maybe you'd like to stand naked in the centre of Swiss Square and roar your delight?'

'I think not.' Scratching my thigh, it suddenly strikes me that I'm naked. Ama must have undressed me. My hands start to pull up the covers, then stop. 'Know what I really want?'

'What?'

'To make love.' Her face darkens. 'I know you love Raimi.

I won't embarrass you by pleading. But for ten years there's been no love in my life. I need to hold and make love to a woman, and I need to do it now. If I have to, I'll go hire a hooker. But I'd prefer it to be you. If you won't, I understand.'

Ama looks away. 'My heart is Capac's. I don't want it to be, but it is.'

'I know. And I won't try and win it, though I wish I could. All I'm asking is that you share this morning with me. If you can bring yourself to lie down with me, just once . . . if you don't think I'm too grotesque . . . if you can forget all the awful things I've done . . .'

She looks at me, eyes soft. 'It's been a long time for me too. And though my heart beats for Capac, I hate him. I want to . . . but . . .' Her jaw firms. 'What the hell. Let's do it. But on the understanding that it's only sex, nothing more.'

Ama pulls her shirt off over her head, then slips off her underwear and stands before me naked, unsmiling. 'I don't know if I can enjoy this,' she warns.

'If you can't, we'll stop,' I promise, then peel back the sheets and invite her into bed. After a moment's hesitation, she joins me, and I toss the sheets over us, covering us, hiding us, bringing us together in the gloom.

Our love-making is slow and gentle. We're clumsy to begin with, but that makes us laugh, taking the tension out of the act, and soon we're moving as one, lips and bodies locked. It lasts a long time, filled with many stops and starts, and by the end we're sweating and panting, despite the leisurely pace of the joining.

Lying on my back, holding her, I kiss her gently. 'Was it OK?'

'Best lay I've had in ten years,' she smirks.

'You know what I mean. Did you enjoy it?'

She nods thoughtfully. 'I feel guilty, but glad at the same time.'

'Has it freed you? Can you forget Raimi and make a new life for yourself?'

She nips my nose and grins. 'You weren't *that* good! I realize I'm not tied as tightly to Capac as I thought, but I'm his by destiny, and even though it's a manufactured destiny, it's not a bond I can break. He'll always be here –' she taps her heart '– whether I want him to be or not.'

'It isn't fair,' I mutter sourly.

'Life wasn't designed to be fair, Al. You know that better than most.'

Ama rises and stretches. She's beautiful naked. I wish I could win her over. I think of reaching for her, loving her again, loving her continuously until I grind away her feelings for Raimi. But I don't have the right to make demands of her, so I let my hand stay where it is, resting on my chest.

'How are the ribs?' Ama asks, slipping on her shirt.

'Tender. Head's worse. Think you could get some painkillers for me?'

'Sure. Any particular brand?'

'I'm easy.'

'Tell me something I don't know!'

I shower while she's gone, water as hot as it gets. My knees and elbows have scabbed over. There'll be scars when the scabs clear, on my forehead as well. More to add to the collection.

I swallow a handful of pills when Ama returns, washing them down with water. Then she makes me lie on the bed and massages my back. She's not very skilled at it, but she's dogged. After an hour I'm feeling much more limber than I was.

'What's next on the agenda?' Ama asks, rolling off.

'Sleep,' I groan, eyes shut, relaxed.

'I mean tomorrow. Next week. Next year. You've been given your life back. What do you plan to do with it?'

My smile turns to a frown and my eyes flutter open. I tilt my head so her face comes into view. 'What do you think I should do?'

'Get out,' she says immediately. 'Catch the first bus, train or plane and take off. It doesn't matter where. Just get away, where nobody knows you, where none of the shit of this city can touch you. Worry about the future later. First you need to escape, from the *villacs*, your father, the riots, everything.'

'You make it sound easy.'

'It is,' she hisses, digging her nails into the flesh of my bicep. 'You're human, Al. I'm not. I don't have a choice. I was made to love Capac and stay by him. I can't leave. But the priests have no hold over you. Get out and don't look back.'

I'm tempted. My mind runs with the idea. Pack a bag, use the credit card Tasso supplied me with to buy tickets and withdraw piles of cash, run until I can't be found, leave this city, its gangsters and Incan priests to go screw themselves.

I limp to the window and gaze at the shaded stretch of street beneath. A few kids are circling bollards on newly acquired bikes, shouting, laughing, unaffected by the riots and the threat hanging over them all. I mean nothing to Ford Tasso or Eugene Davern — useful at the moment, but thoroughly dispensable. And although the *villacs* have a vested interest in me, my disappearance wouldn't throw them too much either. They'd wash their hands of me and turn to another of their fall-guys. But the kids, their parents, my half-brothers and -sisters in the Snakes . . .

Who'll look out for them if I quit? I don't owe them anything – I didn't start the riots, or recruit the Snakes – but I feel responsible. I don't control their destinies, but I can maybe influence them for the better. If I stay.

'I can't leave,' I tell Ama, sensing the outline of a new destiny forming around me. 'I've unfinished business to attend to.'

'Such as?' she snaps.

Answers click into place swiftly as I reel them out. 'The *villacs*. The Snakes. The riots. The Kluxers. My father.'

Definitely my father, if only for what he did to Bill. I always knew he was a monster, but terrorizing a kid into raping and killing his sister goes beyond the bounds even of monstrosity. He could do it all again if the priests free him.

'That's a lot of business,' Ama says sceptically. 'Think you can handle it all?'

'I don't know,' I answer honestly. 'I can confront my father – though I don't care for my chances – and I think I can put an end to the riots by playing ball with the priests. After that . . . we'll see.'

'It's not your place to cure this city of all its ills,' Ama says.

'Of course it isn't. But if I can stop the riots, free my relatives and the local kids from the Snakes, settle matters with my father, spit in the blind eyes of the *villacs* . . . That wouldn't be a bad legacy. And I need to leave a legacy other than one of terror and bloodshed. I couldn't live with myself the way things stand. I'd always be looking back.'

Ama gazes at me silently for long, probing seconds, then sighs. 'You're crazy, but I see you're set on this.' She licks her lips. 'What about Capac? Your bargain with Tasso's off, now that you found Bill. Will you leave Capac to the priests?'

I could. Tasso no longer has a hold over me. I'm free to tell him what he can do with his deal. But Raimi's important to the *villacs*, and they're the key to the Snakes and the riots. If I quit, I'd risk isolating myself. I'm focal as long as the priests need me. Outside the loop of their creation, I'm as powerless as any other pawn in the city.

'I'd happily leave him to rot,' I grunt, 'but I need to restore Raimi to his throne to put an end to the unrest. I also want the *villacs* to think I'm still playing by their rules. The search for The Cardinal continues.'

'Then I'm sticking with you,' Ama says, and she doesn't leave room for me to argue. 'Where do you start and what can I do to help?'

'First,' I yawn, 'I catch more sleep. When I feel ready, I want you to lead me to the *villacs*. I've a proposal to put to them.'

'What is it?' Ama asks.

'I don't know,' I grin. 'But hopefully I'll have thought of one by the time I wake.'

Wednesday, late, the tunnels. My back's killing me but I couldn't put this off until tomorrow. Stuart Jordan launched his counter-attack earlier, taking everyone by surprise for once. He hit the headquarters of the Lobes, one of the larger gangs in the east. Eliminated them swiftly and efficiently. Spreading wide his mixed force of cops and soldiers, he moved on the next four gang strongholds and looked likely to make a clean sweep, when his men were attacked by ghost-like, deadly warriors in dark T-shirts and jeans, with shaven heads and serpents tattooed on their cheeks. The Snakes made short work of Jordan's men – reports put the death toll between fifty and seventy – and forced him to sound a full retreat.

Relief at seeing Jordan's forces repelled was short-lived. The Snakes, having routed the enemy, attacked the gangs that Jordan had targeted, scattering those they didn't kill. The Snakes disappeared back underground, but the gang members are still active, scouring the streets, clashing with each other, hungry for a fight.

Once I became aware of what was happening, I had to intervene, regardless of my condition. Ama helped bandage my ribs. She also disguised the scar on my forehead (I don't want to appear vulnerable). Then she came with me to the underworld entrance, and led me down into the darkness.

I try keeping track of our direction, for fear something should happen to Ama, but it's impossible in the twisting tunnels. If we were going slowly, and I was carefully marking my path, it would be different, but we need to move swiftly. The longer we take, the more lives will be lost.

We encounter nobody until we enter a short tunnel, lit by a torch at the far end, and come face-to-face with a blind priest. He stretches his arms wide and chants.

'Is this who we're looking for?' I ask as we approach.

'No,' Ama says. 'I don't think he speaks English. He's only here to greet us.'

'In that case . . .' I stick out my right arm and pole-axe him. I could break his neck, but settle for dumping him on his ass and leaving him to splutter in the dust.

Four turns later, we enter a large, bare room, where the *villac* I spoke with before is waiting, seated on a high stool. 'Welcome, Flesh of Dreams,' he intones.

'Cut the shit,' I snap. 'I want to discuss terms. Can I do that with you, or is there some other prick I have to go to?'

'I am prick enough,' he says, gesturing to a couple of chairs set by the wall to his left. Once we're seated, he smoothes the folds of his robes. 'You are ready to pledge yourself to us?'

'In a manner of speaking,' I reply shortly.

'You will do as we bid? Lead the Snakes? Assist Blood of Dreams?'

'Yes. But I have conditions.' He smiles and nods for me to continue. 'I want to end the riots. There's been enough bloodshed.'

'We can grant that wish. We will have to strike hard to secure peace and exert control. More must perish. But within a couple of days the fighting will cease.'

'What about the Troops and Kluxers? You think they'll sit back and let the Snakes annex the east?'

'You need not worry about them. Shortly after peace has been restored, we will return Blood of Dreams to his rightful position – assuming he cooperates – and he will see that your authority is not undermined.'

I glance at Ama and catch her relieved smile at the news that her lover is due to return. 'And my father?' I ask.

The *villac* shrugs. 'He is of no interest to us now. He will be released, since we gave our word that we would set him free, but he must go elsewhere to kill. He would be an irritant if he stayed.'

I could make it part of our bargain that they terminate Paucar Wami – I doubt the priest would object too strenuously – but I want him for myself. His fate should be mine to decide, not theirs.

I'm getting most of what I wish for, an end to the riots, the city at peace, the freedom to move against my father. I'd like to see the priests come to grief as well, but I can't have everything. There is, however, one final point. 'When it's over, I want the Snakes disbanded. Send them back to their homes with orders to get on with their lives.'

The priest shakes his head. 'The Snakes are essential. Without them you would stand alone in the corridors of power. They are your bargaining chip when dealing with Blood of Dreams and the others. You need them.'

'I don't want them,' I snap. 'Set them free or it's no deal.'

'Then it's no deal. You are important, Flesh of Dreams, but so are the Snakes. For centuries we worked without an army. We see now that we were mistaken. We need a force of our own, for when political machinations are not enough.'

'But –'

'This is not open to debate,' he interrupts curtly.

I curse beneath my breath, but I know when I'm beaten.

I have nothing to offer the *villacs* except myself. If that's not enough to sway them, I have no other card to play.

'OK,' I sigh, glaring at the white-eyed priest. 'I'll lead them for you. I'll work with you. But if you try and screw me over . . .'

'Flesh of Dreams,' the *villac* chuckles, 'would we do that? Come. We have much to do if we are to realize our plans. Let us begin.' He offers a hand. I stare at the pale fingers a moment – I hate these bastards, but what choice do I have? – then take them and let him lead me through the tunnels, ever deeper beneath the earth, to embrace the destiny of their making that I was for so long so determined to avoid.

TWO – THE SNAKES UNLEASHED

We stream from the tunnels at dawn, three hundred and seventy-eight Snakes, seven Cobras and me, their Sapa Inca, *Paucar Wami*. In a wave we break across the east, the members of each phalanx slotting into his or her designated position, their orders clear, the Cobras of all seven triumvirates in constant communication with their underlings and me. The *villacs* spent the past several hours preparing me for the role of field-commander, talking me through maps, schedules, statistics, lines of assault and defence. This is their battle – they've primed the Snakes, set the targets, issued instructions – but once out of the tunnels, I'm in command. I have to accept responsibility in the field, react to turns in the fighting as I see fit, lead by example. The Cobras will be on hand to advise me but the priests will remain underground.

Ama's by my side, as are the sixteen men and two women of the first phalanx of the first triumvirate — my personal bodyguard. They've been trained to serve the Sapa Inca and they take their job *very* seriously. Apparently it's a great honour and only the cream of the crop are elected to the first of the first.

The primary targets are the gangs who've been roaming freely, falling on anyone who gets in their way. The phalanxes move on the weary members and put them out of action, wounding or frightening-off when they can, killing only when necessary.

We set up in a van outside an abandoned police station and await word from our troops on the streets. Early reports are positive — most gangs break under attack. A few strike back but are swiftly crushed. Within an hour the streets have been cleared of predators. Time for phase two.

Nine of the phalanxes group into their triumvirates and link up, forming a core force of a hundred and fifty-eight Snakes (four died in the fighting) and three Cobras. They congregate in Cockerel Square, the heart of the east. Several gangs have used the Square prior to our takeover, so it's stocked with supplies and weapons. The Snakes set about barricading the entrances and booby-trapping the surrounding buildings. The Square will provide pissed-off enemies with a fortress to target and storm. We'll let them exhaust themselves on it. Those inside will repel as many as they can, for as long as they can, while a fourth triumvirate lays low outside, waiting for word to move in and break up assailants from the rear.

The eight remaining phalanxes go wherever the action takes them, patrolling, breaking up fights, quelling riots, guarding shops and banks, cracking down on looters. They have orders to be kind to women and children, keep the peace, stop the destruction of property, use force sparingly. Most are local kids, eager to protect their friends and loved ones. They'll become the public face of the Snakes – four of my aides are busy contacting news crews to arrange inter-views. We'll make it clear we're not to be taken lightly, but we'll also insist that the innocent have nothing to fear. We're here to help, not conquer. We're the solution, not the problem. At least that's the media line.

As word reaches me that Cockerel Square has been

successfully taken, and that the first reporters are being shepherded through the blockades, I pass control of the van to
one of my bodyguards and step outside to clear my head and
prepare for the long day ahead. Ama follows. 'Think you'll
cope?' she asks.

'It'll be a miracle if I do,' I laugh. 'I'm not cut out to be
a general.'

'You're doing fine.' She leads me aside, out of earshot of
three young Snakes standing guard. 'Have you thought this
through? You're getting in deep.'

'This is the only way I can stop the riots.'

'Maybe you should let them run their course. Do you think
things will be better with these guys in charge? They're
imposing martial law. What happens when order is restored?
The Snakes plan to control everything, who comes and goes,
who owns what and whom. You're handing them the east.'

'That's one way of looking at it. I prefer to think I'm saving
lives.'

'Perhaps you are,' she mutters. 'I just wish there was some
other way. I don't want to see this city under the thumb of
the *villacs*.'

'That won't happen,' I promise.

'You can stop it?' she challenges me.

'Somehow, some way . . . yes. I haven't figured it out, but
I'm working on it. In the meantime I'll do their bidding and
let them think they've whipped me. It'll all come good in
the end.' Trying to sound like I mean it, not just to convince
Ama, but myself as well.

By Friday evening the east is ours. The expected siege on Cockerel
Square never materialized, and although a few ragged bands
made hit-and-run attacks, they were easily repelled, without
the loss of a single life. Two of the triumvirates pulled out last
night and joined the others on patrol, leaving three phalanxes

to hold the Square and propagate the myth that it's our official base.

To my surprise, people have accepted us, freely offering
support and assistance. I suppose any relief from the riots is
welcome, and after all, many of the Snakes are known to
them — friends, neighbours, relatives. They believe we're
their own. They don't know about the scheming *villacs*. Maybe
they wouldn't care if they did. A drowning man rarely stops
to query one who extends a saving hand.

Even more surprising is the eagerness of the gangs to flock
to our cause. For decades the east has been a mishmash of
divided loyalties, gangs resisting the temptation to merge.
Even Ferdinand Dorak was unable to bond them. The gangs
here feared and respected him, and paid their dues, but they
never united behind him. He could crush any gang he liked,
but another would always spring up in its place, and he was
never able to bring the disparate bands together.

That time-honoured standard, which has dictated the way
of life here for sixty or seventy years, changed overnight.
As soon as the Snakes set about spreading the word – that
we're powerful, that we plan to be to the east what the
Troops are to the rest of the city, that we'll fight off the
likes of Eugene Davern and his Kluxers – gangs made a
beeline for Cockerel Square to offer their allegiance. Ama
thinks it's rooted in fear of the Kluxers, the Troops and Stuart
Jordan's forces. The east is under threat and she believes the
gangs have decided it's time to fight as one, at least until the
threat has passed.

I suspect the *villacs* have more to do with the mood swing.
I remember Dorak boasting to Capac Raimi about how he
created Ayuamarcan leaders and sent them among his foes
with orders to bend them to his will. Maybe fresh
Ayuamarcans are at work in the east, and some of the gang
leaders have only recently come into being with the sole

purpose of persuading their followers to heed the call of Paucar Wami and his Snakes.

Whatever their motivation, I welcome the new arrivals warmly, dropping in on the Snakes in Cockerel Square every few hours to make speeches (hesitant at first, but I get the hang of it quickly), promising a new future where those of the east stand among the city's elite. They cheer wildly, keeping any worries they may harbour to themselves.

I've become a highly visible figure, putting myself about, touching base with all the phalanxes, handing out essentials to the needy at food and clothes stations, scowling at the cameras (Paucar Wami doesn't smile), vowing to build from the roots up and lead the east into a new, glorious era. I haven't given any interviews, but eventually I will, making the final transition from mythical killer to public man of the people.

It felt surreal at first, but it's amazing how swiftly you can adapt. I've been head of the Snakes for less than forty-eight hours but feel like I've been doing this for years. I should be alarmed at how naturally I've settled into the role of leader, and how that plays into the *villacs'* hands, but I don't have time. Being in command leaves you with little opportunity to brood about problems of your own. You have to put your head down and get on with it, and somewhere in the middle of all the decision-making you lose your desire and ability to think about yourself — which may be exactly what the blind priests planned.

A spokesman for Stuart Jordan rings at eight, hoping to arrange a meeting, and after that it's non-stop, one flunkey after another, promising the world if the leader of the Snakes will meet with the police commissioner in an attempt to put an end to the violence. What Jordan really wants is to jump on the bandwagon and take credit for the ceasefire. We stall him diplomatically and promise to get back to him soon. In fact we've no intention of having anything to do with Jordan. His days are numbered – someone must be held accountable for the riots, and Jordan's as suitable a patsy as any – so we're holding out for the new man.

While desperate officials jam the lines, I take to the streets for the carnival which is gearing into life. Now that it's relatively safe, people want to celebrate. They've survived the worst outbreak of violence in forty years and witnessed the birth of a new era, where those of the east boast an armed force of their own and need no longer walk in fear of the Troops or any other force. Party time!

The street parties burn far into the night, and it seems as if everyone in the east is dancing in the middle of the roads, lighting bonfires in open squares – carefully supervised, unlike the wild fires of the riots – setting off fireworks, drinking and eating too much, making love in cars and on rooftops. The Snakes blend in with the revellers, accepting their thanks with polite smiles, refusing alcohol, drugs and other gifts, alert to the threat of a sneak raid by the Troops, Kluxers or police.

Ama slips away as the festivities are hitting full swing, to be with her 'father'. She promises to return in the morning but I tell her not to bother. 'Tired of me already, Sapa Inca?' she asks, eyes twinkling.

'The great and mighty Paucar Wami has no time for pleasures of the flesh,' I grunt pompously, then grin. 'Come if you want, but there isn't much you can do. If you'd rather spend time with Cafran, I'll understand.'

She nods. 'I'd like that. It's hard work running an army. If you're sure you can stumble along without me . . .'

'I'll manage somehow.'

She kisses me quickly. I want to make something more of the kiss, but keep my hands by my sides. 'Take care, Al,' she says. 'The coup's gone like a dream but you're bound to hit a glitch somewhere. Don't trust any of these bastards.'

'I won't.'

'Keep me in touch with what's going on, and call when you need me.'

'You think I can't get by on my own?'

'You're a man,' she chuckles. 'Of course you can't.'

I laugh, watching her go, wishing I could keep her.

I run into the glitch quicker than Ama could have anticipated. In the early hours of Saturday I grab some much-needed sleep. I'm stiff when I wake and spend twenty minutes exercizing on the floor beside my bed, limbering up. After checking with my Cobras – all's well – I indulge in a leisurely breakfast. After that I take to the streets with my bodyguards. Many who left at the height of the riots are returning and I ensure they don't feel threatened. I also arrange meetings with some of the looters who've been stripping shops and apartments bare, and ask them to return the goods they stole. I don't come down heavy – I have to keep these people on my side – merely ask that they consider the long-term profits over the short-term, and vow to bear it in mind if they do me this favour. Most cooperate, and by afternoon news cameras are focusing on the incredible sight of thieves returning their plunder to its rightful owners.

It's evening when the glitch hits. I'm watching a news programme, enjoying the positive coverage, when the anchorman cuts in with a report of violence in the centre of the city. Although it hasn't been confirmed, it appears that several of the Snakes attacked a group of diners leaving a restaurant, killing eight people. At least three of the eight were Kluxers.

As my brain races, a radio reporter makes an excited announcement — the lobby of Party Central has been firebombed by the Snakes. The death toll hasn't been established, but several Troops perished, along with a number of civilians.

'Sard!' I bellow, startling the Snakes in the van. Sard's a Cobra. Although they're not supposed to reveal their names, I made them tell me, so I could address them directly without having to remember and repeat their triumvirate numbers all the time. Sard responds to my call immediately, poking his head into the van. 'What the fuck are the Snakes doing at Party Central?' I roar.

'Sapa Inca?' he frowns.

'I just heard on the radio that we've attacked Party Central. And there was a report on TV that we're killing Kluxers too.'

'But, Sapa Inca, *you* authorized the strikes.'

My eyes narrow. 'Get out,' I snarl at the Snakes. They obey without question, clearing the way for Sard. I tell him to close the door, then grab him by the lapels of his leather jacket and jerk him forward. 'When did I tell you?'

'Early this morning, before dawn.'

While I was sleeping. The priests must have sent the real Paucar Wami to issue fresh orders to the Cobras. Those sons of . . .

'What did I say?' I growl.

'You sent the phalanxes of the fourth triumvirate to take the battle to our enemies,' Sard answers proudly. 'I'm not sure what their targets were – only the Cobra of the fourth knows that – but you said we'd hit fast and hard, where it hurt, and warned us to be ready for a backlash.'

'Did anybody question the logic of attacking the two most powerful forces in the city at the same time?' I bark. 'We haven't even consolidated our position here!'

The Cobra shrugs. 'You're the Sapa Inca. We don't question your orders.'

'Brainless fucking . . .' I mutter vile curses beneath my

breath, but they won't change anything, so I snap out of my rage and consider this mess from a cold, unemotional standpoint. 'Recall them,' I tell Sard. 'I was mistaken. The thrill of victory rushed to my head. I want them back before they do more damage.'

'I can't,' Sard says, staring at me oddly. 'You told them to leave their radios and phones behind. They're incommunicado.'

'Fuck!' I kick a stand stacked high with TV sets, then kick it again, smashing the glass of the set lowest down. 'Find them. Send your men and . . .'

I stop when I see him shaking his head. 'I don't know where they are. We could search, but those of the fourth have been trained to lie low and cover their tracks, the same as the rest of us. The odds –'

'Screw the odds. Take a phalanx, split it into pairs, and hunt them down. Look everywhere. Don't stop to draw breath. When your men flag, replace them.'

'As you wish, Sapa Inca,' he says, bowing his head.

'Sard!' I shout as he backs towards the exit. 'Will you do me a favour?'

'Of course, Sapa Inca.'

'Start using your brain.' He blinks uncomprehendingly. 'I'm not a god. I'm prone to error like everyone else. The next time I issue an order that makes no sense, that strikes you as the dumbest fucking thing you've ever heard, tell me.'

'But we've been taught that to question the Sapa Inca is to invite death.'

'Are you afraid of death?' I ask quietly.

The Cobra snaps erect. 'No, Sapa Inca!'

'Then use your initiative in future. Tell the other Cobras to do the same. I need people to challenge me when I make a bad call. Are you prepared to risk my wrath, even at the cost of your life?'

He nods solidly. 'I am.'

I smile fleetingly, then point to the door. 'Now go find those fools and pray they haven't fucked everything up for the rest of us.'

As evening turns to night, reports of attacks by the Snakes increase. The three phalanxes are covering a lot of ground, hitting Tasso and Davern's forces at random. Suddenly the news crews don't care about thieves returning stolen goods. They want to know why the Snakes have overshot their boundaries, where we'll hit next. In the space of a few hours we've gone from being saviours of the east to would-be conquerors of the north, south and west. And nobody likes it.

I tell my media-friendly frontmen to issue blanket denials – we know nothing of the attacks, they're the work of a splinter organization, we don't condone them – then get busy trying to prevent the catastrophe which is poised to engulf us.

I send messengers to track down the *villacs*, so that I can talk about this with them, but the few who speak English can't be located and the others merely babble meaninglessly in response to my call for answers.

As the airwaves fill with the news that a highly ranked Troop was butchered at home, along with his wife, three kids and visiting mother-in-law (comics will have a field day with that in the coming weeks), I dial Ford Tasso's number and hope that he's still in Party Central, not on his way over in a retaliatory strike.

The phone clicks and Tasso snarls before I have a chance to say anything. 'You better have a great fucking explanation for this, Algiers.'

'It isn't my doing.'

'You lead the Snakes, don't you?'

'They're following Paucar Wami's instructions, not mine. The first I knew of this was when the story broke on TV. I'm doing all I can to call them off.'

'What do you expect me to do in the meantime? Sit here, twiddle my thumbs and wait for you to sort this shit out? Do you know how many people I have urging me to stamp you out like the arrogant little upstart you are?'

'I can imagine,' I chuckle humourlessly.

'I've held them off because I wanted to check with you first, make sure you weren't being set up by some sneaky bastards disguised as Snakes.'

'I'm definitely being set-up,' I groan, 'but by sneaky bastards on the inside. The priests are behind this. I don't know what they're up to, but they seem to want you and Davern to attack the east — which should be reason enough *not* to.'

He sighs heavily. 'You're asking a lot.'

'I know. But if you send the Troops in, you'll play into the *villacs'* hands. Stall your men. Give me time. Please.'

He's silent for five seconds. Ten. Fifteen. Finally, 'I want to send someone to discuss this with you.'

'Who?'

'Frank.'

'When can he be here?'

'He's in the field. It'll be midnight before he's back. By the time I brief him . . . How does three a.m. sound?'

'Perfect. Send him in by Blesster Street. I'll have an escort waiting.'

'You'd better,' he growls, hanging up.

I dial the number Eugene Davern gave me. He answers on the second ring with a curt, 'Yeah?'

'It's Al Jeery. I want to talk.'

'The time for talking's past. You had your chance. I've nothing to say except see you on the street, nigger.'

'Don't be a fuckhead!' I snap. 'Negotiate with me now and we might walk away from this stronger than ever. Cut me off and we're both going down.'

He pauses suspiciously. 'What are you talking about?'

'All I want is to make my home turf safe. I've no wish to go to war with you or the Troops. Even if I did, would I start one while I'm still trying to secure the east?'

'You might,' he mutters. 'Nobody was expecting an attack.'

'Because it's suicide. The bastards behind this only want chaos. They don't give a fuck about any of us. I'm meeting a representative of Ford Tasso's at three a.m. Send one of your men along. I'll have him met at Blesster Street. Hear what I have to say. Hold your forces in check until then.'

'I don't know . . .'

'A few hours, Davern, that's all I'm asking.'

He considers. Davern's new to this game, not as seasoned as Tasso. He's smart but itchy, afraid of being made the fall guy. He could swing either way.

'OK,' he says abruptly. 'I'll send Wornton — if you can win *him* around, you'll earn a fucking ceasefire. Otherwise . . .'

I hang up before he can change his mind, dial Sard's number and discover he's had no luck tracking down the rogue Snakes. I tell him to keep trying and suggest detailing another two phalanxes to the search. He advises against it – the fewer people we send, the less conspicuous they'll be. I bow to his assessment – a leader has to trust his aides – then sit back and chew my fingernails, counting off the seconds of the most nerve-wracking hours of my life.

Hyde Wornton arrives first, wearing his trademark white fur coat, blond hair as immaculately combed as before. He casts an eye around the deserted police station which I've appropriated for the meeting, taking in the charred rafters and gaping holes in the roof. 'Don't think much of your choice of HQ,' he sneers.

'It's as good a place as any.' I nod to one of three chairs I've laid out in a triangle. He ignores me and eyes the exposed rafters suspiciously.

'You're sure we're safe?' he asks.

'You've no enemies here,' I tell him — a ludicrous lie which brings a smile to his lips.

'I should live to see the day,' he chortles, but relaxes and takes a chair. 'Who are we waiting for?' he asks, digging out a knife to pare his nails.

'Frank Weld.'

He whistles. 'Should be interesting.' Checks his watch. 'I left two of my men at Blesster Street. If they haven't heard from me by five, they'll call Eugene and –'

'All I'm waiting for is Frank. It wouldn't be polite to start without him.'

Wornton lapses into silence and concentrates on his nails. He's less nervous than I am, which irritates me, but I can't help it. I'm playing a new game, in which maybe hundreds of lives are at stake. Wornton cares only about himself, as I used to. I've let myself start to worry about others, which is a weakness I must hide from Wornton and Frank. They seize on weaknesses, like sharks.

Frank turns up at 03:21, drawn and ill-tempered. He stops in the doorway when he spies Hyde Wornton. 'What the fuck's he doing here?' he bellows.

'The Snakes attacked Davern's men too,' I explain. 'I need to clear the air with him as well.'

Frank glares at Wornton, who smiles back innocently, then levels his gaze on me. 'I thought this was supposed to be one-on-one. I've no intention of discussing private affairs in front of that son of a bitch.'

'Watch your mouth,' Wornton snarls. 'It's not just niggers we string up.'

Frank laughs monotonously. 'That's the sort of scum you hope to strike a deal with?'

'I don't like it, but I'd rather talk with him than fight him. If you want, I can see you one at a time, but I've got the same thing to say to both of you. It'd be a lot quicker if I took you together.'

Frank hovers uncertainly.

'For fuck's sake, sit!' Wornton snaps. 'The nigger's right — if we don't talk today, we'll be at war tomorrow. I'll face that if I have to, but I'd rather not.'

'OK.' Frank takes the third chair, moving it a couple of feet further away from Wornton. 'Impress me, Al.'

'First I want to make one thing clear.' I gaze steadily at Hyde Wornton. 'Call me a nigger again and I'll gut you, regardless of the consequences.'

Wornton opens his mouth to jeer, sees the real intent in my eyes, and closes it. 'Touchy, aren't you?' he pouts.

I face Frank. 'Fifty-five Snakes are responsible for the attacks. They've been sent on a hit-and-run mission by the real Paucar Wami. I'm assuming he was put up to it by –'

'Hold on,' Wornton interrupts. 'What do you mean, the *real* Paucar Wami?'

'You know I borrowed the name, that there was a serial killer before me?'

'I heard stories but I never believed them.'

'Believe. Paucar Wami was real and is real again. The *villacs* used him to lead the Snakes. I stepped in on the understanding that I was to replace him, but he's still hanging around. He's to blame for this mess. I had nothing to do with it.'

'This is bullshit,' Wornton growls. 'How can this other fucker give orders if you're in charge?'

'*I'm* not in charge,' I sigh. '*Paucar Wami* is. The Snakes rally to the image of the assassin. I've assumed his image, so to that extent I control them, but since the real Wami looks just like me, he can obviously step in when I'm not around and issue conflicting orders.'

Wornton raises an eyebrow at Frank. 'You buying any of this shit?'

Frank nods slowly. 'Ford explained some of the situation to me before sending me over. I can't say I understand it all, but he's telling the truth about Wami.'

'So why isn't the other guy here?' Wornton asks. 'If he's the real leader, why aren't we talking to him instead of this pretender?'

'Paucar Wami doesn't talk,' I answer softly. 'He kills. To most intents and purposes, I control the Snakes. I'm the one who can get us out of this mess. Strike a deal with me and I'll do all in my power to call off the renegades. But if you charge in, I'll be helpless. You'll give the *villacs* what they want – a war – and regardless of who wins, we'll all suffer.'

Frank clears his throat. 'What guarantee can you make? If we hold off, how do we know the priests won't use the real Paucar Wami to send more Snakes to attack us?'

'I can't make any guarantees,' I tell them honestly. 'I'll do all I can to curtail the Snakes but I could fail. If I do, the city goes to war and it will be horrendous. But if I'm not given a chance, we're definitely screwed. It will be a war of the *villacs'* choosing and they're the only ones who'll profit in the end.'

Frank lets out a long, uneasy breath and shakes his head thoughtfully. Wornton eyes him, smirking, then studies his nails as if they're of far more importance to him than this meeting.

'The longer we wait,' Frank says, 'the stronger the Snakes will get. If we're to attack, it should be now.'

'The Snakes shouldn't have hit you until they'd established

a stronghold in the east,' I counter. 'The normal rules don't apply here.'

'What do you think?' Frank growls at Wornton. 'Or do you plan to sit there all night, paring your nails?'

Wornton puts his knife away. 'I never trusted a *coloured man* before, but this one's different. He wants to keep the blacks in the east, which is what we want too. Our reasons are different, but as long as our aims are the same, that's what matters. Eugene has final say, but I'll advise him to leave things be, at least for a couple of days. If Jeery can prove he's in control, fine. If not . . .'

'Frank?' I ask.

'I don't want to wait,' he mutters, then sighs. 'But if the Kluxers are willing to hold back, I'll discuss it with Ford. I can't make any promises, but I think he'll grant you a stay of execution.'

I let my head fall back and smile at the sky through the holes in the roof. I've done it! I'm not out of the woods – the Snakes have to be recalled, and I have to think of a way to stop others from obeying the orders of my father – but I've time to play with. I can go on from here and . . .

The self-congratulation dies prematurely as I spy a shadowy figure on the rafters. It's too dark to be sure, but my gut tells me instantly who it is, and I guess what he's here for.

'*No!*' I scream, leaping to my feet and whipping out my .45. Before I can target him, he drops and knocks the gun from my hand. He rolls away from me and rises smoothly. Turns and grins, his luminous green eyes sparkling with twisted delight. I dive after him as Frank and Wornton struggle to their feet. He waits for me to close and throws a lazy punch. I ignore the fist – not enough power to harm me – but then his fingers fly apart and dirt sprays from his hand, into my eyes.

While I'm momentarily blinded, the real Paucar Wami

kicks me in the stomach and I crash backwards. I'm up again a mere four or five seconds later, but that's an eternity to a killer of my father's calibre.

He takes Wornton first. The Kluxer has slipped out his knife and jabs at the assassin, keeping his cool, using his free hand to grab his chair by a leg, utilizing it as a shield. Wami kicks the chair from Wornton's hand, leaving himself open to attack on his left. Wornton seizes the bait and drives his knife at Wami's heart. Wami shimmies, grabs Wornton's forearm and rams an elbow into the Kluxer's jaw, thrusting his head back, snapping his neck, dropping him to the floor, where he groans, alive but helpless.

Frank has drawn a gun, which he fires several times in quick succession, opting for volume over accuracy. Wami rolls across the floor, inches ahead of the bullets. Frank carries on shooting, getting closer each time. I wipe dirt from my eyes and start forward, scrabbling after my .45. Then Frank stops firing. I assume he's out of ammunition, until his arm drops to his side and his pistol falls to the floor.

'Frank?' I pause, eyes flicking between my friend and my father, who's come to a rest. 'Frank, are you . . .?'

He turns slowly and the handle of the knife sticking out of his chest comes into view. 'Al?' he says dully. 'I think the fucker's killed me.'

I stare at him, appalled. The fingers which were holding the gun rise and clasp the knife. He starts to pull it out, grimaces, drops to his knees. 'Killed me,' he whispers, then collapses — dead.

I stumble across the room, ease Frank's fingers off the knife and press them to my chest, as though I can extend my heartbeat to his and bring him back to life. 'Sorry, Frank,' I mumble. 'I didn't mean for it to end like this.'

I'm dimly aware of Wami working on Hyde Wornton, finishing him off. Out of the corner of my eye I see him rip out the Kluxer's tongue with his bare fingers. Wearily I turn away.

I don't think about revenge. It'd be pointless. Even on the off-chance that I got the better of my father, what good would it achieve? Weld and Wornton are dead. Any hopes of a peaceful outcome have been shattered. This means war, bitter and bloody, and neither Tasso nor Eugene Davern will stop until all the Snakes – me included – are dead.

Wami concludes his business with Wornton and stands, wiping his hands clean. 'I would have liked to work on him longer,' he says, 'but time is of the essence.'

'You bastard,' I hiss, not looking at him. 'Frank was my friend.'

'That is why I killed him quickly. I am always thinking of you, Al m'boy.'

I close Frank's eyes, extract the knife and lay his hands over the hole in his chest, covering it discreetly. 'You've pushed me too far this time. What makes you think I won't fight to the death?'

'Actually, I think you might,' he answers. 'Part of me thrills at the prospect. It has been many years since I tested myself against a worthy opponent. But the priests would surely destroy me if I won, and I am not ready for my final demise. So many countries to visit, so many people to kill. I hope you have enough sense not to force the issue, but if you attack, I will meet your challenge fairly.'

'Tell me why you did it.' My fingers are tight on the handle of the knife.

'The *villacs* told me to. The final part of our bargain. I am free now, to leave and torment the good people of the world as I please.'

'But why? What's in this for them? They want to control the city. How can they if chaos is raging and their Snakes are annihilated?'

'The Snakes will not be harmed,' Wami chuckles. 'You are clever, Al m'boy, but not clued-in. The priests wish to run the whole of the city, not just the east. They must create an army greater than the Troops and the Kluxers. That could not happen if the Snakes remained in the east — it would merely lead to a three-way stand-off. Now that their lieutenants have been slaughtered, Tasso and Davern will send in their forces for revenge, but the Snakes will disappear. The priests will lead them underground, leaving only the common folk for the invaders to attack.'

'They'll take it out on them,' I mutter, seeing it now. 'They'll kill hundreds of gang members and any others who get in their way. But that won't be enough, so they'll wage war on each other.'

Wami nods smugly. 'The titans will meet on the field of battle and fight to the death. The Troops will probably win, but their losses will be great. As they try to recover –'

'– the Snakes will re-emerge,' I cut in. 'Recruit new members from among the embittered survivors of the east. Maybe forge alliances with allies of Davern, men prepared to go to any lengths to get even with the Troops.'

Wami smiles. 'You take a while to catch on but move quickly once you do.'

'Those whoresons,' I growl, thinking of the *villacs*. 'They don't care about all the people who'll die.'

'Of course not,' Wami laughs. 'Nor should you. Life is a game, and humans are the pieces on the board. That has always been your failing — you were never able to separate yourself from the common cattle. It holds you back, Al m'boy.'

Wami claps loudly, startling me. 'I would love to stay and shoot the breeze, but the world calls. I do not know what the priests plan for you, but I imagine they are not finished. You might want to consider hitting the road with your dear ole pappy. In the unlikely event that the *villacs* do not ruin you, there will be many eager to string you up.'

'I'll take my chances.'

'As you wish.'

My father crouches, leaps, grabs hold of a low-hanging rafter and pulls himself up. 'Wait!' I call before he vanishes forever into the night. There's an itching at the back of my skull. I don't know what it means, but I've a feeling this isn't as done-and-dusted as Wami believes. 'Why are you in such a rush to leave?'

'The priests do not want me hanging around. They were clear on that point.'

'All the more reason to stay.'

'I do not want to anger them,' he mutters.

'But what if you could hurt them as they've hurt you?'

There's a long pause. 'You think you can turn the tables on the *villacs*?' he asks eagerly. He's played along with them because he had to, but I know he hates the blind priests and would love to find a way to thwart them.

'I don't have a plan yet, but I'll work on one. Stick around a few days and I'll cut you in on the action.'

'And if I do not want cutting in?'

I shrug. 'If you don't like the look of things, you can leave.'

Wami's silent a few seconds. Then he reaches for the roof. My heart sinks, but lifts a moment later when he looks down again. 'I will stay for three days. If you search for me, I will be found. But do not waste my time.'

With that he slips away, leaving me with the two corpses, on the brink of a total disaster, but with the slightest glimmer of hope at the back of my mind. Pushing regrets for Frank and fears for the future from my thoughts, I retreat to one of the small holding cells, immerse myself in darkness, and pan around desperately for a way out of this mess before the walls collapse and the vengeful hordes crash in around me.

THREE – DEALS WITH DEVILS

My thoughts keep wandering back to Frank. I've spent the last decade living with death. I know all its moves and moods. But with a friend it's different. I want to keep Frank's corpse company, arrange for a safe escort to his family so he can be properly mourned. But this is a pivotal moment. I can surrender to self-pity and waste time on the dead, or focus on the living and maybe prevent the waves of bloody destruction from breaking over this city.

With an effort I fade Frank out and concentrate on the task at hand. I don't see what I can do to counter the care-fully laid plans of the blind priests – it's insanely egotistical of me to presume I can outwit them – but a rage burns in my chest, filling me with self-belief. I agreed to assist them. For the sake of my friends and neighbours, I pledged myself to the *villacs'* warped cause. As my reward, they set about wrecking that which we were meant to save.

Thinking ahead, I can imagine the conversation they have planned for me when the Troops and Kluxers invade. 'This is bad, but it will be worse if we don't intervene. We misled you, Flesh of Dreams, but you must stay true to us or chaos will rule completely.'

And the bastards will be right. If it gets that far, they'll be the only ones who can quell the riots. If I don't play along, they'll hold the Snakes in reserve and let Tasso and Davern's men do as they please. I shouldn't have agreed to lead the Troops. That proved that I truly cared for these people. Now that the *villacs* have exposed my weakness, they'll exploit it, do as they like and expect me to dance to their tune.

Maybe *that's* what I can use against them.

My eyes grow cold in the gloom of the cell. Sending Wami to kill Frank and Wornton while they were in discussion with me was an act of contempt, an open admission that the priests believe they can use me any way they wish. Even if that's true, they shouldn't have let me know. The *villacs* are masters at masking their thoughts and feelings. This time they miscalculated and showed their hand. Maybe that one slip is enough.

I find myself focusing on the brace of corpses. On some level I think that I can use them, but I'm not sure how. When Wami dropped from the rafters and killed Frank and Wornton, I thought that was the end. Tasso and Davern's right-hand men were slaughtered on my turf, in my company, while under my protection. Their bosses would have no choice but to come gunning for me and all who stood in the way. Invasion still seems inescapable. Except . . .

I scowl impatiently, then smile as the tumblers click into place. It was *my* turf. *I* invited them to the meeting. As their supposed protector, *I'm* the prime target.

That's the flaw in the priests' plan. By setting me up as leader of the Snakes, they've made me look more powerful than I am. As far as everyone else is concerned, the Snakes are mine and I'm using them to seize control. What if I could convince Tasso and Davern that there was no profit in this for me, if I could show them that I'm as vulnerable as they are?

The Troops and Kluxers fear and distrust me because they believe I'm in this for gain. Convincing them that I'm not couldn't be easier. All I have to do is prove how little power means to me by revealing my true limitations. A sacrifice should suffice. I'll offer them the head they most thirst for — *mine*.

The Snakes outside the police station are startled when I emerge lugging the corpse of Hyde Wornton, but say nothing as I dump him on the front steps and go looking for my motorbike, a newly acquired model, same design as my original. When I return and strap Wornton to the back of the bike, the stand-in Cobra (Sard's still trying to find the renegade Snakes) clears his throat. 'Sapa Inca? Are you going somewhere?'

'Taking my sweetheart for a ride,' I grunt.

'Maybe some of us should accompany you. I can —'

'I go alone.'

'But I'm not supposed to —'

'Soldier,' I say softly, 'I am giving you an order. Do you acknowledge a higher authority than mine?'

'Well, no, sir, but —'

'That is all there is to say.' I finish with Wornton, tug on him a few times to make sure he's tied securely, then nod towards the station. 'Remain on guard and allow no one in. Not even Sard if he returns. *Absolutely* not the priests. With luck, I will return in a few hours to make another pick-up.'

'I don't understand, Sapa Inca,' the Snake mutters.

'You are not here to understand. You are here to obey. Yes?'

He snaps to attention. 'Yes, sir!'

I head west, taking the quieter streets. Bypassing the barricades isn't a problem but the armed forces beyond pose more of a threat. Several times I'm sighted and ordered to pull over. Each time I accelerate and take unexpected corners, losing my pursuers, before tracking back on course.

With the diversions, it's an hour before I pull up outside the Kool Kats Klub. Dawn hasn't broken, but the restaurant's swarming with anxious-looking Kluxers. I spot a platoon of Davern's soldiers unloading rifles from the back of a truck. Unleashing the body of their champion, I hold him length-ways in my arms, like a groom carrying his bride, and stride up to the entrance of the KKK. Remarkably, nobody notices me until I'm almost at the door. Then a Kluxer spots my dark features and the body I'm cradling, and roars dis-believingly, 'What the fuck!'

All eyes snap on me. Guns rise automatically and fingers tighten on triggers. Only one thing gives them pause — they're not sure that Wornton is dead, and don't want to risk wounding him if he isn't.

'I'm here to speak with Davern,' I shout, nudging Wornton's face closer to my chest, hiding his blank expression from his supporters. 'Tell him Paucar Wami requests the pleasure of his company.'

'You've got to be shitting me,' the soldier says, but bolts inside the building, yelling for Davern. The Kluxers around me snarl and spit, muttering murder.

Eugene Davern emerges, looking fragile and stretched. I bet this was never how he planned it when he plotted his takeover. Davern surged up the ranks too quickly and landed far out of his depth. I'm also willing to bet he didn't surge alone. I've been doing a lot of thinking during the ride over, and this all plays too neatly into the *villacs'* hands to be coin-cidence. I'm sure the priests have been using the leader of the Kluxers, just as they've used me, to undermine the power of the Troops and open the city to a force of their choosing. If it wasn't for the innocents Davern would take with him, I'd be tempted to leave him to the mess of his greedy making and let him lead his men to defeat against the Troops.

Davern walks straight up to me, ignoring the warnings of

his guards, and stares at the pale face of his second-in-command, noting the red marks around his lips where my father ripped his tongue out. 'Is he dead?' he asks dully.

'Yes.' I drop the body with calculated disregard. It hits hard and rolls onto its back. There's an angry, collective gasp from the crowd but I ignore it, focusing on Davern, the only one I have to worry about.

'What happened?' Davern asks quietly.

'Does it matter? He came in answer to my invitation. I guaranteed his safety. I was sure I could control the situation. As you can see –' I nudge the corpse with a foot, provoking a flurry of angry shouts '– I was wrong. He was killed under my protection. I accept full responsibility. You don't need to send your men east to exact revenge. You have the culprit here.'

Davern shoots a glance at me, then his gaze returns to the face of his friend. 'I don't understand. Why have you come?'

'To afford you satisfaction. Wornton's murder can't go unpunished — so punish me. You don't need to target anyone else.'

'But . . .' Davern scratches his head, bewildered. 'Why kill him and then offer yourself? That doesn't make sense.'

Exactly the reaction I hoped for.

'You sent Wornton to talk peace. Ford Tasso sent Frank Weld. He's dead too. They were butchered while negotiating a deal with me.'

'Weld's dead?'

'Yes. I'm sure Tasso's gathering his forces even as we speak, just like you are, readying them for war.' I step over Wornton's body and get as close to Davern as I dare. 'I want peace, just like you and Tasso.' I pause to let that sink in, then hit him with the stinger. 'But it's not what the men who control the Snakes want.'

Davern's eyes narrow. 'I thought *you . . .*'

I shake my head, then gamble. 'No more than *you* control the Kluxers.'

He stiffens. 'What the fuck do you mean?'

'People assume you came to power because you're a smart operator making the most of the breaks, but I don't think you're flying solo. You had secret backing, didn't you?' His lips pinch together, confirming what I suspected. 'Did you know it was the priests or did they hide behind others?'

'They hid,' he sighs. 'I guessed it was them but I never knew for sure. I'm still not certain.'

'You are now,' I smile. 'The priests used you, just as they used me. But you've served your purpose, so they're finished with you. They want to take you out. Thus a war in the east with the Troops.'

'With the Snakes,' he corrects me.

I shake my head. 'You won't find any Snakes when you invade. They'll have slithered away. You'll only encounter Tasso's Troops. They'll be looking for the Snakes too, but who do you think they'll lay into when they can't find any?'

Davern doesn't answer but I know his brain is turning and I anticipate his next question before he asks it.

'Are the priests finished with *me*?' I shrug. 'No, but I'm done with them. I've had enough of being their stooge. One way or another, I'm ending it. Death can be my escape if you choose to kill me. Or we can make an alliance and fuck them up that way.' I lean in close and whisper. 'We can beat the *villacs* at their own game. Trust me, plot with me, and we can profit from this.'

Davern stares at me emotionlessly. I can't tell what he's thinking. Then he steps aside and nods at a couple of his men. 'Take Hyde in, clean him up, then call his mother and ask her to come over. Don't tell her he's dead – I'll break that news myself.' He starts back into the restaurant. Pauses and looks over his shoulder at me. 'Well? You coming or not?'

Grinning sickly, I tip an imaginary hat to the stunned Kluxers, then follow their leader into the sacrosanct halls of the Kool Kats Klub.

We talk fast and truthfully, laying our cards clean on the table. I learn things about Eugene Davern and his rise to the top which nobody else knows, and in return I tell him about my past and why the *villacs* are so interested in me. I don't have time to explain it all – wouldn't, even if I had, as I don't want him thinking I'm crazy – but I cover the basics and outline my plan. It's not a great plan but it's better than any he can think of. He's not convinced it will work, and dislikes the idea of my proposed partnership, but by the end of our talk he agrees to follow my lead 'to the bitter end'. We shake hands on the deal – for whatever the gesture's worth – then Davern goes to explain to his people why they have to trust a black assassin who brought the dead body of Hyde Wornton to the Kool Kats Klub on his motorbike.

While Davern does all in his power to win over his supporters – if he fails, it's curtains for everyone – I hightail it across the city to collect the body of Frank Weld. Sard hasn't returned and the Snakes are on guard outside the station, alert as ever. Once I have Frank strapped to the back of my bike, I tell them to get some rest. They depart, yawning and stretching. I watch them go, hoping they make it through the next few turbulent days – hoping we all make it – then set out for Party Central and my second do-or-die meeting of the infant day.

There's an angry skirmish on the border of the east at Stroud Square, between the Snakes and the police. A bank on the west side was broken into and the culprits made a run east. The police tried to follow but the Snakes had other ideas. A fight ensued and is quickly gathering pace. Another time, I'd stop and sort it out, but the confusion aids my purpose and I slip by the battling crowds unnoticed.

After an uneventful journey, I park outside the main doors of Party Central – which hang in scraps in the wake of the bomb attack – unstrap Frank and walk in past the wary Troops on duty. Marching straight through reception, I lay Frank on top of a counter – the receptionists behind it scatter, shrieking – and wait for a braver soul to come see what I want. Finally a seasoned secretary edges towards me. 'May I help you . . . sir?' she asks.

'Tell Mr Tasso that Paucar Wami and Frank Weld are here to see him.'

'Is he expecting you?' she asks, studying my tattooed face, shaved scalp and green eyes.

'No, but he'll see me.'

She hesitates, then picks up a phone and dials. I hear her murmur, 'He says he's Paucar Wami,' and 'I think he's *dead*.' Then she nods and hangs up. 'You can go up now, and you're to take Mr Weld with you.'

I lug Frank's body to the elevator – Jerry Falstaff's buddy, Mike Kones, is on duty again, but he doesn't recognize me – and rise in silence to the fifteenth floor. I make the long walk to Tasso's office, past dozens of ogling Troops, secretaries and execs, all anxious to see if the quickly spreading rumours are true.

Mags is waiting for me at the door to the office. She steps forward to check on Frank, takes his pulse, rolls up his eyelids, then sighs. 'He was a good man.'

'Yes. He was.'

'You knew him?' Like Mike Kones, she doesn't make me for Al Jeery.

'He was my friend.'

She stares at me, then returns to her desk. 'Mr Tasso will see you now. Be advised, the room is under armed surveillance and you *will* be targeted without warning if you make any threatening moves.'

Letting out a deep breath, I clear my head, turn the handle, push the door open with Frank's legs and enter.

Tasso's waiting for me in his chair, massaging his dead right arm, face even stonier than normal. He says nothing as I clear a space on the long desk and lay Frank on it. When I step away, he shuffles over to examine his dead colleague. After a few seconds he mutters, 'I always thought he'd outlive me. He had the luck of the devil.' He returns to his chair and trains his Cyclops-like gaze on me. 'This means war, Algiers.'

'I know.'

'Who killed him?'

'My father. He killed Hyde Wornton too.'

'So it's not all bad news.' He chuckles drily. 'Much as I like you, I can't let this slide. We have to hit now. There's no other way.'

'Again, I know.'

'So why'd you come? To beg forgiveness? Plead for your life?' I don't answer. He's not expecting me to. 'I can't let you walk away. People believe you're head of the Snakes. I know that's bullshit but I've got to play to the public on this one.'

'You've never played to the public,' I demur, 'and unless it suits your purpose, you won't play to them now. You'll kill me because it's what *you* want, not because it's what others expect.'

His lips spread in a granite-cold smile. 'We know one another too well. Next to impossible for either of us to surprise the other.' He frowns. 'But you surprised me by turning up today. What gives, Algiers?'

'I can return Capac Raimi to you.'

His frown deepens. 'That won't save you. It's too late for –'

'It's never too late,' I cut in. 'You've got to go to war, but be careful who you go to war with. The Snakes aren't the enemy, but they can be. Attack them now and you'll not only condemn Raimi to more suffering, but you'll create a military monster which in time will eclipse your own.

'On the other hand, if you hear me out, I can promise you Raimi's return and more power and freedom than you've ever enjoyed. You'll have to share, but it'll be infinitely better than what you've got going now.'

'You're not making sense,' he growls.

'I will if you give me a chance.'

He stares at me warily, his left eye glittering with doubt. Then he glances at Frank's dead face and nods. 'You've got ten minutes. Make it good.'

'I need twenty,' I tell him. 'And I won't make it good — I'll make it *great*.'

Tasso's harder to win over than Davern. He's spent longer kowtowing to the blind priests, and the superstitious fear which the two Cardinals had of them has rubbed off on him. Because the *villacs* were like gods to Dorak and Raimi, Tasso never thought to chance rebellion.

'Capac wouldn't like this,' he keeps muttering, and I have to press home the point that Raimi's a creation of theirs, tied to them in ways that ordinary humans aren't. If we can eliminate them, we'll give this city back its free will.

'But could Capac survive without them?' Tasso asks.

'I've no idea,' I answer honestly. 'But he'll never return on his own terms as long as they're running the show. We might have to sacrifice Raimi, but if that's the price of this city's freedom, don't you think it's worth it?'

'Dorak wouldn't have agreed,' Tasso grumbles. 'He wanted an heir who could run his company indefinitely.'

'But he thought Raimi would be able to work independ-

ently of the priests. Do you think he'd approve if he saw
how they can do as they please? This isn't Raimi's city —
it's theirs. If my way works, at best we'll hand it back to him
and he can proceed as Dorak planned. At worst we'll lose
him, but we'll rid this city of the priests, and I think Dorak
would rather that than how things currently stand.'

Eventually he agrees to consider my proposal. He makes
no promises, but says he'll hold his forces in check while he
mulls it over. He also lets me go and issues orders that I'm
not to be harmed — for the time being. He says I won't hear
from him when he makes his decision. I'll find out along
with the rest of the city tomorrow. I have to settle for that.
In truth, it's more than I had any right to hope for.

I'm hungry and weary, so I visit a nearby café and fill up
with sandwiches and coffee. Then I make one last call, to
the shack of the Harpies and their minder. I make quick time
on the quiet Sunday roads. I'm not sure why I'm including
Bill in this – I could get all I need elsewhere – but gut instinct
draws me to him, and I'm not about to start ignoring my
instincts at this critical stage of the game.

One of the Harpies is digging in a small garden outside
the house, crooning as she fusses over weeds as if they were
prize plants. She gurgles happily when she see me pulling
up – the Harpies associate me with feeding-time. I park and
enter by the unlocked front door.

Bill's downstairs in the living room, reading to the other
two women. I stand in the doorway unseen for a few minutes.
I recognize the text after a couple of lines. Mark Twain, either
Tom Sawyer or *Huck Finn*.

Pausing at the end of a chapter, he glances up and spies
me. A startled look shoots across his face

(*He's come to kill me!*)

then he relaxes. 'Hello Al,' he smiles. 'I didn't expect to

see you again.' Closing the book, he tells the ladies to run along. He remains seated, eyeing me silently. When he hears them in the yard, he asks quietly, 'Come to finish the job?'

'If I wanted to kill you, I'd have done it last week.'

'Why didn't you? You meant to when you arrived. What changed your mind?'

I don't answer, but cross the room and stare through a crack in the boarded-over window. I can't see the Harpies from here, just industrial wasteland, grey and infertile. 'Still having the nightmares?'

His shiver is audible. 'Yes.'

'You know how to stop them, don't you?'

'Kill myself?' He laughs shortly.

'No.' I face him. '*Atonement*. Put right some of the wrongs of the past. Build where you demolished.'

He frowns. 'I don't understand.'

'I need your help, Bill.'

His face creases with astonishment. 'You're asking *me* for help? After all I did to you?'

I nod, hiding a wry smile. 'I'm going into battle with some very dangerous men – your foes as well as mine – and I need to tool-up. I can go elsewhere, but I thought I'd give you the chance to –'

'Yes!' he interrupts, pulling himself to his feet, wincing at the pain in his old bones. 'I'd be glad to help. Overwhelmed! Tell me what I can do, Al.'

'You said you had bombs and bugs in the cellar, from the old days?' He nods eagerly, eyes bright, and I step away from the window. 'Show me.'

FOUR – WAR

Ama's bemused when I call and ask if she'd like to dine with me tonight. 'I thought you'd have more important matters on your mind.'

I smile down the phone. 'The important stuff can wait. Tomorrow's a big day for me. I'd like to unwind before I face it.'

'What's going on, Al?' she asks, perplexed.

'Tell you later. Want to go somewhere fancy or will we snack in Cafran's?'

'Cafran's is fine.'

'Eight-thirty?'

'Sure. Take care, Al.'

'I'll try.'

I hit the shower, then towel myself dry. I begin applying face paint in front of my TV sets, keeping an eye on the latest news. My cell rings — Sard, with mixed news. He's located most of the rogue Snakes, but six are still on the loose. I tell him not to bother with the final half-dozen. 'Take the rest of the night off. Relax. Go bowling. Make love.'

'Sapa Inca?' he replies, startled.

'There's a derelict office block on Romily Street,' I tell him, having chosen the location at random earlier. 'Meet me there at midday tomorrow on the top floor with a dozen of your most trusted Snakes. I've a special mission for you. It may prove the most vital of the entire campaign.'

'I won't let you down,' he vows.

I finish applying the paint, check that the tattoos can't be seen, then slip on the wig and clean clothes. I pedal across the city on my bike as plain Al Jeery, whistling as I go, as if I hadn't a care in the world.

Cafran's is busy but Ama has reserved a table near the back of the restaurant and we sit, shielded from the crowd by tall plastic plants.

'How's Cafran?' I ask.

'Blooming. He's off scouting for premises — thinking of opening a new joint. He could have done it long ago but never bothered. He said he didn't consider it worth the effort, until now.'

'Because of you.' She smiles shyly. 'Think you'll stay here long-term?'

'I'd like to, if I have a choice.' A waitress materializes. Ama orders for me. While we're waiting, she opens a bottle of wine and pours. I fill her in on what's been happening, the plan I'm hatching to pull the city back from the brink of all-out war. She listens intently, venturing little in the way of comment until I finish shortly after the first course has arrived.

'You really believe it will work?' she asks neutrally.

'Can't hurt to try.'

'I don't know about that. If the *villacs* find out what you're up to, they might turn on you. Capac was their golden boy but it didn't stop them slapping him down when he refused to bow to their wishes.'

'It's worth the risk.'

She chews in silence, then says, 'I want to help.'

'I figured you would. You know it's dangerous, that we

might have to sacrifice ourselves? My aim is to stop the priests. If I walk away alive, that's a bonus.'

'I don't care. I'm not going to let you go alone.'

I cough discreetly and wipe around my mouth with a napkin. 'I won't be *quite* alone. I plan to take along my father.'

She blinks. 'The killer?'

'He's a useful addition. Fast. Deadly. Unstoppable. Besides, if I don't include him, he'll leave, and I don't want that, not until . . .' I shrug, not entirely sure what I intend to do about Paucar Wami if everything works out with the priests.

'Can we trust him?' Ama asks.

'In this matter, yes. He hates the *villacs* even more than I do.'

Ama pushes her plate away, frowning. 'What if Ford Tasso and Eugene Davern don't come through?'

'I'll push ahead anyway. I've come too far to back out now. I can't finish off the priests without Tasso and Davern, but I'll do what I can to hurt them.'

Ama sighs. 'We must be crazy to think we can pull this off.'

'Yeah,' I grin.

She mirrors my smile. 'So I guess we'd better make the most of the good life while we can.' She tops up our glasses. 'Cheers!'

We eat slowly, padding out the meal with lots of conversation. Some of it concerns the *villacs* and the troubles, but mostly it's about ourselves, our pasts (what little Ama can remember of hers) and what we'd like to do if we had the freedom to choose our futures. Ama wants to stay here, help Cafran, take over when he retires, squeeze in some travel during her holidays. I remind her of her limitations as an Ayuamarcan – she can only exist for a few days at a time away from the city – but she dismisses that. 'We're talking about dreams, not reality. I'll dream what I like, thank you very much.'

Cafran Reed returns. He looks much brisker than the last time I saw him. He kisses Ama's cheeks, draws up a chair and tells us about his day. He hasn't found anywhere he loves, but has heard about a dockside café which sounds promising. We discuss property and rental prices as the restaurant empties around us.

As we drain the final bottle of the night, I bid Cafran and Ama farewell. Ama rises to see me out, but I tell her not to. Win or lose, she might never again sit with the man who was once her father. These minutes are precious and shouldn't be wasted on a bum like me. 'See you later,' I mutter, and she echoes the adieu, slipping me a pointed look to confirm our arrangement while Cafran smiles and sips his wine.

On the street I stand by my bike, savouring the night, putting off the time when I have to shed the disguise and become Paucar Wami again. People rarely realize how well-off they are. A fine meal, a good bottle of wine, charming company . . . who needs anything more? I'd happily trade the Snakes – hell, the whole city – for Cafran Reed's restaurant and peace of mind.

Monday. Day of decisions. Day of destiny.

Sard and his dozen arrive spot on midday. I greet them as their Sapa Inca in a tiny office – they only just squeeze in – and treat them to an abbreviated version of my plan. They're confused and uneasy, but I impress on them the importance of their mission, how our future depends on it.

'It's time to choose. Either you serve your people or you serve the *villacs*. You can't have it both ways. I know they recruited and trained you, but they did so in order to use you. If you trust me, I'll try to grant you the power you seek, as well as the freedom to enjoy it.'

Eventually I talk them round. The priests did too good a job of building me up. The Snakes think I'm infallible. They pledged their hearts and souls to Paucar Wami. They'll do as I command, paradoxical as it seems to them.

I dismiss the Snakes with orders to carry on as usual if the day doesn't go as planned, then return to my post at the burnt-out police station where various Cobras await my instructions. It's difficult to act as if this is a day like any other, but I focus on their reports and send them about their duties, marshalling them as they expect, taking a few minutes to 'commend' the Snakes who carried out the attacks on the rest of the city.

It's minutes shy of 16:00 when I learn of Ford Tasso's decision. I'm in the van when a Snake on the border of our territory makes the call. 'We're under attack!' he shouts, the sound of heavy gunfire muffling his words. 'It's the Troops, repeat, the Troops! The bastards are invading!'

All eyes snap to me. I keep my face impassive, masking my emotions.

'Sapa Inca?' a Snake asks. 'Should I tell the others in that area to move against the enemy?'

'No,' I sigh. 'Sound a retreat. Tell them to back off slowly, to make the Troops fight for every block, but not to make a stand. And they're to advise civilians to seek shelter. I don't want innocents getting caught in the crossfire.'

The Snake nods obediently and sets about alerting the Cobras. I spend the time it takes to spread the word in silent contemplation, considering the attack, what it means, where it might lead.

As the afternoon progresses, it becomes evident that the Troops have divided into four platoons and are marching on us from the west and south. They haven't been sighted in the north and east. My Cobras think they're lying in wait there, in case we make a break for freedom.

As the four platoons of Troops advance on Cockerel Square – their target was apparent early on, but I haven't withdrawn the Snakes who are there – word breaks that Eugene Davern's Kluxers have smashed through in the north.

'Are you certain?' I bark at the scout who reports over the crackle of a cheap cell phone.

'Fuck yes!' he yells. 'There's maybe a hundred of the fuckers, shooting everything in their path, leaving a trail of burning buildings and cars behind them.'

'Get out,' I snap. 'Head for Cockerel Square.'

'Don't you want us to fight them?'

'Negative. Rendezvous with the others in the Square and await further orders.'

I meet the worried gazes of those in the van and muster a smile. 'Heads up. We aren't beaten yet. Bring me every Cobra that you can. And send a couple of runners to the *villacs* – I'd love to hear what they have to say about this.'

As I wait for the Cobras and priests, another band of Kluxers is reported, moving parallel to the first. They're leaving a trail of fiery devastation, and right about now I'd imagine most people are more concerned about Davern's forces than Tasso's. But the Troops will be at Cockerel Square first. They can dig in and set themselves up as the leading force in the east. I assign two phalanxes the task of slowing the Troops, then break to meet with the first of the arriving Cobras.

It's almost 20:00 before all the Cobras and three representatives of the *villacs* are sitting or standing in the room where Hyde Wornton and Frank Weld met their end. I cast a quick glance around as I enter. The seven Cobras are anxious, but regard me trustingly, banking on me to figure a way out of this mess.

'Seems to me we have three options,' I begin bluntly. 'We focus on either the Troops or the Kluxers and throw everything we have against one of them, then worry about the other lot later. We divide our forces and fight a war on two fronts. Or we stick our heads down and get the fuck out of here.'

The Cobras chuckle – they think I'm joking – but the laughter dies when a priest who speaks English nods and says, 'We would advise a retreat, Sapa Inca.'

'Are you crazy?' a Cobra called Peddar roars. 'Give ground to those bastards? I'd rather kill myself!'

The others nod and agree, except Sard, who gazes darkly at me but holds his tongue. I let them express their feelings, then clear my throat for silence. 'Let us hear him out. I want to know why he is so eager to fold.'

'A withdrawal is not surrender,' the *villac* says, smiling blindly. 'The invaders come to fight. They won't leave until they shed blood. If we are not here, they will clash with each other. We wait until that battle is over, then strike at the weary survivors.'

'And if they don't pause?' I ask. 'If they track us down the tunnels?'

'They will not find us,' the priest says confidently. 'The tunnels are ours. We will repel them.'

'This is bullshit,' Peddar shouts, looking pleadingly to his fellow Cobras. 'If we pull back now, they'll massacre our people. I didn't get into this to make promises to my friends and family, then leave them in the shit when –'

'Soldier,' I interrupt quietly, 'you are relieved of command. Find your second, tell him he has been promoted, and ask him to join us. You will return to your phalanx and await further orders.'

Peddar stares at me hatefully, his whole body trembling. Then he remembers who I am and the pledge he made to obey me. He turns to leave, angry tears in his eyes. 'Peddar,' I stop him. 'We do this for the community. We all got into this because we cared. We won't leave them high and dry. You have my word.'

He smiles weakly. 'Thank you, Sapa Inca.'

When he's gone, I face the *villac*. 'They expect resistance in Cockerel Square. We should leave a couple of phalanxes to put up a fight. They need not battle to the death, just hold the Troops for half an hour, then "quit" when the pressure gets too much. The Troops will hopefully stop to draw breath and secure the Square. Next thing they know, the Kluxers will be upon them. The two of them can fight all they want after that.'

'Agreed,' the *villac* says. 'In the meantime you can lead the retreat.'

'Not me. I'll be in Cockerel Square with my men.'

'Is that wise?' he frowns.

'The Troops will expect me. The leader of the Snakes wouldn't desert his men at a time like this. I'll put in an appearance, make it look genuine. Don't worry, I have no intention of letting the Troops take me. I plan to be around when we move back in to pick up the pieces. I've a score or two to settle with Ford Tasso.'

'Very well,' the priest says. 'We will arrange the retreat.'

'Sard,' I bark, heading for the door, 'choose two of your phalanxes and join me. Make sure your soldiers are prepared for death. We want to make this look as real as possible. Some of us will have to die.'

'We'll do what is required, Sapa Inca,' he vows, and follows me out into the night, leaving the other agitated Cobras to break the news to their Snakes.

It's after midnight when the Troops hit Cockerel Square. Apart from myself, Sard and his phalanxes, approximately sixty gang members are here to greet them. I tried to deter the others – told them this was a smokescreen, that we would retreat, that they should disband – but although most heeded my warnings, these sixty-odd refused to give ground. They're determined to hold off the Troops for as long as possible and inflict as much damage as they can. Cockerel Square is theirs and they'd rather die than concede it. I tell them they *will* die, that we'll quit before the Troops take us, but their hearts are set on a glorious confrontation with a vastly superior foe. You can't save those who don't want saving.

Watching the Troops manoeuvre into position is a sobering sight. Three of the four platoons converge on the Square – they must be holding the fourth in reserve – blocking it off on all sides, throwing up a net of death from which there can be no escape. Their commanders deploy them expertly, covering every exit.

'We were crazy to think we could take these fuckers,' Sard says beside me. 'Even if they suffered heavy losses in the fight with Davern, they'd still be too much for us.'

'Not if we hit them as guerrillas,' I disagree. 'Picking at them from the sides, surprising a squadron in the dark, booby-trapping roads and buildings . . . we could demoralize them to the point where they'd have to strike a deal. That's the *villacs'* plan. They don't want to replace the Troops, merely complement them.'

Without warning, someone fires a bazooka or something similarly heavyweight. Those of us at the walls scatter as the shell hits. Some aren't quick enough and the screams of dying men are added to the shrieks of more shells and the exploding thuds of bricks and plaster.

They focus on the exterior of the Square for five long minutes, demolishing the barricades and most of the walls. They don't lob shells into the centre – they want to keep the interior intact, to utilize once they've driven us out – so that's where we group, a hundred or so men and women, waiting for the bombs to stop and the one-on-one combat to commence.

There's a pause when silence descends, while the forces

outside mass around the new openings, awaiting the order
to advance. We hurry to what's left of the walls and prepare
our defence, laying mines, picking targets, stacking rifles and
pistols by our sides. I look for the commander-in-chief of the
Troops (not to take a shot, just curious to know who Tasso
replaced Frank with) and spot the distant figure of Jerry
Falstaff, running the show with admirable coolness.

A minute passes. Two. The tension should be mounting
but it isn't. The Snakes are safe in the knowledge that we'll
slip away before the finish, while the others have resigned
themselves to a bloody finale. Looking around, I see only
warriors smiling grimly in anticipation of battle, eager for it
to begin, not fearful of the deaths to come.

No trumpets or whistles sound the attack. One moment
the Troops are standing to attention, the next they're surging
forward, firing as they run. We hold off the first wave, forcing
them to break and retreat, but a second wave forms immediately and they rush us. We've no choice but to fall back,
although a few sturdier – dumber – souls hold their position.
They succumb to the Troops within seconds, but take a hefty
number of the enemy with them.

As the Troops mount the rubble, they hit the mines we
planted. The air fills with bloody, fleshy scraps of human
meat and bone. They lose twenty or thirty men in the charge,
but push on regardless. Seconds later the first of them clear
the mines and tackle those waiting within the boundaries of
the Square.

The fighting is brutal and merciless. Three or four Troops
fall for every one of ours, but their commanders have allowed
for that and the soldiers press on without slowing. They could
have arranged a clinical takeover, subjected us to sniper fire
and short, concentrated jabs, but they're after a quick victory,
perhaps motivated by the threat of the Kluxers — they'd
rather not face Davern's forces in the open.

I remain close to Sard and the Snakes, guarding the access to the underground tunnels which we carved out over the last few days, the holes in the net through which we'll wriggle free. I take little part in the bloodshed. I fire off a few rounds, felling at least one soldier, but my heart isn't in this. I've no wish to kill any of the Troops, many of whom I once served with.

I decide we've had enough – I've just seen two of my men obliterated by a grenade – and signal the retreat. Sixty seconds later, not one Snake stands in the Square, apart from myself, last to leave. I catch the eye of a surviving gangster – there can't be more than twenty left – and bellow at him. 'You can come with us if you've changed your mind!'

'Nah,' he laughs, waving me away. 'The party's just warming up.'

I salute him, spare the others one last glance – they're surrounded by Troops, damned for sure – then slip down the hole. I crawl at a sharp angle until I come to a larger tunnel where I can stand. Sard is waiting for me. Once I'm clear, he sets the timer on the explosives which we strung up earlier – all the entrances to the underworld are primed to blow – and we hurry to join the others.

Five minutes later, we're standing in a small room deep under Cockerel Square. The last of the bombs has detonated. We've staged a successful escape. I count heads — twenty-three, including myself and Sard, though two are critically injured and may not live to see the dawn. It could have been far worse.

'How many of the dozen you picked for the mission made it through?' I ask Sard quietly.

'All of them,' he answers. 'I didn't use them in the Square. I left them with orders to meet me later.'

'Good thinking. When are you meeting them?'

He checks his watch. 'They should be in place already. It'll take me half an hour to get there.'

'Everything's set? You've run tests on the equipment?'

'Yes, Sapa Inca.'

I take his right hand and squeeze hard. 'Luck to you, Cobra.'

'Luck,' he replies and slips away to do his reluctant duty.

I disperse the rest of the Snakes, with orders to tell the *villacs* that I'm waiting here in case any survivors make it through. They go without question, spirits low, not because of the battering we've endured, but because they had to run. I hope I live to see those spirits raised again, though I doubt I will.

Alone in the darkness, I wait a while, listening to the faint sounds of the Troops overhead as they consolidate their stronghold in the Square. Then I set off through the series of tunnels which I mapped out earlier, moving swiftly, encountering no one, a ghost in the machine.

The area around the police station is deserted. It's 02:12, the Snakes have slipped away and the locals are wisely keeping a low profile. I've been striding around the rooftops for twenty minutes, in search of my father. No sign so far. I'll give him until half past, then leave without him if I have to.

When my deadline expires, I head down to the street. I'm disappointed he isn't coming but I won't cry about it. For ten years I did a damn fine job of pretending to be Paucar Wami. I can masquerade as him for a few hours more.

As my feet touch ground, a voice speaks from the shadows. 'Leaving your poor ole pappy behind, Al m'boy?'

I smile at the wall, then replace the smile with a scowl and spin to face him. 'How long have you been following me?'

'A while. I was waiting to see if you would spot me. You are not as alert as you should be. Perhaps the Troops and Kluxers unnerved you.'

'I've had a lot on my mind,' I admit, 'but they're not first in my thoughts. I'm ready to take the fight to the priests. Are you in?'

'You have a plan?' he asks eagerly, stepping out of the shadows. The front of his T-shirt's flecked with blood — looks like he's been *enjoying* himself.

'I decided to keep things simple. We find a priest who talks English – a few can – and get him to lead us to Capac Raimi. We grab Raimi, bust through anyone who gets in our way, and escape.'

He frowns. 'That is not much of a plan.'

'There's more,' I grin. 'I'll tell you the rest later. Ama's waiting for us.'

'The lady you met in Cafran's?'

'You've been keeping a close eye on me,' I note sourly.

'Only because I care about you,' he smirks. 'Where does she fit in with this?'

'I'll explain as we go. Where's your jacket?'

'In an apartment I've been using.'

'Then we'll pick up another on our way.'

'I need one?'

'Yeah.'

'May I ask why?'

'To hide the bulge of your vest.'

In response to his raised eyebrow, I fill him in on the finer details as we pad the several blocks to where Ama's waiting with all we'll hopefully need to give us a fighting chance against the accursed *villacs*.

FIVE – THE CLEANSING

Ama and my father both know their way around the upper levels of the tunnels, so we make quick time, avoiding the milling Snakes and *villacs*, circling around them through smaller, seldom used passages. Usually these tunnels would be guarded at some point along the line, but in all the confusion they've been left unprotected.

The temperature drops as we descend and torches become scarce. Often we have to navigate through pitch blackness, linking hands, Ama or Wami leading the way, relying on instinct and memory. When I ask during a pause if they're sure of our direction, they insist they are, though neither knows how. I ask how much further they can take us, but they can't say. They can only look ahead to the end of any given tunnel.

As we progress, Ama comes more into command, her knowledge of the tunnels sharper than Wami's. We move steadily lower, down countless sets of stairs and steeply angled corridors. The priests must have been working on this system for hundreds of years. I'm stunned the city hasn't collapsed in on itself, built on such riddled soil. They must be incredible architects to carve out and maintain all this.

After a long period of blackness, we come to a cavern lit

by several torches. Five tunnels branch off it. We examine them in turn, Ama and Wami venturing a little down the maw of each, waiting for the click of recognition which has guided them this far. But it doesn't come. The tunnels are alien to both. Neither knows which way to go.

We squat in the middle of the cavern, debating our next move. Ama loosens the straps of the vest she's wearing and slips in a hand to massage her back. The vests are lined with explosives, a gift from Bill. The detonators are strapped to our wrists, a pair for each of us. Small bands of hard plastic with a button in the centre. They have to be pressed in turn, first the left, then the right within three seconds, to set off the charges. The explosion of each vest will destroy every-thing within a fifty-foot radius on open ground. Down here in the confinement of the tunnels, they should be even more effective.

The vests are both our safeguard and last resort, to be used to threaten our way out of a tight situation or take our enemies down. My father wears his reluctantly and says he'll use it only as a bluff, but I think, if pushed, he'd rather detonate it and kill a few priests than succumb to their rule again.

I won't hesitate to set off the charges. I've come here to die. I haven't really considered the possibility that I might get out alive. It's destroy-as-much-as-I-can time, consequ-ences be damned.

'What now?' I ask, checking my watch. 06:08. It'll be dawn soon in the world above. I wonder idly what sort of a day it will be, and how the various participants are faring in the war to control the east.

'We have markers,' Wami says, jingling his stash of poker chips. We're each carrying a large packet of chips. Even though we've been dropping them along the way, the bags are still more than half full. 'We take the tunnels in turn, marking our path so we can find the way back, and see where they lead.'

'That could take forever,' I grunt. 'The *villacs* will note my absence soon and wonder about it. They might figure out what we're up to.'

Wami shrugs. 'We knew the plan was makeshift, that we would have to rely on luck. Personally I am surprised we made it this far. The fates have been kind to us. We should not insult them by complaining.'

'We don't have to go forward,' I note. 'We could back-track. There might be a way around this cavern.'

'I doubt it,' Wami says. 'All paths lead here. I do not know why I think that, but I do.'

'Then I guess there's nothing else for it.' I extract my bag of poker chips and move to the mouth of the nearest tunnel. 'Shall we try this one first?'

Ama looks at me, frowning. 'I've been here before. And I've been beyond. I remember a huge cavern, pillars rising from floor to ceiling, a raised circular stone like the *inti watana*, and . . .' She stops, shaking her head.

'Do you know how to get to it?' I ask eagerly.

'No, but . . .' Her frown deepens. 'We should stay here. I have a feeling that if we wait long enough, we'll be shown the way.'

I share a glance with my father. 'I do not like it,' he says. 'We will be targets if we stay. I would rather keep on the move.'

'She's led us this far,' I remind him. 'You ran out of ideas several levels up.'

Wami scowls, then nods curtly. 'Very well. We will wait. But if a way does not present itself within the next few hours, I will search for it myself or abandon this crazy quest. I do not intend to grow old down here in the dark.'

A strained silence embraces us, interrupted only by the

occasional sputter or spit of the torches. I sit by Ama but she's distracted, sniffing the air, studying the walls and tunnels, waiting for something but not sure what.

An hour passes. Two. My father hasn't moved. He sits with inhuman poise, eyes closed, head bowed, breathing lightly. I try to mimic his appearance but I'm too edgy. My eyes keep flicking to Ama, Wami, the tunnels, my watch.

As the third hour draws to its close, Ama stands and moves to the mouth of one of the tunnels. My father's eyes open slowly and he gazes at her. When she turns, she's smiling. 'They come.'

'Who?' I ask, hurrying to where she's standing.

'You can't hear them yet. But they're coming.'

'Who?' I ask again.

'I don't know. But they'll lead us where we wish to go.'

My eyes scan the cavern in search of a hiding place, although I know from the last three hours that there isn't one. 'Will we hide in a tunnel?'

'We do not know which they will choose,' Wami notes.

'If we pick the one they take, we run on ahead. With luck they won't –'

'No,' Ama says softly. 'We stay and present ourselves. This is where we were always meant to come when we were ready.'

'I will not surrender myself to the priests,' Wami says stiffly. 'You may greet them if you wish. I will move on ahead, hide and follow later.'

'No,' Ama disagrees. 'Stay or be excluded. Only the invited may progress. They'll know you've been here. If you don't offer yourself . . .' She smiles tightly. 'We both know what they can do to Ayuamarcans when we displease them.'

Wami growls a curse but makes no move for the tunnels.

'Another thing,' Ama says, sliding out the pair of knives I fitted her with at the start of our trek. 'We must disarm ourselves. They won't accept us otherwise.'

'Does that include our vests?' I hiss.

She pauses. 'I'm not sure. We can't take knives or guns. By rights we should leave the vests too, but . . . No. Let's chance it. If they frisk us, we'll have to take them off, but I don't think they'll expect such weapons. We might be able to sneak them in.'

I lay my knives and pistol on the floor. 'Are you doing this or not?' I ask my father, who's standing unhappily in the middle of the cavern.

'Only a fool voluntarily abandons his weapons,' he says.

'We still have *these*,' I grin, flexing my fingers. 'I've never seen an armed *villac*. If you can't take care of them with your bare hands . . .'

He smiles and disarms. 'Very well, Al m'boy. Hand-to-hand it shall be.'

With all our weapons on the floor, laid out in neat rows, we squat and wait for the guides promised by Ama to appear.

Forty minutes later, they come. Judging by the echoes of their footsteps, there are three of them. 'You two take the left,' Wami hisses, moving to the right of the tunnel entrance and pressing close to the wall.

'No,' Ama says calmly. 'We'll wait for them in the open. They must believe that we pose no threat.'

Wami grits his teeth but he does as Ama says, deliberately positioning himself to my side, giving Ama the cold shoulder. I'm as unsure about this as he is – the plan was to grab a priest and torture Raimi's location out of him, not give ourselves up – but I trust Ama. I just hope that trust isn't misplaced, that she's not a pawn of the priests' sent to betray us from within.

A few minutes later, a trio of *villacs* enters the cavern. I'm pleased to note that the middle priest is the English-speaking one who introduced me to this sub-world the day I first met my reincarnated father. 'Pleased' because it means we can make him talk in our language if we have to resort to torture.

The *villacs* stop when they sense us and the hand of one streaks to a pouch tied to his waist. Then they recognize us by our scent or our auras and their faces relax.

'Welcome, Flesh of Dreams,' the middle priest says, bowing. 'And welcome, Dreams Made Flesh.' He nods at Ama and Paucar Wami in turn. 'It is good that you found your way here. We have waited a long time for this.'

'We've laid aside our weapons,' Ama says. 'We offer ourselves freely and ask to be guided to . . .' she hesitates then concludes weakly ' . . . wherever we're supposed to go.'

The priest smirks. 'Your memories are incomplete, as they were meant to be.' He faces me and his smile fades. 'Are you prepared to accept your destiny, Flesh of Dreams?'

'Yes.'

He frowns. 'You sound uncertain. Perhaps this is not the right time. Maybe you should return to the surface and come again when –'

'It's now or never,' I cut in. 'The city's yours, or soon will be. If you're to divide it up as you wish, this is the time to do it. Take me to Capac Raimi. Let me talk to him and see if we can reach an agreement.'

One of the other *villacs* says something in their own language. The middle priest replies, then addresses me again. 'We would rather you had come to us in the cave of the *inti watana*, where our brothers could have borne witness to your pledge. But the most important thing is that you *have* come. We'll lead you, and introduce you to the one who will look into your heart and judge your true intentions.' His blind eyes fall on my father and his features darken. 'This one is not desired. The woman was your guide and is welcome, but the killer was meant to have departed this realm. Send him away.'

'No,' I shoot back. 'He comes with me. I promised him answers.'

'He is untrustworthy,' the priest warns. 'He will turn on you.'

'Maybe. But he's my father and I'm taking him.'

The *villac* cocks his head at his brothers, inviting comment. When they say nothing, he sniffs. 'So be it. He is your charge. You will answer for any of his indiscretions.'

The priest walks to the second tunnel from the right. We start to follow but he stops us and enters the tunnel alone. A few minutes later he returns with three sets of white robes. 'Undress and put these on. You can only be presented to the *Coya* in the attire of her chosen.'

'What's a *Coya*?' I ask suspiciously.

'You will see once you have donned the robes.' He holds them out to us.

I stall, thinking of the explosives-laden vests. Then Ama presses against me and whispers, 'They can't see. Take off your clothes but leave on the vest.'

Smiling – it's easy to forget that the priests are blind – I do as Ama says, and so does my father. I have a few uneasy moments when I take off my T-shirt – I keep expecting the priest to burst out with a sudden, 'What the hell is *that?*' – but the vests go undetected and moments later we're in the robes. I grab my packet of chips, slip the bug from the collar of my jacket – we're all wearing miniature units – and attach it to my new garment. Wami and Ama do likewise.

'If you're quite finished . . .' the priest says, bemused by the delay.

'Ready and waiting, captain,' I laugh buoyantly.

He moves to the tunnel on the far left and leads the way into a long stretch of darkness. Ama, Wami and I follow, the other priests bringing up the rear.

*   *   *

For half an hour we wind through twisting, unlit tunnels, our eyes as useless as the *villacs'*. As we turn yet another bend, I glimpse a dim light far ahead of us. I also fix on a dull thundering sound. I've been aware of it for several minutes but I only now realize what it is.

'That's a waterfall,' I mutter, the first words anyone's uttered since we left the cave with the torches.

'All must be cleansed before communion with the *Coya*,' the lead *villac* says. 'You have nothing to fear. It is merely part of the ritual.'

A short while later we're standing on a platform above a stream, facing the waterfall. It falls from a cleft high above us and gurgles away through a gulley in the floor below the platform. A narrow wooden bridge runs to a ledge on the other side, passing beneath the falling water. There are torches on either side. I wonder why the blind priests bother with lights. I mean to ask, but before I can, the *villac* speaks.

'Do as I do,' the priest says, walking into the spray and spreading his arms. He turns in a slow circle, the water soaking him, drenching his hair and robes. Stepping out, he continues to the far side of the bridge and faces us. 'Come.'

My father steps up beside me. 'Will the explosives be affected by the water?'

'No. But the microphones will.' I raise my voice, addressing the priest. 'How much further is it?'

'Why?'

'I don't like the idea of marching through these cold tunnels soaked like a water-rat. Can't we skip this part?'

'The cleansing is essential,' he snaps. 'Besides, you won't have to walk far, and you are required to rest in a room of steam before progressing to the hall of the *Coya*. That will warm you.'

'Wonderful,' I mutter, dropping a couple of poker chips by the side of the path. Then I shout, 'I'd rather be anywhere but here right now!' That's the signal to Sard. Once it's been given, I walk into the spray and immerse myself. I hear the crackle and hiss of the bug as the water hits. If there was a problem with the signal when I spoke, or if Sard was distracted, we're finished. All we can do from this point on is cross our fingers, play for time . . . and pray.

When we're together again, dripping and shivering, the two *villacs* at the rear move to the front and join their companion. They set off, chanting. Although they don't tell us to follow, we're obviously meant to. Sharing a wary glance, we wring out the wet folds of our robes, then hurry after the priests, to cover the last leg of the subterranean march.

We arrive at a pair of doors twelve feet high, carved out of dark wood, adorned with gold-lined murals of mountains, rivers and warped human figures. At the top, spread across the two doors, are representations of the sun and moon, a face visible at the heart of each, a man's in the sun, a woman's in the moon. The symbols must have been daubed with luminescent paint because they glow softly in the gloom.

The English-speaking *villac* steps forward, hammers twice on either door, then kneels, lowers his head and covers it with his hands. The other priests stay on their feet, so we do too. After a lengthy wait, the doors swing inwards. Thick clouds of steam bubble out. At first I can't see anybody, but as I peer intently, I realize someone is standing just inside the doors. It's a woman.

The woman addresses the priest on the ground. He replies in his arcane tongue. She responds sharply, her gaze directed at my father. The priest speaks again. There's a pause when he finishes, then the woman steps forward out of the steam and into the glow of the sun and moon.

The first thing I notice is that, apart from a pair of loose sandals, she's naked. Once I recover from that brief shock

– the last thing I expected to be greeted with was a nudist –
I swiftly note her characteristics. Short, stocky, a flat face,
broad nose, painfully white skin, hair tied back, curved fingernails at least three inches long, her pubic hair shaved away
except for a small circular mound which has been dyed bright
orange — a tribute to the sun, I guess. And she isn't blind.
Her eyes are large and brown.

The woman bows and makes a snake-like sign in the air
with her left hand. I glance at Ama and my father, then smile
shakily and half-wave. 'Pleased to meet you too,' I chuckle
edgily. The woman frowns and holds up a hand, instructing
us to stay, and retreats into the shadows.

Minutes pass without the priests moving or talking, or the
woman returning. I want to ask about her, these doors and
what lies beyond, but I sense this isn't the moment for questions. Instead I pick at my robes, readjusting them around
my vest, trying to hide the bulges of the explosives. Ama
and my father do likewise.

Finally the woman reappears, flanked by eight others, who
march in pairs, all as naked as she is, similar in height, build
and looks. As they come through the door, the women branch
out, encircling Ama, Wami and me. They pivot around us,
lips moving faintly as they chant softly. My father studies
their naked bodies openly, turning as they turn. Ama stands
stiffly, ignoring them. I focus on their eyes, trying to hold
their gaze so they don't notice the shapes beneath my robes.

Wami reaches out to touch one of the naked women. She
flinches and subjects him to an angry barrage of Incan
gibberish. When she stops, the priest on the floor says, 'It is
not permitted to make contact with the *mamaconas*. No male
hand may maul their sacred flesh, except in the time of
mating. If you attempt to touch her again, you will be disposed
of. That goes for you too, Flesh of Dreams. As much as you
mean to us, certain taboos cannot be broken.'

'You must let me know when it is "mating time",' my father murmurs.

'Who are the *mamaconas*?' Ama asks.

'The priestesses of our *Coya*,' the *villac* says. 'Hand-servants of the queen. They see to her needs and assist her in the time of creation. They are her daughters and sisters, her ever-constant companions, our wives and mothers.'

'It sounds deliciously incestuous,' Wami smirks.

The priest takes his hands off his head, stands and faces us. 'It is almost time to meet the *Coya*. She is old and wise. She does not speak your language, but will know if you are belittling her, and will react without humour if slighted. Do not test her, Dreams Made Flesh, if you value your life, for she endowed you with it and she can just as surely rid you of it again.'

Wami smiles, but I sense the tension behind his grin. The naked women come to a standstill and lower their chins to their chests, resting their long fingernails on the pale flesh of their stomachs. The three *villacs* form a file in front of us and chant. The air smells of incense, but that might be psycho-somatic — I feel as if I'm in church, so perhaps I'm imagining the sickly scent.

The priests move forward. The heads of the *mamaconas* lift and they nod at us. I share a worried glance with Ama and my father, then start ahead. Ama, Paucar Wami and the *mamaconas* follow. When we're all inside, the doors close, plunging us into steam-ridden darkness and mystery.

SIX – MAMA OCLLO

We stumble forward blindly until the English-speaking *villac* snaps, 'Stop!' The clouds of steam intensify, warming my damp robes. 'We remain here until the cleansing is complete. It may be some time. Keep still and do not speak. Any inter-ruption will necessitate an even longer delay.'

We stand close by one another while the steam envelops us and the *mamaconas* slither around, whispering, occasion-ally breathing in our faces or scratching us teasingly with their nails. I don't like this. It's surreal. I imagine all sorts of monstrosities circling us. I want to break free of the steam, shove the priestesses away and run. But I hold myself in check and remind myself that every minute wasted is a bonus, as long as they don't keep us here *too* long.

Eventually the *mamaconas* withdraw and the priest says, 'Advance.' We stagger through a set of heavy drapes, into a candle-lit tunnel a hundred feet long, blocked at the far end by more drapes. I pause nervously at the second set of drapes, then rotate my neck left and right, working the tension out of it. When I'm calm, I part the drapes and step through.

I find myself in a cavern with a low roof – no more than seven feet high in places – supported by dozens of thick, wooden pillars. The room is lit by many candles, set in the floor, casting their light upwards. Women crowd the area close to the entrance, spread in a semi-circle, naked like our guides, eyes bright. When they see me, they squeal like groupies at a rock concert and point excitedly with long, curved nails.

'You seem to be a hit with the ladies,' my father grins.

'But do they want to screw me or sacrifice me?'

'Possibly both. But if you are lucky, they will fuck you first.'

Ama moves up beside us and eyes the women critically. 'I don't think it would kill them to buy some clothes.'

The English-speaking *villac* sniffs. 'The *mamaconas* have been blessed by the goddess of the moon. They are pure, and must exist in a state of purity. They cover the soles of their feet because this earth is not worthy to receive their touch, but otherwise parade as nature intended.' He sighs. 'It is because of their purity that we surrender the use of our eyes. We are not fit to gaze upon them.'

'You let yourselves be blinded so you can't look at your priestesses?' I blink slowly. 'Didn't you ever think of blindfolds?'

'One does not blind oneself to heavenly beauty with a strip of cloth,' he retorts. 'It is an honour to give one's eyes in the service of the *mamaconas*.'

Ama moves ahead of us and studies the women. They don't attempt to shield their nakedness. Some pick at her clothes, frowning, as if they've never seen such garments. 'These are servants of the moon goddess?' Ama asks the priest.

'Yes.'

'I thought you worshipped the sun god, Inti.'

'The creator of all things was Viracocha. When he created the first people, Manco Capac and Mama Ocllo, he split himself in two, becoming the sun and the moon. Our men worship the male form of the god, our women the female. But you will learn more of this soon. Come — the *Coya* awaits.'

The priest claps and the women part. As I walk, I whisper out of the side of my mouth to my father. 'Do you think the pillars support the roof or are they just for show?'

'They look like they are integral,' he replies.

'If we set off our explosives here . . .'

He smiles bleakly. 'If not for the fact that it would mean my destruction too, I would love to bring the house down. But it is better if we wait. Do not be in a hurry to embrace death, Al m'boy.'

I spy a massive red sheet hanging from the roof. It's maybe sixty feet wide and the hem touches the floor. As I get closer, I see that two more run at ninety-degree angles to it at either end, and I guess they're connected by a fourth at the back to form a square.

The *villacs* stop at the red sheet of cloth and the *mama-conas* drop to their hands and knees. They're crooning softly. The priests wait until the tune stops, then the English-speaking one faces us. 'It is time to meet our *Coya*. This is a great honour. As I said earlier, you must treat her with respect or suffer the consequences.' This is addressed to Paucar Wami, who adopts as innocent an expression as he can muster. 'By rights, I should present only Flesh of Dreams to her, but I assume you wish for your allies to accompany you?'

'Yes,' I answer promptly.

'Very well. But you alone have the privilege of addressing her. The others must speak to her through you or me, and they should do so only if they feel it is imperative. This is not a time for idle questions. One last point.' He pauses, and now his white eyes settle on Ama. 'There must be no emotional outbursts. Control yourself, no matter how difficult it may prove.'

'I'm not a child,' Ama huffs.

The priest catches hold of the sheet and lifts. I bend low to pass under it, as do Ama and Paucar Wami. The priest follows us, but his companions remain on the other side of the sheet, along with the *mamaconas*.

I stand inside the veiled room and allow my eyes to adjust to the light, which is much dimmer here. As objects swim into focus, I realize that much of the room is taken up by an enormous bed – no mattress, just a base – on which rests the largest, most gruesome-looking hag I've ever seen. She's lying on her side, thighs obscured by the hanging folds of her sagging stomach. It's hard to guess her height, but I'd put it at ten or eleven feet. Layers of fat encircle her like boa constrictors. Her face is double the normal size, her skin grey and mottled, her teeth sharp and uneven, her eyes a dull red colour. The nails of her fingers and toes are all but invisible – the flesh of the appendages bulges out over them – and her breasts hang to her pubic mound, her nipples huge and black, leaking a dark liquid. She's naked, but there's nothing remotely appealing about her.

The *Coya* casts an eye over us, then puts a question to the priest, who's holding his hands up by the sides of his face, lightly touching his temples with his fingers. He answers with a grunt. She looks at me and smiles. Moves her left hand in under the layers of fat to her vagina. Wets the fingers, lifts them to her nose, then speaks to me in words I can't understand.

'She senses loneliness in you,' the *villac* translates as I gaze distastefully at the creature on the bed. 'She offers to use her juices to create a mate for you, one who will be all that you wish.'

'No thanks,' I mutter, stomach churning at the thought of having anything to do with this foul monster's *juices*.

'Al,' Ama says tightly. Her face is rigid and I can see that she's struggling to hold herself together. 'On the floor, near her feet.'

I look down – I haven't had eyes for anything but the *Coya* until now – and notice a mass of chains and locks. As I stare, something moves beneath the chains and a face swims into view. It's a man. His features are bruised and bloodied, and his ears and nose have been cut off, but I place him instantly — Capac Raimi. He looks fit for nothing but death.

I reach out a hand to steady Ama, afraid she'll disobey the priest's warning and bring the wrath of this monster down upon us. 'I'm OK,' she says, then looks at the *Coya* and gulps. 'Will you ask her if I can go to him?' I raise an eyebrow at the priest. He speaks to his queen, who snorts but waves a hand magnanimously. Ama dashes forward to check on the welfare of the man she was created to love.

'Capac?' she moans, shoving the chains away from his face. He stares at her with his right eye — his left has been poked out and dangles down his cheek, making him look like a waxwork dummy on a ghost train. 'Capac?' she says again, the word breaking into a sob on her lips.

The Cardinal's eye widens. '*Ama?*' he croaks, and as his mouth opens I see that most of his teeth have been extracted. He raises a hand, stops, lets it drop away. 'No,' he groans. 'Just a vision. A trap. Can't be. You're dead.'

'No, Capac, it's me!' she cries, grasping his hand and kissing the bloody fingers. 'They brought me back. They used me to tempt you down here, but they're not using me now. We've come to –'

'Ama,' I interrupt hastily. 'You'd better leave him. Talking can't be easy in his condition.'

'It's easier than it was a couple of weeks ago,' the *villac* laughs. 'We cut out his tongue. It has only recently grown back.' The priest walks over to where Ama is weeping and gazes cynically at the battered Cardinal. 'He thought he was more powerful than us. He assumed, since he could not be killed, that we could not harm him.' He stoops, grabs a chain

and tugs. Raimi grunts with pain and his single eye snaps
shut. 'He was wrong.'

'Leave him alone!' Ama screams, thrusting her nails at the
priest's face. But he anticipates the move and slaps her hands
aside, then releases the chain.

'He forgot that if he's taken to the verge of death, but not
beyond, his body will heal, even to the extent of regener-
ating parts that have been removed.' The priest faces me
proudly. 'We have kept him here since abducting him,
subjecting him to torture and mutilation. We focus on a
different part of the body each day. After a while, when that
part has healed, we return to it and start over.'

'Mother . . . fuckers,' Raimi wheezes, glaring at his
tormentor.

'Be careful, Blood of Dreams,' the priest retorts. 'We can
take your right eye as simply as we took your left.'

'I'll kill you,' Ama hisses, pointing at the priest with a
shaking finger.

'Please,' he yawns, 'let us dispense with threats. We did
what had to be done. He needed to learn the price of
disobedience. If he doesn't do as we command, we can
keep him here forever. There is no escape unless we
grant it.'

'I killed myself . . . a couple of times,' Raimi sighs. 'They
were waiting for me on . . . the train. Took me before . . .
consciousness returned. Drugged and brought . . . me back.
Made me watch as they . . . castrated me.'

'The cruellest cut of all,' Wami murmurs, stepping
forward to study the work of the priests. Raimi's eye fills
with fear at sight of the killer, but he doesn't cringe from
his touch. 'A professional job. I could do better, but my
standards are higher than anyone's.' There's an almost
melancholic gleam to his green eyes. 'A victim with self-
healing powers, who lives forever . . . What a time I could

have with him! If there is an afterlife, and I am to be
rewarded in it by a god or devil, I can think of no greater
a treasure than this.'

'You're real, aren't you?' Raimi says, glancing from my
father to me and back again. 'The other's Al Jeery. But you're
the real Paucar Wami.'

'The original and best,' my father grins.

'Have you come to make good on your promise?'

Wami frowns. 'What promise?'

'You swore, if you survived . . . Dorak's passing, you'd see
me suffer . . . for making him jump.'

The assassin shrugs. 'I never thought I would hear myself
say this, but I think you have suffered enough. Besides, I
have new enemies. You are nothing next to them.'

'Where are the keys?' Ama asks, sifting through the locks.

'He will not be freed until he agrees to work with Flesh
of Dreams,' the *villac* says. 'When he is ready to commit
himself to our cause, we will cast the chains aside and all
shall be as it was. If he persists in defying us . . .'

'Go fuck yourself,' Raimi splutters. 'I can take as much of
this . . . as you can dish out.'

'Perhaps,' the priest sneers. 'But can you take more from
my son? And his? Our line is endless, Blood of Dreams, as
your suffering will be if –'

He's interrupted by the *Coya*, who says something while
waving at the captive on the floor. The priest frowns and
replies uncertainly. She repeats herself, sharply this time. He
nods and fiddles with the chains, unlocking them with a set
of keys that he's been carrying in a pouch.

'Our *Coya* says that there is no further need for violence,'
he says, freeing the wary-looking Cardinal. 'Your closest
mortal ally, Flesh of Dreams, has come of his own free will,
bringing the woman you loved and lost ten years ago, who
has now been restored — by us. Once you talk with your

companions, and dwell upon this in the safety of Party Central, you will see that it does not benefit you to defy us. We want the same thing — a peaceful, strong, independent city. Why not work together to build it?'

'Fuck you,' Raimi growls, hobbling to his feet, wincing, pausing to snap his loose eye free of the strands attaching it to its socket. He throws it away with a curse, then faces the *Coya*, ignoring the blood dripping down his left cheek. 'One thing kept me going these long years.' I don't correct him – this isn't the time to tell him he's only been down here a matter of weeks. 'The thought of wrapping my hands around your filthy fucking throat and throttling you. Now that I'm free, I'm going to . . .' He's about to mount the bed when he stops and squints at the grinning *Coya* and priest.

'Blood of Dreams,' the *villac* laughs, 'do you really think I would have freed you if there was the slightest chance that you could harm our queen? You may attempt it if you wish, but in your present state I would not advise it. Her sleeping place is sacred, as the *inti watana* is, and you would be repelled the instant you made contact.'

'Bullshit,' he snarls.

'It's true,' I tell him. His head turns slowly. 'I don't know about the bed, but the *inti watana* stone is charged with some kind of magic. You can't set foot on it unless you've been cleared. The jolt's savage at the best of times.'

Raimi holds my gaze until I look away – I don't like staring into the bloody maw where his nose should be – then takes a step back. 'What brings you here, Jeery?' he asks, brushing some of the dried blood from his cheeks. 'I thought you knew better than to get into bed with these fuckers.'

'The city's gone to hell since you were taken. This is the only way to restore order.'

'You're a fool. This city's all they have. They won't irreparably damage it.'

'Maybe not, but they've killed plenty of my neighbours and friends.'

Raimi shakes his head and spits blood onto the bed, splattering the *Coya's* legs. She only grins. 'I always suspected you had a soft side. Even when you killed, you only went for scum, never the babes or innocents.'

'You and my father have an advantage over me,' I respond. 'You're inhuman. I have a conscience.'

'I used to think I had one too,' Raimi sighs, scratching the spot where his right ear should be. He looks around the sheeted room at the *Coya*, Ama, Paucar Wami, me, the *villac*. 'What now? We all go home, play happy families and jump when you say?'

'More or less,' the priest smiles. 'I would hold you here if it was up to me, but our queen thinks differently. She says you will come round to our way of thinking when you have time to weigh up the pros and cons. If you do not, we will haul you down here again. It's not like you can flee the city and hide from us, is it?'

Raimi mutters something dark and terrible, but he knows he's beaten. I don't think for a second that he means to take his defeat lying down – as soon as he's back in Party Central, his thoughts will turn to revenge – but for the moment he's prepared to throw in the towel.

Not me. This is the only chance I'll get to hit back at the *villacs*. If all is going as it should, the first blows have already been struck. Now I have to play for time, to ensure the queen and her *mamaconas* don't slip away to hatch fresh schemes and renew their grip on the city.

'We're going nowhere until our questions have been answered,' I say, grasping Raimi's elbow and forcing him to sit. 'We're not as lost as we seem,' I hiss in his ear cavity.

'We need to keep them talking.' The Cardinal shows no sign of having heard, but lets me lower him to the floor, where he starts to shake and moan.

'Capac!' Ama reacts instantly, rushing to his side.

'It would be easier to kill him,' the priest says. 'That way he can re-form on the train, physically whole. Otherwise he faces a slow, painful recovery.'

'Later,' I say. 'He's got a right to the answers too. Give us a few minutes to clean his wounds.'

The priest looks to his queen, who shrugs lazily. 'Very well. But be quick. I wish to take word of this momentous occasion to my brothers. We have waited so long for the blood lines to merge. There will be much celebrating tonight.'

'We'll do the best we can,' I lie blithely, and step aside to let Ama tend to her lover's wounds. She works slowly, wiping away blood with her robes, fetching water from a barrel near the foot of the bed. There's not much she can do about his nose and ears, but she fusses over the gaps, stretching out the minutes, as aware as I am of the need to procrastinate.

'We need to stitch these,' Ama says, examining gashes on his skull and chest.

'That won't be necessary,' the priest replies. 'We have wasted enough time.'

'But it will only take –'

'No,' he snaps. 'Our *Coya* is tiring of your company. Put your questions to her now or take them with you.'

I can't think of an excuse to delay further, so I settle into my role of inquisitor. 'Let's start with the Ayuamarcans. As I understand it, Ferdinand Dorak created them with your assistance, and when he died, they died as well. So how come this lot –' I wave at my back-from-the-dead companions '– are up and walking?'

The *Coya* answers slowly, the priest translating as she speaks.

'There was much Ferdinand Dorak didn't know about our powers. He saw what we wished him to see, no more. Where there were gaps, he overlooked them or filled them in with logic of his own. We never corrected him when he was wrong. We never even spoke to him in words he could comprehend — we had not bothered at that time to learn the language of your people.

'The generation of the Ayuamarcans was not as straight-forward as he believed. When he wished to create a person, he chose a face from his dreams, then came to our *villacs*. Having shared his dream, they constructed a doll in advance, which they daubed with their blood and his, then cast a spell on it. He thought that was the end of the process.'

The *Coya* shakes her head and chuckles. 'It was not so simple. Every act of creation requires a mother and a father. That was why Viracocha split himself in two when he wished to create the first humans. As a single entity he could only replicate himself. Divided, he was able to give life to new creatures, to Inti Maimi and Mama Ocllo.'

'Wait a minute,' I interrupt. 'You're not trying to tell us that thing on the bed is the same Mama Ocllo of your legends, are you?'

'No,' the priest answers directly, 'but she is a direct descendant. Each of our *Coya*s lives for more than a hundred years, giving birth to thirty or more children. When her body withers, her spirit finds a home in one of her children and lives again, carrying on with only the briefest of inter-ruptions.'

'These children,' Paucar Wami says to the queen, then stops and re-addresses his question to me. 'Do they breed with one another, or with outside stock?'

'The *villacs* and *mamaconas* are of pure blood,' the priest replies huffily. 'Our Incan followers – those who helped escort us here – bred with the Indians who were indigenous to this region, and later with the Europeans, but we have always remained apart.'

'That explains a lot,' Wami murmurs. 'The pale skin, the thin hair, the various genetic oddities.'

'Don't mock us,' the priest growls. 'We are not cursed with the weaknesses of in-breeding. Our people long ago discovered ways to combat such defects. We are as strong of constitution as any race.'

'Let's get back to the creating business,' Raimi mutters. 'I want to know what they held back from Dorak.'

The *Coya* recommences. 'Creation requires a man and a woman. Our *Watanas* have traditionally served the function of the father. Our priests could have adopted that role, but we chose to include members of the communities which we ruled, partly to strengthen the ties between us, mostly to prevent internal conflict — a *villac* who possessed the powers of a *Watana* would have been a threat.

'Ferdinand Dorak was the last *Watana*. With your creation –' she points to Raimi '– we abandoned the practice. This world has changed faster than our forefathers ever imagined. We needed a new breed of representative to face it. Thus we had our *Watana* create an immortal being, one with the power of –'

'We know this part,' Raimi snarls. 'Get back to how we were created and how you reanimated Ama and Paucar Wami.'

The priest glares at Raimi, then looks to his queen. She ponders the request, then nods. Walking to one of the hanging sheets, he parts the folds and calls to the *mama-conas*. There's a scuffling sound, then two naked priestesses enter with wooden trays, upon which lie a number of dolls. They lay the trays on the bed, bow low to the *Coya* and depart.

We study the dolls in silence. A doll of my father is there, and one of Ama. There are others I recognize — Conchita Kubekik and Inti Maimi.

'Leonora Shankar,' Wami murmurs, pointing to the doll of the once-famous restaurateur.

'And Adrian Arne,' Raimi adds, reaching for the doll of a young man, stopping before he touches it, slowly withdrawing his hand. He glances at the *Coya* but speaks to me. 'Ask her if these have been stolen from Party Central.'

'No,' comes the answer. 'What Dorak didn't know was that there were two of each doll. There had to be, just as you need a sperm and an egg to make a baby. The blood he gave to his doll was combined with the blood our *Coya* gave to hers, and the pair were used to produce the Ayuamarcans.'

The *Coya* picks up a doll – Ama's – and runs a cracked nail over the top of its head. Ama shivers violently, then steels herself and stares impassively at the queen of the underworld Incas.

'When Dorak destroyed a doll by piercing its heart,' the *Coya* continues, 'he eliminated its body but not its spirit. For that to happen, the other doll's heartbeat also needed to be stopped. Until it was, the spirit of the dream person remained at our disposal, to be recalled any time we wish.'

I frown. 'But you said a male and female were needed. If Dorak was the last of the *Watanas*, how can you bring the Ayuamarcans back to life?'

'Restoring life is not the same as creating it,' the *Coya* says. 'We cannot create new beings without the *Watana*, but we can restore the essence of those who have walked before. Thus we brought back Paucar Wami when we needed a figurehead to front the Snakes. And Ama Situwa when we needed to lure Capac Raimi to us.'

'Care to tell us how you pull that trick off?' Raimi asks sourly.

'Good magicians never reveal their secrets,' the priest

chuckles without asking his queen. 'And we are the very best magicians.'

'It makes sense,' Raimi mutters, 'in its own crazy way. It explains why Dorak always had to wait a day or so for his Ayuamarcans to appear — the *Coya* had to weave her magic over the other doll. And it accounts for you being here —' this to Ama and Wami '— in your original forms. Your dolls never aged, and since they used those restore you, you look the same the second or twentieth time round.'

'Couldn't they have had one doll instead of two?' Ama asks. 'I understand that both the blood of the *Watana* and *Coya* were needed, but I don't see the need for the duplicate dolls.'

'We could have used a single doll,' the priest says. 'Indeed, we did with Capac Raimi, which is why you don't see a doll of him on the trays. But by creating twins, we gave our *Watanas* a degree of control over their creations.'

'You let them think they were running the show,' Raimi says, 'while all the time you were really pulling the strings.'

'Of course,' the *villac* smiles.

'There is another thing I have difficulty understanding,' Paucar Wami says. 'Any time I disobeyed your orders, you took my body apart with magic. Did you do that by piercing the heart of my doll?'

'No. There are other ways to disassemble an Ayuamarcan. By removing a doll's head, we render the human inert. Once the head has been reattached and the proper procedures followed, life can be restored. The heart of the doll continues beating until pierced. As long as it does, the Ayuamarcan may be recalled. Once pierced, that is the end, the spirit can never be summoned again.'

My father stares at his doll, eyes narrowing. I know what he's thinking — if he gets hold of it, the priests have no further claim on him. He'd be free to do as he pleased. Unfortunately for him, the *Coya* has also read his thoughts.

She picks up the doll and holds it close to her grotesque breasts, stroking its bare chest with a sharp nail.

'The removal of the doll's head also explains how we keep our creations bound to this city,' the *villac* says smugly. 'Dorak thought his Ayuamarcans could not survive beyond these boundaries, but with the exception of Capac Raimi, they *can*. The reason most never did is that we unpicked the flesh of their bodies every time they left. It was our way of keeping them in check.'

Ama stares at the priest. 'You mean I can leave? My body won't disintegrate?'

'Only Raimi is bound. We knew we could not kill him once Dorak was dead, so we took steps to ensure we could control him by tying him physically to the city. The rest of you were always free to wander if we'd let you.'

While Ama and Raimi mull that over – my father isn't bothered, having been able to come and go anyway – the *villac* consults with his queen, then says, 'You now know how you came to be and why.' He turns to Raimi. 'You also have a further reason to pledge your cause to ours, so we expect no more trouble from you after this.'

'How's that?' The Cardinal replies sceptically.

'Your woman.' The priest waves at Ama. 'You sacrificed her once, when you thought it was necessary. But by uniting with us, you can keep her, and not just for this life. When she reaches the end of her mortal days, we can resurrect her. She will not last unto eternity – her doll will eventually crumble, and her essence with it – but we can promise you a millennium together, maybe longer.'

Raimi's eye softens and he looks to Ama for her response, which comes more quickly than he anticipated. 'If you have any feelings for me at all, you won't do that.'

'You'd say no to a thousand years of life?' Raimi asks, surprised.

'Don't subject me to the misery *you* endure, Capac. I don't want to come back time and time again. One life's enough. I don't crave another.'

'How about you?' Raimi asks my father. 'Would you accept their offer?'

'If I could accept it and be free, I would,' Wami answers thoughtfully. 'But to be a slave for ten centuries . . .' He shakes his head. 'I could never tire of killing, but I would know I was at their beck and call, and that would sour life for me.'

Raimi faces the *villac* and grins. 'We all agree — go fuck yourselves.'

The *villac*'s face darkens. 'It seems you have not yet learnt your lesson, Blood of Dreams. We will have to tie you down again and . . .' He stops at the sound of commotion. Voices have been raised and the alarmed cries of *mamaconas* ring around the cavern. In the distance there are the dull thuds of gunfire. The priest strides to the sheet and swipes it aside. Through the parting I see naked priestesses gathered around a small group of shaken *villacs*.

'What's going on?' Raimi whispers as the priest hurries to his companions to determine the meaning of the interruption. The *Coya* is peering over our heads.

'A little surprise Al cooked up,' Ama grins, kissing The Cardinal's bloody forehead. 'Just sit back and enjoy the show. We'll explain later.'

The English-speaking *villac* consults with his harried brothers, impatiently at first, then fearfully. He races to the door of the cavern and is almost knocked down by several priests as they surge through. He makes it to the entrance, stands there listening, then pushes ahead out of view. A minute later, he returns at full speed, face warped with terror. He cuts through the *villacs* and *mamaconas*, ignoring their plaintive cries, and screams at the *Coya* before he's even halfway to her bed-cum-throne.

The massive queen bolts upright and snaps something in reply. He falls over a shrieking priestess, rises, kicks her out of his way and answers. The *Coya's* gaze settles on me and the hatred in her eyes would floor a lesser man. She points a finger at me, Ama and my father, then roars to the approaching *villac*. He grabs two of the priests closest to him and barks an order. The three draw daggers and move on me, while the *Coya* grasps the dolls of Paucar Wami and Ama Situwa and prepares to drive her nails through their hearts.

My father reads the queen's intentions and hurls himself at her. He gets no further than the base of the bed. As soon as his foot touches it, he's propelled backwards and he crashes through the red sheets, falling heavily on a circle of candles. The *Coya* roars maliciously and holds his doll above her head.

'Wait!' I bellow as the priests close in. Grabbing the hem of my robes, I hoist them over my chest, exposing my body to the bloated queen — along with the vest of explosives.

The *Coya* doesn't know what the vest means – I imagine she understands little of the world above – but she knows I'm not flashing for the fun of it. She screeches a command to the priests, who stop within striking distance of me. I turn to the one who speaks English. 'Come here,' I growl. 'Feel what I'm wearing.'

He lowers his knife and stretches out a hand. He frowns when his fingers touch the material of the vest. Then his fingers explore further and his face collapses.

'Make any further moves on me or the others and I'll blow you all to hell,' I tell him sweetly.

'You would perish too,' he moans.

I laugh. 'I came here to die. If you think I'm bluffing, try me. Now, tell her to give me the dolls or I'll bring this roof down on the whole lot of us.'

The *villac* gulps, then speaks to his queen. Her flabby jowls quiver indignantly and she starts to berate him. He snaps at her irately, and even though I don't speak their language, I know what they're saying. He tells her about the explosives and my demand of her, she questions my sincerity – would I truly take my own life? – and he puts her straight in no uncertain terms.

The *Coya* snarls at me, but then the sound of gunfire fills the cavern – the invaders must be almost to the doors – and she realizes she has no time for a duel. She hurls the dolls at me, then rattles off a list of orders to the *villac*. Reacting with admirable coolness, he summons several priests, along with a dozen or more *mamaconas*, and issues instructions. They obey without question, hurrying to the side of the cavern and returning with two long poles which they slide into grooves along the sides of the *Coya's* bed. The Incas group around each of the four protruding handles, then lift at the *Coya's* command. Facing the back of the cavern, they set off with surprising speed.

The English-speaking *villac* squares up to me, his white eyes tinted orange by the flickering lights of the candles. 'This is not the end,' he snarls. 'We've had to flee before and build anew. We shall do so again. This city is ours and we will reclaim it as surely as the sun will rise in the morning.'

I smile and hit him with a sly, stinging retort. 'In your dreams.'

The priest's upper lip curls, but he can think of no suitable comeback, so he races after his *Coya* and her retinue, quickly disappearing from sight.

'Shouldn't we go after them?' Ama asks.

'There's no rush.' Tucking the dolls of Ama and Paucar Wami between my vest and chest, I lower my robes and wink at her, nodding towards the remaining *villacs* and *mamaconas* as they face the barbarians spilling into the cavern. 'Let's enjoy the grand finale. I've been waiting a long time to see these blind bastards take a good beating. I wouldn't miss this for the world.'

SEVEN – PIZARRO MK II

The Incas mount a surprisingly stout defence, the naked priestesses and blind priests hurling themselves at their assailants, brandishing fingernails and knives with lethal expertise. But they're outnumbered and their opponents pack guns, so it's no real contest. Within five or six minutes the last of the howling *mamaconas* is being put down like a rabid dog – the soldiers have orders to kill all who they find – and a beaming Eugene Davern strides towards me through the mixed ranks of Troops, Kluxers and Snakes.

'You're alive!' he laughs, throwing his arms around me. I'm sure he'll wince when he recalls this later, but for the moment he's been carried away by the swiftness and ease of the crushing victory.

'So it seems,' I grunt.

He stands back and studies my robes. 'Don't think much of your get-up. We could have shot you in gear like that.'

'I didn't have much choice. We had to bow to their whims to delay them.'

Behind Davern, Sard enters the cavern and hurries over. 'Sapa Inca!' he shouts proudly, wiping blood – not his – from his face. 'The hour is ours!'

'You did well, soldier.' Looking around, I see that the Snakes

in the cavern are from various phalanxes, not just Sard's.
'Did you have any trouble convincing the others to unite
against the *villacs*?'

'None,' he grins. 'They knew I wouldn't invent such an
order by myself.'

'They did not question my motives?'

'You're the Sapa Inca,' he replies simply. On the floor, my
father groans and sits up, regaining consciousness. Sard's eyes
widen when he spots the second Paucar Wami and he takes
a step backwards. 'Sapa Inca?' he asks uncertainly, right hand
going to the knife on his belt.

'We needed to confuse the priests, so I had this man
disguised to look like me.'

'A decoy?' Sard frowns.

'Yes.' Stooping, I grab Wami by the elbows and hoist him
up. His eyes are cloudy but otherwise he appears unharmed.
'Are you OK?'

'I feel like I've been kicked by a horse,' he growls, rubbing
his neck. Gazing at the soldiers and dead Incas in the cavern,
he smiles. Then he realizes the bed's no longer where it was
and his smile vanishes. 'The fat bitch — where is she?'

'Some of her subjects spirited her away. Don't worry, I
can't see them getting very far. We'll set after them shortly
and finish them off.'

'My doll! If she pierces its heart . . .'

I start to tell him I've retrieved the doll, then stop, fixing
on an image of Bill Casey weeping as he told me about his
sister. I think for a moment, then mutter, 'She's too frantic
to reason clearly. You've nothing to fear. We will track her
down presently.'

While my father fidgets, Raimi hobbles forward and confronts
Eugene Davern. The leader of the Kluxers flinches when he
spots the bloody, barely recognisable figure stumbling towards

him, then realizes who it is and smiles shakily. 'Capac,' he greets him nervously.

Raimi runs his eye over Davern, then looks to me. 'What the hell's going on?'

'An alliance,' I explain, nodding at the Troops, Kluxers and Snakes, who are gazing uneasily at one another, branching off into their respective groups now that the fighting's over. 'The *villacs* pushed your Troops and Davern's Kluxers to the brink of war, using the Snakes – the guys with the bald heads and tattoos – to spark it off. I cut a deal with Tasso and Davern. They staged an invasion of the east, giving the priests the idea that they were going to battle for real. To avoid the chaos, the *villacs* retreated underground. Once I gave the word, the Troops and Kluxers linked up and surged down the tunnels with the Snakes. The three forces cut all the priests they could find to ribbons, while a combined spearhead raced here, tracking a trail of poker chips we left for them to follow.'

Raimi thinks that over, his battered face creased with doubt. 'Tasso and Davern working together? The Kluxers in league with a gang of blacks? A lot's changed while I've been away.'

'It was time for change. The *villacs* had arranged it. I simply stepped in and readjusted their plans, turning the new deal to our advantage instead of theirs.'

'And what exactly does this "new deal" entail?' Raimi asks.

'The finer details haven't been thrashed out yet. You can take care of that when you're back in charge. The way I sold it to Tasso and Davern, the Troops, Kluxers and Snakes get to carve up the city between them. There's enough to go round, especially now that the priests have been taken care of. The final say is yours, of course, but I think you'd be crazy not to take advantage of the peace now that it's been established.'

Raimi nods thoughtfully, then cocks an eyebrow at Davern. 'I thought you wanted to run me out of town and take over the show.'

'I did,' Davern smiles, 'but that was then, this is now. Our dark-skinned friend has shown me the light. I'll settle for a third of the city — if it's the *right* third.'

Raimi laughs hollowly. 'There's a lot of negotiating to be done. But we can do that another time. There are a few loose strings I want to see to first.'

'Leave that to us,' I tell him. 'You're in no fit shape to go chasing after –'

'I'll slit the throat of any man who tries to stop me,' he vows.

'We won't go slow on your account,' I warn him.

'I'll keep up, even if it kills me.' He grins. 'Which it probably will.'

Nodding, I ask Davern to fetch arms for us. 'There are more of the bastards?' he asks.

'A couple dozen or so. They're ours. Don't follow. Finish your job here, scour the tunnels above in case you missed any priests, then return to the surface with your men and wait for The Cardinal to contact you.' I face Sard. 'I'm placing you in temporary control of the Snakes. If I don't make it back, the promotion's permanent. Work with Davern and Raimi. Make sure they cut us a good deal. Use your power to build and improve.'

'Why this talk of not coming back?' Sard frowns. 'You're the Sapa Inca — you always come back.'

'Maybe not this time. Be prepared if I don't, and deal with it. That's an order, soldier.'

His heels click together and he salutes. 'Yes, sir!'

Sard and Eugene Davern stare suspiciously at each other, but don't draw guns. It's a start, not of a beautiful friendship, but hopefully a working relationship.

I face Capac Raimi, my father and Ama. All have armed themselves and Raimi has borrowed a dead *villac's* robes. They're ready for action.

'Let's go finish this,' I snap, and we set off in pursuit of the fleeing *Coya* and her consorts.

There are several tunnels leading out of the cavern, but only one is large enough to accommodate the *Coya*'s bed. There are no lights, but we take torches from the floor. The tunnel runs straight for three hundred feet, then divides in two, each passage the same height and width. We pause at the junction, searching for signs of our quarry, but they've left none.

'We will split into pairs,' Wami decides. 'Ama and her beau can take –'

'No,' Raimi interrupts, stepping forward. His left leg drags, but he's kept the pace so far, running on sheer determination and hatred. 'They went left.'

'You are certain?' my father asks.

Raimi nods. 'I've spent my time here chained to that foul bitch. I could sniff her out from the other side of the city. Left.'

Wami looks to me for confirmation and I shrug. 'I'm happy to go with his call.'

'Very well.' The killer sets off down the tunnel. I hurry after him, Ama and Raimi not far behind.

We come to a number of subsequent junctions, and each time Raimi chooses the way. If he's wrong about this, we've lost them, probably forever.

We scramble over several small cave-ins as we progress, the first time we've encountered structural flaws. I mention them to my father and ask what he thinks. Raimi answers before he can. 'The other tunnels and caves are upkept, but they haven't bothered with these. They've grown arrogant and lazy. This path was laid many decades ago in case they needed to retreat, but they came to believe they were invulnerable, especially with Dorak and me affording them so much leeway.' He shakes his head, disgusted. 'If I'd known they would be this easy to defeat, I'd have come after them years ago.'

'You wouldn't have found them,' I tell him. 'They'd have slipped away into the shadows and struck back at you when you weren't expecting it. We've only rumbled them now because they were so close to victory that they couldn't see the ruin on the flip side of the coin.'

Finally, as we turn into one of the narrower tunnels – there are marks on a wall, where the edges of the bed scratched it, proof we're on the right track – we hear the sound of voices and digging up ahead. 'They must have hit a more serious cave-in,' my father grins, drawing a knife and testing its blade. 'They are ours.'

'Wait,' Raimi says, tugging at the assassin's robes. 'I want to do this alone.'

'You are in no fit state to take them on,' Wami snorts.

'I wasn't planning on a duel,' Raimi smiles, his face twisted with pain and exhaustion – but also triumph. 'Lend me your vest.'

'Ah,' Wami purrs. 'I see. But I would rather dispose of them the old-fashioned way if it's all the same to you.'

'It isn't,' Raimi growls. 'I don't care about the priests and priestesses – you can have them if any escape – but the queen is mine. Don't push me on this.'

My father cocks an eyebrow. 'Be careful who you threaten, little man. You rule the roost up in Party Central, but down here you are nothing more than a mess of flesh and bones.'

'Can't we do this together?' I ask. 'We've come this far as a team. Why not –'

'You'll all die if you challenge them,' Raimi says softly. 'I sense death in the air. I'm as sure of this as I was of how to track the *Coya*.'

'Nonsense,' Wami snorts. 'Al is almost as good a fighter as his pappy. We will make short work of them, hmm, Al m'boy?'

I don't reply. Raimi's right. Death lies waiting for me — *if* I go to meet it.

'I'm not afraid of dying,' I mutter. 'And I won't regret it, not if I take that lot with me.'

'I believe you,' Raimi smiles. 'But you don't have to. I can do this alone. You can live, Mr Jeery, or you can sacrifice yourself. Choose.'

'His choice is irrelevant,' Wami snarls. '*I* will not step down under any —'

'Your doll,' Ama interrupts, and he glances at her sharply. 'If you attack them, the *Coya* will destroy your doll.'

'Not if I cut her fucking head off first,' he barks.

'Do you want to run such a risk?' Ama asks. 'This world's full of people for you to kill. Are these few worth risking everything for?'

He stares at her, then chuckles grimly. 'When you put it that way . . . Very well, Cardinal, the *coup de grâce* is yours. Enjoy.'

'I will,' Raimi beams, then turns to Ama. 'See you in a few days?' The hope in his eye is pathetic.

'I guess,' she sniffs.

He looks at me and winks. 'It's been fun knowing you, *blood-brother*.'

'Same here,' I grin.

'Visit me when I return. We have important issues to settle.'

'I'll come,' I promise. I start to undo the straps of my vest, remember the dolls stashed there, and fake a groan. 'Give him yours,' I tell my father. 'I pulled a muscle earlier. My shoulder's killing me.'

Wami wriggles out of his vest, straps it over Raimi's robes and shows him how to detonate the charges. The Cardinal waves to us, then hobbles down the tunnel after the *Coya*, leaving the rest of us to withdraw and strike for the lights of the world above.

I'm in agony that no ordinary man could endure, but that's nothing new. I've spent the last few months exploring all the stars, planets and moons in a universe of pain. The *villacs* put me through every kind of torture imaginable, while that she-bitch looked on and laughed. And then they put me through it again. And again. What's different now is that I'm a free agent. I could stop, sit, rest. Any small measure of relief would be a blessing. But if I pause, I won't be able to rise. I'll just lie there until I die.

Dragging my left leg behind me, gritting the few teeth I have left, I march onwards, enduring the pain, welcoming it — the worse I feel, the sweeter it'll be when I send those bastards to hell. I gave my torch to Jeery, so I'm operating in darkness. That doesn't worry me. I don't need to be able to see to find that cow. I could zero in on her if I was deaf, dumb and blind.

I'm not sure what will happen to me when I kill the *Coya*. I was created to last through eternity, immune to death, but that power came from the queen and her priests. Perhaps, when they are no more, I'll cease to exist as well. If so, so be it. I've spent ten years training myself to accept a life without end, but immortality hasn't been easy to adapt to. Genuine death isn't an altogether unwelcome prospect.

I'd miss Ama though. Seeing her again almost made all the pain and humiliation worthwhile. I thought the woman the priests sent to lure me underground was an illusion. I'd dismissed her from my thoughts during my long days and nights of suffering. I hadn't dared believe she could be real.

Now that I know she is, I long to spend time with her, tell her what she meant to me, how much it pained me to sacrifice her. I want to explain that I had no choice, I was a puppet incapable of severing its strings. I want to touch her, even if it's just one last time, hold her, kiss her, whisper words in her ear that I can whisper to no other because I can love none but her.

But I'm afraid. What if she rejects me? What if she hates me for what I did to her? I'd rather die the one true death than have her spurn me. She fussed over me in the cavern of the *Coya*, but that might have been a sympathetic reaction. Perhaps it will be for the best if my spirit's set free by the destruction of the Incas.

I'm close now, a turn or two away. Their voices are loud and clear, as are the sounds of their fingers and knives on the rubble they're frantically trying to burrow through. The flickering lights of torches make the tunnel seem warm and homely. The priestesses can't navigate as capably in the dark as the *villacs*, even though they've spent their lives out of sight of the moon they worship.

I was supposed to bring them to that moon. If I'd accepted the priests as masters, and worked with Jeery and the other sons of Paucar Wami, they'd have risen from the depths. With the Manco Capac statue dominating the city, the *Coya* would have established herself as queen, the *mamaconas* would have been the most sought-after women, and the *villacs* would have been the most powerful of men. They'd have ruled supreme. That dream kept them going in the miserable gloom. It was all they had to live for. A nobler man might feel pity for them – they were born to their lot, they didn't ask for it – but I'm a savage son of a bitch and I feel nothing but hateful glee at the thought of wrecking their carefully laid plans.

I'm almost upon them. A brief pause to draw breath and

flex my fingers, careful not to touch the buttons nestled in
my palms. Then I plaster a smile in place, force a weak
whistle, and stumble around the final turn, into view.

The tunnel is narrower than the others, only just wide
enough for the bed, with a low ceiling. The cave-in isn't
impassable – the Incas could wriggle through if not for
their oversized queen – but it's a tricky one to clear. All
the priests and priestesses are working on it, but as they
scoop rocks and pebbles away, fresh stony trickles cascade
from the sides and overhead. If they're not careful, the roof
will collapse. It's a delicate operation, requiring finesse and
time, which they don't have any more.

'Having fun?' I bellow, and two dozen alarmed faces shoot
around. The *Coya* is closest to me and she hisses with fear,
making a sign with her huge, fleshy hands, as if that could
ward me off. Her priests and hand-maidens race from the
rocks and line up in front of her. I grin at them. 'Heard you
were throwing a party. Thought I'd drop in.'

'Where are the others?' snarls the English-speaking *villac*
from earlier.

'Gone.'

'Dead?' he asks, surprised.

'No, you fucking moron. They've returned to the city.'

He frowns. 'You have come alone?'

'Shut up, you asshole,' I sigh, stepping forward for a better
view of the *Coya*. 'It's the queen bee I'm interested in, not
her drones.'

The priest starts to launch a retort but the *Coya* silences
him with a bark. Drawing herself upright on the bed, she
glares at me, then studies the vest I'm wearing over my robes.
'You have come to destroy me,' she sneers in the ancient
tongue which is as natural to me as my own.

'Sure as shit,' I laugh in her language.

'This is foolish. We are your parents, Blood of Dreams,

your destiny. We have amazing plans for you. We can keep you
intrigued through the long, interminable millennia. Alone,
you would have only humans for amusement, and they will
cease to amuse you far more quickly than you imagine.'

'I've already lost interest in them,' I sigh. 'But you don't
interest me either. I don't care about your plans. I have my
own. The mistake you made in letting The Cardinal create
me was thinking I'd feel a bond with your kind. You mean
nothing to me, you fat, ugly, Incan cunt.' I've never relished
anything as much as the delivery of that insult. If I survive,
I'll play that moment over and over, possibly until the very
end of time.

The *Coya* snarls savagely at me, then shouts at her underlings. 'Get him!' A ridiculous choice of final words, but there's
no time for her to reconsider and add a fitting coda. The
villacs and *mamaconas* rush me. I have no more than four or
five seconds.

Closing the fingers of my left hand, I press the slim button
at the heart of my palm. A brief pause, then I press the
button on my right. There's no click and no poised moment
of heightened tension. The vest explodes instantly, a fer-
ocious blast, obliterating me and the nearest of the Incas,
knocking the rest off their feet, bringing the roof down on
a screeching, hateful *Coya* and her clan.

The end.

epilogue

life goes on

ONE – INTO THE LIGHT

Ding-dong, the bitch is dead.

It's been almost two weeks since the Troops, Kluxers and Snakes joined forces to rid this city of its Incan rulers, and although it's early days, the signs for a favourable future are positive. Raimi and Davern are cooperating cautiously, and Sard and I have been representing the Snakes, making sure we're not frozen out of the negotiations. The days of a divided, isolated east are over. From now on the gangs here operate under a single, unified banner. We had to crack some heads to begin with, and that will continue for a while, but in time people will see the benefits of doing it our way. They'll flock to the cause and the new era of peace and prosperity it heralds.

Or so goes the plan.

The city never looked sweeter than it did when I broke clear of the tunnels with Ama and my father. It was evening, the sun was setting, and for the first time in a decade the ruby red sky didn't remind me of the colour of blood. We'd heard and felt the explosion on our way up, and knew that Raimi had succeeded.

'So!' Paucar Wami boomed after a few minutes, as we lay

on a bank of burnt grass and gazed at the sky in solemn silence. 'We have overcome the *villacs* and their queen, united the warring factions of the city, and laid the foundations for a long and lasting peace. Not a bad day's work, hmm, Al m'boy?'

'It could have been worse,' I deadpanned, then shared a laugh with him, Ama looking on, smiling wistfully (probably thinking about Raimi).

Done laughing, Wami stood and scanned the towering buildings of the city, his green eyes thoughtful. 'It is over,' he said softly. 'I am truly free for the first time in my life. No Ferdinand Dorak or *villacs* to tell me what I must and must not do. I can be my own man, live for myself, do as I want.' His fingers flexed slowly, hungrily, by his sides.

I cleared my throat and stood beside him. 'There'll be no more killing here.' He didn't give any sign that he'd heard. 'Go elsewhere for your sick kicks. This city's off-limits.'

'Says who?' he whispered, eyes still on the skyscrapers.

'The leader of the Snakes.'

'*I* lead the Snakes.'

'No. Paucar Wami does. In this city there can only be one Paucar Wami, and that's *me*. We can fight about it if you want, but there seems little point. It doesn't matter to you where you kill. Why pit yourself against me when you could be out there –' I gesture to the world beyond '– slaughtering freely?'

He considered that, then nodded calmly. 'Very well. The city is yours. I will depart immediately and leave you to it.'

'I'd rather you didn't.' He glanced at me, surprised. 'The next few weeks could be difficult. I might have need of you. I want you to stay, hidden and inactive, ready to step in if I call.'

'Why should I?' he asked. 'I am eager to be about my new life. I care not for the people of this city and their problems.'

'I'm asking, as your son — please hang around.'

'If I do not?'

I shrugged. 'I can't force you to stay. You'll do it or you won't.'

He thought about it, then nodded again. 'I am grateful to you for including me in the rousting of the *villacs* – that was sport I shall not forget in a hurry – so I will stay for a fortnight, lie low and heed your call. But,' he warned, 'if you *do* call, you must accept the nature of the beast which you summon. I will not kill while in hiding, but if directed, I will consider those you sic me on fair game. I will show them no mercy.'

'Agreed.'

'I will be near the burnt-out police station. Come if you need me. Otherwise I will contact you before I leave.' He paused, tugged at his robes and grimaced. 'I hate these rags.' He pulled the robes off, stood naked before us – he winked lewdly at Ama, but she gazed back blankly, unimpressed – then turned and set off at a leisurely pace, whistling as if out on a casual stroll.

'I despise that monster,' Ama said as we watched him leave, 'but there's no denying the man has style.'

'Come on,' I chuckled, taking her arm. 'The Snakes and their *friends* should be finished in the tunnels. Let's go separate them before they turn on one another.'

I got virtually no sleep the next few days. There was a lot of work to be done in the east – fires to extinguish, roads to unblock – and the Snakes made sure all went smoothly, providing escorts for the police, medics and clean-up crews who were soon swamping the streets. We kept tabs on dissident gangs, knocked them into order if necessary, safeguarded the public by patrolling the neighbourhoods, securing the peace.

I faced a constant stream of meetings with public officials, on top of the head-to-heads with Ford Tasso and Eugene Davern at Party Central. I involved Sard and the other Cobras as much as I could, getting them accustomed to the politics of self-control, but as the Sapa Inca my presence was expected. I had no intention of saddling myself with the job in the long run, but in the short term there was nothing for it but to bite down hard and go with the flow. No point rescuing people from the wolves, only to leave them for the vultures.

Raimi returned on Friday, fresh and unscarred. Tasso stepped aside without a murmur and The Cardinal was soon locked in negotiations with Davern and Sard. When anyone asked where he'd been, he grinned and replied, 'On vacation.'

It soon became clear that The Cardinal had changed, and everyone agreed it was for the better. Before his disappearance he'd been arrogant and aloof, conferring only with the elite in Party Central, having nothing to do with the ordinary people, spurning media interviews. Now he was on the news all the time, pitching in to rebuild the east, sponsoring shelters to house the homeless, liaising between the Troops, Kluxers and Snakes. He also worked closely with the police, even going so far as to publicly run Stuart Jordan out of the city and allowing an honest cop to replace him.

I have my doubts about how long The Cardinal's change of heart will last. He's come through a terrible ordeal, and I think he's over-compensating for the torment he endured. It's probably only a matter of time before his old personality reasserts itself. But I keep my doubts to myself. Everyone thinks he's a new man, and that gives them hope – if The Cardinal can change, *anyone* can. I don't have the heart to piss on their parade.

*   *   *

It's a beautiful June day, and all's well. *So* well, I've decided
to cut out before the job takes me over and I find myself
stuck here, head of the Snakes for life, tied to this city until
the day I die. The east's at peace, the gangs have been brought
under the thumb of the Snakes, there's harmony between
them, the Kluxers and Troops. I'm not needed any longer.
Time to pass control of the Snakes over to themselves and
hope they don't go wild with power.

As Al Jeery, I told Flo and Drake of my decision last night,
and sat up late with them, drinking and reminiscing about
Fabio and the past. Now, as Paucar Wami, I tell Sard and
install him as leader of the Snakes. He asks me to reconsider
but he doesn't plead. I've spent a lot of time with Sard, and
I think he's come to realize I'm not the immortal Sapa Inca.
He's never mentioned the man he saw in the cavern, but
I'm pretty sure he knows that the 'double' was the real Paucar
Wami. He acts as if I'm their leader, but I sense his relief
when I say I'm leaving. He doesn't want the others figuring
it out and splintering.

'What will I tell them?' he asks. 'How will I explain your
departure?'

'Just say I've gone away. That will be explanation enough.
The Sapa Inca does not have to account for his actions.'

After passing the baton of power to Sard, I drop by the
abandoned police station where my father has been hanging
out and find him perched on the rafters, paring his nails.
'You can leave now,' I tell him.

He drops to the floor and faces me. 'You no longer require
my services?'

'Peace has been restored and life's moving on. I have no
need of you.'

'Once I go, you will never again be able to find me.'

I smile thinly. 'I'll never wish to.'

'Al m'boy,' he purrs. 'If I did not know better, I could

almost believe you were anxious to see the back of your dear ole pappy.'

'I don't know what gave you that idea,' I laugh.

Wami grows thoughtful. 'There was something I failed to consider when Raimi went after the *Coya*. By blowing her up, he should have blown up my doll too, thus destroying me. Yet here I am. What do you suppose happened to it?'

I shrug. 'She probably dropped it while they were fleeing.'

'I thought about that. I returned to the tunnels and re-traced their route. I did not find it.'

'Then it must be buried under the rubble, trapped in an air pocket. You always did have the luck of the devil.'

'The dark one favours his own,' Wami chuckles, then waves his worries away. 'It has been fun, Al m'boy. I will miss you, and I mean that sincerely.'

'In a strange sort of way, I'll miss you too,' I mutter, gazing at his shaved head, his cruel lips, the tattoos, his cynical green eyes, one final time. 'If I begged you to stop killing,' I blurt out suddenly, 'do you think you could?'

'Of course not,' he says. 'Why make such an absurd request?'

'I don't know,' I sigh. 'Guess I'm getting soft in my old age.' I offer my hand. 'Take care, you evil-hearted son of a bitch.'

'You too, O misdirected spawn of my loins,' he grins, clasping my hand. 'You could have been a legend, Al m'boy.'

'It's better to be human,' I reply.

'Perhaps,' he says, releasing me. 'That, however, is something I could never aspire to. I was made to be vile.' Stepping back, the assassin salutes, turns, walks through the door and slips away, never to be seen in these parts again.

Ama's face lights up when I walk into Cafran's, my tattoos painted over, stubble coating my skull, the beginnings of a new head of hair, my first in a decade. I don't know what it will look like – I imagine I'll have more than my fair share of grey – but it'll be interesting to find out.

'Howdy, stranger,' she greets me, standing on her toes to kiss my cheek. I haven't seen much of her lately. I've been busy elsewhere.

'How are you doing?' I ask as she leads me to the back, out of earshot of the busy lunch crowd.

'Can't complain. Business is good, the city's booming, Cafran's bought a new restaurant and has said I can run it. I've got my life back.'

'I hope you take care of it this time. It's your last.'

'Don't worry, I've no intention of wasting it.' We nudge into an alcove in the kitchen, out of the pathway of the waiters. 'What's happening with you?' she asks. 'How's the dividing-up of the city going?'

'Pretty good. I'm going to see Raimi after this, bid him farewell and warn –'

'*Farewell*?' she interrupts. 'You're leaving?'

'This afternoon. I'll catch a train out.'

'Where to?'

I shrug. 'Away.'

'You're not coming back?'

'Don't intend to.'

She stares at me in silence, then smiles. 'Good!' She takes hold of my hands and squeezes. 'Don't return, no matter what happens. You've served your time and done all you could for this city. You owe it nothing more.'

'That's the way I figure it too. It's why I'm going to see Raimi, to clear it with him.'

'How is Capac?' she asks hesitantly.

'You haven't been to see him?'

She shakes her head. 'I'm afraid. I know people say he's changed, that he's a new man, but . . .'

'An Ayuamarcan can't change. He is what he was made to be — The Cardinal. He can be benevolent when it suits his purpose, but when the time comes to be ruthless again, he will be.'

'I feel sorry for him,' she mutters, then coughs. 'Can I come with you? I don't want to face him on my own, not the first time. If you don't want me in the way, I'll understand, but —'

'No problem,' I tell her. 'I wasn't looking forward to being alone with him either. I'd appreciate the company.'

'We're a pair of fools, aren't we?' she giggles. 'If we're that afraid of him, we should have left him underground, in the hands of the *Coya*.'

'No,' I disagree, stepping out of the alcove. 'Raimi's dangerous, but she was worse. He's the lesser of two evils. And in this city, that's as good as it's ever going to get.'

TWO – LONELY AT THE TOP

I stand by the window, gazing down on my city, drawing out the moment. Mags buzzed me a few minutes ago, while I was in conference with a couple of Davern's men, to say that Al Jeery and Ama Situwa wished to see me. I brought the discussion to a swift conclusion, but I've kept the pair waiting while I compose myself. I'm almost as nervous at the prospect of sitting down with Ama now as I was when The Cardinal first summoned me to Party Central that long, eventful decade-plus ago.

Far across the way, cranes are working on the Manco Capac statue, dismantling it. I'm going to remove every trace of the Incas from this city, starting with the glorious centre-piece which was meant to herald the dawn of their all-powerful reign. By the time I'm finished they'll have disappeared as completely as the Ayuamarcans. Nobody will ever know they were here, except me — and in time, perhaps even I'll forget. I've plenty of time for forgetting.

Turning my back on the statue, I walk to the door and open it. Jeery and Ama are chatting with Mags. I study them, unnoticed, then call out, 'The doctor will see you now!'

Ama flinches, but Jeery regards me calmly. 'Mr Raimi,' he greets me with his usual, cautious show of respect.

'I told you, call me Capac.' Holding the door wide, I gesture them in. As they pass, I tell Mags not to disturb me. 'Not for anybody or anything.'

'Sure thing, boss,' she smiles.

Jeery and Ama are taking their seats when I close the door. I walk around them and lean against my desk, gaze settling instantly on Ama. I know it's an embedded reaction, that I'm only attracted to her because I was designed to be, but knowledge can't stop the excited flutter of my heart.

'How have you been?' I ask.

'Alright,' she replies neutrally.

'Still with Cafran?' She nods. 'I must call and see him sometime.'

'I'd rather you didn't.'

I shrug, trying not to show that her words stung me, and face Jeery. 'This is the first time you've come without any of your Snakes, the first time we can speak freely, one to one. Do you want to discuss the future now?'

'What's there to discuss?' he asks.

'You. Me. How we share the city.'

'I thought it was already being shared.'

I laugh. 'That won't last. A year or two from now, the Kluxers will be back at the throats of the blacks and the Snakes will disintegrate into factions. It's the way it's always been.'

'But not the way it *will* be,' Jeery grunts. 'You'll see to that. You'll keep them in check, act as the go-between, chastise them when they step out of line, reward them when they play ball.'

'Why should I?'

He shrugs. 'I'm not sure. But you will, until it suits you not to. We've had our fill of chaos, enough to last a lifetime. Of course, you've many lifetimes to look forward to, and I'm sure you'll stir things up again some day when you get bored. But for the time being I think you'd like to keep it peaceful, secure your clutch on the city, bring the Kluxers and Snakes fully into the fold, so you can use them as you'll use the Troops — to conquer the world.'

I stare at Jeery, impressed. He's read my intentions with eerie accuracy. This is a time for consolidation. It's what I was working towards before the Incas abducted me, only then I was fighting Davern and the gangs in the east, even my own disenchanted people. Now that I have them working with me, it should be possible to grow serenely. Eventually the conflict will start afresh, when we try to take over other cities, but for the next few decades we need to build quietly and unobtrusively.

'Where do you see yourself fitting in?' I ask.

Jeery smiles. 'I don't. This is your city and you're welcome to it. I want out.'

'*Out?* Out where?'

'I'm leaving,' he says. 'This afternoon, as soon as I'm finished here. That's what I came to tell you. I know the *villacs* were building me up to be your human counterpart - the first of an endless number of Sapa Incas, loyal lieutenants bound to you by blood - but I'm not interested. I set out to put a stop to the riots — I did. I wanted to free the Snakes, so they could operate independently and protect the interests of my people — that's been achieved. The *villacs* are history. As for the rest, I couldn't care less.'

'You plan to just walk away?' I ask, startled.

'Yeah.'

'But . . .' I pause. I was worried about placating this man, not sure how I'd keep him happy and at arm's length at the same time. I should be delighted that he's quitting, but I'm not. Part of me wants him to stay. The Incas thought I needed a partner. I never trusted those blind meddlers, but they were experts at understanding people and sensing their weaknesses. They believed I was incapable of ruling alone.

Do I have an Achilles' heel? Will I one day regret it if I let this man go?

'You don't have to leave,' I tell him. 'You could stay, if not as leader of the Snakes, then as part of the Troops. That's what Dorak wanted. He saw you as a replacement for Frank Weld.'

'How do you figure that?' Jeery snorts.

'It was in his notes, the private files only I have access to.'

'Head of the Troops . . .' He winces. 'No thanks.'

'Some other position?'

'No.' His eyes – their natural colour now, minus the contact lenses – are firm. 'I've had enough. I want out.'

'As you please,' I sigh. 'That just leaves us with your payment to settle.'

'Payment?' he echoes.

'Ford Tasso hired you to find and rescue me, which you did. In return, he said he'd tell you where Bill Casey could be found. I decided to spare him that job and reward you myself. This contains the address.' Smiling smugly, I hold out an envelope which I prepared last week, knowing this day would come, but he doesn't reach for it.

'I already tracked Bill down,' he says softly.

I blink, astonished. 'When?'

'Shortly after the riots started.'

'Did you kill him?'

'That's my business, not yours,' he retorts.

'Prickly customer, aren't you?' I mutter sourly, but inside I'm grinning. I like Al Jeery. He's not rotten at the core or interested only in what he can get out of life. He's a good man, better than most I know – far better than me – yet with the drive and determination of a demon. A dangerous foe, as the Incas found out to their cost, but a powerful ally. I wish I could convince him to stay.

'Very well.' I clasp my hands, then open them. 'You're free.

Go with my blessing. If you ever need help, I'll be here and I'll do what I can. But I won't come looking for you. I won't drag you back.'

'Thanks.' He stands and hands me a credit card. 'Ford gave me that. I withdrew some cash earlier, to get me started. Is that OK?'

'Christ, Jeery, keep the damn thing,' I laugh. 'You've earned it.'

'No,' he says tightly. 'I don't want your money. I'll make my own way. I'm not sure how, but I'll figure it out as I go along.'

'As you wish.' I take the card from him and toss it on the desk, then look at Ama and lick my lips. 'Would you mind leaving us alone?' I ask Jeery.

'Ama?' he says.

She stares at me coldly, then sighs. 'Will you wait for me outside, Al? I won't be long.'

'OK. Holler if you need me.'

Jeery looks back once, makes a half-wave – I return it – then marches to the door and exits, leaving me alone with the woman whose love I crave, whose hatred I fear.

'Been a long time,' I grin sickly. 'You're as beautiful as ever.'

'You sacrificed me,' she says softly, coming straight to the point. 'Dorak put it to you – me or his empire – and you chose the latter.'

'I had to,' I mutter shamefully. 'He made me to need this above all else. My choice wasn't my own — you know that.'

'Do I?' she replies icily. 'I love you, Capac –' my hopes flare '– but I don't want to.' And fade just as swiftly. 'The love's buried deep within me and I can't ignore it.'

'Nor can I!' I protest. 'I love you now, as I did ten years ago, but I had to put this city first. I'll always have to. The Cardinal instilled that in me, just as he filled us with love for one another. I'm as helpless as you are.'

'I don't think so,' she disagrees. 'He made you differently. You had to be unique and free-thinking to take his empire to the heights he desired. I think you had the strength to choose me, if you'd valued me over the power on offer. But you didn't.'

'You'd have died anyway,' I remind her stiffly. 'All the Ayuamarcans did.'

She smiles sadly. 'That hardly justifies your choice.'

'I did what I had to,' I insist, but I don't know if I believe that. For ten years I've told myself I was a pawn, but part of me has always queried it. Maybe that's why I suffer with nightmares in which I re-live that moment of choosing and burn with shame at the memory of it.

'Let's not argue,' Ama says, closing her eyes. 'I'm here now. I came back, as I had to. I'm yours. Do with me as you wish.'

I start towards her, to take her in my arms, then stop uncertainly as she opens her eyes and stares at me hollowly. 'No,' I croak. 'Not like this. It's not enough that you love me. You've got to *want* me. I won't take you against your will.'

'You'll have to,' she says, 'because I *don't* want you. I'll *never* want you. But I love you and I'll give myself to you. I don't know how long I'll be able to endure it – I guess I'll wind up slashing my wrists in a tub late one night – but you can have me for as long as I last. You'll get your money's worth.'

I feel my lower lip quiver and bite down on it quick. I'm The Cardinal, and The Cardinal doesn't cry, no matter what the circumstances. Steeling myself, I force a sneer. 'You flatter yourself if you think I'd give my heart to a whore.'

Her jaw drops. 'What?'

'That's what you're offering yourself as. You'll give me your body, to do with as I please, while you lie back, close your eyes and dream of . . . who? Jeery? Is that who you'd rather be with?'

'I'd rather be with anyone than you,' she snarls, angry tears building.

'Then go,' I shrug, my soul disintegrating with the gesture. 'The city's full of whores. I won't have difficulty finding another, one who'll at least pretend her heart's in it.'

'You . . . you don't . . . want me?' she mumbles.

'Not like this. If you'd come to me with love, I'd have turned you into a queen and placed you above all others. But chaining yourself to me as a slave . . . that doesn't tempt me. I can't love a woman I can't respect.' I turn my back on her and walk to the window, forcing the words from between my reluctant lips. 'And I can't respect a whore.'

The brutality is necessary. To free her, I must drive her away. She'll never get over me, just as I'll never get over her, but if I convince her that I don't want her, maybe she can live without me. Ferdinand Dorak loved a woman who couldn't love him back. Rather than imprison her, he behaved as a human for perhaps the only time in his life and set her free. I must do the same, even though I'm more of a monster than he ever was.

'Capac . . . I don't understand . . . I thought . . .' She stops and stands. I'm captivated by her reflection in the glass. She's staring at me, crying but smiling. I almost turn and run to her — but don't. If I did, I wouldn't be able to let her go. The monster would overwhelm me and she'd be devoured.

'Thank you,' she whispers. I pretend not to hear. Wiping tears away, she walks to the door, turns the handle and steps through, closing it gently behind her.

I stay by the window, gazing at the rear yard of Party Central, thinking about how I sacrificed Ama before and how I've given her up now. It was easier the other way. Life's simpler if you face it as an emotionless beast.

I spot them exiting, black and white specks fifteen floors down. They go to their vehicles – a bicycle and moped – then stop and talk. I wish I could hear what they're saying. A car pulls up and they exchange words with the passengers in the back. Jeery laughs, slaps the roof of the car, and it drives on. The pair share a few more words, then Jeery hands something to Ama. She ends the conversation by throwing her arms around him and kissing him. I'm too far up to tell whether it's a kiss of passion or friendship. Then she turns, climbs aboard her moped and departs. Jeery leaves soon after, pedalling slowly, passing through the gates one last time.

I back away from the window and stare around my office, considering my position. I have everything Dorak made me to desire — power, influence, wealth, an army, a city . . . one day, perhaps, a world. I have more than any man before me, all the attributes and possessions of the gods, and I may well become one before I'm through.

But I'd give it all up if I could trade places with Al Jeery, receive that kiss from Ama, and just walk away to live a normal life and die and never come back.

THREE – ADIOS!

We say nothing in the elevator going down. Ama's crying. I'm not sure what went on in Raimi's office, but I think things didn't go quite the way she expected them to. I take my time walking from the elevator to the yard, knowing this is the last time I'll ever make the walk, remembering my years as a Troop, the good years with Ellen, the lost years of drinking . . . the human years.

When we reach our bikes, I clear my throat. 'Did you tell him where to get off?'

Ama smiles. 'I told him the truth, that I loved him and would give myself to him, but if I had a choice I'd have nothing to do with him.' She pauses, eyes misting over. 'He set me free.'

'Come again?'

'He said he didn't want me. Told me I was a whore. Kicked me out with orders not to come back.'

I stare at her. 'But I thought he was created to love you.'

She nods. 'But he always enjoyed more freedom than the other Ayuamarcans. He had the ability to cast me aside. And he did, even though it pained him, for my sake.' Tears trickle down her cheeks, but they're tears of happiness. 'He's alone, and always will be, but he set me free because he loved me and couldn't bear to see me suffer.'

'Maybe he really didn't care that much for you,' I suggest, but she shakes her head confidently.

'He's in agony but he'll endure it – for me.' She glances up at the fifteenth floor, then looks down morosely. 'It's almost enough to make me want to go back to him. *Almost.*'

'What will you do now?' I ask curiously.

'Carry on with Cafran,' she shrugs, drying her cheeks. 'Run his new restaurant. Make friends. Try and forget about the past.'

'You could leave with me if you wanted,' I mumble, not daring look at her as I make the proposition.

'Inviting me to elope, Al?' I sense her smile.

'We got on well together that time we . . .' I cough discreetly.

'*Very* well,' she giggles.

'So how about it?' I raise my eyes, grinning hopefully.

'No,' she sighs. 'I'm not saying I don't want you — I just don't want you *now*. I have to find out who I am, discover what I need from life. This city's a cemetery for you, but it's a nursery as far as I'm concerned. I want to grow here and learn. One day, maybe, I can leave too. But not now.'

'Think you might want to look me up when that day comes?'

'I might,' she smirks. 'Will you keep in touch, let me know how you get on and where you wind up?'

'Sure. By the way, there's something I have to give you . . .'

As I'm reaching inside the bag attached to the back of my bike, a car pulls up. The tinted glass in the rear window rolls down and the grinning faces of Ford Tasso and Jerry Falstaff are revealed.

'Doing a runner, Algiers?' Tasso bellows.

'Bet your wrinkled old ass I am,' I laugh, leaning down for a better view. 'How you doing, Jerry?' I haven't seen him since the attack on Cockerel Square, though I've heard he stepped down as head of the Troops shortly after.

'Not too bad,' he smiles. 'Getting some grief from the new boss, but with a bit of luck he won't be around very long.'

'Watch it,' Tasso growls. 'I'll out-last you and all the rest of your soft-as-shit generation.'

'You're back in control of the Troops?' I ask, mildly amazed. 'What happened to your retirement?'

'Fuck that,' Tasso snorts. 'I wasn't meant to grow old gracefully. I got such a buzz being back in the game, there wasn't a hope of me walking away from it again. I'm in this for the duration, Algiers, however long that might prove to be — and the way I'm feeling, there could be a few decades left in me yet.'

'You're an insane old bastard,' I chuckle, shaking my head admiringly.

'In this city, you have to be,' he retorts, winking with his one good eye, sitting back and calling to the driver, 'Home, Thomas!'

I laugh, step back from the car and slap the roof, seeing them off. I smile as I watch them go and silently wish them well, though I doubt whether they need my good wishes. Some people were born to succeed in this city, and Jerry and Tasso are two of its favoured sons. They'll flourish.

'You'll miss them, won't you?' Ama asks.

'Yeah. The old son of a bitch especially. But I'll survive.' Reaching into the bag, I hand her the doll I was going to give her before the interruption. It's her Ayuamarcan doll, the one I brought from the hall of the *Coya*. 'Take care of that,' I warn her as she turns it around, studying it warily, lifting it to her ear to listen to the tinny beating of its heart. 'If anything happens to it, you're done for. Keep it somewhere safe. *Very* safe.'

'I will,' she replies, slipping the doll inside her shirt.

She clears her throat. 'It's not any of my business, but your father's doll . . . what happened to it?'

I let out a long breath and pat the bag behind me. 'Don't worry. I wasn't sure what to do with it – what I *could* do with it – when I came up from the tunnels. But I've had time to think. I know how to deal with it now.'

'You'll make things right?' she asks.

'As right as I can,' I smile.

Ama nods, satisfied, then wraps her arms around me and kisses me deeply. The kiss takes me by surprise and for a few seconds I don't respond. Then my arms tighten around her and I return the embrace. When we break, we're both grinning. Maybe I'm kidding myself, but I don't think this is the last kiss we'll share. Some day, in some far-flung corner of the world, we'll kiss again. I'd stake all I have on it.

'See you later, Mr Jeery,' Ama smirks.

'Not *too* much later, I hope.'

Blowing me a kiss, Ama mounts her moped and takes off, not looking back, putting the monster on the fifteenth floor behind her forever, surrendering herself to the random uncertainties of the future. I wait until she's out of sight, then cycle slowly through the gates of Party Central – '*Adios!*' I roar as I pass the bemused Troops on guard – and head for my final port of call before catching the train out.

The Harpies are absent – they must be with Jennifer – and Bill's upstairs, painting snakes on a wall. He's working on a huge rattler when I walk in, using a tiny brush to get the colours *just* right. I don't announce myself, just toss my gift – the Paucar Wami doll – at his knees and await his reaction.

Bill's eyes narrow when he spots me. Then he looks at the doll and slowly picks it up. He studies it silently, running the tip of a finger over the tattooed snakes. 'This is the man in my dreams,' he whispers.

'The original Paucar Wami,' I confirm. 'The one who tricked you into killing your sister.' Bill's eyes harden and his fingers close around the doll. 'Let's find a couple of chairs. I've a story to tell you . . .'

Seated in a bare room at the back of the house, I run Bill through the history of Paucar Wami, how he and the other Ayuamarcans were created by The Cardinal, the part the *villacs* played in it, how I became aware of my father when Bill drove us together ten years ago, his death, my years mimicking him, his revival, what happened in the tunnels, how the killer's linked to the doll. I don't think Bill takes all of it in, but he grasps the most important element. The doll he holds can be used to terminate the assassin of his nightmares — forever.

'I can't do it,' I finish. 'As barbaric as he is, he's my father and we've come through too much together. But I can't let him roam the world freely either. He has to be stopped. And I think you're the person most entitled to stop him.'

Bill stares at the doll, saying nothing, his face a blank.

'It's what you wanted,' I whisper. 'The son to rise up and destroy the father. I'm giving him to you, letting you take him down. Your revenge is complete. Once you drive a pin through the doll's heart, it's over. You'll be quits. I think you'll enjoy some measure of peace. It might even stop the nightmares.'

Bill's eyes lift slowly, painfully. 'You think I can escape them?' he croaks.

'Maybe.'

'A life without snakes,' he murmurs, gaze returning to the doll. 'I've forgotten what that was like. It's been so long. To sleep again and not dream of serpents and death and terrible things . . . It's too much to hope for.'

'A good night's sleep isn't that much,' I disagree. 'I think you've earned it.' Standing, I search my thoughts for a final comment, but what's there to say? This man destroyed my life, killed those closest to me, set me on the path to madness and murder. Yet without his interference the *villacs* would still rule the city, immersing it in chaos whenever it suited their purpose. Ama would be theirs. The Snakes would be puppets in their hands. And maybe I'd belong to them too. The priests were intent on winning me over to their cause. If Bill hadn't pushed me too far, perhaps I'd have succumbed to their call. I can't hate him, not any more. I'm not sure what I feel for this pitiful old man who's played such a crucial role – both for good and bad – in my life, but it's not hate.

Abandoning the search for a memorable farewell, I settle for the simplest of all. 'Goodbye, Bill.' And after pausing to set down my second gift to the wizened old man – the varnished finger which has hung from a chain around my neck these past ten years – I leave him to his wreck of a house and ruin of a life, sitting on the floor, surrounded by snakes, cradling the Paucar Wami doll to his chest, weeping softly at the thought of the freedom and peace that are his for the taking.

The train station. The sun's setting in the west and I'll be heading after it, at least for an hour, before the train turns north. Riding off into a long, rosy sunset like a cowboy. My ticket will take me to the end of the line if I want to travel that far, but I suspect I'll get off somewhere along the way, in a quiet town or village, or maybe just hop off in the middle of nowhere. I'd like to find a nice spot by a river and do some fishing for a year or two, push all other worries from my mind. Travel later if I feel like it. Sit by the river and grow old slowly if I don't.

The train pulls out on schedule and I lean back in my seat, casting my weary gaze over the landmarks one final time. Hard to believe I spent so much of my life here, confined by grey buildings, beating blood-drenched streets, living so tensely, so brutally. What keeps people in cities when there are the wide open spaces of the world to explore? It must be madness or an addiction.

I find myself staring at my reflection when the train enters a tunnel. With my snakes painted over, my short crop of hair, and a hunger for new challenges in my eyes, I can almost pass for the man I was ten years ago, before my descent into the subterranean world of the Incas. I must keep the snakes covered. Perhaps one day I'll pay a surgeon to remove them. Or maybe I'll hang onto them, reminders of the darkness. It might be good in later years to wipe the paint away every now and then, study the coils of the insane past, and appreciate how fortunate I am to have come out of it alive, intact and in some way human.

Across the aisle, a young boy – four, maybe five – pulls away from his tired mother and makes a break for freedom. She lunges after him but misses. I catch him before he escapes and hand him back. 'Thank you,' she smiles, then scolds him in a low, harsh voice. Out of the jumble of words, I hear her warn him, 'If you don't behave, Paucar Wami will come and eat you!'

I turn away to hide a wry smile. Paucar Wami won't ever eat any little children again, but let him live on in legend if that's how people want it. I like the idea of him surviving that way. He stepped, fully formed, out of a fantasy and it's only fitting that he should now return to the land of shadowy myths.

Me? I'm through with legacies. I don't want anybody telling stories about Al Jeery. I'll happily pass into obscurity when my time comes, and leave nothing but the dust of my bones behind. Let Capac Raimi have his eternity, and Paucar Wami his notoriety. I'll settle for whatever years I have left and a soothing, dark hole in the ground at the end.

The train clears the suburbs and picks up speed. I look for a sign to say we're leaving the city but none materializes. Maybe kids have made off with them, or perhaps nobody bothered to erect any since the city always seems to be expanding, devouring more ground with every passing year. One day it may cover the entire planet, but that's not my problem. Let future generations deal with that one.

As we head into the glow of dusk, away from the shadows of the city, I lie back and close my eyes, basking in the warmth of the sun through the glass, listening to the whine and screech of the engine and the wheels. After a while I doze, not a sound sleep, but that state halfway between dreams and the real world. In that in-between realm, I'm sitting on the greenest bank of grass in all the world, fishing in a river of purest blue. Bill's close by, fixing bait

(*not a worm, but a tiny snake*)

to a hook. He catches my eye, winks and casts off. Behind us, ghostly figures flit in and out of the scene — Ellen and Ama, Capac Raimi and Ferdinand Dorak, Nicola Hornyak, Rudi Ziegler, Sard, Ford Tasso. Frank Weld hits the party with Hyde Wornton, both bitching about the way they were killed. My father doesn't appear. I'll dream about him often in the years to come, but he has no place at a friendly gathering like this.

There's a barbecue sizzling in the background. Someone tells Bill and me to get busy – there's a lot of hungry people need feeding. We look at each other, laugh, crack open beers and engage in the mother of all contests. Soon the bank around us is overflowing with fish, every shape and variety, but all pale-skinned and blind.

'That's it!' Bill cries, abandoning his line to the river. 'You win.' He stands, claps my back, then vanishes into the crowd behind me, to dance with his young, giggling sister and a smartly dressed, prim and proper lady who would have been